BLOOD BROTHERS

A DYING TRUTH EXPOSED, BOOK FIVE

HOW FAR WILL THE LOVE OF A BROTHER GO...
MARCUS ABSTON

Blood Brothers (A Dying Truth Exposed, Book 5)
Copyright © 2024 by Marcus Abston, Chas Novels

For more about this author, please visit www.marcusabston.com

This is a work of fiction. Names, characters, businesses, places, events, locales, and incidents are either the products of the author's imagination or used in a fictitious manner. Any resemblance to actual persons, living or dead, or actual events is purely coincidental.

All rights reserved. No part of this publication may be reproduced, distributed, or transmitted in any form or by any means, including photocopying, recording, or other electronic or mechanical methods, without the prior written permission of the publisher, except in the case of brief quotations embodied in critical reviews and certain other noncommercial uses permitted by copyright law. Please do not participate in or encourage piracy of copyrighted materials in violation of the author's rights.

For permission requests, write to the author at www.marcuscabston.com

Editing by The Pro Book Editor
Interior and Cover Design by IAPS.rocks

Paperback ISBN: 979-8-9865965-2-5

    1. Main category—Fiction

    2. Other category—Historical Fiction

First Edition

CHAPTER 1
A Changing World

Sunlight illuminated Albert Brooks's living room as brown eyes stared at old photos and writing encased in plastic. "Like every snowflake that falls from the sky, each child is unique," Albert said. "Any good parent can tell you, the feeling of knowing your child is in danger does not only affect your heart and mind but also your spirit and soul. No matter how well a person can control their emotions, the reality of not having control can be difficult. Being ignorant on the current danger does create a different storm, leaving us more vulnerable to situations we did not think possible. From a young age, Annabelle experienced many things adults in our time would never experience. She and Mr. Brown's daughters had developed a forbidden friendship, with Judy Mays becoming her best friend."

Albert's daughter looked at him as she held one of the old letters, saying, "I never understood their mindset, Daddy. How can you befriend what you hate?"

"Judy Mays and her sisters viewed Annabelle as family."

"I couldn't imagine my best friend becoming the greatest threat to any of my children."

"It's not that simple, especially with the laws in place. She was not only seeing Joseph but now feeling all the emotions she had for years."

"Annabelle fought so hard to move forward with her life; she married a Cherokee man and created a family with him, with Joseph being her missing puzzle piece. Did Judy Mays try to destroy the beginning of our family?"

"We often make the mistake of believing that good intentions will give us the desired results, but life doesn't work like that. Life can be cruel. That's why we must walk by faith and not by sight a day at a time. Be careful with which wolf we feed. The Father uses these life events to grow and mold us. Joseph was going through his trials just like his mother and Judy Mays. A missing Joseph was a thorn in Annabelle's side, but it was also her mentor that Jesus was using to grow her faith. No different than now, Judy Mays was confronted with a choice she had never seen coming."

"They look so happy in these old pictures." Liz's eyes shot open as her jaw unhinged, and she held up a picture in front of her father. "Wait...is this who I think it is?"

Albert stared at the old picture with a woman and a young man. "I guess that picture alone creates a lot of questions. Let's continue to answer those questions..."

On April 12, 1861, the American Civil War began with the attack on Fort Sumter. The field slaves remained unaware of the war, but Dorothy and the other house slaves heard about it through the Pleckers' conversations. Five days after the battle of Fort Sumter, Kenneth approached Calvin and Wilma. An argument arose in the mansion when Kenneth told Calvin and Wilma he was seriously thinking about joining the Confederate Army. The argument rattled Dorothy and Riza as they stood silently in the room.

Kenneth stormed out of the mansion, and Calvin and Wilma quickly walked after him. "Joseph, come here!" Kenneth bellowed.

A shiver ran up Joseph's spine as he looked at the white mansion. "I didn't do anything wrong," he said.

"Go on, so Master Kenneth don't get angrier," Bo said. The

slave man put down some nails on a wagon. "Hurry, I know you not do nothing wrong. So don't be scared. Do as you told."

Joseph sighed. "Okay." He ran to the mansion up the dirty road. As he approached the mansion, he could hear Kenneth arguing with his mother. He slowed down once he saw them and slowly walked up to Kenneth. "Yes sir, Master Kenneth?"

Kenneth pointed at the horse's barn, "Bring out Gallant."

"Joseph, stay right there or I'll have your hide beat," Wilma said, her voice elevating and her green eyes narrowing.

"Momma, I've made up my mind."

Wilma turned to Mr. Plecker, frowning. "Calvin, do you hear this disregard for my words?"

"Wilma, calm down," Master Plecker said. "He is a man, and if it wasn't for so much going on here, I'd be going with him. I support your decision, son."

Wilma growled, "He needs to be focused on getting married!"

"Things seem to be going well between him and Miss Reece; now, you will stop these dramatic acts and let the boy live."

Wilma pouted, stomped her foot, and marched back to the mansion. "Riza, Dorothy, come on," she commanded.

Kenneth threw up his arms, saying, "Momma, don't walk away like that. I'll hold back on going to fight."

Each of Wilma's footsteps echoed through the mansion. With Dorothy walking beside her, her rant continued. Her voice elevated the farther she got away from Mr. Plecker and Kenneth, and the men could hear her push open the patio door.

Master Plecker sighed. "Women." He looked at Joseph and then pointed at the horse barn. "Hurry up, boy, and bring Gallant here."

"Yes sir, Master Plecker," Joseph replied. He jogged to the horse's barn and greeted Gallant. The kind horse reminded him of home. He prayed for Annabelle and the rest of his family before he brought the large horse to Kenneth.

Later in the evening, Dorothy visited Kenneth. "Your momma seems really worried," she said.

"She shouldn't be. I know how to fight, and I should be defending the South," Kenneth said.

Dorothy slightly frowned. "I'm worried. I don't want to see you go away."

"What does that make me if I don't defend this house?"

"That still makes you a father and, if I'm honest, a smart man. Do you believe in what they're fighting for?"

Kenneth looked away from her and started pacing in a small circle. "I would be fine with the end of slavery, but the North forcing their will on us, I'm not okay with that."

"Why not take me and the children? Let's go somewhere the fighting hasn't started."

Kenneth sneered. "I'm not a coward!"

"And I don't want to have to tell the girls that their daddy died fighting in something he doesn't fully believe in! They need you!" Dorothy began to cry, and Kenneth stepped up to embrace Dorothy, but she pushed him away. "No, you can't make this okay." Kenneth forcefully hugged Dorothy as she cried. "I don't want to lose you. It would kill my soul."

"If I have to go, I promise to come back to you and the girls. I won't rush into fighting." Dorothy stayed with Kenneth and tried to persuade him to let the other men fight. However, she could tell in Kenneth's heart he wanted to fight and defend what he believed in. She kissed Kenneth and was permitted to leave the room. She left the mansion deeply worried he would leave without warning, feeling powerless to stop him.

On April 15, 1861, Riza turned fourteen, even though she could not celebrate it. To her surprise, Wilma allowed another chicken to be fried to award her. As the field slaves were allowed a lunch break, Joseph saw Susie approaching the old cookhouse.

Susie smiled as she carried a piece of cloth with something in it. "Come with me," she said in Cherokee.

Joseph followed her, and they sat together behind the old cookhouse. Susie opened up the cloth and presented Joseph with the fried chicken. "Oh chicken, why are you bringing this to me? You could get in trouble," Joseph said in Cherokee.

"This is a little of what Mrs. Wilma allowed Riza to have for her birthday."

"Today is Riza's birthday! I wish I could see her, but Master Rice and the others watch us so much."

Susie cocked her head. "It's okay. She knows you and Tom can't see her right now."

"Is some of this for Tom?"

"Yeah, some of it is for Tom. He can have the wings. Riza said you can have the thighs."

"I should leave a thigh for Tom."

"Don't worry about it. I'll throw away the bones so he won't know. He likes the wings anyway."

"Okay, I'm so hungry I had to eat that nasty corn again for breakfast."

Joseph ate the fried chicken thighs while Susie talked with him. While he ate, they tried to guess which birds were singing. Guessing was the only game they could think of since he had little time to rest. After Joseph finished, Susie gave Tom the wings and hurried to the white mansion.

She walked back into the cookhouse and entered the mansion through the kitchen pathway. She picked up a clean cloth to polish the grand piano. "Did you give both of them a wing and a thigh?" Riza asked.

Susie turned around with a smile. "Yes. They said thank you," she said politely.

Riza smiled at Susie. "Good. They don't deserve to be eating that slop stew. I better grab these stupid crackers before Mrs. Wilma starts screaming for me."

"All right, I better go clean the piano since Master Kenneth is done playing on it." The two separated and did their assigned tasks. As Susie polished the piano, she could see her reflection and smiled at herself. "Hello, Mr. Piano," Susie said in Cherokee.

"I like your black color and the beautiful sounds you make. One day, I'll try to make pretty songs from you."

"Susie," Master Plecker said. Susie jolted and turned around. "Are you talking Indian gibberish?"

"No, Master Plecker, I wasn't speaking any of it," Susie nervously said.

Master Plecker walked down the stairs and stood before Susie. He towered over her. "I hope you weren't because you know the punishment for speaking that junk. You be careful not to pick up any of Riza's bad habits now."

"I will never speak that way, Master Plecker."

Master Plecker slightly squinted. "You'll never speak what?"

Susie gulped. "I'll never speak Cherokee in your home."

"That's right. Not in this house or in the house you sleep in. You better remember it's a privilege for you to clean that piano. Otherwise, I'll send you out there to clean the pig pens, you understand me?"

"Yes, Master Plecker. I understand you."

Master Plecker brushed back Susie's hair and caressed her face. "You keep doing as you're told, and you'll keep that pretty face. Don't disappoint me."

Susie's eyes widened. "I'll do as you say, Master Plecker."

"Good girl." Master Plecker exited the living room, entered the study, and left Susie's sight. Susie grabbed the cleaning supplies and deeply breathed when she went upstairs. The moment she entered one of the guest rooms, she closed the door and sat against the door to cry. "Father, please free us from these evil people," Susie cried in Cherokee. Susie forced herself to stop sobbing and cleaned the room. Susie remained anxious for the rest of the day to end so she could sing to herself in Cherokee.

In Tahlequah, the Lightning-Strongman family remained deeply focused on finding Joseph but was forced to plant their crops for the next season. The work required all the men, frustrating John. He wanted to start looking for Joseph as soon as the snow melted. The outbreak of the Civil War also complicated how they could now travel, creating worry they would encounter a military regiment of the South.

On April 21, 1861, Paul strolled through the dirt streets of Tahlequah and entered the supply store. Lizzie stood behind the counter. "Good afternoon, Lizzie. I'm surprised that you're here and not Grace," Paul said.

Lizzie smiled as she played with a string. "Well, she had the baby two weeks ago," Lizzie said. "She gave birth to a healthy baby boy and named him Gabriel. I guess she wants some hope he'll grow up to be a great man."

Lizzie saw Paul's eyebrow lift slightly. "I'd think you would be more excited having a new nephew."

Lizzie half-shrugged. "It's been two weeks. My excitement doesn't live for long. My only thoughts are to make sure we can buy or grow enough food for him and the others."

"So you here alone?"

"No, Lisa is out feeding the chickens with Sunni. Sunni likes the chickens. I don't know how the child is going to feel when she has to learn how to cut one up."

Paul chuckled. "You funny."

Lizzie narrowed her eyes. "It's you're funny, and I wasn't being funny…what do you want?"

Paul cleared his throat. "I was here for two bags of flour for Mrs. Nancy."

"Still working for that blue-eyed snake? I thought you would've looked for something else by now."

"Well, she give me a place to sleep and pay me now. Mr. Scott speaks to me kindly, and I enjoy seeing those girls grow up. They good peoples now."

Lizzie rolled her eyes. "Right…"

She entered the supply room and walked out with two sacks of flour. "Let me get those for you," he said.

Lizzie glanced at Paul, showing aggravation. "I can carry them myself, so don't ask me that again. Put the money on the counter, and take these."

He put the money on the counter, took the flour sacks from

Lizzie, and walked toward the door as Lizzie held it. "Be careful walking back to your wagon."

"I will, and thank you."

Lizzie smirked while she watched Paul put the sacks on the wagon. "The next time you see a bloomed flower, bring it to me."

He looked up at her with big eyes. "What did you say?"

"You heard exactly what I said," she bickered. "I'm not repeating that!"

She stormed back into the store and slammed the door. He looked around to see if other townspeople had noticed and joyfully got into the wagon. "I best watch my words. If she had something to throw at me, I think she would have hit me."

Later in the day, Lizzie and Lisa strolled home with Sunni. The women entered the family house and saw Grace nursing Gabriel in a rocking chair. "Look at him. He's such a quiet baby. I like it," Lisa said in Cherokee.

"He wasn't quiet last night," Grace said.

Lisa joked, "I didn't hear anything last night, so I'm happy."

Grace giggled. "Get away from me. You're starting to sound like Tsula." Lisa laughed and walked to the kitchen with Lizzie following her. "Lizzie, wait a moment."

"What do you want?" Lizzie asked in Cherokee.

"Someone sounds like they're hiding why they had a big smile on their face," Grace said in Cherokee.

"I'm having a good day and happy to see him. Also, I smile all the time."

"I know you. You were thinking and smiling. So, do you want to talk about it?"

"No, I don't." Lizzie put her hand on the kitchen door and looked back at Grace. "Is Annabelle in the kitchen?"

"She's in there."

Lizzie continued walking into the kitchen as Grace laughed to herself.

"You've been so serious these past few months. I know that smile meant something," Grace murmured. Grace looked at Gabriel as she nursed him, "I think something good has your Auntie Lizzie's attention. What do you think?" Grace continued to look into Gabriel's brown eyes while she nursed him. "Someday you'll see your older cousin again." Grace kissed her son's forehead. "That I can promise you."

Days passed as the cotton fields grew, the walnut and apple trees bloomed, and Joseph and Tom were given more tasks. Joseph's mornings remained hard. He was forced to eat nasty cornbread and pieces of beef or pork for breakfast. When they brought corn to the cattle and pigs, they would eat some of it when no one was looking. One day, while feeding the cattle, the boys took handfuls of corn to eat.

As Joseph took a handful and began to eat it, he noticed Rice was standing behind him and immediately stopped chewing while Rice stared him down. "So this is what you little niggers do when y'all supposed be feeding these cattle?" Master Rice asked. "Y'all eating their corn?" Rice slowly walked around the cattle pen as Tom nervously watched him approach Joseph. "I suggest you spit out what's in your mouth."

Joseph swallowed slightly and said, "There's nothing in my mouth, Master Rice."

Rice smacked Joseph upside his head and grabbed Joseph by his hair. Joseph groaned as he held onto Rice's hand, dropping the bucket of corn and grains. "You little nigger! Get your dirty hands off me!" Rice threw Joseph to the ground, and Tom froze with fear. "Pick every piece of corn and grain off this ground, the both of you!" Tom put down the bucket he was carrying and began to pick up the spilled food. Joseph angrily picked up the corn kernels and grain while Rice watched. "Y'all not going to do this again, are yah?"

Tom nervously replied, "No, Master Rice."

Rice looked at Joseph as he remained silent and continued to pick up the spilled food. "You better learn your lesson, half-breed redskin." Rice kicked Joseph, causing him to hold his stomach in pain.

Joseph pouted as he looked up at Rice and continued to pick up the spilled food. "Nothing but an evil man," he mumbled.

"I see you forgot already." Rice pressed his foot on his back, forcing him to moan in pain. "Now this is what you are going to do…you're going to eat all leftover food, including that grain…now eat it!"

Joseph began to cry while he ate the corn on the ground, and Rice pressed his foot into his back. Tom frantically picked up the spilled food.

Rice grunted and kicked Tom in the face. "What do you think? I wouldn't see what you were doing?"

Tom hesitantly replied, "I was doing what you told me to do, Master Rice."

Rice rubbed his chin as he stared at Tom. "You two half-breeds must think I'm stupid, or has Riza been telling y'all how to act up?" The boys remained silent while they looked at Rice. "I see. This ain't got anything to do with Riza, right? Well, y'all can deal with the consequences like a man." Rice grabbed Joseph by his hair, grabbed Tom by his hair, and pulled the boys to follow him. "I wonder how much I would get for bringing in your scalps."

"Stop, Master Rice, you hurting me," Joseph yelled. "Please stop!"

Master Rice angrily replied, "See…I know that's you boys' problem right there. Y'all must think because y'all got Indian blood, it make you special. Well, y'all wrong." Rice continued pulling Joseph and Tom toward a short brown barn with a wired mesh door and bones lying outside. He pressed the boys' faces onto the mesh gate, and four dogs charged the gate. The dogs growled, barked, and attempted to bite the boys. "Now, these dogs here have been trained to attack any nigger. The dogs don't see any half-breeds, just some Negro children and the dogs don't lie."

"I'm not a nigger," Joseph cried.

"Did those whippings wear off, boy? Do you need some more?" Rice yelled. "Smell that dog breath. I swear if I catch either of you eating more corn, I'll cut you up and feed you to these dogs. Y'all hear me!"

As Rice pressed the boys against the gate, one of the dogs scratched Joseph. "Yes, we hear you, Master Rice," Tom cried.

Rice arrogantly replied, "Well, I hear one agreeing."

As blood started to run down Joseph's cheek, he cried, "Yes, I hear you, Master Rice."

Rice let the boys go and spit on the ground. "Y'all watch yourselves. Don't follow Riza," Rice snarled. "Y'all not worth half of what she is." Joseph looked at Rice with his dilated narrow eyes and turned to walk away when he heard a whip crack. Pain went through Joseph's body as he fell to the ground. "Did I say I was finished?"

Joseph cried, "No, Master Rice."

"That's what I like to hear. Now, you boys feed those horses and get out to the cotton fields. Move quickly, I said!" Rice cracked the whip on his back again. He immediately got up and quickly ran to the horse barn with Tom behind him while Rice watched. "Curse Riza...I know that rebellious Mohawk is poisoning those boys' minds. I'll have to remind her to watch her mouth."

A few days passed, and Joseph remained intimidated by Rice, doing his best to avoid eye contact. The welts caused by the whip lasted two days. Stella used a cloth soaked in cold water to help the swelling go down on Joseph's back, but it did little to take away the pain as he slept. During a break, the slaves quickly ate what they could, but Joseph noticed Clint wasn't around eating. Joseph was surprised because he always ate and talked about food. Clint snuck up to the white mansion.

Clint stood at the cookhouse door and knocked on it. Emma opened the door and snobbishly looked at a smiling him, who kept one hand behind his back. "Boy, what do you want here?" Emma asked.

"Hi Emma, I was hoping to see Riza for a minute," Clint said.

Emma snobbishly replied, "I guess you would want to see her, but you can't. She is with Mrs. Wilma all day. You gone have to wait for the evening to even talk to her. So go on back to the fields where you belong."

Riza walked into the kitchen carrying a silver tea set. "Clint, what are you doing here?" she asked.

Clint smiled and looked past Emma's shoulder. He cheerfully answered, "I was here to say hi. Master Kit said we can have a short meal."

Riza placed the silver tea set on the counter and went to the door. "That was nice of you."

"Mm-hmm, more like stupid," Emma snarled.

Riza replied, "I appreciate that he came to see me." Emma scoffed and exited the kitchen. She lightly chuckled as soon as she left. "She's strong on rules."

"I think she hate me," Clint said.

Riza smiled. "I don't think so. I think she wishes she was somewhere else. So, did you come here only to say hi to me?"

Clint blushed and avoided eye contact with Riza. "I thought you might like a flower from one of the trees. Here."

Clint moved his hand from behind his back and showed her a large yellow flower. "Wow, a magnolia flower! Thank you. That was nice of you." She could see Clint was blushing. "When I was healing from getting beat, you left blue flowers and a rose flower by the slave house, didn't you?"

"Yes, it was me, but don't tell nobody. Mrs. Wilma still mad about the rose flower. I...I do it for you and Susie. I hope you liked them."

Riza continued to smile. "I think it's sweet of you to bring me this. You're welcome to visit me when I get done working for Mrs. Wilma. We can look at the stars."

"You would look at stars with me?"

Riza nodded. "I would like to look at stars when you want."

Clint deeply inhaled and grinned. I blessed to know you all this time."

Riza cocked her head, looking up at Clint. "I'm happy I know you too. You know the boys always talk about you. Please keep an eye on them when you're out there with them."

"I can do that. They strong for they size, but I guess it that Indian blood. I think the Lord gone do good with them."

A mild breeze began to sway the grass along with Riza's wavy hair. "I think that too. Well, go back before you get in trouble. I don't want you getting in trouble for me."

Clint smiled at her and began to walk away. "I take whippings for you, Riza."

"No, you don't, Clint Plecker," she said with a playful tone. "I don't want you to go through that," she murmured.

Clint cheerfully snuck back to work through the willow trees and went past the slave houses. "Clint, where were you at, boy?" Rice asked.

Clint froze and slowly turned around. "Master Rice, I was looking at them flowers on the trees," he said. "I got done with the horses."

Rice scratched his chin. "Was you now? I could have sworn I saw you going up the path to the mansion with a flower in your hand. Where is that flower now?"

"I don't have it, Master Rice."

Rice chuckled while he stared at Clint. "Boy, who did you give the flower to?" He stood silent as Rice stood in front of him. "I asked you who was it?" He remained silent and shifted his gaze around the field. Rice slapped him. "Who was it?" Rice slapped him again and kicked him in his knee.

Clint kneeled on the ground to comfort his knee as he grunted. "Master Rice, please, I do no evil."

"I determine what's evil here, you understand that?" Rice slapped and spit on him. "Now you going to tell me who was it, or we gone have a hanging."

Clint moaned while he held his knee. "I give it to Riza so her day nicer. She have good heart."

Rice squatted down and looked at Clint. "Let me tell you something, nigger. You ain't got nothing that girl wants; she'll use you like a dog. What, you think she like you? A nappy-headed field nigger? She wouldn't let you touch her with your dirty hands."

"I wanted to say hi and make her happy. When she did what she did, it make me sad."

"So you think you being nice gone do what? Boy, don't you go back up there today if you ain't got no instructions to do so, or I'll give you a new color on your skin, and it will be red."

"Yes, sir, I won't."

Rice pointed to his head. "She playing with your mind. Don't let her trick you into thinking you a smart nigger. Ain't no smart niggers out here. Riza still got that savagery in her, and you know what they do to niggers like you if you wrong them? They scalp you…that's right, they gone cut your hair off your head, and you going to pray to the good Lord to let you die. Now get back to those fields before I beat you."

"Yes, Master Rice." Clint stood up and limped to the cotton fields as Rice watched.

Rice got on his horse and rode to the mansion. He knocked on the door, and Dorothy answered the door. Rice demanded for Riza to be brought outside. Dorothy went to Mrs. Wilma and told her about Rice's request. Riza went to the front of the mansion door and stared at Rice. "Come on out here, Riza," Rice said.

Riza walked out of the mansion and kept her eyes on Rice. "Yes, Master Rice," Riza said.

Rice slightly chuckled while he looked at Riza. "You think you smart, acting nice like I can't see through that pretty face. Don't get that nigger's hopes up. I told that boy not to come back up here unless he gets instructed to."

"Clint did nothing wrong, Master Rice. He didn't even come inside the mansion."

"Did I ask for an explanation? You better watch yourself, or me and Master Plecker gone have a talk about you."

Riza pressed her lips. "Why do you care if he brings me a flower?"

"Whoever said this was about you?" Rice stepped up to her.

"I will gladly give you some lashes if you try your mind games on me. This ain't about you. That nigger needs to know his place."

"You smell like pig crap," Riza murmured.

"What did you say?" Rice grabbed her by her hair. She grabbed onto Rice's arm. "You lost your mind putting your hands on me and talking to me like that! Maybe I should cut this hair again so you keep being reminded how much you look like those field niggers."

Riza growled, "I didn't do anything wrong."

"You testing my patience." Rice let go of her hair as she took deep breaths. "You think you going to turn these Negroes against me with your charm?"

"I've done no such thing! I have no thoughts of that."

Rice caressed Riza's cheek with his finger, but she stepped back. "Who said you could move?" Rice saw Dorothy standing by the stairs, watching the entire incident. "Who said you could stand there, Dorothy? Go do what you supposed to." Dorothy walked away to the dining hall and quickly looked back at Riza. "Now you look here, you going to follow the law in this land, or like I told you. I'll make you a woman." Rice grabbed Riza's shoulder and grabbed her butt with his other hand. Rice whispered, "You not that little girl you were; you almost a woman. What you think Clint see in you now?"

Rice let go of Riza. Tears of disgust and rage filled her brown eyes. "I'm sorry, Master Rice, but he ain't you. I think every Negro man is better than you."

Rice's brown eyes enlarged. "What did you say to me?"

Riza gulped, looking into his eyes. "You heard what I said. So why don't you go meet with your pig by the big willow trees."

Riza ran for the door with him trying to give chase, and she slammed the door in his face. "Riza, you little redskin she-demon, I'll tear your hide!" Rice furiously opened the door and marched through the mansion. "Where is she? Where is Riza?"

Rice stormed through the hallway leading to the living room, only to be met by Wilma. "Rice, how dare you walk into my home in such a manner," she yelled. "This behavior is inexcusable!"

Rice humbly replied, "Ma'am, I apologize for my rudeness."

He saw Riza standing behind Wilma. "That little grass nigger got a mouth on her, and she needs to be beat for her rebellious manner."

Wilma looked back at Riza and Rice. "No, I won't have my day ruined by a few smart words coming out of Riza's mouth," Wilma confidently said. "Besides, when Riza did rush in here, I saw the tears she was quickly drying from her face. Rice, your job here is to help maintain the order and keep them field slaves in check. Not torture Riza. As we speak, Wade and Kit are out there with all them slaves where you should be."

"Mrs. Wilma, I promise I do nothing improper to her. She plays mind games."

Wilma's voice elevated. "I know how she operates, and those were not fake tears! Don't put any more time into Riza. She's a house slave. Stick to the niggers in the fields. I should be working on my knitting and drinking tea while you keep those Negroes in line. However, here we are because you can't be a man and ignore the words of a young woman who's only fourteen years old!"

"Mrs. Wilma, she fourteen years, but she think like a seventeen-year-old woman."

"We've had peace for months now, and I won't tolerate you giving her reasons to even think of trying another rebellion. Are we clear?"

Rice angrily looked at Riza while she stared at him. "Yes, ma'am, I will do my best here."

Wilma crossed her arms. "Good, I know you will."

Rice left the mansion, and Wilma walked to the living room. "Well, now all of that confusion is over. I have a puzzle to build. You may stay and watch, Riza, but bring me my crackers first."

"Yes, Mrs. Wilma," Riza said. She went into the cookhouse to get Wilma's crackers and brought them into the living room on a silver platter. She spent the rest of her time with Wilma and Dorothy, listening to Wilma talk about whatever subjects came to her mind.

On the night of April 30, 1861, in Tahlequah, Annabelle and John sat in their room illuminated by a lamp while they prayed together. There was a soft knock on their door. "Come in," John said.

The door slowly opened, and David walked inside the room. He was now almost as tall as John. "I'm sorry to come so late," David said.

"What is on your mind?" Annabelle asked in Cherokee.

"I want to go with Father and the others to find Joseph. Please allow me to go."

John replied in Cherokee, "No, David. We need you here to tend to the crops and protect the family here. Watching over your sisters, Jonathon, and the rest of the family is as important as looking for Joseph."

David pouted. "Jacob and Michael will be here. Please allow me to go with you?"

"The travel is too dangerous, and the White men have started a war between themselves. There's even talk of war coming our way, and soon we'll have to choose a side."

"I can fight. You know I can fight. I'm not scared of the White men."

John sighed. "It's not a question of whether or not you're scared. It is about protecting the family. It is better for you to stay here."

Annabelle could see the anger building on David's face as his nose wrinkled. "David, come here," she said. He sat on the bed next to her and looked at his parents. "I know you want to help. I see your pain, and I understand it, but we can't risk you going out there. You're too young, too inexperienced. I won't lose another child to these White men. You're too special to me and your father for us to let you go out there."

"I feel powerless here," he said in Cherokee.

"You're growing into a strong young man with a good heart. Don't let the pain these White men have caused us to grow evil in your heart." Annabelle hugged David as he wept. "There's nothing wrong with being angry, but I refuse to watch it kill my son. That loving boy I know." David continued to weep angrily as

Annabelle embraced him. "We need you here, okay, to help protect what we have here." Annabelle wiped the tears off David's face. "Do you understand me? Your siblings, your cousins, your aunties, Uncle George, Maria, and me, we need you here."

David nodded. "I understand, Momma."

"I know you miss your brother. It may not seem like it to you, but me and your father miss him so much, but we have to do things right so we bring him home safe. Those White men would rather shoot your brother dead than for us to save him. We have to be careful."

David frowned. "Okay, Momma. I'm sorry if I woke you and Father."

Annabelle smiled. "You didn't, but I can tell you this. We're proud of you. Stay focused on following Jesus and praying for your brother's return before this war becomes more dangerous."

"I will."

"Good. We need as many prayers as we can send." Annabelle kissed him on the cheek.

"You've always had a kind spirit, David," John said in Cherokee. "And your spirit has always been strong. As your mother has said, I'm proud of you."

David half-smiled and walked to the bedroom door. "Goodnight."

"Goodnight, David," Annabelle and John said in Cherokee.

He left the house. Annabelle watched him walk back to the family house to sleep. She walked back into her bedroom. Annabelle and John cuddled in their bed but remained awake. "This time must be a success. I don't know how much longer he can take the pain," John said in Cherokee.

"It's so hard," Annabelle said in Cherokee. "I felt it when I looked at him. Those were tears of anger, not sadness. I don't want to see my other son poisoned by what they did to our family."

"We have enough supplies in the carriage to last us three months and some extra money to buy more so we can stay out there longer. I have faith we'll find our boy this time."

Annabelle placed her hand on top of John's hand. "I do too.

That's the best thing we can do. If things don't go as planned, don't blame yourself. I know Elder Joyce received a strong word from Heaven."

John kissed Annabelle's hand and held it. "If such a thing happens, we will go and search for him again. Years ago, I would have cursed the Father and would've wanted nothing to do with him. But being the man I am today, I know this happened because this world is broken, and it allows evil to survive."

"I think that's all evil can do is fight to survive in some way until Jesus comes back. Well, I think it's time to sleep. You have a long ride tomorrow." Annabelle kissed John and smiled at him. "Goodnight."

"Goodnight, beautiful."

The next day, John, Eli, and Samuel double-checked their supplies before they left for Louisiana. The family gave each other hugs and kisses, and George led them in a prayer of protection. When the men were getting on the carriage, John approached David and gave his son another hug. "Remember, I'm relying on you, and I'm proud of you," John said.

David replied in Cherokee, "I won't fail you."

John nodded at him and he gave each of the twins a kiss on the cheek. "Papa, we made this for you," Rain said in Cherokee.

Rain presented a wooden knife to John, and he chuckled as he held the sharp piece of wood. "I see the both of you have learned a lot from Auntie Lizzie," he said in Cherokee. The girls gave big smiles as they heard his approval. John gave Annabelle another hug. "All for one and one for all," he whispered in Annabelle's ear. Annabelle quietly giggled as he got onto the carriage, and the men rode off to Louisiana. Days passed while John, Eli, and Samuel rode through the country in hope of finding Joseph.

CHAPTER 2
Hidden within Those Eyes

On May 9, 1861, David's seventeenth birthday arrived, but David was uninterested in celebrating it. Annabelle saw David leaning on the cornfield fence as he watched a small herd of bison and walked to him. "David, Michael was looking for you," Annabelle said in Cherokee.

"I'm not interested in playing cards, Momma," he said in Cherokee.

"You can't remain in mourning. If you remain this way, it'll make you sick or bring darkness into your heart. Enjoying this moment isn't ignoring that your brother isn't here to celebrate it with you."

Annabelle noticed his lowered eyes and slight frown, which echoed his frustration and sadness. "It doesn't feel honorable to celebrate with Joseph gone. I don't know how to let this pain go."

"You let it go by having faith, David. You let it go by being grateful. We have a list of all the possible places your brother could be at. Many families don't have that much. It's okay if you don't want to celebrate Jesus giving you another year, but I want to celebrate having my son here for another year."

David turned around and exhaled. "Will Joseph be the same when they bring him home?"

Annabelle frowned. "No, he won't be the same, but it will

help more if you have some joy to give him. He'll need a lot of love when your father brings him home."

Annabelle saw Rain, Jannie, and Rosita running to the field. "David, come play with us!" the girls yelled in Cherokee. "Michael is waiting for us!"

"Go on," Annabelle said in Cherokee. David approached Annabelle, and she gave him a hug and a kiss on the cheek. "I love you so much." The girls anxiously grabbed David's arms and pulled him so that he would start to run with them. The persistence of the girls gave Annabelle hope that David would try to have some joy while waiting for Joseph's return. "Please help his disbelief, Jesus."

During the night in Caledonia, Joseph sat outside the slave house looking up at the stars while the other slaves spent time with each other. "Joseph, why are you watching the stars?" Susie asked in Cherokee.

"I was thinking about my brother. Today was his birthday," Joseph said. "I miss him."

"I know he misses you too."

Joseph pouted. "Not being around David makes me hate this place more. I never thought I would miss his birthday."

Susie sat next to Joseph and handed him a dinner roll. "Eat. It'll make you feel better." Joseph took the roll and started to eat it. "I miss my family too, but I pray to Jesus all the time that I will see them again. I believe I will see them again. I hope you haven't given up."

"No, I haven't given up. I feel angry. We don't belong here."

"Be ye angry, and sin not; let not the sun go down upon your wrath." Joseph was surprised by Susie's response. "My momma used to always say that to me when I was younger. She would always say it's okay to be angry, but remember who you are... remember what would make Jesus happy."

"Do you get tired of listening to Master Plecker read us the Bible?" Joseph asked.

Susie huffed. "I do and I'm happy when Mrs. Wilma says we

don't get to listen to the good word because we didn't clean parts of the house fast enough. Master Plecker lies a lot about the scriptures."

"Yeah, that's the way I feel about it. Thank you for reminding me how we should act."

"You help me, and I help you. We're Cherokee, and we're good people. I'm sorry I didn't accept you earlier. It was wrong of me. You probably have heard it your whole life."

"Yeah, I have heard a lot of different things because my momma is Negro, but I've met many that accept me. Like you. It makes me happy, but I realized I was ashamed to be half Negro. I embarrass my momma by thinking that way."

"You don't embarrass her anymore if you understand what you did and don't act that way. I think it would make her proud…if you're proud to be half-breed."

Joseph's eyes slightly widened. "You think so?"

Susie grinned. "Yeah, I think so."

"What is your momma like?"

She laughed as she looked at Joseph. "My momma is like me. People say we have the same spirit. She likes to sing to herself a lot. Even when we didn't have enough food, she would sing through our home. I wish I had her voice."

"My Auntie Lizzie can sing. She only does it in church and when she walks alone. It's pretty." They continued to look at the stars and talk more about their families. "Thank you for making me feel better."

"You're welcome, Joseph. We will see each other again." Susie snuck through the weeping willow trees to the slave house as Joseph went inside Bo's slave house.

On May 12, 1861, Judy Mays visited Wilma again along with Daphne. Joseph recognized the carriage and the two brown horses that pulled it. As Joseph and Tom worked in the cotton fields to kill pest insects and scare off any rodents. Susie was sent out to ask for Joseph. He followed Susie to the white mansion. He wondered if Judy Mays was going to take him away to be a slave for her if she was going to ask more questions, or if she was willing to free him.

As they were about to enter the mansion, a familiar white carriage arrived at the mansion. "Susie, Joseph why are y'all standing in the doorway? Come inside," Dorothy said.

"I think Miss Reece just arrived," Susie said.

Dorothy calmly walked up to Joseph and Susie and looked at the white carriage sneeringly. Reece's driver got off the carriage, and was about to open the carriage door. "The two of you go on to the living room. I know Mrs. Judy Mays is waiting for y'all right now."

"There's no need for that," she said. "Come inside, Joseph." He and Susie walked inside the mansion. He felt his heart race when he stood before her. "Good afternoon, Joseph."

"Good afternoon, Mrs. Judy Mays," he nervously said.

"I can tell by those dirty trousers you've been out in those cotton fields. Susie, you may go back to your tasks so Mrs. Wilma doesn't scold you."

"Yes, Mrs. Judy Mays," Susie said. She went up the stairs to continue her duties.

She leaned over to him and placed her hand on his cheek. "What caused those wounds?"

"Those cuts on his face were caused by one of the hunting dogs," Wilma said. "He was caught eating the corn for the cattle of all things. Rice felt it was necessary to punish him by putting his face in front of the dogs."

Judy Mays replied, "What an unnecessary cruelty. That man doesn't even know how to be proper to a lady."

"Mrs. Wilma, Miss Reece is here," Dorothy unenthusiastically said.

"Good, good I was hoping she would arrive soon," Wilma said. Reece walked up to the front door in her light blue Victorian dress as Dorothy forcefully smiled. "Ah, Reece, come in, come in. I'm so excited you could join us."

"Why thank you, Mrs. Plecker. It was my pleasure," Reece said.

"Hello, Reece, I'm Judy Mays. Wilma has spoken highly of you."

Reece gleefully replied, "I'm grateful to hear such words. Why is one of the half-breeds here? He is so dirty."

"He is here at the request of Judy Mays. She finds him entertaining," Wilma said.

"Entertaining... how such a dirty thing could be entertaining puzzles me," Reece said. "I can't tell the difference between his skin and the actual dirt."

Wilma giggled, but he slightly narrowed his eyes at Reece. "Well, that's none of your concern, is it?" Judy Mays said. "I do enjoy seeing this child display intelligence."

Reece laughed while she looked at Judy Mays. "You're a funny woman to think of a half-breed having any real intelligence. The only thing they're smarter than is a Negro."

Judy Mays raised an eyebrow. "I think your ignorance is amusing. Are you so blind or prideful that you believe they have no intelligence? I hope there's more to you than that pretty face."

Reece scoffed. "I find it hard to believe they have any true form of intelligence. They're nothing but a crossbreed between two lower forms of man."

Judy Mays gave a fake smile. "So sad you know so little. I'd consider it a blessing you don't have an Indian slave like Riza. She nearly burned down this house in a disturbing but clever way." Riza, listening to the conversation, quietly stepped back, not wanting to be seen. "It makes me wonder what kind of capacity you have in your mind."

"Judy Mays, don't bully her. She's a bright young woman," Wilma said with an appealing tone. "She is seventeen and still learning, but I trust she's more than capable of controlling a slave."

Reece slightly crinkled her nose and snobbishly said, "I would never be careless with my authority of a slave. I know what needs to be done when a slave needs to be reminded of their place." Reece noticed a slight smirk on Dorothy's face and abruptly slapped her. Dorothy held her face and stared at Reece with her combative hazel eyes. "Don't think I didn't notice that little smile, you frizzy-haired mulatto."

Wilma groaned, "Enough of this. Dorothy, go and prepare our sandwiches while we talk. Reece, please remember your place here."

Dorothy humbly replied, "Yes, Mrs. Wilma." Dorothy gave Reece an instigative look and walked to the kitchen.

"Mrs. Plecker, you should have seen the way that mulatto looked at me," Reece said. "The amount of disrespect is absurd."

"That wasn't surprising," Judy Mays said. Reece pouted as she looked at Judy Mays.

"Enough of this small bickering. There's no need for it. Come, let us enjoy some tea and fresh crackers," Wilma said. "Susie, come here." She immediately came downstairs. "Susie, please escort Joseph back to the fields so I don't have to worry about the boy being accused of not working."

"Yes, Mrs. Wilma," she said. They left the mansion as Judy Mays frustratingly watched.

The women entered the luxurious living room with its brown grandfather clock ticking away while sunlight reflected off the piano. Daphne patiently waited on a crème-colored sofa. "Daphne, I want you to meet Reece. Her and Kenneth are courting," Wilma said.

"So this is the beautiful young woman I heard about. Such a pleasure to meet you," Daphne said. "Kenneth must be excited about meeting a young lady like yourself."

"Why thank you," Reece said. "I'm grateful to have been introduced to Kenneth." Reece looked to her right and saw Riza standing by the grandfather clock. "I...wait, who is that?"

Wilma replied, "Reece, are you feeling all right? That's Riza."

"Shocking, she's almost as tall as me."

"Well, she's fourteen years old now. She's on her way to becoming a young woman like yourself. She is still the same Riza, dear."

"It's called a growth spurt," Judy Mays sarcastically replied. "I'm sure you experienced one yourself at least once."

"Don't mock me," Reece irritably said with her eyes narrowing.

"I see you've met Judy Mays completely. Don't let her sarcasm bother you," Daphne said. "Most of the time, she is much more enjoyable."

"Please relax, Reece. Take a seat. There's no need for more drama," Wilma said. "The ongoing war is enough. As ladies, we need to be peacekeepers. Now come sit down and enjoy some tea. Riza, go and bring us some crackers while Dorothy finishes making our sandwiches."

"Yes, Mrs. Wilma," Riza said. She gave Reece a slight smirk when she left the living room to the cookhouse.

"The fear of the Lord needs to be beaten into her," Reece griped. "I don't like the way she looks at me."

"Poor dear, did Riza stick her tongue out at you," Judy Mays said.

Reece sneered at Judy Mays as Daphne chuckled. "Enough, Judy Mays, please act your age," Wilma begged. "No more of these insults. We're supposed to be having a good time and getting to know each other."

"Good afternoon, ladies," Kenneth said.

"Kenneth, there you are. I was wondering where you were," Reece said.

"I would've been down here sooner, but I was distracted by the view from my balcony. The spring weather always cheers me up."

"Edgar says you should come back to Columbus for a day and go hunting with him," Judy Mays said. "He's missing having someone around that he can have intelligent conversations with. He thinks the northern men are arrogant."

Kenneth scoffed. "I think the northerners are arrogant. That's why we're at war with them now, and we'll win. They aim to destroy our way of life without any compensation. Lincoln is leading a pack of fools. Forcing a change on land that isn't ready for change."

Judy Mays leaned forward, folding her hands. "Do you think our country needs to change? There's a difference between being ready to change and needing to change."

Kenneth stepped forward. "I think our country does have some issues needing to be dealt with, but they should be dealt with politically. This is no longer a country…I believe the North underestimates our resolve."

"Are you going to join the war?" Daphne asked.

"If things progress for the worse, I believe it would be my duty to fight alongside my Southern men," Kenneth said. "I see no honor in taking a life, but to defend this home and my family, I would do so."

"Come sit with me, Kenneth," Reece said.

He replied, "Actually, Momma, would you excuse us for a moment? I wanted to speak with Reece privately out on the patio."

"Of course, but please be quick about it," Wilma said. "We'll be having sandwiches in here soon."

Kenneth cheerfully replied, "Yes, ma'am." Reece followed Kenneth out to the patio. During this time, Daphne, Judy Mays, and Wilma continued to talk about their thoughts on the war.

Wilma kept her eyes on the hallway. "Please keep voicing your opinions on this war before Riza returns. I feel uncomfortable with her hearing about the freeing of slaves," Wilma said. As the women talked, Kenneth and Reece soon returned to the living room and sat down smiling.

In the kitchen, Dorothy could hear cheering. She walked out of the cookhouse with the sandwiches on a silver platter down the covered walkway. She strolled into the living room and saw Wilma giving Reece a hug. "Mrs. Wilma, I have the sandwiches ready," Dorothy said.

"Great Dorothy, this is a time to celebrate! Kenneth asked Reece to marry him, and she accepted! Wilma shrieked. This is wonderful news!"

Dorothy felt her heart drop when she looked at Kenneth and

forgot she was holding the silver platter. The silver platter and sandwiches fell on the floor, and Dorothy immediately started to pick up the ruined sandwiches off the floor.

Daphne laughed, saying, "She's more surprised than we are!"

Riza hurried to help Dorothy pick up the sandwiches. "I'm so sorry, Mrs. Wilma. It will never happen again," Dorothy nervously said.

"Quickly clean this mess and bring us some more, Dorothy," Wilma snobbishly said. "I know the news is shocking but please try to contain your excitement next time. Your father is going to be so excited to hear this. He should be back soon."

"Thank you, Momma," Kenneth said.

As they finished cleaning up the spilled food, Judy Mays watched with a raised eyebrow. Dorothy stood up with the platter of ruined sandwiches and slightly gazed at Kenneth. He looked away toward a smiling Reece. "I make some new sandwiches right now, Mrs. Wilma," she said.

"Yes, please hurry, Dorothy," Wilma said. "Riza, go help her quickly."

Dorothy and Riza left for the kitchen. Inside the kitchen, Dorothy began to sniffle, but she took deep breaths to stop herself. "All right, Riza. We need to do this quickly for Mrs. Wilma," Dorothy said.

"Are you okay?" Riza asked with a skewed frown.

Dorothy huffed. "Why wouldn't I be okay? I'm fine...not surprised he would ask that woman to marry him."

Riza grimaced. "She is pretty and...well, I see why it would make you upset."

"He could do better. That's all I have to say." Dorothy's seriousness was obvious while aggressively making the sandwiches. Riza frowned and worked to keep up. As they made the sandwiches, Dorothy placed one sandwich on the side and spit on the inside of it. Riza's jaw dropped, but knew not to question Dorothy. "That sandwich is for Reece. She can give that cute smile all she wants!" Dorothy said with her voice rising with each word. She placed the sandwich on the edge of one of the platters.

Dorothy and Riza brought out the platters, and Riza placed her platter down. "I'm so pleased to see that you're happy with the good news," Reece said. Dorothy presented her platter to Reece. Reece reached for the sandwich and began to eat it. "Maybe I'll let you help me put on my wedding dress, Dorothy." Daphne and Wilma chuckled while Dorothy gave Reece a fake smile.

"How kind of you, Miss Reece. I hope you enjoy your sandwich," Dorothy said with a subtle sarcastic tone. Judy Mays's brow somewhat lowered upon hearing Dorothy's tone, but she remained silent while Reece ate. Mr. Plecker later arrived at the mansion and was informed about the proposal. He was pleased and congratulated the young couple. Dorothy continued to serve while she struggled to contain her emotions and avoided eye contact with Kenneth.

As the group ate lunch, Judy Mays pouted, hearing Daphne and Reece's dominant wedding talk. "Wilma, how has Joseph been behaving?" Judy Mays asked.

"He and Tom have been serving well from what I hear," Wilma said. "I believe they would be next in line to be a slave driver."

"Let's not be so quick to say so dear," Mr. Plecker said.

"Why not Calvin?"

"I'm waiting to see if those boys continue to work like they supposed to. I haven't forgotten Joseph's involvement in Riza's rebellion. I need to see more loyalty before I put either of the boys in charge over any other slave. Those half-breeds are liable to lead more slaves astray than to keep them in check. They're not commanding nothing until I say."

Wilma submissively remained quiet as Calvin looked at the others. "Well, I'm sure in time those boys will make you proud, Mr. Plecker," Judy Mays said. "I do think they have potential to keep the others in line if you needed such a thing."

Mr. Plecker replied, "Well, the boys do have some more smarts than the other niggers. I can be honest and say that's true, but as I said earlier. I'm not giving them anything yet."

Judy Mays smiled. "Well, trust is earned. I admire your wisdom."

"Pardon, but I couldn't care less about hearing about some half-breed nigger when I've just been proposed to," Reece bickered. "I think you care too much for the boy."

Judy Mays's pinched her mouth, her eyes shifting from Wilma and back to Reece. "Actually, this slave is of interest to Judy Mays because he may be a link to a runaway from years ago," Wilma said. "That's why he's of so much interest." Wilma scoffed. "Not because she cares about the boy."

Reece politely replied, "Oh, well, my apologies. That does change things. No slave has the right to ignore their duty." Riza slightly scoffed while she stood next to the grandfather clock. Reece turned to Riza. "What was that?"

Judy Mays chuckled, saying, "Please don't tell me you're offended now. Riza, more tea, please."

Riza replied, "Yes, ma'am." Riza poured the tea, ignoring Reece.

"Well, enough of this talk. Let's negotiate a wedding date, shall we," Wilma said.

"Indeed," Reece said. Reece snobbishly looked at Judy Mays, and a conversation on setting a wedding date began. In the late afternoon, Daphne and Judy Mays prepared to leave. The mood between the women became peaceful as they prepared to leave the mansion. Dorothy stood by the opened front door, and Daphne and Judy Mays walked out of it. Kenneth and Reece stood behind them.

"What a day," Kenneth said.

Reece beamed. "Yes, it was. Goodbye, you handsome man. I'll see you in a few days," she said.

"I look forward to it," Kenneth said. Kenneth kissed Reece on the hand and walked outside, avoiding eye contact with Dorothy to say his goodbyes to Daphne and Judy Mays.

Wilma stepped out of the mansion after Kenneth to talk to the young women as Riza followed her. At this time, Reece and Dorothy gave each other a blank stare. "You know you don't fool me for one moment," Reece irritably said, her face slowly scrunching. She slapped Dorothy and looked at Dorothy with a strong leer. "You can fool the others all you want, but I know you didn't drop those sandwiches because you were surprised. I can see in those pretty eyes. You don't like me. Well, I don't like you either, and I don't like Kenneth talking about you."

"Is that all, Miss Reece," Dorothy said.

Reece obnoxiously laughed. "If I could have that pretty face beaten, I would. I'm no fool, and I feel this"—she dismissively waved her hand—"unnatural feeling to want to slap you again. You're nothing but a slave...a frizzy-haired mulatto."

Dorothy sarcastically replied, "As you say, Miss Reece."

Reece slapped Dorothy again. "Don't think I can't see through that. Maybe I will have you help me put on that wedding dress." Reece and Dorothy stared each other down intensely with narrowed eyes while Judy Mays's carriage door could be heard closing. "I have no favorites. A nigger is a nigger. I will greatly look forward to seeing you soon again." Reece's upper lip lifted showing her irritation. "Yes, I will. Mulatto." She turned around, exited the mansion, and gave Wilma a hug. Reece confidently approached Kenneth and gave him a kiss on the cheek. "You've only made me happier."

"You've made me happier too," Kenneth said. Dorothy stood in the doorway with hazel eyes piercing like daggers at Kenneth as he continued to talk to Reece. She marched back into the mansion and continued the rest of her duties.

After the Pleckers' supper, the house slaves cleaned the supper table, dishes, glasses, and utensils. Dorothy remained mostly silent while she helped Riza and the others clean up. Riza and Susie were concerned as they watched Dorothy clean systematically in deep thought. "Doris, Daisy are you done in there," Dorothy yelled.

Doris walked through the other set of doors leading to the living room. "We almost done, Momma," Doris said. "We finished cleaning all the cabinets, Momma."

"Good, I want you to take your sister with you and follow Riza or Susie back to the house," Dorothy calmly said. "We're almost done here. You're not a nigger in the fields, so don't talk like them, sweetie."

Doris cheerfully replied, "Yes, Momma." After the house

slaves finished cleaning, Dorothy reluctantly left the cookhouse with a small loaf of bread and a glass of water. Riza frowned when she heard her mumbling. Riza took the two young girls with her to the slave house.

She cautiously looked around to make sure Calvin and Wilma were finally asleep and knocked on Kenneth's door. He opened the door, and was presented with the small loaf of bread and glass of water on a silver platter. "Dorothy, I didn't ask for you to come here," he whispered. You can take all of this right back downstairs."

She walked into his room and placed the silver platter on his brown desk. "Master Kenneth, you seemed to not eat as much as you normally would, so I brought you some extra food," she calmly said.

He agitatedly replied, "I said to take that platter back to the kitchen. I'm not going to tolerate any of this behavior, Dorothy. You do as you're told."

"Why didn't you tell me you were going to propose to Reece?" He closed the door and calmly approached her. "I know…I have no right to ask such a thing, but I thought you would say something to me."

"I believe she is what's best for me. I actually do like her and it's time for me to really be a man with my own property, my own profits."

"I see. I do hope in some way she makes you happy."

His brow furrowed. "Don't lie to me. I saw your face when you dropped all that food. Now leave. I don't want you here right now."

She slightly frowned. "Do you love her?"

Kenneth looked away from Dorothy. "What kind of question is that? Don't ever question me on how I feel. I'm doing what is best for me, and I do like her. It doesn't matter if you approve of this or not. I need to tell you we won't be meeting like this anymore. I'm a Christian man, and I won't embarrass my family with any act of adultery."

"And I'm a Christian woman, Kenneth. I've done everything you have asked of me. I lov—"

He raised his voice, "What about what Riza did? Our agreement was for you to tell me everything. I knew she was planning something, but you told me nothing."

"That's because I knew nothing! She isn't a fool! You know she didn't tell me about the plan at all. I've also been worried about her."

Kenneth scoffed. "Why, why worry about her?"

Dorothy's face twisted. "Because of how Master Rice looks at her, I know that lustful look. I'm terrified for her. She already looks older than she is, and I'm terrified he'll force himself on her. I know it would break her spirit."

"Maybe that's what she needs…to be broken."

She tearfully replied, "I've never been raped! You're all I know! But I've heard stories from many different slaves from this plantation and others. Please don't allow her to experience such a thing. I know what she did was evil, but she doesn't deserve that."

Kenneth huffed. "Fine, but I need you to leave me."

"Please don't send me away like that."

"I said leave, Dorothy." Sadness surged through her body as she stood her ground. She leaned forward and kissed him. She looked into his brown eyes and kissed him again. Kenneth grabbed Dorothy by the arm and forced her to the door. "I said go!"

Dorothy turned around and took a deep breath as if she was about to cry. "Kenneth." He sympathetically looked at her, but she aggressively wrapped her arms around his neck and softly kissed Kenneth again.

"No, Dorothy," Kenneth whispered. Dorothy kissed Kenneth again. "Dorothy, I said stop!" Dorothy continued to kiss Kenneth and moved his hands onto her butt, alluring him to fall into his feelings for her.

Dorothy had seduced Kenneth again. *The law says you can't marry me, but she'll never give you love like me. Even in the shadows*, she thought. After being with Kenneth, Dorothy returned to the slave house. While everyone slept, Dorothy prayed, *Lord, I'm sorry for my sins, and I'm asking for any way to be with the man*

I love. You know my heart, and these girls you blessed me with are the most important thing. I love him, and sometimes I hate myself for it. Your will be done on this Earth as it is in Heaven.

A few weeks went by while the relationship between Dorothy and Kenneth remained unstable. Riza noticed the change as he tried to limit his interactions with Dorothy but remained kind to her. Susie also noticed it, and the girls wondered if she had spoken up about her dislike of Reece. One day in June of 1861, Susie strolled to an old cookhouse to quickly see what Joseph and Tom were doing. Joseph saw a few chickadees fly over the old cookhouse from the direction of the willow trees. He looked at the path and saw Susie approaching him and Tom. The boys greeted Susie and talked for a moment. Susie waited behind the old cookhouse for the boys to finish eating. Joseph noticed Susie was watching chickadees in the trees.

"I'm done eating," Joseph said.

"You didn't have to eat that fast," she said.

"Today was the beef stew, so it was better than that pork."

She grunted. "I don't like pork either, it makes my stomach hurt. Does Master Wade still make you and Tom pick bugs from the plants?"

"Yes he does, and it's terrible even with this straw hat on. I hate killing the bugs and someone got bit by a spider yesterday but it was one of the colorful ones so he is okay."

"Yeah, I'm not having a good day. Mrs. Wilma made me iron her dress twice today. I think her eyes are going bad because she kept saying it had wrinkles in it when it didn't."

"Is Dorothy still acting strange?" Joseph asked.

"A little, but I'm happy she's not upset. I think she really hates Miss Reece. That woman is mean, and she looks—"

"What is this I hear?" Rice said. They froze as they stood before Rice. "I know you know speaking Indian garbage isn't allowed anywhere on this plantation, Joseph."

He nervously replied, "I didn't say nothing bad, Master Rice."

Rice folded his arms while he looked at the Cherokee children. "Boy, you think I'm stupid, don't you? I think you've learned too much from Riza, and I ain't about to tolerate none of that."

Susie replied, "Master Rice, he didn't say nothing."

Rice angrily replied, "Little girl, I heard gibberish clear as day! And what are you doing out here? You know what? Don't even try to explain. I don't have time for it. Come here, Joseph, and get your lashes." He stood still as he fearfully stared down Rice. "Boy, is you deaf?"

He replied, "No, Master Rice."

Rice growled, "Then come here, boy." Joseph remained still as she reached for his hand. "I see, y'all think y'all gone disrespect me well...y'all wrong." Rice went to a small tree and ripped a fresh branch off of it. "Susie, you best back up, or you getting it too."

She looked at Joseph as he took a deep breath. He shook off her hand and frowned. She saw the fear in his eyes, but he stuck his hand out.

She began to tremble. "You don't have to do this alone," she said.

As Susie was about to grab his hand, Rice struck him across the head with the branch, knocking him down. "I see you want to do things like a man," he said. He hit him across his back with the branch. "Then you gone follow the laws of this land like a man." Rice continued to strike him on his back and his legs while he rolled around in pain. "Stop moving, you little nigger!"

Susie watched as he was being beaten. Trembling, her heart rapidly paced. Susie screamed and jumped on Rice's back. "Please stop, Master Rice," she screamed. The commotion had now caught the attention of the other slaves, and they went behind the cookhouse witnessing Susie hold onto Rice's back.

Rice managed to shake off Susie ripping his brown vest. "You little grass nigger," Rice howled. "You must've gone insane!" Rice looked down at Joseph and saw him shaking in pain.

"What's going on here?" Wade asked.

"I caught this half-breed speaking Indian gibberish and was

giving him the proper beating when this little redskin decided to get in my way. You see, she tore one of my favorite vests."

Wade looked at Joseph as he continued to shake in pain and looked at Susie. "Give her ten lashes and send her back to the mansion," Wade said.

"Ten…ten lashes after this nigger gone ripped my vest!" Rice yelled. "Come here, you little savage!" Rice grabbed Susie by her hair, and she screamed.

"No," Joseph murmured.

Rice angrily replied, "Did he say no?" Rice kicked Joseph in his stomach. "Boy, you be grateful she's not getting it like Riza. Especially after what she did to my vest." Rice grabbed Susie's face. "I think you best be grateful the next time you see Susie. She still gone have this cute face of hers. Still trying to be Indian…that's why she's getting her whippings. When you gone realize you ain't one of them no more?"

"Rice, that's enough. Take her to receive her punishment the girl needs to finish her duties," Wade commanded. Rice grabbed Susie by her hair and pulled her to the old tree stump to be beaten. Susie grabbed his arm and pulled back, causing a struggle. She fought Rice the whole way to the stump. "The rest of you get back to work now, or y'all be getting twice the beating that little redskin is gonna get." The other slaves quickly moved to the cotton fields and their workstations. Wade forced Joseph to stand. "Walk boy. We ain't got all day out here." Joseph began to walk with a limp and when he moved around the cookhouse, he saw Tom standing there wiping away his tears. "Y'all finish y'all duties or the whip is going across both of your backs."

"Yes, Master Wade," Tom said. Tom helped Joseph walk as Joseph began to weep for Susie. As the boys slowly walked to work, they could hear Susie's screams. Hearing Susie's screams angered the boys. They could only imagine what Rice was doing to her to force her to scream.

Susie was later returned to the mansion quivering as pain flowed through her body. The whippings gave Susie two new flesh wounds and several welts on her back. Rice stood in the doorway as Dorothy quickly took Susie inside to clean the wounds. Wilma pouted and watched Susie struggle to move.

"Next time, don't damage her so much over a vest," Wilma said. "We will gladly purchase you a new one for all your hard work, but next time, if such an occasion like this happens again, I want her brought back more functional. She probably thought you beat the boy to death. They're from the same tribe, after all."

Rice replied, "I apologize, Mrs. Plecker, but that little redskin got a lot of fight in her for her size. I will pay more attention to her tolerance next time."

"Hopefully, there won't be a next time. Thank you, Rice." Wilma nodded and marched to the living room.

Riza stood in her place as Wilma moved past her and grimaced at Rice. Riza went to the door to close it. "Did I do something you didn't like, young lady?" Rice said with an instigative tone.

"I think you're a smart enough to know what I think, Master Rice," Riza murmured.

"What was that?"

Riza continued to squint at Rice. "Nothing, Master Rice."

"Mm-hmm I see it in those eyes of yours. I suggest you think twice about pulling some mess again. I don't like the looks you give me."

Riza sharply replied, "My apologies, Master Rice my face has a hard time not reacting."

"Don't test me now. I'm a Christian man."

Riza scoffed. "Master Rice, even Judas was a disciple."

Rice's eye bulged. "When you get a little older, I'm gone have a real fun time with you. You will jump when I say jump, and you will bend over when I say bend over."

Riza thought, maybe you should go to the war and show how much of a Christian man you really are. "I've been summoned." Riza slammed the door in Rice's face.

Rice looked around and took deep breaths. "Clock is ticking for that prairie nigger...the clock is ticking."

Days passed before the boys saw Susie again. When the boys did see Susie, Joseph tearfully apologized to her, but she refused his apology. She felt it was something she should've done. The friendship between the three Indian children remained strong, but Susie was now on a shorter time scale.

CHAPTER 3
My Friend, Espionage

On June 18, 1861, Peter Avail opened the curtains in his living room, revealing a partly sunny day. A sandy-colored couch sat in the middle of the sunlit living room, with a beige-colored grandfather clock standing to the right of it. A gray upholstered armchair sat to the left of the couch. He turned to Ruthanne, saying, "He is supposed to arrive today?"

She answered, "Yes, Leonard should arrive today. The railroads have been quite consistent."

"Hopefully, we can benefit from his assistance."

"Well, he will be coming from Saint Louis. It must've been the Lord's timing when I wrote him the letter."

"Ruben's last letter to you gave us another door. Who'd ever think your brother's angry rant in calling Leonard an abolitionist sympathizer and traitor gave us what we needed. I believe God has his hand on this, and Joseph will be saved."

"I wish I could leave for Mississippi and search for him myself."

Peter put his hands in his pockets. "Yes, but we've talked about this. With the outbreak of this war and your less-than-desirable reputation in your own hometown. You would have a difficult time looking for him, and we can't risk a random battle taking place. Who knows if Columbus will become a battleground."

Ruthanne rubbed her pregnant belly with the sound of the grandfather clock ticking. "I know, Peter. I can't risk my life or my freedom."

"Momma," Belle cheerfully yelled.

She looked at the kitchen door frame and looked back at him as she sighed. "What do you need, sweetie?" she asked.

"I spilled my water."

She groaned and marched into the kitchen.

Suddenly there was a knock on the front door. Peter opened the door and saw Marilyn standing there in a blue and white Victorian dress. She was holding a brown grocery bag filled to the top and had Naomi on her right side. The hazel-eyed toddler grinned at Peter, and he smiled back. "Good morning, Peter," she said.

"Good morning, Marilyn," he replied. "What's with all the food?"

"Well, this is for our expected guest. Ruthanne wanted to make sure he felt fully welcomed."

Peter rubbed his forehead. "Ah…I see my wife has decided he needs a very hospitable welcome." He welcomingly waved his hand. "Come in, come in. Hello, little Naomi."

"Good morning, Pastor Avail," she said with a dimpled grin. They entered the sunlit home and calmly walked across the wooden floor. Naomi immediately went toward the grandfather clock with widened eyes.

"I hope us making him a meal isn't a problem," Marilyn said.

He calmly closed the door. "No, we need to appease him the best we can. I was a little wary of Ruthanne writing him the letter. But we need to use every resource we can to help Annabelle. If he's against slavery as she believes…he will be a great ally to our cause."

The corners of Marilyn's mouth curved upward slightly, revealing her dimples. "I hope she is right. Ruthanne, I'm here."

"I'm in the kitchen cleaning up Belle's mess," Ruthanne shouted.

He calmly approached the kitchen, with Marilyn following a few steps behind him. He entered the kitchen with his young daughters, Belle and Christina, sitting at a small table to his right. "Well, I'm off to the church," Peter said, stepping up to the girls and kissing them both on the cheek. He then gave Ruthanne a quick kiss.

"I'm sure Jonah will be awake when you return," Ruthanne said.

"He's a calm baby boy," Marilyn said.

"I expect nothing less of my son," Peter said with an uplifted chin and a grin.

Ruthanne scoffed and dismissively waved her hand at Peter. "Go on before he wakes up."

"Good day, Marilyn," he said.

"Good day, Peter," she replied. On the way out of the house, he grabbed his black top hat and black walking cane.

A few hours later into the afternoon, there was a knock on the front door. Ruthanne opened the door with Marilyn and Belle standing right behind her. Her green eyes widened, and the corner of her mouth curved upward, forming a welcoming smile. "Leonard, you made it," she said.

Leonard held a brown suitcase in his right hand. He had an average build and was the same height as Peter. He tipped his brown top hat, replying with a Southern accent, "It's a blessing to see you, Ruthanne. I do try to keep my word to old friends." His brown eyes anchored on her pregnant belly, and he grinned. "Seeing you with child is truly a beautiful thing." His head turned toward Marilyn. "And who is this welcoming young woman? I see she has your piercing green eyes, Ruthanne."

"This is my good friend, Marilyn."

"Truly, a pleasure to meet you, Marilyn."

"It's a pleasure to meet you as well," she said.

"Well, come on in and have a seat on the couch," Ruthanne said. Leonard entered the home and put down his suitcase. "Let me take your waistcoat." He took off his brown waistcoat and held onto his top hat. Belle's green eyes dilated as she looked at the blond-haired man. She confidently walked up to him and took his brown top hat from him. She looked at the hat and then beamed at him. "Belle! Don't take without asking permission," Ruthanne scolded with a furrowed brow.

"Belle," Marilyn sternly said with her hands on her hip.

"It is all right. She's a little girl," Leonard said. "I'm amazed how much she looks like you."

"Why, thank you, Leonard. I know it baffles Peter as well," Ruthanne said.

"Please don't call me Leonard. I know we're adults now, but please, call me Leo. I hope to see a sermon of his before I have to return to Mississippi."

"He will be preaching tomorrow. It'd be nice if you could attend."

"This war is becoming darker by the day with no end in sight."

Ruthanne's brows drew together. "Are you going to fight?"

He huffed. "Not at this moment, if I do. I'll join the Union and help end this reign of slavery once and for all, but for now, I feel it is more important for me to help any Negroes that have escaped. There's so much at stake with this war. It's like the gates of hell have opened up and have cursed our country."

The beardless man followed Marilyn and Ruthanne to the sandy-colored couch. Jonah moaned as he lay in his wooden cradle, which sat next to the armchair. "Oh, looks like someone will be up from his nap," Marilyn said.

"Oh, is this your son, Ruthanne?" he cheerfully asked.

"Yes, that's Jonah," she answered.

Ruthanne sat down in the chair and Marilyn sat down on the couch to her right. Leonard sat on the other side of the couch. "Belle, go play with Naomi and your sister," Ruthanne calmly said. Belle quickly walked away to the bedrooms. "Leo, are you returning to the Benedict plantation to visit your sisters and their children?"

Leonard rubbed his chin. "Good question…my brothers-in-law have foolishly decided to join the Confederacy leaving my sisters and the children alone. We have working servants instead of slaves now that Pa has passed away. I feel greatly uncomfortable about them being there without a White man there."

"If you don't trust your former slaves around your sisters, why are you here?" Marilyn asked.

Leonard folded his hands on his knee as he slightly leaned forward. "I do trust them. I don't trust some of our neighbors. The only ones I can trust is Edgar and Judy Mays Reynolds. You would never think of Judy Mays coming from such a stern pro-slavery family."

Ruthanne's eyebrow lifted. "What do you mean?"

"Well, she still has slaves on that plantation, but they receive wages, and the Reynolds refused to buy anymore. I know for a fact two of the women slaves have managed to pay for their freedom but remain on the plantation to work, much to the disgust of her parents for sure."

"Does she have any half-breed Indian children there?"

Leo shrugged. "If she does have any children there with Indian blood, they were born there and less than half Indian, though. Three of her women slaves are clearly mixed with that blood. Why do you ask?"

"Can you search the plantations in Columbus and Caledonia for an Indian child for me? The child was not born a slave but was taken from his family. He's the son of an old friend of mine I met over a decade ago."

Ruthanne looked over at Jonah as he slept. "I couldn't imagine it, Leo. Someone coming onto my property and kidnapping my son, my only son, nonetheless. The more time that goes by, the harder it will be to find him."

Leonard sat back with his hands still folded. "What exactly do you want me to do? I'm terrible at confrontation."

"I have a listing of each plantation in Mississippi that's known to have Indian children there or those almost in adulthood. I just need to know if he is at any of those children in Columbus or Caledonia."

"Why those two towns?"

They locked eyes with lowered brows and then looked at him. "Because...the boy's mother is linked to Columbus and also connected to Judy Mays. If Judy Mays or her family finds out who the boy's mother is, we may never be able to bring him home.

If Judy Mays is anything like her younger self, she'll make this war look like a tea party."

Leo leaned forward with his elbow resting on his leg. "The boy's mother was a slave of the Browns, I take it?"

Ruthanne exhaled. "The boy's name is Joseph, and his mother's name is Annabelle."

He sat back in his chair with his mouth agape while Marilyn and Ruthanne looked at him. His brown eyes shot open, and his voice elevated, "You mean Annabelle Brown!? The slave the Brown family ripped through all of Mississippi looking for and placed a $1,400 bounty for her live return? That Annabelle!?"

"Yes."

"Ruthanne. How did you get involved in all of this?"

Jonah began to cry, and Ruthanne leaned over to pick him up.

"Oh, I'm so sorry, Ruthanne," Leonard said.

"It's all right. His nap time is basically over," she replied, with Jonah now sitting on her lap. The baby boy quieted down as she swayed with him.

"We know this is shocking information to take in," Marilyn said.

"Yes, well, you're talking about one of the richest and most powerful families in Mississippi. And that's who you angered, Ruthanne. Even though your family is in the same tier, you certainly erased any boredom in Mississippi. Especially to outsmart your brother."

"That story is for another day, but Joseph is in a lot of danger if he's in either of those towns."

His brow drew together. "But…what makes you so sure Judy Mays could even possibly find him? She's not even looking for him, so what are the chances?"

"Judy Mays is different than me in one major way, she's a socialite. She's always spent a lot of time in Columbus and Caledonia. Only woman I knew that knew the names of slaves she didn't need to know. If there's a situation where she even gets a hint that Annabelle is Joseph's mother, who knows what she'll do. I fear for the boy."

"All right, I think I can do that much. If I can locate the boy, I'll send a message to you immediately, but I feel taking the boy will be out of my power."

"Leave that part to Joseph's family. He's a child of the Cherokee. As we speak, I know they're looking for him."

"What makes you think they haven't found him?"

"It has been almost a year and no word from Annabelle or the others. Normally Joseph's father would have visited Mercy for supplies with a letter from Annabelle. We've heard nothing from them."

"Then I will do the best I can. There is no sense in me trying to talk my way out of the pleas of a pregnant woman."

Ruthanne chuckled as she caressed Jonah's brown hair. "I'm doing quite well, don't you think? Nothing emotional here, just a lot of concern and baby number four on the way."

"We have to be careful," Marilyn said. "Annabelle ran away without a word to Judy Mays. They were friends. Having her son would be the greatest revenge."

"Momma, my hair needs help," Naomi said.

Leonard's eyes bulged as he watched the hazel-eyed girl walk around the couch. Marilyn exhaled. "Come here, sweetie." She quickly redid Naomi's ponytail as she looked at Leonard.

"Good afternoon," Naomi said.

His eyebrows raised, and he smirked. "Well, good afternoon."

"There you go. Now quickly go back to playing with the girls," Marilyn said as she gave Naomi a quick kiss on the cheek. As Naomi walked past Leonard, his smile faded. Marilyn rubbed her hands and exhaled while Naomi cheerfully went down the hallway.

"I see, there's more going on here," he said.

"I'm a married woman. All of my children are mulatto," Marilyn said with her brow lowered.

Leonard huffed as he wiped his mouth. "Ruthanne, you do keep it interesting."

"If my daughter's or my presence bothers you, we will leave. I will not be a reason for you to not help us."

"You are a bold woman, Marilyn. To give birth to more than

one mulatto child. God must've placed a special man in your life. I'm shocked, not offended by your choice. Besides befriending rebels, Ruthanne, is there anything else I should know?"

"Like what?" Ruthanne asked with a blank face.

"Have you been aiding abolitionists on the Underground Railroad?" he asked.

"I haven't been directly involved in those activities."

"I had to ask, even though my viewpoints on slavery have changed. We are living in an era of hate. I have to play it carefully."

"As you should, and please keep in mind, I wouldn't have asked for your help if I believed it would endanger you or your family. I'm trying to help a friend, a good friend, the best I can. It was pure evil what they did to her. Snatched her son, her baby boy, off of their own land, Leo." Tears escaped her eyes, and she wiped them away. "I can't even go back to Mississippi without facing the possibility of being harassed or maybe even being put back behind bars. Because everyone knows what I did. That's why I swear to you. I wouldn't ask if I believed it was risky."

Leonard nodded with a smile. "You and Judy Mays are the smartest women I've ever encountered. I think you're right. The littlest hint Joseph is Annabelle's son may lead to something even more tragic. I'll do it, my old friend."

Ruthanne replied with watery green eyes and a smile, "You are a blessing to us, Leo."

Peter later arrived at the Avail home and greeted Leonard. Ruthanne told him about the plan. The plan was exciting for him, and he thanked Leonard for his willingness to help. He had been praying for more answers to help Annabelle and felt in his spirit this was the answer. Afterward, Leonard had supper with all of Annabelle's old friends, and it weighed on his heart even more to help them. The next morning Peter and Ruthanne gave Leonard their blessings after he attended Peter's morning sermon. Leonard then left for Mississippi by train.

Weeks went by as Joseph and the others suffered enslavement. The slaves attempted to have any form of happiness they could, and Susie would sneak to Stella's slave house at nightfall to pray with the others. For Joseph, Susie, and Tom, it was hard not having Riza with them when they prayed, but having the other slaves pray with them helped them hold onto hope. Over time, Joseph noticed Clint would eat his supper and quickly leave. Out of curiosity, Joseph followed Clint and watched him walk through the old willow trees to the slave house. "What are you doing, Joseph?" Tom asked.

"Nothing, I wondered why Clint has been eating and leaving so much," Joseph said. "That isn't like him to eat and leave. He always stayed after eating to talk with us."

"I think we can ask him later when he returns or tomorrow morning where he goes."

Joseph sighed. "I think he's going to the slave house."

"Well, he's going to talk to Riza or Susie. Let's go back inside. The mosquitoes are really bad tonight." Joseph swatted a mosquito on his shoulder and followed Tom inside Stella's slave house.

CHAPTER 4
War Games Chess Not Checkers

A FEW DAYS LATER ON THE night of June 30, 1861, Clint snuck to the slave house again after he ate supper. He quietly moved through the willow trees to the house-slave house, and saw Riza leaning against the house. She noticed him and smiled. "I was wondering if you were going to watch the stars with me tonight," she said.

"Stella took longer to cook the stew today," he said. "I wouldn't want to miss looking at stars with you."

"Well come sit with me under the apple trees." Clint anxiously followed Riza to the apple trees and sat down. The many stars baffled her and reminded her of how she spent time with her family. She enjoyed his sweet nature, and liked his boldness for approaching her.

Through the night Riza and Clint continued to talk about their favorite foods, and other things they were unable to enjoy on the plantation. "Riza, what you know about the war?" he asked.

"All I know is White men are fighting other White men. I know some of it has to do with the abolitionists, but I think there is more to it."

"Who is abolitionist?" he asked with a skewed frown.

She laughed as she looked at him. "Well, it's not one person.

Abolitionists are the White people that want to end slavery. I met a few when I was a child."

"What they look like?"

"Like other White people. Sometimes I think those people do nothing but talk. However, I did hear about an Underground Railroad that will take escaped slaves to the North."

"Are you thinking about trying to run away again?"

"No, not right now. It's not the right time and that's the reason we failed the first time." Riza nudged Clint. "What? Were you going to miss me?"

"Well I...I was hoping you take me with you. You said you was gonna teach me to read, and yeah I know I miss you. It wouldn't be nice without you here. That's why I would go with you and the others."

Riza smiled and gave him a kiss on the cheek. "Don't tell anybody about that."

Clint blushed while he looked at the stars. "I promise I won't."

She giggled when she noticed he blushed. "If I can find a book around here I can hide from Master Plecker. I'll start to teach you then."

His eyes widened. "Really you do that for me?"

"Yeah, I would but remember you can't tell nobody." Riza looked down at a small twig, and traced her name in the dirt. "R-I-Z-A, that's how you spell my name."

He became excited and stared at her written name. "How do you spell my name?"

She rubbed out her name and drew his name into the dirt. "C-L-I-N-T is how your name is spelt."

He smiled. "Wow, you so smart."

She grinned. "Yeah well, come back tomorrow night if you can, and I'll teach you so more."

"Okay, well goodnight, Riza."

"Goodnight, Clint." He returned to the slave houses as she watched him. Her grin faded while she looked down at the grass.

"What are you doing, Riza?" Dorothy asked.

Riza looked up, replying, "I was looking at the stars."

"Come on, before someone sees you and says you were at

the field slave houses." The two continued to talk while walking toward the house-slave house with the moonlight and stars lighting their path.

A few days passed and she kept her word to teach Clint how to read, but to his confusion, she wouldn't sit close to him. Her limited time to see Joseph and Tom further frustrated her. She continued to send messages through Susie to keep communication between her and the boys. Judy Mays's visits also unusually declined and it held the Indian children's curiosity.

On July 5, 1861, Judy Mays's carriage arrived at the Plecker mansion. Judy Mays and Daphne walked inside the mansion with smiles. Wilma took them out to the patio with a large grin etched across her face and had Dorothy and Riza bring them drinks and snacks. Daphne and Wilma talked about the upcoming wedding, but Judy Mays's eyes remained fixed on the cotton fields. She sat with a forced smile, and took a sip of tea when the sound of Daphne's nasally voice annoyed her. Talks about the wedding plans continued, but her eyes widened when she saw Joseph and Tom putting cotton baskets on a wagon. "Hmm... some of the cotton must be ready for the first harvest," Judy Mays murmured.

"What did you say, dear?" Wilma asked.

"Nothing, I think I'm as excited as you are about this wedding. When is it again?"

"In two weeks, on July 20. It will be fabulous. Of course, Reece's family will be paying for the wedding cost while we host it here. I get more and more excited about the idea of having grandchildren."

"Wilma, you already have six, or did you forget?"

Wilma sighed. "I didn't forget about them, but I barely get to see the babies since my daughters live in Tennessee, with the exception of Sydney. You know that. She hardly brings over my granddaughter, if at all. Cornelius's three little boys, I barely see them. I know Reece will give Kenneth many children."

Judy Mays scoffed. "Do you really want that?"

Wilma lifted her finger. "Don't start your rudeness about my future daughter-in-law. She is a proper girl and what Kenneth needs."

Judy Mays tilted her head. "I apologize, but as the scripture says, he that walketh with wise men shall be wise, and Reece is wise on a diabolical scale…she's a manipulator. I have no doubts in her love for Kenneth, but I'm telling you. I can tell that girl would do some questionable things if she had to."

"All speculation…really. In what way would she do something in such a manner?" Daphne asked.

"Yes, please tell me if you have seen her do something inappropriate," Wilma said, her brows drawing together.

Judy Mays replied, "I know you haven't noticed or thought nothing of it, but I see the way she looks at Dorothy."

"Really, Judy Mays! You bring Dorothy into this!?"

Judy Mays's lifted an eyebrow and the corner of her mouth pinched. "I think Reece is jealous of Dorothy." Daphne and Wilma began to laugh while they drank their tea. "I do, I've seen the way Reece looks at her. Kenneth treats Dorothy kindly. I think it bothers her."

"Well, I've tried for years to get Kenneth to be sterner with Dorothy, but what do you do? The two of them grew up with each other and are a year apart in age. Even the promise he made to her to keep those two girls together is bothersome and unheard of, to a degree. He sometimes worries me."

Judy Mays took a sip of tea. "I still think Reece is jealous of Dorothy."

"Hmph, Reece, jealous of a mulatto slave. If you keep this up, Judy Mays, I won't be able to finish my tea because you making me laugh so much," Daphne said. "I doubt it's jealousy. She's probably used to a stricter environment on house slaves."

Judy Mays smirked. "Time will tell."

"What do you mean?" Wilma asked.

Judy Mays leered and shrugged, "I bet the moment her and Kenneth are married, she'll want to imply that more restrictions be put on Dorothy. Especially since they are living here for a moment. That will be the biggest clue she's actually jealous of Dorothy."

"All right, I'll take that challenge," Wilma proudly said. "Though I can't possibly think of the ways she would try to restrict Dorothy's interactions with Kenneth. I'll only tolerate so much. Dorothy needs to be able to complete her duties, and that's a priority for me. Not the insecurities of a new wife. She has been back here several times since you were last here, so she could get ideas on decorating the room she'll be sharing with Kenneth."

"Isn't she moving into his room?"

"Oh no, I'm giving them our largest guest room which is only proper. Ah, before I forget, come see how well the apples are growing this year. I'm greatly pleased with them this year. They're absolutely beautiful."

Daphne and Wilma stood up, but Judy Mays remained seated. "Give me a moment so I can finish my tea. I'll meet you there with Riza escorting me."

"Very well, but don't take too long. I do want you to see how beautiful the apples look right now."

Daphne and Wilma cheerfully traveled to the apple trees as Judy Mays sipped her tea and watched them walk away. "The conversation you heard does not reach Dorothy. Is that understood, Riza Moon?" Judy Mays calmly said.

"I guess I can keep a promise for a certain amount of time," Riza calmly said.

"What would cause you to break your word?"

"If Dorothy gets hit or beaten for no reason. If I see it killing her spirit, I will gladly say something."

Judy Mays cocked her head. "Such a bold statement. You do know that increases the chances of you seeing a whip again. I would think someone of your intelligence would avoid that at all costs."

Riza half-smirked. "I try to be brave."

Judy Mays huffed to stop her lips from forming a smile. "Better to have some courage than to be a complete coward. How is the boy?"

"Joseph is doing better."

Judy Mays's eyes slightly narrowed. "What do you mean by better?"

"He was beaten by Master Rice for speaking Cherokee. We're not allowed to speak our Indian languages here. Susie was also beaten badly for it."

Judy Mays smacked her lips. "Mr. Rice, I must admit, bothers me in many ways. I hope Joseph has learned his lesson. Speaking that stuff will get him nowhere around here."

Riza pouted. "It's his real language, English is his second language. He is proud of where he comes from, and Susie is too."

Judy Mays's eyebrow raised. "A proud slave. I once knew a proud slave, and I guess God did have better plans for her than being a slave. I imagine you must have many questions running through your mind after my short talk with Joseph."

"I haven't thought of it."

Judy Mays crossed her legs and grinned. "Riza, let's be honest now. You certainly have thought about my questions toward Joseph. You're a clever girl...too smart for your own good, but I've always enjoyed that about you. You will certainly grow into a remarkable woman. What more of his family has he told you?"

"He's told me nothing more, Mrs. Judy Mays."

She chuckled as she put down the white teacup. "Still trying to protect the boy, that's...honorable of you. I could tell you I'm of no threat to Joseph or his family, but what reason would you have to believe me? All these years of me watching you grow into a young woman isn't enough."

Riza's brow lowered. "You haven't freed me. I also took two bullets for starting a fire. My ability to trust is limited."

"Hmm, I'll do what they won't. The law prevents me from taking you away for one thing, but I understand your anger. You weren't born a slave. I'm sorry you received such a harsh beating. I saw the look in your eyes after you saw the ruined dining hall. It surprised you."

"I'm sorry, there's nothing more for me to say about Joseph."

"Okay, what do you want to know, Riza? Go on…ask the question you want to ask."

Riza's eyes shifted from Judy Mays, and she inhaled. Her brown eyes anchored back onto Judy Mays with a blank expression. "Is Joseph your Annabelle's son?"

Judy Mays crossed her arms, and her eyes quickly fixed on Wilma's location and back to Riza. "I'm not entirely sure. Even if I was certain, what do you think would happen?"

"I don't know what you would do."

"I'm sure you've thought of the possibilities. My one talk with Joseph already tells me he's not just a scared boy. He's a sweet one. It's very easy to bond with someone with a good soul."

"If he was your Annabelle's son, would you free him?"

"What's your definition of freedom, Riza? Remember our little games, everyone does not have the same point of view. For those who think Negros belong in those cotton fields, Joseph is free. However, someone like you, who comes from a powerful bloodline. Your definition of freedom would be akin to mine."

Riza's brows drew together, and the edges of her mouth turned downward slightly. "Please tell me the truth."

Judy Mays sighed. "I wish I could say you have no idea what real loss feels like. But you've experienced more at your young age than most adults in their thirties, I'd say even their forties. The truth is Annabelle broke the law." Judy Mays's nose scrunched. "She abandoned me. She ran without saying a word. By law, she belongs to my family, but…" Judy Mays's face relaxed, and she bit her lower lip. "The law isn't always right. Even so, it'd be hard to get him out."

"So you would free him?"

Judy Mays uncrossed her arms, reached for her teacup, and held it out to Riza. "More tea Riza, I have to make you work. Otherwise, our little talk is going to get interrupted sooner." Riza deeply exhaled while she poured Judy Mays more tea. "Goodness Riza, you could show more patience…and trust."

Riza's eyebrow raised with her eyes locked with Judy Mays's blue eyes. "What do you want out of this?"

Judy Mays grinned. "And there it is. My dear, all I want is information...just like you. I've been telling you the truth."

Riza's eyes went downward. "My tribe?"

"Yes, your tribe. You're not the last Mohawk."

Riza's left eye began to well up as she looked up at Judy Mays. "Are you sure?"

"I'm absolutely certain of it. I'm sorry Mr. Plecker went as far as to lie to you about them. Now what more has Joseph told you?"

"Nothing you haven't heard."

Judy Mays's smile dropped from her face as her pointer finger tapped on her teacup. *Ugh, this child*, she thought. "I understand your concern. What proof do you have that I won't go after his mother or siblings he has if, Annabelle was his mother, which I know you know the law. Any child Annabelle brings into this world will belong to my family. That's the law. You do disagree with this law, though?"

Riza's nose crinkled. "I think any Christian with a heart would disagree with it."

"Ah! There she is...there's the fire. Careful though, such an outburst can send the wrong message."

Riza's eyes widened, and she gulped. "I meant no offense by it, Mrs. Judy Mays."

"I'm sure you didn't. I imagine those scars on your back remind you to be careful every day."

Riza frowned and narrowed her eyes. "My scars remind me of the fear I bring them."

Judy Mays huffed and with the corners of her mouth forming a leer. "And fear can bring out the worst in people. I'm sure you're wise enough to only speak so boldly with me, little girl. No surprise you wouldn't trust any White person, but I'll continue to be honest with you. All I want is your honesty, Riza."

"Why don't you ask him things yourself?"

"Oh, I will, but why not ask you when you care about him? You know...I was heartbroken when you were punished. If I had it my way, I would've spared you."

"If I set your dining quarters on fire...you'd spare me?"

"You'd be punished…but not by spilling your blood or cutting off your beautiful hair. I believe in education, not brutality."

"I…I want to know more if…you want me to tell you more about Joseph. But I won't tell you any more about his family."

"I see." Judy Mays looked down at her teacup. *Gaining her full trust is going to take more effort,* she thought. *I enjoy her intelligence too much for my own good.* Her blue eyes refocused on Riza and she leaned back in her chair. "The Lord has a way of bringing out the truth. The clock is ticking, Riza Moon, but I agree with you. What else do you want to know?"

Riza took a deep breath with her eyebrows slanting upward, answering, "My mo—"

"Mrs. Judy Mays, Mrs. Wilma wants you to join her quickly," Dorothy said. Judy Mays and Riza quickly turned their heads toward Dorothy.

Judy Mays smacked her lips and moaned. "Well, enough of this, for now. Let us see these apple trees before Wilma begins to complain."

Dorothy nodded. "Yes, Mrs. Judy Mays."

"At least the weather isn't unbearable today. Go on ahead, Dorothy." Judy Mays put her teacup down on the coffee table, stood up, and stretched her arms. She adjusted her white sun hat and began to follow Dorothy.

Riza immediately followed alongside Judy Mays to the apple trees. A frown remained fixed on her face, and her head slightly slouched. Judy Mays noticed the frustration on Riza's face and took a deep breath. *Unfortunately, Dorothy arrived when you started to feel comfortable,* she thought. *I know what you were going to ask. You'll just have to wait for the answer, little girl. After all, you're my key…and I need you to open doors for me.* Her blue eyes anchored on Riza, and she noticed with a raised eyebrow. "I guess I may not see the boy today. There are more important things at hand. Let's play our guessing game you're so fond of, Riza, before I'm forced to look at apple trees." Riza struggled to withhold her smile, and Judy Mays played with her. As they approached the trees, Judy Mays kept her focus on Riza, and managed to even get a smile out of the girl. Dorothy even glanced back a few times as she heard the exchange between the two. Once they arrived at the apple trees, Riza stood behind Judy Mays while Wilma boasted about the trees.

Afterward, Daphne and Judy Mays exited the mansion, but before Judy Mays stepped into her carriage, she heard the slaves singing hymns in the cotton fields. Her eyes scanned the fields. "Judy Mays, what are you looking at?" Daphne asked.

Judy Mays's gaze remained fixed on the fields. "The horizon Daphne. It's filled with uncertainty. Let's go. I've already promised another visit within the week." Judy Mays stepped into the carriage, and they left the Plecker estate.

Meanwhile, in Tahlequah, the Lightning-Strongman family struggled to remain focused on current events, including increased war talk. Stand Watie's voice had already been heard throughout the Cherokee territory, and it divided the tribe. The Lightning-Strongman family became furious with those who sided with Stand Watie and saw his viewpoints as non-Christian.

On July 10, 1861, David worked the fields along with George, Jacob, and Michael. The work was tedious as they struggled to keep the crops healthy due to a short spring, uninvited critters, and persistent insects. During his time in the fields, his frustration grew. He saw Jannie and Rain watching him as they sat by the old redbud tree. He went to the young girls as he dried off his forehead with a dirty rag.

"What do you want?" David asked in Cherokee. "Both of you are supposed to be with Rosita feeding the chickens right now."

Jannie replied in Cherokee, "She wanted to do it alone today."

He angrily replied, "None of you are supposed to be alone. Not ever!" She suddenly began to cry. "What are you crying for?"

"I miss Joseph. When is Papa bringing him home?"

David looked at Rain and noticed her watery eyes. "Papa will bring him home. I know he will. Believe Elder Joyce's prophesy. We will bring him, and we will be together again."

Jannie began to hyperventilate, so Rain embraced her. "We have to have faith, Jannie. We can do that," she said in

Cherokee. "Auntie Lizzie said we are stronger when we remain faithful even when we can't see."

Jannie replied in Cherokee, "It's hard. I miss him so much."

"I miss him too. I'm sure Papa can bring him back this time."

David kneeled down and wiped a tear off Jannie's face. "We're a strong people, and as long as we keep our faith in Joseph's return, it brings us hope," he said. "Momma told me all we have to do is our role and trust in Jesus's plan. I don't know if Papa will succeed this time, but I know one day we'll bring him home. I know if we keep praying and fight to find the happiness that's still here, it'll give us strength to push away the pain and look for the day Joseph comes home."

Jannie replied, "If Joseph doesn't come home this time, will we look again?"

"We will never stop looking for him. Come, you can ride on my back. We can't leave Rosita alone. It doesn't matter if she wanted to feed the chickens alone." Jannie got onto David's back. He stood up and calmly reached for Rain's hand. He walked the girls over to the chicken coop next to John and Annabelle's house. "I know the three of you are becoming big girls, but you must never go anywhere alone. I know Momma has told you both that, but promise me. No going anywhere alone."

"We promise," the girls said in unison. He dropped the girls off at the chicken coop and gave Rosita the same speech.

"The three of you have school tomorrow. I'll be happy to hear how it goes." David returned to the fields with a troubled heart after he saw how heartbroken the girls still were. At supper, he made a conscious effort to tease the girls and make them laugh. He said nothing to Annabelle about what happened and remained in deep thought as to how he could help even as he slept.

In Caledonia, the July heat was now almost unbearable. Joseph and Tom had now been placed to follow behind field slaves and pick any missed cotton before filling the cotton baskets on the wagon. Joseph hated picking the cotton but tried to hum along with Cecil as he and the other slaves sang hymns. He could feel his hands burn in the sun as sweat dripped down his face with the only comfort coming from his straw hat. When Joseph and Tom were finishing one of their rounds, Joseph missed a cotton plant. "Joseph, you missed that plant over there," Pearl snarled. Looking at Pearl, Joseph pouted, scrunched his nose, and snatched up the cotton. "I saw attitude, grass nigger. What you mad for?"

Joseph angrily replied, "If you did a better job, I wouldn't have to go behind you, nigger."

Tom gasped as Pearl's eyes narrowed on Joseph. "So you think you better like Riza? Boy, I beat you! You ain't nothing but a slave picking cotton like me."

"I'm not better than you, but I don't accept being a slave like you. I wasn't born to be a slave. My momma said nobody is born to be a slave."

Pearl scoffed. "Well, yo momma lied to you." He was about to approach Pearl when Tom grabbed his arm. "Maybe you need to try combing that nappy hair before you say you ain't like me. Maybe that Indian blood touched the roots of yo hair."

"See now, Pearl, why are you talking to them boys instead of working?" Master Kit authoritatively said.

Pearl nervously replied, "Master Kit, I sorry. I was telling them they got all my cotton."

Kit struck Pearl with a switch. "Then keep picking more," Kit yelled. Kit looked at Joseph and Tom. "What you boys staring for? Get that cotton to the barn before you both get some lashes." They quickly put the last cotton baskets on the wagon, and Louis drove it away. When the wagon rode away, Joseph twisted his face as he looked at Pearl, and she stared back at him while picking cotton.

"She'll always be against us because we stand with Riza," Tom said.

"I shouldn't have called her a nigger," Joseph said. "I sounded like a White man, and I hate it."

"But she called you a grass nigger."

Joseph frowned. "That doesn't make it okay for me to call

her a nigger. My momma would've been sad to hear me say that word." The boys continued to talk about their frustrations with Pearl while they sat in the wagon.

A few days later, Reece arrived at the Plecker mansion for the sixth time in two weeks. Reece's latest visit tested Dorothy's and Riza's patience with all of her petty requests. Reece had Dorothy and Susie rearrange furniture in the guest room designated to be hers and Kenneth's until they found a home of their own. It was an exhausting day for the house slaves, and an obvious hostility remained between Dorothy and Reece.

Reece was later taken to Sydney's home to stay the night causing the house slaves to silently celebrate with humming, and excitement for the day to end. As they celebrated in the darkness of the willow tree pathway, Pearl sat against the willow tree furthest away from the slave houses.

Pearl wiped away a tear while she sat under the tree bending blades of grass. "There you are, right on time," Rice said. He stepped up to Pearl as he rubbed his thin mustache, "Have you heard of anything new from the Indian boys?"

Pearl humbly replied, "No, they ain't said nothing, Master Rice. I think they too scared to run away again."

Rice caressed Pearl's face and chuckled. "You think they won't do nothing again? I tell you what I know, you wrong…do you want to know why I know you wrong?"

Pearl hesitantly replied, "Yes, Master Rice. I want to know why."

"Because Riza will give into her savage ways and get them to follow her again, and I'll catch them again. It will be my moment of fun seeing Riza fail again." Rice stared at Pearl lustfully. "Well, what you waiting for? Take it off. I don't have all night." Pearl reluctantly took off her undergarments, and Rice raped her behind the tree. While Rice raped Pearl, she wiped away any tears she couldn't stop from coming out. When Rice finished, Pearl put her undergarments back on. "Is that a tear on your face?"

"No, it not, Master Rice. I got some dirt in it, and I was getting it out."

"You know what I say about crying out here. I don't like it, and it's disrespectful to me."

"I swear I wasn't crying…I swear I ain't cried in a long time."

"You better not have been crying. You know not to test me. Don't stay out here long."

"I won't, Master Rice." He walked away to his quarters as Pearl watched. When she couldn't see Rice anymore, she began to cry. After a moment of consoling herself, she strolled through the willow trees and saw Clint going to the house-slave house. "What he walking to they house for?" After he arrived at the house, he knocked on it, and Riza came outside. Pearl watched as he walked with her to one of the apple trees. In the shadows, she enviously watched as they sat together and watched the stars. As they sat and talked to each other, he tried to put his arm around her, but she turned her body toward him. He scratched the back of his head, but she comforted him by touching his shoulder. "I know how to play a game you ain't ready for." Pearl continued to watch them and returned to the slave houses before Clint to avoid being seen.

On July 20, 1861, after the slaves worked the cotton fields, Kit decided to allow the slaves to have lunch. Clint cheerfully went to the old cookhouse with the others when Pearl began to casually walk next to him.

"Ain't this a blessing, Clint? Master Kit must be in good spirit today," Pearl said. However, he ignored Pearl as they entered the cookhouse. "So you still mad at me about telling on those Indian children?"

He replied, "All of it was yo doing. You tell Master Rice and got them all beat."

Pearl pouted and continued to walk next to him. "What if I told you I know about you and Riza? Master not gonna be happy about it."

"You know nothing."

She grinned. "I know more than you know. I watch you and

Riza under the apple tree last night, and it not first time I see y'all there."

He stopped walking. "Please don't tell nobody. Riza said we can't tell anybody."

"So she tell you what to do? I see how she act around you. I know how to make her like you more."

She noticed his eyes slightly enlarge. "What you mean?"

She put her hand on her hip. "I know why she won't let you hold her. You not man enough. You a boy."

"What I need to be a man?" She left with a smile on her face to get her meal, but he hesitated to follow her. He rested his chin on his palm as he ate, and after he ate he immediately returned to the cotton fields. Clint later came across Pearl in the cotton field. "What I need to be a man?"

She grinned, and she began to play with a cotton bulb in her basket. "I can teach you what she can't. I can make you a man. You want me to show you?"

He paused for a moment. "Yeah, what you gone teach me?"

She winked. "How to be a man…that what I teach you. I look for you tonight but don't tell nobody."

"Okay, I do what you say."

"Clint is your basket full," Joseph said.

He turned around, startled. "Joseph, you scare me… it not full," he said.

"Negro leave, we talking," Pearl bickered.

Joseph angrily replied, "I'm doing what Master Wade said to do. What are you saying that I can't hear?"

Pearl angrily replied, "Ain't nobody say something you can't hear! You wouldn't know nothing anyway. You ain't nothing but a boy."

Joseph sneered. "I know more than you. I can read."

Pearl clutched her cotton basket as she stared down Joseph. "Ain't nothing here for you, half-breed nigger."

"Well I hope your basket is full when me and Tom come back to get them, or Master Wade might beat you. Better move fast Clint. Pearl is trouble."

"Says the one that helped burn down Master's house," Pearl

snarled. Joseph rolled his eyes at Pearl and walked toward other slaves who were gathering cotton to see if their baskets were full or not. "You see Clint, Joseph a boy. You see, Riza not give him special smiles, and he's half-breed. I teach you everything. When they all asleep, you come out, and I be waiting for you."

"Okay, I see you tonight," he said. Pearl continued to pick cotton, and he focused on his row.

During the night, Clint quickly ate and interacted with the others while they talked. When everyone went to sleep, he snuck out of the house and saw Pearl sitting in front of her slave house. "You did good," she said. "I see you being more of a man every day. Follow me."

He followed her to the willow trees and noticed her looking back to make sure none of the other slaves saw them. Pearl stopped by one of the trees furthest away from the slave houses and the mansion. "Why we come so far?"

She replied in a seductive tone, "I can teach you a lot in one night. So you not worried about someone seeing us, walk closer to me." He stepped closer to her. She placed her hand on his face. "Have you ever kissed a girl, Clint?"

He looked away. "No, I too scared when one of the girls wanted to kiss me before."

Pearl grinned. "And now you want Riza. I can tell you she knows how to kiss."

His eyes widened. "She does?"

"Clint, a young woman like Riza, I promise she know more than she's telling you." She placed her hand softly back on his face and kissed him. "Don't be scared. I promise I won't tell." Pearl kissed Clint again and seduced him into kissing her for several minutes. "See, it not hard. Did that feel good?"

"Yes, I didn't think it would feel that good."

She giggled as she looked at him with a leer. "Well, I think tonight I can make you into a man. You learn how to kiss so fast. No wonder Master Wade always have you cut wood for the animal houses. You a special one."

Clint grinned. "You think I special?"

"Yeah I do. I know that why Riza like you, but like I say, you not no man."

"I ready. I want to be a man."

Pearl smiled and placed Clint's right hand on her left breast, causing him to blush. "Don't be scared. I know you like how that feel. It okay to say you like it. Do you like it?"

Clint nervously replied, "Y-yes, I like it."

"Good, 'cause what happens next gone feel *real* good and make you a man." Pearl took off her brown cotton dress in front of Clint, causing his heart to race and his eyes to widen. "Come here and hold me." He stepped up to her and hugged her. She kissed him. "Now I gone show you how to be a man. Lay down."

Clint nervously lay down on the grass. Pearl got on top of him and began to take off his brown trousers. "No, wait. I scared."

She caressed his face while she looked into his innocent brown eyes. "I promise you be fine, and I make you feel good, make you a man. I'm gon' make you feel so good. So you ready? I promise I go slow for you." He nodded. "Good, and after this, you'll know how to make Riza fall in love with you." Pearl continued kissing Clint and soon succeeded in seducing him twice, taking his virginity.

As they strolled back to the slave houses, Clint couldn't stop blushing. "I don't know what to say."

Pearl smirked at him. "You ain't got nothing to say. You did good…better than I thought. We need to do this one more time tomorrow night. That way, you really know what to do. Like I say, Riza gon' fall in love with you, now that you a man."

"Okay, I wait for you again."

The two went into their houses with Pearl smiling at him as she went inside. He remained wide awake, staring at the ceiling with big eyes. The next day, they met by the old willow trees again and slept together. She promised him it was what Riza wanted, and now he was a man she would want as a husband.

A few days passed, and Riza agreed to meet with Clint but remained reluctant to let her feelings for him grow. On July 26,

1851, Clint was on his way to the slave house as Riza waited. Clint asked her if she could meet with him during the day when the other house slaves would be working. She agreed, knowing Wilma would be taking short naps on certain days. Clint snuck to the house-slave house, trying to make sure the overseers didn't see him leave the barns. "Hey Clint, come on," she said.

Clint jogged up to Riza. "Hey, I'm glad you here. I don't have much time," he said.

Riza smiled. "So am I. Let's go see what we can before we both have to leave."

"I was hoping we can talk inside so nobody see us."

Riza raised an eyebrow. "Okay, we can go inside." The two walked inside the house, and Clint closed the door. "What did you want to say?"

Clint caressed his hands while he stood before Riza. "I...I wanted to say that you so beautiful. You so beautiful, the most beautiful girl, I mean woman, I ever see. I mean, Dorothy and Susie pretty, but I think you more pretty."

"Well, thank you, Clint. That was nice of you. I think you're a good friend and—"

Suddenly, Clint kissed Riza.

"Oh, Clint, I'm so—"

He kissed her again, and she pushed him off.

"Clint, what is wrong with you?"

"I trying to show you...I love you. Riza, I love you."

"No, Clint, you can't love me. It takes a long time to know that you love someone."

He frowned. "I know what I feel, and I know you feel that way too. I can show you." He grabbed her and tried to kiss her again, but she struggled to pull away from him. "Please stop fighting me. I know I can make you feel good."

"Clint, let me go!"

They fell on the floor as he struggled to hold her down.

"Please, Clint, stop it!"

He reached up her skirt and tried to pull down her undergarments.

She screamed, "Please stop it! Stop it, Clint!"

"I have to have you before Master Rice have you. Pearl said it will make you happy. It's the only way you gonna love me. I a man now."

Riza slapped Clint. "No, you're not!" She slapped him again when he tried to pull down her undergarments and then clawed his neck.

He let go of her and screamed as he held his neck, but when she went for the door, he grabbed her shoulder and pulled her back. She slapped him and then he slapped her, knocking her head against the door. He gasped and tried to catch her, but she landed on the wooden floor. He kneeled down and tried to hold her, but she pushed him away.

"Stop it!" She struggled to balance her head and began to weep while she crawled on the floor.

"I sorry, please stop fighting. Pearl told me what Master Rice gonna do to you. I don't want him to have you first and hurt you. Please, Riza. I love you."

As she crawled on the ground toward the stove, he grabbed her shoulder to turn her around, but she punched him in his eye.

"My eye!" He stumbled back as she used all her strength to get up and stumble to the old stove.

Howling in pain, Clint tried to open his eye. The moment he forced his eye open, Riza swung an iron pan at him. The pan rang once as it hit him in the face, knocking him off his feet.

She took another swing, hitting him on his arm. "No!" she screamed. She took six swings with the pan while she screamed, "No man can have me without me letting him!" Blood splattered onto her dress and dripped off the pan. Shaking, she slowly limped to the door while she held the blood-soaked pan. Opening the door, she squatted down in her blood-soaked dress and began to cry as she held her side. "How could you try to do this, Clint?"

Clint, lying on the blood-soaked floor looked over at Riza with his bloody face and began to weep. "I thought that what you wanted. Pearl say I couldn't have you 'cause I too nice. She say I wasn't a man so she can make me a man. So I can make you a woman before Master Rice hurt you. She say you never love me if Master Rice get you first. I don't want him to hurt you."

"You mean she gave herself to you?"

"Yes," he cried.

She gagged while she struggled to stand and vomited. She screamed as she threw the pan to the ground. "I hate her!"

"I sorry. Please forgive me. I do love you…I sorry."

The sun shined off Riza's tears. "I can't look at you the same anymore." She wiped tears and snot from her face as she saw him struggle to hold himself up. She frowned. "I can't trust you anymore. I don't know what other lies Pearl put into your head."

"Please don't say that."

"I need a lot of time away from you. When I say no, I mean no."

"Riza what's going on here?" Dorothy yelled as she marched out of the kitchen. "I heard you scream all the way at the mansion." Her eyes bulged as her jaw dropped. "Oh my God! Is that your blood?"

Dorothy ran over to Riza while she limped over to her and began to hyperventilate. "I-I hurt Clint really bad," she said, her voice breaking.

"Girl, what do you mean? Is this your blood?" She shook her head and looked at the house. Dorothy looked inside the slave house and saw him covered in blood and barely able to hold himself up. "Oh Lord, Riza why…why would you do this? Tell me!"

"Pearl tricked Clint into trying to rape me! She told him that if Master Rice raped me first, I'd never love him."

"Curse that spiteful witch! Go tell Emma to come here and help me clean him up."

"I have to go do something important first." Riza picked up the pan and began to march away.

"Where are you going? Clint needs help. Riza?" Dorothy shrugged her hands and ran to him to begin treating him.

Out in the cotton fields, the slaves' hymns could be heard, but suddenly some of the slaves in the field stopped singing and looked terrified as the cotton plants parted with Riza's approach. Slaves gasped when they saw Riza's blood-soaked dress. Breathing heavily, she approached Pearl and said with a deepened voice, "Pearl." Pearl turned around, and the pan slammed into her head. She fell to the ground. Riza screamed, hitting her again. She lay in the cotton field motionless while Riza walked away. The other slaves watched in awe. Kit saw the commotion, rode up on his horse, and jumped off to check on Pearl. Kit looked up and saw Riza storm off to the mansion with an unremorseful strut.

Two hours later, a battered Riza and Pearl stood before Master Plecker and Wilma in the living room. The ticking of the grandfather clock terrified Pearl. She believed it increased Master Plecker's anger while Riza, with her wounds, remained unremorseful. "I don't even know where to begin in all of this unnecessary chaos," Master Plecker bickered. "I see my second-best house slave in a dress covered in the blood of another slave…a good slave. Two Christian women. Fighting like men. What is this world coming to?" Wilma tugged on Master Plecker's sleeve, "Oh yes, to be corrected one fighting like a man, and another provoking the action from what I understand."

Dorothy calmly entered the living room doorway. "Master Plecker, may I speak?" Dorothy asked.

Master Plecker casually replied, "No, now leave us."

Dorothy frowned and glanced at Riza and turned around to leave. "Wait a moment Dorothy," Wilma said.

"I said she is excused. I don't want to hear another version of this chaos," Master Plecker snarled.

"Please dear, I believe Dorothy will speak the truth."

Master Plecker gave a dismissive wave. "Fine, so be it. Dorothy, what did you have to say?"

"Master Plecker, I can't lie and say what Riza did was proper, but you should know the truth. Pearl tricked Clint into trying to rape her, and she fought him. I believe she could've been more proper as a Christian woman, but believe Pearl received what she deserved."

Master Plecker looked back at a bleeding Pearl. "Dorothy, you can go now." Dorothy anxiously walked toward the cookhouse. "What to do…what to do with the both of you. Riza, that temper may come to use, and I think I know how." Master Plecker stepped up to them as his shoes echoed in the living room. "Pearl, I consider you a valuable asset, but even valuable things can make dangerous mistakes. You tricked that dumb nigger into attacking Riza for what?" Master Plecker began to circle them, imitating a shark. "I said for what!"

Pearl jumped with the echo of Master Plecker's voice. "M-master…I was…I was mad at Riza, s-she throw pig droppings at me, threw apples at me, and got no punishment," Pearl hesitantly said. "She think she better than me."

Master Plecker stopped in front of Pearl, asking, "And what if she is better than you?"

A tear went down Pearl's swollen face. "I don't believe she is."

"Well, Pearl, she is better than you. The girl can cook, clean, wash clothes, care for small children, hell, the way her body is shaping, she'll pop out some strong children one day, and we all know she's smarter than you. So what makes you think you're better? She ain't never known a man. I know you have." Master Plecker rubbed his forehead. "I wonder, is that why you sent that boy after her? You wanted to kill the only pure thing about her?"

Master Plecker began to cackle, but Pearl began to tremble. "Calvin, please. Don't laugh about such a serious nature," Wilma said with her brows furrowed. "Pearl, is that true? You sent that boy to rape her?" Pearl remained silent as her body quivered. "I said speak, nigger!"

"She already like him Mrs. Wilma, I swear she already like him," Pearl wept. "And he love her."

"In what way does that excuse this?" Wilma yelled. "I see no fault of this being Riza's. I think Pearl needs something more severe than getting hit with a pan on her face. Riza clearly hasn't been an angel…but this sickening behavior. I want none of it here!"

"Well, I have a solution to dealing with both of them," Master Plecker said. "Letting Riza off without no punishment isn't happening. She was supposed to be working, but instead she got one of my best slaves to ignore his duties. She marched out onto that cotton field instead of telling us about this. Clint may not be of any use to me for the rest of the week." Master Plecker looked at Wilma and saw her pouting.

"If that nigger had succeeded in raping her and gotten her pregnant, it could've ruined our future plans for the next generation."

Master Plecker groaned, popped out his gold watch, and stared at the opened watch. "Wade, take both of them out to the old stump."

Wade walked around the corner of the living room. "Yes, sir. Who do you want tied down first, Master Plecker?" Wade asked.

"We'll deal with that once I get there."

Wade approached Pearl and Riza and pushed them from behind. "Go on, you two." They reluctantly moved to the foyer after exiting the front door. Wade escorted them to the old tree stump. Wilma grunted and marched upstairs, saying nothing to Master Plecker. He scoffed and left the mansion toward the old stump, whistling while he took his time.

As Pearl and Riza marched to the old stump, Pearl struggled not to cry. Scowling, Riza thought, *I don't care...she deserved it. He knows she deserved it.*

Pearl and Riza waited as Master Plecker strutted up behind them. He pointed at Pearl. "Tie her down, Wade."

Wade replied, "Yes, sir."

Wade grabbed Pearl, forced her to take off her brown dress, and pushed her onto the old stump. "Please, Master Plecker! I sorry," Pearl cried. Wade held Pearl down strongly as she begged. "I won't do it again. Riza better. I know she better! Please, Master, please have mercy!"

"Pearl, who do you think you talking to?" Master Plecker asked. "Only mercy out here is from the Lord, and it ain't for you. Now, things would be different if you had said something to Riza, and she beat you with that pan. However, the only vengeance going on out here is mine. Did you think she wasn't gonna fight back?" Master Plecker scoffed. "Never mind. You didn't think about that…that's your problem. You don't think, and Riza does."

Wade grabbed the whip and cracked it in the air. "How many you want me to give her?" he asked.

"She getting twenty for all this time wasted," Master Plecker casually said.

"No," Pearl cried.

"No…did she say no? Well, make it thirty now." More sobs escaped her mouth as snot ran from her nose. Wade raised his hand to crack the whip, but Master Plecker placed his hand out in front of Wade. "Now, wait a moment, Wade. We're not done yet. Come here, Riza." Riza hesitantly walked over to Master Plecker. "Give her the whip." Wade gave Riza the whip and stepped back. "Now Riza, you going to give her fifteen good lashes on her back, is that understood?"

Riza looked at Pearl and looked back at Master Plecker. "Me?" Riza asked.

Nonchalantly, Master Plecker answered, "Oh yes, you or you gone take those thirty lashes for her. Riza, you better hit her good, or do you need to be reminded of your place? Do you understand, my sweet Mohawk?"

Riza's lips quivered. "Yes Master Plecker."

"Please, Master Plecker, I learn," Pearl cried.

"Pearl, you created all this drama you see here!" Master Plecker yelled. "You wanted to make Riza bleed between her legs. Well, now you're gonna bleed from your back and your legs!" Master Plecker pointed at Pearl and commanded, "Crack the whip, Riza!"

Riza gulped and took one practice swing, cracking the whip. She stepped behind Pearl as her right hand shook and cracked the whip across Pearl's back.

Pearl screamed in pain. "Now, Pearl, you repeat after me. I ain't better than Riza!"

"I ain't better than Riza," Pearl sobbed.

Master Plecker pointed at Pearl. "Strike her again."

Riza exhaled and struck Pearl again.

"That was a good one!"

Riza looked at Master Plecker. "I did as you said," she calmly said with a deep inhale.

"You keep that up now."

Riza grimaced and cracked the whip across Pearl's back again. "Now say it again, Pearl, you ain't no better."

"I ain't better than Riza," she wailed as blood slid down her back.

"Again, Riza!"

She repeated the lashes each time Plecker commanded her to declare she was no better than Riza. Tears went down her face when she felt the whip hit Pearl. Master Plecker and Wade counted down with each strike and laughed as a few slaves working on equipment, including Bo, noticed.

When Riza gave Pearl her thirtieth strike, Wade took the whip away from her. "Well done. I knew this young lady had some power in those arms," he said. "Why the tears, Riza?" Wade chuckled.

Pearl moaned as the sun reflected off the blood drizzling down her back and legs.

"I think she feels guilty. Well, that's life," Master Plecker said. "Now for yours." He sucker-punched Riza in the cheek, knocking her down. "I can't have anyone thinking I have favorites, now can I. Now get back to the mansion before I decide to tie your redskin behind to that stump next."

Riza stood and quickly ran to the mansion, holding her cheek while the pain throbbed.

"Woo, look at her move. All right, have Pearl cleaned up."

The news of what Pearl did angered the other slaves, and few wanted to care for her wounds. Stella reluctantly cleaned Pearl's wounds and prayed for her. Stella frowned while caring for her childhood friend. Pearl remained mostly silent as she lay on the wooden floor, and Stella continued to check her wounds to make sure they didn't become infected. Joseph walked past Pearl's slave house and stopped once he heard Pearl and Stella talking. "Thank you, Stella. I don't deserve help," Pearl said with sadness in her voice.

"Don't say such things. We been friends since we was children," Stella said. "You all I got besides Bo and Mary. Mary the only niece I got, and she might get sold one day."

"I gave up wondering. I know I will never see them again—my momma, my papa, my sisters…I know it's true. We won't see each other again."

"Don't say that, Pearl. God good, we gone see all of them again before Heaven."

Pearl moaned in pain as Stella continued to check her wounds. "You always hope. Maybe that why Bo love you."

"We have to hope, and I would like it if we be friends again."

Pearl chuckled but began to weep. "I do need a friend. I need a friend." Stella laid her head against Pearl's while she cried. Joseph frowned when he heard their conversation.

"It doesn't matter if we Indian or Negro, the pain is the same," He mumbled. He walked away from the house frowning as he looked back at the mansion. The tragedy only made him want to return to Tahlequah even more.

CHAPTER 5
When the Heart Breaks

On August 1, 1861, Wilma went upstairs, with each step echoing authority. *Cornelius better not be slowing Kenneth down on his special day*, she thought. She entered Kenneth's room. "Ah! So handsome! I'm so proud of you Kenneth," Wilma said with the corners of her mouth forming a large grin. "This will be a day to be remembered. Doesn't he look handsome, Dorothy? With his blue morning coat, nice gray trousers, gray vest, and lovely blue cravat."

Dorothy forced a smile when she looked at Kenneth. "He looks very handsome, Mrs. Wilma," Dorothy said. "I think Master Kenneth looks like the most handsome man I've ever seen. Miss Reece is a blessed woman."

"Bah, he's not that good-looking," Cornelius remarked as he dismissively waved his hand.

Wilma pointed to the door and commanded, "Downstairs. This is your brother's day."

Cornelius scratched his blond head and replied, "Okay, Momma." Cornelius, standing eye to eye with Kenneth, left the room, giving Kenneth a smirk.

Wilma squealed with excitement, "Now, doesn't he look handsome, my baby boy, all grown up. I'll let you take a good look at yourself...I want to see if your sisters are here yet." Wilma anxiously left the room and went downstairs.

Dorothy slowly approached Kenneth while he looked in his mirror. "I meant what I said, Kenneth," Dorothy calmly said. Dorothy adjusted Kenneth's blue cravat and kissed him on the cheek.

Kenneth looked at Dorothy and gazed into her hazel eyes. "Stop looking at me like that," Kenneth whispered. Dorothy could feel his heart race as she continued to look directly into his eyes. Kenneth's brow lowered. "No, Dorothy, not today." Kenneth spun on his heel and quickly walked away, leaving Dorothy in the room. Dorothy exhaled, her mouth curved downward, and her head lowered before she exited the room.

At this time, Joseph and the other slaves were preparing the courtyard for Kenneth's and Reece's wedding celebration. Joseph and Tom were assigned to bring cut-up meat to the mansion so the house slaves could cook it. He thought, *I can't believe they made us wake up so early for this.* He saw the Pleckers leave for the church in a row of carriages. Dorothy came out of the mansion and continued to direct the slaves. He asked her if he could go to the well to get some water, and he rushed to the water well. The well sat several feet to the right of a white-painted shack that was the cookhouse for the slaves. He sent the bucket down into the well, pulled up the filled bucket, and used a ladle to drink out of the bucket. He heard a chair move in the shack and walked up to the under kept building. He cracked open the door and Pearl was standing before a table. She was staring at a bowl that was sitting on the table. He was about to leave the shack but saw her struggling to reach for a bowl of stew. His brows lowered when she sighed and lowered her arms. He entered the building and walked up to the table. Pearl slowly turned around but said nothing as the young boy approached. Joseph picked up the bowl and gave it to Pearl. She frowned and said, "Thank you, Joseph."

He half-smiled, replying, "You're welcome."

"I sorry for what I say about your momma. I sorry if I make it hard for you to hope."

"I forgive you, Pearl. I'm sorry you got whipped."

"Thank you."

Joseph nodded and left the shack to work. After a few hours, the boys finished those tasks and were instructed to bring drinks and appetizers to the arriving guests. From the courtyard, he could see that Mr. and Mrs. Plecker had returned from the church. More carriages soon arrived at the plantation, and the cheerful voices of guests could be heard. *I've never seen a fancy celebration like this before*, he thought. Even though he was forced to serve, he enjoyed seeing all the different hairstyles and colorful outfits. His main concern was pleasing Dorothy, whom seemed unusually short-tempered throughout the morning. Dorothy had her hair put into a ringlet style.

As Joseph and Tom stood at attention by the guest tables, Riza exited the mansion. Her dark brown, wavy hair had now grown down to her upper middle back. She had her thick hair braided into two braids, and they swayed as she walked to the guest tables carrying silverware and plates. She was now wearing the blue house slave dress. She waved at the boys before continuing her tasks. The young boys waved back at her and continued their work as Dorothy directed them. Over an hour later, Mr. and Mrs. Plecker arrived from the church. While Riza placed items on the tables, Master Plecker saw her. "Wilma, why is Riza wearing that blue dress?" Master Plecker bickered with his eyes widening. "When we left for the church to speak to Pastor Macray, she had on her brown rags like she's supposed to."

"So she would look nice for your son's wedding celebration," Wilma argued.

"She's taking that dress off and putting on the brown one. I will have no other way!"

"I had her and Little Susie change out of those rags. Riza is wearing that dress, Calvin. The other dress was ruined by all that blood and dirt," Wilma snarled. Wilma's voice deepened with her index finger, now pointing at Master Plecker, "She's wearing that dress!" Master Plecker shook his head, crossed his arms, and walked away to greet the arriving guests.

The sound of guests conversing and a live orchestra created the background as Daphne and Judy Mays arrived at the Plecker estate in their elegant Victorian dresses. Daphne wore a blue and white Victorian dress, while Judy Mays wore a flowered green and white Victorian dress with a white trim. Both women wore white sun hats. "Ah, there you ladies are!" Wilma said, waving her hands with a wide smile. "Looking as lovely as ever. I'm sorry Thaddeus couldn't be here since he decided to join the war, Daphne. Where is Edgar, Judy Mays?"

"He already had business plans with the railroads, but he will arrive later today," she said.

"Wonderful, I hope his efforts will help our Confederacy. Too bad your parents couldn't be here due to a prior engagement."

Judy Mays inhaled and forced a smile. "I know the good Lord has my husband and, of course, Thaddeus since he is out on the battlefields."

"Amen to that," Daphne said.

"Well come on, we have special seating arrangements," Wilma said. "I'm so glad the two of you were in the church." She took the young women to a round wooden table that was painted white with a vase of flowers set in the middle. The women sat, adjusting their sun hats. "I'm so overjoyed, I will be back with you ladies shortly. My baby boy is married!" Wilma left as Daphne and Judy Mays watched. While Joseph and Tom worked the guest tables alongside the house slaves, Judy Mays whistled. Joseph turned around and saw Judy Mays playfully waving at him. "Joseph, come here," Judy Mays said.

He walked over to Judy Mays as her and Daphne watched him. "Look at that. They cleaned him up," Daphne snobbishly said.

"I see you have healed up quite well from the last incident," Judy Mays said.

"Yes, Mrs. Judy Mays, I did," Joseph humbly said.

"Do you remember what I told you? I said to behave, now didn't I?"

"Yes, ma'am, you did."

"It seems you didn't listen to me at first but seeing you haven't had any trouble for some time it looks like you learned. I expect nothing less from you."

"What can you expect Judy Mays. He's a half-breed from a redskin father," Daphne said. "I still can't believe Wilma decided to have these Indian children serve us after all they have done." "Especially Riza, with her savage, unpredictable ways."

Judy Mays's nose crinkled, and her lips tightened. "The recent occurrence was not entirely Riza's fault, and she defended herself from a dangerous situation. She was in her right."

Daphne scoffed. "You find her moments entertaining. That's the only reason you defend her. She nearly killed one of the slaves and knocked the other out cold. I would've had her hanged."

Judy Mays scoffed, her upper lip lifted slightly. "Well then, it's a good thing she isn't your slave. You almost sound like your aunt."

Daphne gasped and put her hand to her mouth. "I'm not cruel and you know that! I'm just saying, Riza should be missing a hand or an ear for all she's done. Look at her, not a scar on that pretty face."

"I'm sure you would feel differently if she didn't have a pretty face." Daphne sneered as Judy Mays looked at her with her clever blue eyes. "Joseph, I'd like some lemonade."

"Yes, Mrs. Judy Mays," Joseph said.

Joseph poured the lemonade into a glass, and gently placed it down in front of Judy Mays. She calmly grabbed the filled glass. The corners of her mouth curved upward. "Ah, well done. I—"

"Judy Mays, Daphne, it's good to see you both," a blond-haired man said. The man wore a blue waistcoat, which complemented his blue-brown checkered vest and pants and brown top hat.

"Why Leonard Benedict, I didn't think you would come here," Judy Mays said.

"Well, I did bring Clarissa, and we haven't visited here in

about two years, so the visit is long overdue," Leo cheerfully said. "I see you're getting great service."

"Why yes. Joseph is one of the best slaves the Pleckers have, and he's quite the interesting half-breed."

Leonard leaned over and looked at Joseph. "Oh yes, the eyes. I can tell he's a half-breed, or is he less?"

Judy Mays shook her head and pointed at Joseph. "Oh no, Leo, he's half. His father is an Indian, and his mother is Negro."

Leo's eyebrows lowered, and he rubbed his chin. "You surprise me, Judy Mays. You know much about this one. You must find him entertaining. Why?"

Judy Mays put her elbow on the table. "He's unique...not many slaves have a parent that's full-blood Indian." Her eyebrows drew together. "Why do you ask?"

"You seem to be showing the boy off. Are you thinking of purchasing the boy from the Pleckers? I thought you weren't interested in the purchasing of new slaves."

Judy Mays's jaw slightly dropped. She looked at Joseph, and her eyes fixed on his face. "Purch— I'm not. The boy is simply an interesting case. I find it interesting how the half-breeds show more promise than the Negroes. Joseph and the other Indian children nearly burned down the mansion not too long ago. He wasn't the one who set the fire. That honor belongs to that full-blood young lady, Riza. However, he did almost escape with her."

Leonard put his hand in his pocket. "Ah, so the fire incident I heard about was started by children. We have a bunch of rebellious children on this plantation."

"I told Wilma she should've had Riza's hand cut off. That girl is a savage," Daphne said.

"Well I think it is best she isn't in your care," Leonard said. Judy Mays giggled while Daphne scrunched her napkin and pouted. "Well, do you mind if I borrow this boy for some service?"

Judy Mays bit her lip but exhaled with a smile. "Of course not Leo, but I do want him back," she said tapping her finger on the table.

"Thank you, come boy, and bring some lemonade to me and my wife."

"Yes, sir," Joseph said. He got the lemonade and hurried over to Leonard and Clarissa while Judy Mays watched. He carefully put down the glasses and stood at attention.

"Well done, Joseph," Leonard said. "You know Mrs. Judy Mays is taking great interest in you. I'd say that's a good thing. You don't want to be on her bad side. I have an old friend named Carl who can attest to that. How old are you?"

Joseph replied, "I'm ten years old, sir."

"You can call me Mr. Benedict. Were you born a slave?"

"No, I wasn't, Mr. Benedict."

"Hmph, no wonder you and the Riza girl rebelled. Where are you really from, boy?"

"I'm from Tahlequah."

"That's one of the Indian towns in Indian Territory. Yes, I've heard of it. It's one of the Choctaw or Cherokee towns."

"It's Cherokee, Mr. Benedict."

"Well, we can't tell the difference between any of you anyway, but how long have you been here?"

The corners of Joseph's mouth fell, forming a frown. "I have been here for over a year."

Leonard took a sip of lemonade. "You seemed to have learned quickly as you needed to. What is your mother's name, boy?" He remained silent as Leonard's wife sipped her lemonade. "Did you not hear my question?"

"Annabelle."

Leonard's eyebrows shot up a little. "What a different name, but I've heard it before. Was your mother a slave?"

"No, she was not Mr. Benedict."

Leonard rubbed his chin and took a sip of lemonade. "What is your mother's last name?"

"Lightning."

"Are you sure? Sounds like an Indian name the Cherokee gave her. It must be Cherokee if that was your last name too, is it?"

"Yes, it is, Mr. Benedict. My momma said her last name was Mays."

Leonard smiled and took another sip of lemonade. "Judy

Mays was right. You are an interesting boy. You must've had an interesting family."

"They will find me," Joseph murmured.

Leonard leaned forward. "What did you say?"

"Nothing, Mr. Benedict."

He lightly chuckled when he looked at Clarissa. "She was right. Judy Mays. That woman's perception must be a gift from God. Hmm, she's a woman not to be played with. Go on back to her before she comes over here to get you. I see her counting down before she wants you all to herself."

Joseph quickly returned to Judy Mays. Leonard watched as he and Clarissa waved at Judy Mays and Daphne. "Leo, what are you talking about?" she asked.

He answered, "Ruthanne gave me the exact description of that boy, and he fits in all the right pieces without even knowing it. I was beginning to wonder if we would find him after we visited a couple of other plantations."

She leaned into Leonard's ear. "So that's the boy Ruthanne spoke of? What do you want to do?"

He whispered, "Play it carefully, Clarissa, and send Ruthanne a letter tomorrow. I'm worried Judy Mays almost has it all figured out."

"You think she wants the boy?"

"She shows too much interest in the boy. I think she might, but maybe there's more to her wanting the boy. She's chosen to entertain herself with him. I can't tell if it's to learn more about him or if it's something else. We can't risk aggravating her. She already put a bullet in Carl. All we can do right now is enjoy the wedding, and I'll deal with this tomorrow."

"I'm concerned for the boy, and he's not even my child."

Leonard rubbed Clarissa's hand. "Keeping Judy Mays happy is the best way to play this, especially if she's figured out who this boy is. This world is filled with surprises."

Joseph continued to serve Judy Mays while she welcomed wedding guests who greeted her.

Joseph was later called away by Dorothy to help with other tasks. Judy Mays forced herself to smile with her gaze fixed on Joseph as he walked further away. As Riza left the family table carrying a glass pitcher of lemonade, Daphne waved at Riza while she rolled her eyes and scoffed. "I imagine you enjoy this, Judy Mays," she groaned. "All these other niggers are serving but only Riza is available."

"I take no enjoyment in you being scared of her," Judy Mays joked with a light chuckle.

Daphne leaned back and pouted at her friend. "Scared, I'm not scared. I don't tru—"

"Mrs. Judy Mays, Mrs. Daphne, y'all wanted some lemonade?"

"Yes dear, we did," Judy Mays said. She held out her glass, and Riza poured her some lemonade. She smiled. "I see your hair has mostly grown back."

"Yes, Mrs. Judy Mays, about half of it."

"Really, only half? My goodness, Riza!"

Daphne held out her glass and she poured lemonade into it. "As if it matters," Daphne griped. "This creature deserves no form of praise. It's beneath you to even speak of it, Judy Mays."

The corner of her mouth pinched. "Oh please, Daphne. You're ruining the moment."

Daphne pouted. "I'm sorry, I don't mean to be so negative. After all, we need to be together more than ever now."

"Would you like an extra biscuit, Mrs. Judy Mays?" Riza asked.

"No dear, I'm fine," She answered.

"I do love the setup of their celebration. The church seemed to glow even brighter during their wedding," Daphne stated before taking a drink of her lemonade. "I'm sure Reece will give Kenneth plenty of children. Is there no greater way to honor your husband?"

Judy Mays forced herself to grin and tilted her head. "Well, I'm sure you truly believe that dear."

Daphne smacked her lips. "Judy Mays!"

"What? I didn't disagree with you." Judy Mays's eyes slightly narrowed and took a sip of her lemonade. "I agree bringing children into the world is a beautiful thing. There's nothing like holding your own baby in your own arms." Her gaze fixed on Riza. "One day, you'll get to experience that kind of love, Riza."

Daphne cackled. "Love, love, really Judy Mays?" She pointed at Riza. "This creature doesn't know what love is, how could she? And the way she is, she'll never know real love."

Judy Mays's eyes dilated, her nose flaring while she cocked her head. "Don't speak so ignorantly! Even the lowest of us are capable of love. You test me, Daphne."

Daphne's jaw dropped, and her head lowered. Riza let out a little giggle but quickly covered her mouth.

Daphne looked up at the Mohawk girl, her nose scrunched, her upper lip lifted, and she gritted her teeth. She bobbed her head, uttering, "I can't help but feel there's still some savagery in you, Riza..." She leaned back and leered at Riza. "I heard your momma begged for you." Riza's eyes widened. "Her only daughter...it's bad enough her husband was a gambling cheater, but I imagine it hurts even more when you're missing the only daughter you have. You don't even know what happened, do you?" Riza's chest began to inflate with her deep breaths. "Oh, Riza, she undoubtedly begged for you."

"Daphne, that's enough," Judy Mays said, with each word deepening in timbre.

"I understand you can tolerate this grass nigger, but she should've kept her mouth shut," Daphne growled. "Don't think I didn't notice you didn't offer me a biscuit!"

Riza replied, "I apologize, Mrs. Daphne. I meant no disrespect."

Daphne continued to leer. "You think I'm gonna say something? Is that what you're thinking? As much as I would love to see you get whipped, I've gotten something even better. Your whore momma offered her body to get you back. It wasn't surprising, though. Your momma was a squaw, from what I was told. It was only second nature for her to behave like a whore." Riza's right hand slowly began to ball into a fist. "It's what your momma was best at, the only reason she knew you were your daddy's is that brown skin."

"Daphne, enough," Judy Mays said with a stern whisper.

Daphne's leer dropped from her face. She rested her elbow on the table and pointed at Riza. "No, I've been waiting to tell this savage, Judy Mays! Your momma took a bullet for you! It's the best secret I was ever told, but why let it be a secret. Why lie to a redskin that burns down homes?"

Riza's dilated eyes narrowed and locked onto Daphne's remorseless blue eyes. "Oh, did the truth take all your laughter away? I'll say it again, there's nothing but ashes left of your momma. Redskins can have any dollar amount drawn on their body, but you're an exceptional girl. Your momma was a worthless squaw who took a bullet for a worthless yet exceptional savage. You have no family left, and you'll never have a family. I imagine it doesn't mean much to—"

"Daphne, you've said enough," Judy Mays growled as slapped her hand on her thigh.

Riza's lips began to quiver.

Daphne scoffed, and she leaned forward. "Don't tell me you didn't know that's how your momma was paying bills, Riza. Seducing men and pushing out bastard babies is the only thing you grass niggers are good at."

Riza aggressively grabbed one of the knives sitting on the table as tears began to well up in her eyes. Daphne's eyes shot open. She gulped and grabbed onto Judy Mays's arm. "I told you, she's a savage," she screamed.

"Riza," Judy Mays shouted. A couple of guests turned their attention to the table with calm sounds of band filling the background.

Riza's dilated eyes widened. "I… I have to wash this silverware off…" Riza grabbed the other silverware. "I'm so sorry I scared you, Mrs. Daphne. I promise I'll bring them back immediately." A tear escaped Riza's eye and landed on the table. She immediately took off to the cookhouse.

Judy Mays's face began to turn red as she took a deep breath. "Get off of me, Daphne."

Daphne let go of Judy Mays, replying, "I'm sorry, she scared me. Did you see that? She was about to stab me!"

"I'm sure she would've just stabbed you if she wanted to. After all, she is only a savage, right?" her tone dripping with sarcasm. Riza soon returned and placed down the silverware accordingly as the young women watched. "Thank you, Riza."

Riza forced a smile. "You're welcome, Mrs. Judy Mays, Mrs. Daphne." Wilma then called for her, and she left to attend to what Wilma needed.

Judy Mays now remained mostly silent while she drank her lemonade while Daphne continued to socialize with guests who walked by their table. Judy Mays's finger tapped on the table as her eyes followed Riza, ignoring Daphne's conversations. *What am I supposed to say now?* She thought.

More guests continued to arrive at the celebration. Reece came into the courtyard in a white wedding dress and awed everyone with her beauty. She greeted all the guests, and as she went to greet one table, her blue eyes locked onto Dorothy. Reece leered, and she side-eyed Dorothy while continuing to greet the guests before the celebration started. The ceremony for the wedding commenced as all the guests watched, including the slaves. Dorothy watched, frowning, while Reece smiled and held Kenneth's hands. "God, give me the strength to serve as I'm supposed to," Dorothy whispered. However, when they finished their vows and kissed, Dorothy broke the neck of a glass she was holding and entered the mansion wiping away tears.

As the wedding celebration went on, Dorothy was forced to serve at the family table along with the other house slaves. "Come pour me some more lemonade, Dorothy. This heat is getting to me," Reece said. Dorothy walked over and poured Reece a cold glass of lemonade. "Well done. I think I'll gladly see your face every day."

"Yes, Mrs. Reece," Dorothy said.

Reece wiggled her finger, signaling Dorothy to bend down toward her. "Do you really believe I can't see it in those hazel eyes?" Reece whispered. "Your disapproval of me. I promise to make sure you will never give me that look again, and I promise we're going to have some interesting times together." Dorothy rose and returned to her post as Reece giggled and drank her lemonade.

Dorothy mumbled, "I promise to spit in your food every chance I get you blue-eyed Delilah."

Judy Mays entered the mansion through its white back doors with Wilma and a few guests. Her eyes brightened when she saw Edgar turn the corner, with Riza walking behind him. He wore a white high-collared shirt, a green cravat that complemented his shirt, a gray waistcoat, a green vest, and gray trousers. She quickly approached him, gave him a hug, and he gave her a kiss on the cheek.

"Edgar, how did everything go?" she asked.

"Hello, my love. It went very well. I'm sure we can talk about it later," Edgar said with a grin.

"Edgar, looking well-groomed as always," Wilma said with open arms. "I'm so happy you're here to join in on the celebration."

"I'm happy to be here to celebrate a friend's next journey in life. After receiving a very proper greeting from Riza, I'm sure it will be a great celebration. Oh, and before I forget, Austin will arrive too."

Wilma beamed and calmly brought her hands together. "Oh good! Your brother is coming. That's what I like to hear. I was about to show my guests and Judy Mays the new mahogany table seat we got for our dining room, but that can wait. I'm sure Kenneth will be overjoyed to see you! I'm sure Calving will also want to know about your continued railroad deals. Wilma stepped up to Edgar and put her hand on his upper back. Come on, dear, the day isn't over yet."

"I'll join you in a moment," Judy Mays said. Edgar glanced back at her and nodded. The other guests followed and chatted with Edgar and Wilma.

"Did Mrs. Daphne tell me the truth?" Riza asked.

Judy Mays's gaze remained fixed on the glass windows. *If I lie to her, I'll never gain her trust again. Daphne, what have you done*, she thought. Judy Mays turned around, seeing a blank expression on Riza's face, but sunlight reflected off the tears resting in Riza's eyes. "I don't know Riza," she answered. "I was never directly told what happened to your momma or the rest of your family."

"Please, I only want to know the truth."

Judy Mays began to slowly approach Riza. "Believe me when I say I'm so sorry, Riza. I do not know if she is alive or not. I know this answer only creates pain for you. From the depths of my heart…I'm sorry Daphne said what she said."

"I used to say to myself; even if my momma was gone, I still had my little brothers. Now I know the truth…they don't care if we are children. Those White men probably killed them too. They are that evil."

Judy Mays's eyebrows slanted upward and then lowered. "Riza, I—"

"If my momma is gone, then they're dead, or they're slaves like me. This is the truth. How can people like this…call themselves Christians?"

A tear escaped her left eye, and Judy Mays felt her heart drop. "I'm sorry, dear." She wiped away her tears and put her hand on her cheek. "You are a strong girl."

She closed her eyes and turned her face downward, but Judy Mays forced her gaze back to hers. She opened up her eyes, and tears streamed down her face. "No matter what people say to you, walk in faith. Because the people here will say whatever they can to break your spirit…it's what they want."

"Have you ever heard anything about my momma?"

Judy Mays wiped her face again. "I promise you, I haven't. I told you the truth about your tribe, didn't I?"

"Yes."

"Okay, then trust my words on this. If I can find out the truth about your momma, how would that make you feel?"

Riza took a step back and wiped her face. "Why would you do that for me?"

"Because I've watched this amazing, beautiful little girl grow up before my eyes, and I can't stand to see you in pain, not knowing the truth."

Riza's brown eyes remained locked with Judy Mays's, the corners of her mouth slightly curved downward, forming a half frown. She deeply inhaled and turned around. "Is Joseph your Annabelle's son?"

Judy Mays bit her lip, and she exhaled. "I don't know. I don't have enough proof."

Riza turned around, side-eyeing Judy Mays. "You said he has his momma's smile."

Judy Mays felt her heart skip a beat. "I did… but other people can have that same smile. It's not like it's the rarest smile in the world. Riza, a smile isn't—"

"If Joseph is Annabelle's son, would you free him?"

Judy Mays's nose crinkled. "You know, it's not that simple."

"Says a woman with power…"

Judy Mays's jaw dropped, and she scoffed. "I shouldn't be surprised by the words that come out of your mouth, Riza Moon."

Riza quickly wiped away a tear that escaped her eye. "You're the only White person that calls me by my real name. Why?"

"Because you do remind me of Annabelle, and I have watched you grow up. I'd imagine she'd be just like you if she didn't grow up a slave."

"Would you free me if you could?"

"I w—"

"Judy Mays! Come on out here and dance," Reece shouted.

She rolled her lower lip and huffed. She turned around and smiled, "Sure, dear, I know you're excited about your day."

"Looks like you were having a talk with this…Mohawk."

"She has served me well. Riza, when I get done with these dances I'll take some lemonade."

"Of course, Mrs. Judy Mays," she replied.

Judy Mays followed Reece, while Riza followed the young

women. Judy Mays saw where people had gathered to dance as a live band played. A few guests greeted Reece and Judy Mays and began conversing with Reece. Judy Mays slowed her pace as Reece became distracted by party guests. She glanced back at Riza, seeing her lips were now forming a pout. Her eyes centered forward and one of the guests greeted her as they slowly walked to the crowd. Judy Mays forced herself to smile, and after a short talk, the guest rejoined the conversation Reece was having with the other guests. Judy Mays inhaled and stopped walking until Riza caught up. Judy Mays walked with Riza, whispering, "We will continue this talk later, little girl. You are right. I do have power…but not as much as you believe." The pout dropped from Riza's face. "I hope you do see that." The celebration ended when sunset arrived, and guests went home while some stayed overnight.

Joseph and the other slaves toiled to clean the mansion, so Master Plecker would wake up to a clean home in the morning. The removal of all the trash and rearranging of the mansion was completed, but the slaves who cleaned it all returned home sore and exhausted. Joseph had never been so happy to sleep on a wood floor but gladly fell asleep next to Tom and Mary.

In Tahlequah on August 3, 1861, the Lightning-Strongman family remained faithful in the hopes of Joseph's return. After Grace and Lizzie locked up the supply store, they strolled home as Grace played with her son. Suddenly, they heard a horse neigh and saw Brock slowly riding up to the women. Grace held Gabriel tighter to her chest while the women stood their ground. "Well, I haven't seen you ladies in a few weeks," he snobbishly said.

"We have no interest in seeing you, Mr. Jackson," Grace said.

"Don't be that way, Miss Grace. I haven't had any quarrels with your family for some time now. I see your son is growing well."

"What do you want?" Lizzie asked.

"I want nothing. I was curious with your progress in finding that Negro boy. It's been over a year since the unfortunate incident."

Lizzie angrily replied, "Who do you think you're fooling? You don't care about Joseph. We're sure you were involved."

He grinned. "Young lady, I was not there and had no knowledge of the incident."

"I doubt Mr. Sawyer acted without telling you," Grace said. "Not stopping him is as bad as you being there."

He replied, "I disagree. After all, your doing got him shipped off to the capital. The boy could've been returned if an agreement were to be made."

Grace angrily replied, "If that agreement involves you seeing that little girl, then no. You'll never be in her life, and she'll never know of you. You White men think you rule the world. Well, you don't."

He sneered. "I think you need to rethink your tone with me. We rule this land, and we rule your people."

"Why don't you go off to war," Lizzie growled. She pursed her lips as Brock began to take deep breaths. "Oh, I see. It's easier to threaten a woman than it is to fight for something. I hope those Union boys kill ever last one of you slave lovers."

He huffed. "What kind of hypocrisy is that?" "Your people thrive off of slave labor."

"Maybe my people that support the White man's way should catch a pellet too. Did you want to say anything else because you're terrible at begging?"

His brows furrowed. He hopped off his horse and approached her while Grace held her Gabriel closer. "Begging? What would I beg you for, redskin?"

"For us to talk to Lisa so you can see the girl."

"I have no intention of ever begging to see my daughter, so you can be silent. She's my daughter. I don't need permission to see her."

She put her hand on her hip. "She'll never be your daughter, and I promise to keep my word if you come on our farm if Lisa doesn't get you first."

"Are you threatening an officer of the United States, Lizzie Lightning?"

Her brown eyes dilated. "I'm threatening a coward, a rapist, a man that claims to be Christian, but all your actions oppose your claim." He started to turn red as she stood her ground against him. "I think we're done here." Grace and Lizzie walked away as he angrily watched.

"We'll have our time soon."

Lizzie squinted and turned her head around, her voice dripping with sarcasm, "Allow me to give you an invitation to hell scented with lilac. I'm sure you'll make an effort." She and Grace continued down the road.

Brock got onto his horse. "You won't see it coming, prairie nigger. I'll enjoy it." He signaled the horse and slowly went past the townspeople. While Grace and Lizzie moved away, she kept looking back to make sure Brock wasn't following them.

In Caledonia, things remained the same for the field slaves but drastically changed for the house slaves with Reece's agenda. She was determined to have things her way and began to limit Dorothy's interactions with Kenneth. Dorothy was quick to notice the personal attacks and often spit in Reece's food or drinks. Her attention even expanded to the other house slaves as she purposely made things harder for them. Riza never thought she would see the day she'd be happy. Wilma wanted to spend most of the day out on the patio. Wilma's wants took Riza out of the house, and she was far more willing to listen to her rants than submit to Reece.

On August 10, 1861, Stella announced her pregnancy to Bo. He excitedly told the other slaves, and after slaving, they celebrated. The men danced around an open fire, clapped, and stomped on the ground to make a beat. Joseph and Tom watched, amused by the excitement, and were happy for Bo and Stella.

"What are you thinking about?" Tom asked.

"My little brother Jonathan. He'd already be two years old,"

Joseph said. "His birthday was in June. I never got to see his first birthday."

Tom slightly frowned and said, "Yeah, my little sister would be eight, and my little brother turned five two weeks ago. I wonder if he remembers me."

Joseph pulled up a blade of grass. "Yeah, Jonathan probably doesn't know who I am. It's scary thinking your family doesn't know who you are."

"I think Jesus will somehow get us home someday so we can see them."

"I think so too, but how long will we have to wait?"

"Try not to think about it. Maybe Riza will think of a better plan, and this time I won't be afraid."

"I won't be afraid either."

The next night, Susie came to the slave houses, hoarding extra food for them. While eating the extra food, Joseph thought, *I remembered how much Momma ate when she was pregnant.*

He gave his extra pieces of bread to Stella. "What you doing, Joseph?" Stella asked.

"For the baby, I'm not hungry anymore anyway," he said with a smile.

Tom looked down at the tin plate with the bread he was eating and shifted it over to Stella. "I'm full too," Tom said.

Stella calmly replied, "Boys, please eat if you're hungry." The boys shook their heads no, and Bo nodded at both of the boys showing his appreciation. "Well, thank you both."

As Stella ate, the others talked about the day. "How is Riza?" Tom asked.

Clint looked up while he sat against the wall, and Susie pressed her lips. "She is doing a lot better. She stopped having the nightmares again," Susie said. "Mrs. Reece is always finding things for us to do. Two days ago, she made me and Dorothy help her try on different dresses for two hours. She's different from Mrs. Wilma."

"That sounds worse than washing dishes," Joseph said.

Tom lightly giggled, but Susie pouted. "It's worse than washing dishes. I'd rather wash dishes the entire day than help that woman put on another dress. The air in the room changes when Mrs. Reece and Dorothy are in the same room. Like when one of the great storms is coming. I thought they were going to fight with all the mean things Mrs. Reece kept saying about Dorothy and the looks Dorothy was giving her. I thought Dorothy was going to stab her with a needle."

"Are Mrs. Reece and Master Kenneth going to move away soon?" Tom asked.

Susie answered, "I don't know, but it looks like they'll be here for a few months."

"I think you have to keep smiling so she won't have a reason to get you into trouble," Joseph said. "She's scarier than Ms. Wilma."

Susie giggled. "Don't tell nobody but Dorothy spits in Mrs. Reece's drinks." The boys started to chuckle when Susie began to laugh louder. "Well, I better leave so I don't get into trouble. I miss seeing all of you more often. May Jesus bless y'all with protection."

Susie stood up and was about to leave. "Please tell Riza I said hi," Clint said sorrowfully.

"I have little to say to you, Clint," Susie sniped. "You hurt Riza badly and because of you she started the nightmares again."

"I want her to know. I sorry."

Joseph and the others remained silent as Susie stared Clint down. "I hope you do mean it. If Riza does feel like talking to you again, don't touch her. She won't like it." Clint wiped away a tear and exhaled. "I'm glad you healed, but you have to earn trust… bye everyone."

Susie left the slave house and smoothly walked through the willow trees without anyone seeing her. Clint continued to mourn as he leaned against the wall.

"Clint, you need to understand the pain Riza feel," Bo said. "You did a evil thing. You let Pearl change your mind. Would you have kept fighting if Riza cried or force yourself on her if she scream for you to stop?"

Clint sadly replied, "No, I would've stopped."

"Then why you not stop after the first no?" Clint looked at

Bo frowning. "When Riza get ready, the day gone come when she ask you. She not gone be nice about it, and she may take another swing at you."

"Should I try to go speak to her?" Clint asked.

"No and Mrs. Wilma has forbid you from going to the house-slave house," Stella said. "You did wrong, and sometimes we don't get to fix it. Maybe like what Bo was saying, when she ready, she'll find you." Joseph could see the regret etched into Clint's frown but was still disappointed he had hurt Riza. Most of the other slaves continued to ignore Pearl, who was slowly healing. Before everyone went to sleep, Bo led them in prayer. He thanked God for what they had prayed, for a better future, and for healing among the slaves.

The backbreaking work increased as the cotton grew. The overseers patrolled the land with an iron fist and had no patience for anyone that wanted to take a break. The repetitive tasks tested Joseph's faith. However, he listened to Tom's advice and ignored how many days were passing so hope would remain. He often listened to the songbirds when he could to help him have some form of joy. The birds had no care in the world, and he hoped to be able to experience such a day.

On August 20, 1861, Joseph and Tom stopped by one of the cotton fields to collect baskets from the other slaves. Joseph came up to Pearl and she handed him her basket. "That's all I can carry right now. I still healing," Pearl said.

Master Rice rode up on his horse and looked down while Joseph calmly took the basket from Pearl. Rice halted the horse and got off the animal. "Pearl, what is this?" he asked.

"Master Rice, I sorry. I still healing. I can't carry more right now."

He agitatedly replied, "You trying to get out of work?"

Pearl nervously replied, "I swear I not, I not Master Rice." She began to shake as he stared her down. "I swear I work faster so I can get as much as I used to."

He scoffed while he ran his hand down his brown mustache and new beard. "Joseph, take the basket and come out here more often to make sure she getting the amount she supposed to." He got onto the horse and began to ride slowly to the mansion. Joseph placed the basket in the wagon and gave Pearl an empty one. He watched Rice travel up to the mansion and scowled.

During this time, Riza went outside to give fresh leftover food to the pigs at Reece's command. Riza felt it was Reece's way of trying to make them suffer. She rebelled by eating the fresh bread that Reece didn't even touch. As she dumped the food into the pigs' pen, she saw Rice slowly riding up to the mansion. She quickly began to go to the mansion. "Riza, where are you going so quickly?" Master Rice yelled. She kept walking and was about to reach for the front doorknob. "You run inside that mansion, and I'll make sure you get that tree stump!"

Riza stopped and turned around, scowling. "I apologize, Master Rice. I didn't hear you," she said. What did you say?"

He got off the horse and arrogantly approached her. "You lying little prairie nigger. That must be fun for you. Lying so much I don't know what to believe. Go get me an apple."

"Mrs. Reece will be looking for me soon."

"Do I look concerned about that?"

"There are many things you look like," she murmured.

"What did you say?"

"I said I'm going to the apple trees right now, Master Rice." She quickly marched over to the yard with the apple trees behind the mansion. He followed her. She jumped up and grabbed a fresh apple. The second she turned around, he grabbed her shoulder and held her against the tree. "Why—"

"I don't know how to show you how angry you make me feel. You damage one of the best field slaves we got to the point that she can't carry as much as she used to. You damage the other one, forcing me to put him on feeding some dumb animals until now. You have a debt to pay."

"Let me go!" She forced her shoulder free from his grip and stood her ground against him.

"Careful now. I like the ones that fight back. What you think, 'cause you wearing a blue dress now that gone change things? I'm gone have you and you gone know your place. What you gone do hit me with that apple?" He took a step forward, and she posed to throw the apple at him. "So you think you gone win?"

"I have to go inside, Master Rice," she snarled.

"No, you following what I say right now. Now put down that apple." She held her ground while she slowed back up to try to position herself to run. "I see we not gone have an agreement."

"What's going on out here?" Kenneth said. She dropped the apple and began to walk over to Kenneth. "Well?"

"Master Kenneth, I was getting an apple Master Rice told me to get and held me against the tree," she pleaded. "I did what he asked of me."

"Go inside, Riza, before Mrs. Reece starts looking for you."

"Yes, sir." She side-eyed Rice and ran into the mansion.

"Rice, why aren't you out in the fields?" Kenneth boldly asked.

He answered, "I was trying to make sure she was doing what she was supposed to be doing. I saw her outside the mansion, and I wanted an apple."

Kenneth replied with an irate tone, "I think you focus too much on Riza when those field niggers out there are on their own. What's going to stop one of them from getting ideas with you not there?"

"I apologize, I guess I have a hard time trusting her. She's a clever redskin."

"As I said, keep your eyes out there. I'd hate to tell my Pa you're not watching those slaves."

"I'll go now. I'm sorry." Kenneth nodded, accepting his apology. Rice went around to the front of the mansion while Kenneth watched. He turned to go inside the mansion when he saw Dorothy standing in the doorway with a slight frown. He nodded at her as he returned to the mansion.

Kenneth walked past her when she gently grabbed his arm. "Please tell me you could see how he going after Riza," she said.

"I can't accuse that man of anything unless he is caught in the act or at least caught attempting," he said. "Even if he was caught, my father wouldn't have him removed from this land."

She released his sleeve, and he began to go toward the double door. "Does it really mean nothing to you if he hurts Riza?"

He abruptly replied, "Don't question my form of justice. Is that understood?"

She gulped. "Yes, Master Kenneth." He looked away from her as he stared at the door. "I miss you, Kenneth," she whispered. He looked back at her and sighed. He walked around her and went through the doors leading to the foyer. Dorothy smiled and left to wash the dishes. As she washed the dishes, she could hear him playing on the piano and grinned.

CHAPTER 6
Hope in the Darkness

As the American Civil War grew and created a greater division among the people, a much-awaited letter arrived in Mercy, Missouri. The letter arrived at Ruthanne's home on August 22, 1861. Ruthanne's eyes shot open when she read it was from Leonard. She ripped open the letter. She read,

Ruthanne I have surprisingly located Joseph after searching nine different plantations. Even more shocking is Judy Mays has managed to encounter the boy and shows unusual interest in him. It seems almost certain she knows who he is. I believe Judy Mays's socialite behavior made this possible. However, I can't determine if her motives are to harm Joseph. I asked her about purchasing Joseph and she stumbled on the idea of it. She seemed more interested in having Joseph near her rather than him leading her to Annabelle. As we both know, though, Judy Mays is a clever woman, and she may be using Joseph. Annabelle has done an impressive job hiding her past from Joseph. Unfortunately, his naivety was obvious, as you would expect with a child. I do worry for the boy, and with this war, time is not on his side. Who's to say what Judy Mays's plans are or what ugliness this war may bring out of her. The Cherokees need to act now before the war makes it impossible to travel. I do wish the best for the boy especially since he is in Judy Mays's vision.

Ruthanne sat back in her rocking chair while she rubbed her pregnant belly. "This beyond troubling," Ruthanne said. "What game is running through your mind, Judy Mays? Why haven't claimed on him?" Ruthanne rubbed her forehead.

"Momma, is something wrong?" Belle asked.

Ruthanne looked into Belle's green eyes and smiled. "Why, no. Nothing is wrong. Momma was thinking about an important thing," Ruthanne said with a playful tone. "Mr. Benedict has found a person Momma was looking for."

Belle joyfully asked, "Is Mr. Benedict coming back?"

"No baby, not for some time. It's too dangerous now."

"Why is it too dangerous?"

"The war Daddy has been praying about has grown stronger, and a lot of bad men are doing bad things. So for now, Mr. Benedict can't visit us. We'll see him again."

When Peter returned home from church, Ruthanne told him about the news. She wanted to leave immediately.

"Ruthanne, you are pregnant, and a war is raging," Peter said. "You're not going to Indian Territory."

"Annabelle needs to know immediately that Joseph has been found," Ruthanne argued. "I believe Leo is right. Judy Mays has figured out the truth. Time is not on his side. I'm not sure what she's planning, but this is dangerous." She wiped a tear away from her green eyes. "All of this is worrisome."

Peter rested his chin on his hand as he sat at the supper table and looked at their son Jonah, standing in the crib. "I'll go to the Cherokee territory," he said. "I believe that's the quickest solution to telling them about Joseph's whereabouts."

Ruthanne replied, "Peter, you can't go alone. It's too dangerous. You've never even fired a gun before."

"I'm sure I can find a few good men to accompany me. And let me further add that God's word is stronger than any weapon."

"Then don't forget your Bible when you make the trip. Who did you have in mind to accompany you?"

"I'm not sure. I guess I'll have to ask one of our younger members to go."

"Peter think…the men you're thinking about are hoping the

Confederates win. How do you think they'll react when they find out you're carrying a letter to some Indians with information that will help them free a slave?"

Peter rubbed his forehead. "Well, yes, that does create a problem. Who should I ask at such short notice then?"

"Why not Allen Keys."

"You think Allen would come? All right, I'll ask him tomorrow morning."

"You need to go ask him after supper. I don't want any more time wasted while that boy is chained, or you're not eating any of this!"

"All right, you don't have to be so hostile." Ruthanne picked up Jonah and started to bounce him on her hip with a slight frown. "Was there someone else you wanted to go?"

"Yes, another addition that wouldn't cause trouble in Indian Territory. I do have someone in mind."

"I'm scared, Peter."

"The Lord allowed Judy Mays to run into Joseph. We have to have faith…if we're going to question why. I'm very concerned too."

Ruthanne placed Jonah down, took a roasted chicken off the stove, and put it on the table. "Children, come and eat. Walk by faith and not by sight."

Peter exhaled but then smiled. "And with boldness and the strength of the Lord." Later in the evening, Peter told Allen and Rebecca Keys the news. The excitement was so loud that the Williamson family walked over to check on the family but worry soon matched the excitement. Peter spent the rest of the evening making a plan after Allen accepted the offer to go to Tahlequah. The other person of interest also accepted the offer to go to Tahlequah.

Three days passed while the men rode through the prairies and sparse forests in a carriage with two brown horses. The men finally arrived in Tahlequah. The townspeople stared at the men as they slowly rode through the dirty roads. The men found it slightly difficult to find someone who spoke English and was willing to speak to them. Hours went by as the men slowly rolled through the town. Peter saw a young teenage girl with long, wavy hair that was put into one braid who looked at them. "Excuse me, young lady, do you speak English?" Peter asked. The teenager stopped but decided to keep walking, "Ma'am, please wait. Do you know Annabelle Lightning?"

The teenage girl stopped and turned around. "Yes, I know Annabelle," the teenager said. "Why are you looking for her?"

"My name is Pastor Peter Avail from Mercy, Missouri, and my wife is a good friend of hers. Me and my friends here have a very important message for her. It is a letter about her son, Joseph."

The teenage girl came up the carriage. "What do you know about Joseph?"

"All of that information is in this letter. That I swear."

"I will show you where her family lives."

"What is your name, young lady?"

"My name is Lea. My grandma spent a lot of time with Annabelle."

Lea greeted Allen and the other man who sat on the driver seat of the carriage next to Peter. Lea got on the carriage, and they rode off to the Lightning-Strongman farm. While they drove through Tahlequah, Allen and Peter noticed how different Tahlequah was compared to Mercy. Few buildings and homes were made of brick or stone, and the sight of impoverished people made them uncomfortable. The carriage soon stopped in front of the family cabin of the Lightning-Strongman family. Rain and Jannie were carrying buckets of grain when they saw the carriage and put the buckets down.

Lea jumped down from the carriage and smiled at the girls. "Go get your momma," Lea said in Cherokee. "I have important words for her." The girls immediately ran to the family house. The men got out of the carriage, and Peter stepped down from the driver seat. "It's best you stay here. The family has remained careful since Joseph was stolen." Suddenly, the front door of the cabin opened, and Lizzie came out with a bow and her quiver. Lea saw Lizzie's blank face and immediately walked forward. "These are good men, Lizzie."

Lizzie opened the log cabin door and shouted in Cherokee, "Annabelle, come outside."

She walked outside and saw Peter, Allen, and Daniel. "Oh my God," Annabelle said. Annabelle moved toward the men as Lizzie followed. "Oh my God! Pastor Avail, Allen, and Daniel what brings you here?"

"Annabelle, it's a blessing to see you. We were worried that we were going to have a harder time finding you," Peter said. "We have promising news. We know were Joseph is."

Annabelle's tears escaped her eyes and she began to cry with her hands over her heart. Lizzie embraced Annabelle as she cried, and she started to tear up. Lea smiled as she heard the news. Her grandmother's prophecy was starting to come to past. "Where is he? Why haven't you brought him?" Lizzie asked.

Allen replied, "Ruthanne received a letter from a friend that lives in Mississippi, and he has no doubts about a boy he met on a plantation. Because of the war and because of social issues we can't just go down to Mississippi and take him. Doing things in that manner would be too dangerous."

Lizzie exhaled and slightly pouted. "He's alive, which means we can bring him home," Annabelle said. "That's what matters, which town is he in?"

Peter frowned, replying, "He's in Caledonia, Annabelle."

Annabelle gave a skewed frown. "I never heard of it. Is it far from Columbus?"

"It's not far from Columbus it's actually a little south."

"Well, at least my boy isn't in Columbus." The three men looked at Annabelle with their eyebrows slanting upward. "What is it? Daniel?"

"That woman, your friend, Judy Mays, she's met Joseph. Her behavior is showing she probably knows who he is," Daniel said.

Annabelle's eyes shot open. "Impossible! How is that possible?" Annabelle asked with a frightened tone, her eyes widened.

"Annabelle, people travel from Columbus to Caledonia all the time," Peter said. "It isn't a far trip, and her family has been friends with the family that has Joseph for decades. The family that has him is very wealthy and well-known. Ruthanne said she is a sociable woman, so it's not surprising she would somehow meet him or come across the plantation he's located."

Annabelle put her hand on her forehead. "If she really knows he is my son, I don't know what she's going to do. I ran away without even saying goodbye to her. I didn't get to show how much she meant to me. Why hasn't she claimed him, if she really knows? She would claim him as her property, wouldn't she?"

"Leonard is the man who found Joseph, and he is even confused with Judy Mays's actions. He's not sure if she's enjoying his enslavement though she isn't behaving in that manner. We've all been thinking about it, maybe she's protecting him."

"Protecting him? From who?" Lizzie asked.

Annabelle felt her chest become heavy, her body quivered, and she said, "Her papa...Mr. Brown. I've been so scared of how she would react. I haven't been thinking of the person that would hurt him. Either way, we need to bring my boy home."

"Come inside. We've started making supper. I left the girls to prepare food," Lizzie said. "We can talk more about this over food."

"Thank you for your kindness, ma'am," Peter said. All of them went into the family house and continued to talk about Joseph's situation. Tsula and Maria were thrilled with the news and had Rosita run to the fields to tell David and the men. Peter gave Annabelle the original letter from Leonard as they talked. David and the others arrived at the house, and the situation was explained to them. Grace and Lisa later arrived from working at the supply store, and Luke from patrolling Tahlequah. The family was excited about the news, but they were also concerned with Judy Mays's motives. When supper was prepared, George blessed the food, and they all ate with Allen, Daniel, and Peter talking about their pasts and their families. The time reminded Annabelle of the great times she'd had in the Keys' home, and Grace proudly showed off Gabriel entertaining the men.

As the family and friends continued to eat, Michael looked at David as he played with his food and remained uninterested in their guests' stories. "Speak your mind, David. You know better than to remain silent," Michael said in Cherokee.

"We should leave tomorrow and bring Joseph home," David said.

Everyone stopped talking and looked at David. "David, we don't have what we need to make the trip," George said. "Your father and the others have the carriage and the supplies that would be needed to make that journey. The White man's war also makes it worse. We'll have to wait for them to return so another trip can be made to bring Joseph home. They might even make it to that plantation and bring him home."

David then slammed his fist on the table. "I don't want to wait! It has been over a year!" David shouted.

"Calm yourself. Your anger won't bring him home," Michael said. "Be grateful our guests have brought us hope. Our family has experienced many bad things, but Jesus remains faithful to us."

"Why do we suffer like this? Has Jesus decided we suffer in blood?"

"We were never promised this world would be fair, David," Luke said. "Was it fair for Jesus to die for us when he did nothing wrong? It was a sacrifice no man could do. Listen to our words and be patient. Have faith or did you forget Elder Joyce's words? She prophesied Joseph would return home to us. This information brings us closer to that day."

David angrily replied, "I don't want to wait! Who knows what those White men are doing to him."

"Be aware of your words, David. They create fear," George said. He slightly nodded to signal David, causing him to look to his right and notice his sisters and Rosita were wide-eyed.

David looked down at his plate. "I'm sorry for my anger. Thank you for telling us about my brother."

"You're welcome, young man," Peter said. "You have a lot of wisdom in your family. I can see you're also growing in wisdom."

"Thank you, Pastor Avail."

"I believe Elder Joyce's words, but I also agree with David," Lizzie said. "As soon as John and the others return, another trip needs to be made quickly. Joseph has been there long enough."

"I agree," Grace said. The rest of the evening was spent with the family playing cards with their guests. Peter also showed them on the map exactly where Caledonia was and how far away it was from Columbus.

During the night, Allen, Daniel, and Peter slept on the floor of the family house in front of the fireplace. During this time, Annabelle had laid Jonathan in bed. She went into her living room and sat down in front of the fireplace in a rocking chair. She frowned and began to pray. The front door slowly opened, and Annabelle quickly turned around in the chair. She looked at the door. "Gra—Lizzie," Annabelle said, her eyes widening a little. "Where are the girls?"

Lizzie stepped into the candlelit home. "In my room, snoring and drooling," she said. "I'm tired…Jonathan is sleep?"

"Yeah, he's sleeping quietly."

Lizzie approached Annabelle and started to unbraid her wavy hair. "How are you? Ever since they told us about Joseph, you've been unfocused. You were losing count of things when we cooked, you stopped talking when he wasn't our focus. I know when you're forcing yourself to smile."

Annabelle sat back in her chair. "I hate waiting. I hate being here because I know I can't go to the South." She breathed. "I feel powerless. I'm his mother and I can't go after him. It makes me feel sick."

Lizzie sat down in the other rocking chair. "We have to hope."

"What if she tells everyone who Joseph is?"

"If she tells to keep Joseph enslaved, she's not the woman you knew anymore."

Annabelle shook her head. "It's my fault. I should've left her a note or something. She must be so angry at me."

"I believe you did hurt her feelings when you ran away. Any good friend would've been hurt, but if she still loves you. I believe she'll try to help Joseph."

"What can she do? He's not under her rule."

"Maybe give us the time we need."

Annabelle's eyes lowered, and her brows furrowed. "I've already lost two children. I don't have the strength to lose my baby boy."

"You know I want to leave today, but the Father knows why we can't leave now." Lizzie's eyes shifted off Annabelle to the fire. "I'm not sleeping well. I can still hear his scream." Her eyes locked back onto Annabelle. "We won't lose anyone else in our family."

Annabelle's lips quivered a little. "I hope you're right. The only reason I won't leave for him is because of David, the girls, and Jonathan."

"I'll bring back their heads if you want me to."

Annabelle grinned as she lightly chuckled, but her grin dropped due to Lizzie's blank expression. "Lizzie, no."

Abruptly Lizzie quietly cackled. "I'm joking." She shrugged. "Sort of...but I promise we're bringing him home before the next winter."

Annabelle folded her hands. "I never started to understand how my momma was so quick to let me go until I got pregnant the first time. But when I held Joseph for the first time, I fully understood. As a mother, you're willing to even sacrifice your own happiness for your children."

Lizzie leaned forward, and the corner of her mouth arched into a half-smile. "I hope I can understand what you feel someday."

Annabelle smiled. "I think you will. And I think you'll be great."

"Can I pray for you?"

Annabelle put her hand on her chest. "Did Lizzie Lightning just ask that question?"

Lizzie smacked her lips. "Forget it."

"Oh, don't be like that now. I'll take all the prayer I can get." Lizzie scooted the rocking chair closer to Annabelle and placed her hand on her shoulder. The two women prayed for each other and then went to bed. In the morning, the men left, with Annabelle and the others giving their thanks and praying over them for a safe journey.

As days passed, tyranny reigned in Caledonia. The long hours, demeaning insults, and brutal ways of the Plecker plantation kept the slaves under control. On September 1, 1861, the Plecker family returned to the mansion after church. The slaves were forced to sit in the front of all the slave houses to listen to Master Plecker read scriptures to them. Master Plecker spent the majority of the time making up scriptures while he read and agitating Joseph and the other Indian children who could read.

"And the good Lord said thou shall work the fields and tame every beast," Master Plecker said. "Ye shall work as thee White master commands and give praise to ye master for the food that's giveth. Servitude is the role of all persons not of pure White blood, and thee are to rejoice in serving thy higher race. For only angels, the Holy Ghost, our Lord and Savior Jesus, and our Father God in Heaven are of a higher rank than the White man." As Master Plecker continued to read, Joseph slightly scoffed as he waited for him to finish. Master Plecker observed his attitude while Wade and Kit stood at attention behind him. "Little Joseph, do we have a problem here?" Master Plecker asked.

He gulped as he sat up and said, "No, Master Plecker, there's nothing wrong here."

"You don't seem to be listening to the good Lord's word here. Do you have a problem with me talking?"

He anxiously replied, "No, Master, I don't have a problem with listening to you. I was a little tired."

"Tired? So you're trying to tell me you're too tired to listen to the good Lord's word? Boy stand up." He looked at Master

Plecker, and slowly began to stand. Master Plecker raised his voice, "I said get up!" He quickly stood up while the other slaves watched. "Come here, boy. I know you're tired so let's make this quick."

He slowly stepped forward and stood before Master Plecker as his heart began to pump faster. "Master Plecker, I'm sorry. I learned my lesson."

Master Plecker s rubbed his blond hair as stood before Joseph. "What lesson would that be boy?"

"I learned to always listen to the good book when you read it. I promise I'll always listen."

Master Plecker ran his hand across his blond beard. "You think I'm like these niggers sitting here, boy? I see your disbelief, and it is disturbing. It's not the first time either, and I'm tired of it." He walked up to Wade and gave him the Bible he was holding. He picked up his black cane and approached Joseph. "Joseph, your learning lessons are only beginning. As the good book says, ye are to respect the master the good Lord has giveth you." Master Plecker placed the black cane on Joseph's chest and began to walk slowly in a circle as he rubbed his blond beard. "So much time wasted on this foolishness, don't you agree, Mr. Wade?"

Wade replied, "Yes, I do, Mr. Plecker."

"Well, I guess a lesson will be learned today." Master Plecker went up to the other slaves and pointed his cane at them. "Joseph, which one of these do you care about the most?" He turned around and Riza slightly shook her head no. He began to rub his fingers together in his right hand. "Who did you look at boy?"

He replied, "No one, Master Plecker. I don't care about any of them."

Master Plecker laughed as he walked up to him. "These half-breed redskins give me a show. That almost sounded as smart as something Riza would say. Is that who you care about the most here? Riza Plecker...the redskin...the homewrecker? Well I think it's a good thing I pay attention to you boy. Otherwise she might be my person of interest but I know better." Master

Plecker returned to the group of slaves. "I'm always watching you boy. I know how to get what I want, and you gone learn not to disrespect me again."

Abruptly, Master Plecker struck Susie in the back with the black cane. Susie screamed in pain, and he struck her again. "Please, Master Plecker, stop! I swear I won't do it again," Joseph begged.

Master Plecker tone dripped with sarcasm, "You swear? What good is that if it's a lie?" He grabbed Susie by her hair, and dragged her to Joseph as she screamed. He let go of Susie's hair once she was a few feet away from Joseph, and began to give her several more strikes. She tried her hardest not to scream, and took the beating silently as Master Plecker grunted. He trembled while Master Plecker took pleasure with every swing. "So you want to be a strong Little Susie? I know this hurts sweetie, but he will only learn if you get the punishment. How about we give that pretty face a scar or two so when he looks at you he remembers it was his doing?"

Master Plecker raised the black cane to hit Susie in the face when Joseph screamed and charged him. He attempted to tackle him, but Wade tackled him to the ground with Kit standing right behind him. "I got him," Wade said. "Oh, he's gotten stronger. I'll go take him to the old stump right now."

Master Plecker slowly approached him with confidence lightly patting his black cane on the palm of his hand. "No, that's quite all right," he calmly said. "I already know how to fix this boy." He looked over to Riza and saw her staring with a slight pout. "Isn't that right, Riza? Kit, please bring me the hot stick so we can conclude this."

"Yes, Mr. Plecker," Kit said. He quickly went over to the blacksmith shed, got the hot stick, and heated it. He returned to the others with the hot stick glowing hot orange. "See now, it's nice and ready as you want it, Mr. Plecker."

"Nicely done," Master Plecker said. He strutted up to Joseph as Wade held him. "The next time you're going to enjoy when I preach, boy. Like the rest of those niggers over there." Master Plecker stuck out his hand, and Kit handed the hot stick to him. He looked at Master Plecker with blazing eyes while Master Plecker raised the hot stick to his face. "You still don't get it. I said you gone learn to always respect me."

Master Plecker quickly marched over to Susie, and grabbed her by her hair. "Joseph, this isn't your fault," she said in Cherokee. A tear went down her face as Master Plecker pulled her, and she stumbled. "We're still friends no matter what they do to us."

"Look at that! You even have Little Susie breaking one of my major rules of no Indian gibberish on this plantation," Master Plecker complained. "On your knees!" She got on her knees and Master Plecker forced her head onto the ground. He pressed the hot stick on her lower neck. She screamed and a leer slowly etched across Master Plecker's face as he glared at Joseph. He took the hot stick off, and she groaned in pain as his hand pressed on the back of her head. "Come here, Kit, and pull back her collar," he commanded.

"No!" Susie screamed.

"Did you just tell me no?" Master Plecker yelled. Kit pulled her dress collar back, and Master Plecker slid the hot stick across the base of her neck and scorched her upper back. Her head pushed back against Master Plecker's hand. "Woo-wee, talk about getting stronger. She's trying to fight me." He pulled the stick out of her dress as she breathed heavily with sweat going down her forehead.

"See now, what you want us to do with him," Kit asked.

Master Plecker chuckled as he walked over her body whose fingers had dug into the dirt. "Nothing. Do nothing to the boy," he said. "However, since I spared this little prairie nigger's face, cut her hair like we did Riza's. Make sure she gets back to the mansion in one piece. The new in-laws are coming for a visit, and I want all my house slaves functional."

Wade released Joseph. He tried to go over to Susie but Master Plecker raised his black cane to stop him. Kit grabbed Susie's arm and forced her to stand while she moaned in pain. "Please, Master Plecker," Joseph begged.

Master Plecker replied, "Please what, boy? Let me guess you want to say you sorry?"

Joseph replied, "Yes, sir."

"Well, that's too bad. You don't have my permission to do so." Joseph felt his chest tighten as he looked Susie who was shaking uncontrollably. "What lesson did you learn today boy?" Joseph eye's remained wide as he looked at Master Plecker. "Hmph, I'll let you think about that. So your nigger mind can catch up with that rebellious redskin side. And next time, it will be Riza." Master Plecker moved toward the other slaves with a leer. "Well, that concludes church today, and I hope all of you have learned as Joseph has today. Take Susie away."

Mr. Kit aggressively tugged her arm, and she groaned in pain. Her face scrunched to fight back tears as she was led away to have her hair cut. The slaves dispersed and went about their business discouraged. However, Riza quickly went up to Joseph while Dorothy and Tom followed her. Sobs abruptly escaped his mouth. Riza embraced him as he cried and said, "Be strong, Joseph."

"Riza!" Master Plecker barked. "Enough of that or do I need to make another example?" Riza released him and backed away from him. Dorothy placed her hand on Riza's shoulder calmly persuading Riza to follow her to the mansion. Dorothy went away holding Riza's hand. Tom walked up to up Joseph, and the two boys quickly left.

Later in the day Susie was forced to help the other house slaves prepare supper. Reece, with her twin hair bun style, mocked Susie's short haircut throughout the day. Once her parents arrived at the mansion, she made Susie embarrassingly present herself. Dorothy, Emma, and Riza could tell bending over caused Susie a great amount of pain, and she felt ashamed to have so little hair. "I must say this is entertaining seeing an Indian with hair like a nigger. Her hair is barely at the base of her neck," Reece said. Her parents chuckled as Susie placed fresh tea on the table and struggled to not cry.

"She does look more like a Negro now than what Riza did," Sydney said. "What an interesting thing. Susie, do you have Negro blood at all?"

She replied with a saddened tone, "No, ma'am."

"Well, she does look better than any other Negro on this plantation, even with her hair cut," Reece blurted. Everyone at the table laughed at the comment except Kenneth and Wilma. "As if that's hard to do." Reece, her parents, and Sydney's husband laughed as the onslaught on Susie continued.

"I must admit. I'm not pleased with this altercation," Wilma said. "I don't like how your father corrected Joseph's disrespectful attitude."

"Momma, Susie is all right. You know these Indian girls can take more damage than us White women," Sydney said. "Look at her moving around like Papa did nothing to her."

Wilma scowled when she looked at Mr. Plecker. "All I have to say is the next time Joseph should be the one to be disciplined if he makes another mistake." Mr. Plecker passively enjoyed his wine while Wilma continued to look at him.

As conversations continued Reece gave Dorothy another instigative leer as she chewed her chicken. Dorothy noticed and took a deep breath. "Susie, more mashed potatoes," she said. Susie walked over and began to put more mashed potatoes on her plate when pieces of her cut hair fell onto Reece's plate. "What is this?" Reece screeched.

"What's wrong?" Kenneth asked.

Reece angrily replied, "Her nasty hair fell onto my plate! Disgusting!"

Kenneth huffed. "Calm down. It's not like she was given time to make sure all of her loose hair was brushed out. Susie, go brush out the rest of your loose hair."

Susie quickly exited the dining as Reece angrily watched. "Stupid grass nigger ruined my food. Can you believe this? Dorothy, get over here and bring me a clean plate!" Dorothy came over and picked up Reece's plate, and went to the kitchen. Dorothy brought back the plate and placed it down in front of Reece. "Now give me my mashed potatoes." As the others at the table talked, Dorothy gave Reece her mashed potatoes. The tension between the two women grew as Reece stared at her with her vindictive blue eyes, and tapped her fingernail on the table. "Now give me some chicken wings and corn." She placed the items on Reece's plate. When she was about to leave, she rubbed against Kenneth's shoulder causing him to spill his wine on his vest.

"Ah great," Kenneth snarled. He took a napkin and tried to rub out the wine, but it didn't work. "I'm sorry I need to change this."

"What's going on? First, that savage's dirty hair gets into my food, and now you spill wine on yourself! This supper is a disaster."

"Don't overreact, Reece. Accidents happen," her mother said.

"Dorothy, go help Kenneth clean himself up. I don't want him taking all day," Reece commanded.

"I can handle this on my own dear," Kenneth said. He quickly left as Dorothy watched.

Reece growled, "Dorothy, did I stutter? Go after him and don't take no for an answer." Dorothy exhaled while she walked away from the supper table and followed Kenneth upstairs. "I swear she likes to test my patience, Momma Wilma."

"Well, I keep telling you to be patient with her. Dorothy has been our most efficient slave," Wilma said. "She is a treasure." Reece jealously remained silent and snobbishly listened to the conversations.

As Kenneth took off his vest and high-collared shirt, Dorothy entered the bedroom and closed the door. "Get out, Dorothy," he commanded.

She calmly replied, "Reece commanded me to make sure you come back looking representable, Master Kenneth."

He turned around and put on a white high-collared shirt as he looked in the mirror. She calmly walked up behind him and ran her hands down his arms. "The shirt looks good on you. Let me button it for you."

He agitatedly turned around. She began to button his shirt while she gazed into his eyes and gave him a seductive smile. He pushed her hands away. "No, stop it…stop looking at me like that. Don't anger me, woman!"

She smiled and placed her hand on his left cheek, but he pushed her hand away. "Are you really mad at me? The wine really was an accident. Is that why you're mad at me, or is it because you miss how I feel?"

"Don't ever accuse me of such a thing! I should have you tied to that old tree stump and beaten for saying such a thing."

She calmly stepped up to him and softly kissed him. "I miss you too. Every morning and every night, I miss you. I miss looking into your eyes. I miss hearing your strong voice tell me your ideas. I miss how you would hold me and the excitement you gave me."

"Dorothy, get out of my room. I won't break my covenant, not for you or any other woman."

"You made a covenant with me first!" She gave him another soft kiss causing him to start to back up. "I'm a proud Christian woman, and in my heart, I have the man that's meant for me." She kissed him again as he kept stepping back from her. "She'll never have you like I do. I've given you two beautiful girls, and what has she given you…nothing but headaches. You know I love you, Kenneth Plecker." She stared into his eyes with her hazel eyes begging for his acknowledgment.

She exhaled and turned around to leave, but he grabbed her arm. "I remember a young girl that brought me soup when I was sick when my momma didn't even ask for it. I remember the young girl who watched me play the piano. I also remember listening to the smart young woman who would sit outside and watch the moon with me." A tear suddenly went down his face. "Most importantly I remember my friend I grew feelings for when I wasn't supposed to."

She turned around. "I forgive you, but I also need you. I know you feel the same way. Please stop pushing me away."

"I need you to stop. Please stop. The way you look at me every time it pulls me in closer to you. I love Reece and I'm protecting our girls. I'm doing what's best, and I need you to stop pulling me back."

She frowned. "But I miss you. I miss our real conversations. I miss all of it. I don't care if we have to continue to keep it a secret." She stepped up to him and calmly placed her hand on his cheek. "Look at me and say you don't love me."

He placed his hand on top of hers while he looked into her eyes as she smiled at him. He leaned in and kissed her. "I miss you too." Kenneth walked around Dorothy, grabbed his black vest, and left the bedroom. She sat down on the bed and took a few breaths before she exited the bedroom.

When Kenneth arrived back into the dining hall, he sat down next to Reece while the others laughed and continued to talk. "What has been taking you so long?" She quietly asked.

Kenneth murmured, "I was not gone for that long. Why are you so concerned?"

She snobbishly replied, "I'm not concerned. I didn't want you to miss all of our conversations. Hmph, Dorothy did a terrible job of telling you I wanted you back quickly."

He looked away from Reece, and saw Dorothy standing in the dining room doorway. "I told her I would come down when I was ready. She did what she was supposed to do."

Reece leered as she watched Dorothy walk over to Riza and stand at attention. "Why do you always defend that mulatto?"

He scoffed. "I'm not defending her. I'm telling you what I told her to do, and she obeyed. Don't try to give her grief for obeying me."

Reece looked back at Dorothy, and she looked back at her. Her confident gaze caused Reece's grip on her fork to tighten and her face to scrunch slightly. "I've never encountered a slave willing to show their dislike of me," she mumbled. She leered. "I'll be glad to break Riza's and Dorothy's spirits even more."

A few nights later, when Kenneth and Reece were about to sleep, she leaned over on his shoulder. "Kenneth, we need to talk," she said.

He sat up and saw her slightly frowning. "What is it?"

She calmly replied, "I've been thinking about this for some time and thinking of ways to improve things before we get our own home. I don't want Dorothy talking to you at all. Anything you need, Riza or the others can do it."

He angrily replied, "What kind of suggestion is that? What difference does it make that I talk to Dorothy?"

Her eyes' widened. "What difference would it make if you didn't talk to her? She's a slave. She's nothing."

"Dorothy doesn't deserve to be treated in that way. She's been loyal to my family for her entire life. I believe a loyal slave deserves some form of favor."

She pounded her hand on her chest. "She doesn't respect me! You should see the looks she gives me, her and Riza. I can take it from Riza because I'll break that little girl, but with Dorothy… there is something there. She welcomes it."

His brows drew together while he shook his head. "Welcomes what?"

"I don't know how to describe it." Her voice became deeper with each word, "She doesn't fear me, she doesn't respect me, and she should be wiping my shoes every time I step inside this mansion! She looks at me as if I'm in her home…like this is all hers."

"She needs time to trust you more, and you being unnecessarily cruel to her won't help that."

She crinkled her nose. "Time? Me give time to some mulatto woman because she's served you well? What will I look like when I invite my friends over, and she gives me one of her looks? You have let her kindness blind you."

Kenneth raised his voice, "I've done no such thing! Now you're going to treat Dorothy kindly and even Riza. They will do as they're told."

"Be nice to a slave? How could you ask that of me? I would rather watch Wade crack a whip on both of their backs." She could see his brows furrowing deeper, and realized she wasn't going to get her way. "How about we just go out to the patio, and look at the moon? You used to do that, didn't you?"

"I'm in no mood to do that. I haven't done that in a long time."

"Why not? Let's go to bed a little later."

He sighed. "No, I really want to be rested for tomorrow."

Reece started to squeeze the bedsheets. "Is it because you used to do that with Dorothy? Are you saying that I can't go out there because you used be out there with that mulatto?"

"It has nothing to do with Dorothy, and if you must know, I would make her come out there with me. You need to check your imagination. I always made Dorothy do things with me."

"Why didn't you tell your parents?"

"I was young, and I would've been scolded. She would've been beaten. Why get a good slave beaten for my mistake? That's heartless to me."

She smiled at him while she rubbed his arm. "Wow, that's noble of you. I swear you always manage to find a way to remind me why I fell in love with you. Your kindness and your wisdom amaze me. I guess I did make a crazy assumption. I apologize."

Kenneth raised an eyebrow. "What assumption would that be?"

"Oh no, I'm too embarrassed to say. It would only anger you and I'm tired of fighting." Reece laid her head on his chest. "How about we talk about other things like what color our home should be." Throughout the rest of night, they talked and laughed about various things. He lowered his guard and she gave him fake smiles. Reece thought, *I hate that he's so defensive of her. I can feel it. She has feelings for him, but I'll give him something that frizzy-haired slave can't.* She continued to entertain him leading to them making love.

On September 11, 1861, while the slaves worked the fields, Master Rice's brutality toward them grew. He had no tolerance for any cotton that was missed and refused to allow the slaves to have a break. Joseph believed his increased brutality was the result of a runaway slave named Ronald. He had no family on the plantation and always remained somewhat unattached to the other slaves. The moment it was discovered he had run away, Rice rushed to the dogs' house, and let them out to chase after Ronald. Wade later decided to hunt Ronald down and pass out fliers around the town.

Joseph and Tom were loading up the cotton baskets as quickly as they could when Rice lost his temper. He saw a slave named Bishop had missed a few of the cotton plants and began to beat him. Kit came over to calm Rice down, and commanded Bishop to finish picking. Joseph watched attentively because he had never seen an overseer stop another one from beating a slave. "See now, what's going with you?" Kit asked. "You still mad about Ronald? See, it's been three days. I'm sure if Wade don't catch that nigger, someone will."

Rice angrily replied, "I can't believe that nigger got away when I decided to give them an award for picking good. Honestly, I'm thinking about joining one of the regiments, and fighting to protect our rights. No Negro, no Indian should have the right to tell me what they will and won't do."

"See now, you not still sore over what Kenneth told you?"

Rice scoffed. "What would that be?"

"See, don't play dumb with me. You know he said to back off of Riza. Is that it? See, you been looking at her since last year."

"It's not like that. I can't stand that redskin. She ain't sorry for what she did, but there she is in that house when she should be out here."

"See now, I agree. Riza should've gotten some more beatings, but I know you also need a woman. Sherry was wrong for leaving you, but I know you can get another one. Good-looking White man. See, we can go out to the tavern after we get done with these niggers, and I introduce you to some nice young things. See, don't lower the standards, going after some prairie nigger. You already know, you go after Riza she's gone leave her mark on you."

"Maybe I want a mark or two. I know you've had yourself Indian girls, so don't act like your hands ain't dirty."

Master Kit adjusted his brown trousers. "See now, I took what I could before I met Theresa." Kit placed his hand on Rice's shoulder. "You'll be good too once we find you a new one, someone you want to marry."

A horse could be heard coming to the plantation with the dogs barking. Joseph looked over and saw it was Wade. He had captured Ronald. Ronald had his foot and leg roped and wasn't moving. Rice and Kit quickly got on their horses and rode toward Wade. Joseph frowned as he watched the men got closer to Wade. "Do you think he's alive?" Tom asked.

"I can't tell. He wasn't moving when Master Wade stopped," Joseph said. "Are they going to take him to the old tree stump?"

Tom replied, "I don't—"

"What you boys doing? We got to get more baskets," Louis snarled.

Joseph angrily replied, "Master Wade brought Ronald back, and we're trying to see if he's okay."

"I don't care. The nigger is getting beat. He not gone be running nowhere any time soon. He a dummy for running from Master Plecker."

"You talk a lot for a coward," Joseph bickered.

"I do what I supposed to do. You don't see me out on the stump."

Joseph and Tom got into the wagon, and he tightened his grip on the wagon. "You don't have any family, do you?"

"I don't have any, don't want none."

"I'm sure they wouldn't want you either." Tom began to chuckle as Louis looked back at the boys. "Drive, or you might get the old tree stump." Louis clinched his rotten teeth and drove the wagon.

As Louis drove the boys through the plantation to collect cotton baskets, they arrived at the cotton gin barn where Bo was fixing a wagon. The boys exhaustedly unloaded the cotton baskets. Mary began to take the cotton out of the baskets when Stella came to the barn. "Bo, they found Ronald," she worrisomely said.

"Stella, what you doing here? Go back to the field," Bo yelled.

She frantically replied, "Master Rice said for all of us to go by the old elm tree right now. I was told to tell you."

Bo put down his hammer and looked at Joseph and Tom. "We best go now." The boys, Mary, and Stella followed Bo while Louis slowly followed them. Bo frowned as he patted dirt off his brown cotton shirt. "Bo, what's so bad about the old elm tree?" Joseph asked.

Bo avoided eye contact with Joseph while he walked. "Y'all gone see, but I don't know what Master Rice gone do," he said. "But we see when we get there. Don't talk so they ain't got nothing to say to you." His words caused Joseph to feel his throat tighten. When they arrived at the old elm tree, all of the slaves were there except Doris and Daisy.

Joseph gasped when he saw Ronald tied to the old elm tree and the overseers standing by him. Two of the large branches were missing pieces of bark rubbed off. Joseph looked at the other slaves with a skewed frown. Ronald looked exhausted, with bruises on his face and an open wound on his arm. Master Plecker exited the white mansion smoking a cigar when a strong summer wind blew in the direction of the elm tree intensifying his tyrannical nature. He pulled his gold watch out of his vest to look at the time. He leered as he stood before the slaves with the gold watch shining in his hand.

"Well, I'm so pleased that all of you are here as commanded," Master Plecker said. "I didn't think I would have to give this type of punishment anymore, but my watch tells me that Ronald here has been gone for three days. Three full days. How unfortunate. You got anything to say, boy?"

Ronald lifted his head and breathed heavily. "I sorry, Master Plecker, I sorry. Please forgive me," he begged. "I won't do it again."

Master Plecker walked closer to Ronald. "I see you tried to fight off Master Wade there. He didn't have a bruise on his face when he left this plantation." Ronald began to tremble as Master Plecker stared him down. "I see we have a different problem with this one. What kind of Christian man lies to his master and, even worse, runs away from doing what he was put on the Earth to do? Mr. Wade, I imagine he tried to give you a good fight."

"He did," Wade said.

Master Plecker tilted his head. "Sad, very sad. Didn't I tell y'all one of the commandments is for y'all not to ever strike a White man? Mr. Kit, please give me the breaker."

"Yes, sir," Kit said.

Kit gave Master Plecker a medium-sized sledgehammer. "Now y'all better remember this day," Master Plecker boldly said. "Nobody enjoys this, but I won't tolerate any disrespect. Don't make me feel like you need to be reminded who the master is and who the slaves are!" Master Plecker quickly swung the sledgehammer, and it hit Ronald's ankle. He screamed in pain while the other slaves watched in horror.

Master Plecker took another swing causing Ronald's ankle to crack. "Please stop, Master Plecker. I won't do it again," Ronald cried.

"Did you tell me to stop?" Master Plecker looked at the other overseers as Ronald moaned in pain. "Well, that must take a lot of courage telling me to stop, but boy… you expendable." Master Plecker punched Ronald. "I can get another one of you. Gentlemen, take him off the tree." The men loosed the ropes on Ronald leaving his hands bound in front of him. Ronald stood on one foot, avoiding his broken ankle.

Only a noose around his neck remained while Ronald struggled to balance himself. Master Plecker abruptly hit him in his stomach, causing him to kneel on the ground as the pain coursed through his body. "What's wrong? Come on, boy? Stand up, you thought was a man, didn't you?" He hit him in his back with the sledgehammer, causing him to fall to the ground. Ronald screamed in pain while Master Plecker laughed. He hit him in the back two more times with the sledgehammer as Joseph and the others watched. Joseph avoided eye contact with Master Plecker, terrified to be made an example.

"Rice, did you bring those grease sticks?" Master Plecker asked.

Rice replied, "Yes, I did. He's greased up on his lower legs."

Master Plecker leered. "All right, let's get this done and over with I want to finish my lunch."

"Yes, sir." Rice picked up small twigs six inches long and

started to place them in Ronald's shoes. When Rice finished putting the sticks in his shoes, Wade walked over and helped Rice force Ronald to stand up on one foot.

"Mr. Plecker, we ready," Wade said.

Master Plecker stopped smoking his cigar and casually looked at Ronald. "String him up," he said.

"Yes, sir." Rice, Kit, and Wade pulled on a rope, and it strung him up into the tree. Wade tied the rope around the tree, and the noose partially strangled him. The other slaves watched with widened eyes.

"Well, now look at that. You can still breathe, can't you, boy?" He continued to struggle for a breath as he desperately tried to break the rope binding his hands. Master Plecker slapped his broken ankle. "I said you can breathe, can't you, boy?"

"Yes, Master Plecker," he said with a garbled tone.

Master Plecker subtly replied, "Well, good boy. You see, I never wanted to lynch you. No, that's the easy way out." He looked at the horrified slaves with a smirk. "I expect none of you to follow this nigger's disrespectful ways. Look at him…weak, cowardly. Now, are those tears, Ronald?" The overseers cackled while Master Plecker continued to circle Ronald. "Well, let's give you a real reason to have tears." Master Plecker placed his cigar on one of the greasy sticks, and it caught fire. He screamed in pain as he shook around. Master Plecker then lit another stick by his broken ankle, and he shrieked in pain. The other slaves watched in horror while Stella covered Mary's eyes.

The fire grew intensely as it scorched his body. "Woo! See now, look at that. I didn't think the fire would catch quickly," Master Kit said.

"I made sure they were nice and greasy with Riza's help over there," Rice arrogantly said. He looked over at Riza and smiled seeing her tighten her lips. "Didn't have a clue what those sticks were for, did you?" He shouted over Ronald's screams. Riza's eyes remained forward.

The overseers continued to cackle as the fire crept up Ronald's body. "All right, that's enough. He's starting to fade out a bit," Master Plecker said. Wade took a big wooden bucket and splashed it on him. The smell of burnt flesh dominated the air. He barely remained conscious. The overseers lowered his badly burned body while Master Plecker mercilessly watched, "Well done, boys. Bo, I want you to have two strong men take this nigger here to one of the slave houses. Have one of the women tend to his wounds. If he survives, so be it."

"Yes, Master Plecker, we do it now," Bo said. Bo gathered two men to carry Ronald away as his body throbbed in pain. While the men carried him away, Joseph could see both of his legs were burned beyond recognition, and the fire had scorched his left abdomen. "Dorothy, come help his wounds."

Dorothy stood and began to follow Bo quickly. "No, not Dorothy, that nigger there doesn't deserve no help from our best caretaker. Dorothy, you sit down."

Dorothy sat immediately as Bo looked baffled. "May Katie help?"

Master Plecker rubbed his blond beard as he looked at Bo. "Yes, she may; I guess it's fitting since she is named after my Katie. Go on now, Katie." She immediately stood up and rushed to follow the two men while they continued to carry Ronald to one of the slave houses. "My daughter has interests in the medical arts. How fitting it would be if she does a good job, don't you think, Dorothy?"

"Yes, it would, Master Plecker," Dorothy said.

"I want to see top production…good slaves get the Lord's blessing, and the rest will be given damnation in whatever form I choose. Well, that'll be all. Now get back to work." Joseph quickly stood up while he tried to shake off the fear and saw that Tom was in shock like him. The boys began to walk back with the other slaves, speechless. As the boys strolled, Joseph saw Mary clinging to Stella with tears covering her face. The talk of escaping the plantation now seemed taboo to him. He felt the overseers were keeping a stronger watch on the slaves.

Days passed while he struggled to rise against the feelings of depression and fear. Ronald could be heard moaning when he went past the slave house housing him. The slaves bonded through song and prayer. It was the only time he felt any form of peace. Susie managed to sneak away from the Plecker mansion after their supper and would often pray with Joseph and the other slaves. Bo led the prayers, and each person prayed about something different. When Susie arrived, it gave them time to speak their native tongue, but Joseph remained haunted by his guilt. Susie's short hair was a painful reminder that his actions could affect the people he now cared about. The scars on her neck were also visible making him believe his foolishness brought more problems. Through the pain, he refused to give up on trusting God and greatly believed they would find a way to escape or be saved. He knew his faith was the one thing Master Plecker couldn't take away. The extreme drama had run through his mind so much that he had only recently noticed Judy Mays and Daphne hadn't visited recently. It made him wonder if Reece's conceited attitude was even unbearable for them.

On October 4, 1861, Joseph was tasked with feeding the cattle and bringing over freshly butchered beef to the mansion. As he was giving the meat to Riza, Reece entered the cookhouse in her pink Victorian dress. "There you are Riza... Joseph," she said. She began to sniff the air as she walked closer to them. "I can tell you've been working with the animals. You smell like them or is that those field slaves?" He remained silent while he slightly gulped. "I did want an answer."

"I believe it's the animals, Mrs. Reece," he said.

"How cute...defending those nappy-headed cotton pickers. I can see why Judy Mays shows interest in you. You're an entertaining half-breed. Riza, after you finish here, immediately come upstairs. I feel like taking an afternoon bath."

"Yes, ma'am," Riza said. Reece left the kitchen, and Joseph began to hand her the rest of the meat. "I can't stand her. I'd rather listen to Mrs. Wilma talk."

"I think she's crazy."

"She is, but don't spread that to the others. She purposely makes Dorothy do things two or three times and always threatens to have my hair cut. Mrs. Reece makes Susie uncomfortable, always talking about her hair. She is the complete opposite of Master Kenneth."

After he finished giving her the meat, she quickly went upstairs to Kenneth's bedroom. Riza opened the door and Reece was sitting on her bed. She pointed to the tub. Riza forcefully smiled. She rigorously prepared the bath water. When it was done, Reece got into the tub. She laid in the tub relaxing as songbirds could be heard out on the balcony. She looked over at Riza, leering. "I can tell that you care about Joseph. Even though he's a half-breed," Reece casually said. "I guess you have no choice especially after that nigger tried to rape you. I imagine you have a strong disgust for him…Clint is his name, right?"

"Yes, ma'am, and to answer your question, I've forgiven him," she softly said. "It wasn't fully his fault." Reece began to lightly chuckled and glanced at her. "Clint was tricked by Pearl."

"You should've ended that nigger when you had the chance. It would've sent a stronger message to the rest of them." Reece noticed Riza's nose slightly crinkled. "You don't think so? Well I'll tell you something…when you get old enough and those half-breed boys get old enough." Reece turned back around. "One of them will be paired with you. Consider it a merciful gift from Momma Wilma. Even though I don't believe you deserve such mercy considering your rebellion."

Riza's eyebrows shot up. "What?"

Reece's eyebrow raised and she dismissively scoffed. "Riza, do you really want that arrangement to be changed?" She looked over at her with a smirk. "I know why Judy Mays likes you." Reece's smirk went away while she analyzed her. "You have a hard time hiding what's really in your mind. I don't like it, so I suggest you work harder to hide it, or I'll have the rest of your finger removed. I could barely tell that you disliked what I said. Keep it that way."

"Yes, ma'am."

"Move here and scrub my back." She stepped up to the tub as she picked up a scrub brush and began to scrub Reece's back. "You know your people should thank us for what we've done for them. We civilized them in this wild land, taught them proper trade, and brought your people true religion, not that superstitious spirit worshipping." She tightened her grip the wooden handle of the brush hard enough to make a minor tightening sound. Reece slightly turned around and flicked her blonde hair while she stared at her. "Did I say something you didn't like?" She remained speechless as Reece stared at her. "I'll admit. You're the only slave to bring out my curiosity. Only this once will I allow you to say what's on your mind, but be careful with your words, Riza Plecker."

She slightly hesitated while she looked at Reece. "My people weren't uncivilized, and we've always prayed to the Creator," She calmly said. "My years of being around White people has taught me that only some actually practice Christian values. When your ancestors first came here they picked and chose what they wanted to follow."

Reece slightly lifted her eyebrows. "In what way did we pick and choose? We've always followed our Christian morals while your people practiced savagery."

"I know in the Bible it says to love everyone not just the people that look like you. No tribe is greater than the other. That's what my family taught me."

"The fact you're not hanging from a poplar tree is proof mercy is being given to you. Mercy is a form of love and you must be loved, or did you forget about what you did?"

"Your people brought us more hate and sickness. Even when your people spoke truth about Jesus, their hate made it hard for my people to hear it."

Reece sneered. "Your people needed to learn their place and they will continue to learn their place or hear the sound of guns."

Riza's eyes dilated while her nose flared and her brow furrowed. "Your people are afraid of us! That's why y'all won't take a lot of Indian slaves. It would be like the old days when entire plantations would burn to the ground!"

Reece lunged halfway out of the tub and strongly grabbed her by the collar of her blue dress. Reece looked at her with her furious blue eyes. "Was that a threat?"

Gasping, her eyes widened. "No, ma'am."

"My great-grandfather survived one of those vicious attacks. I think we made a mistake focusing so much on these Negroes. Your people so easily forget you were slaves too. Not all slaves have chains on them." Reece let go of her and slid back into the tub. "I want you to tell me the truth about something. Does Dorothy have feelings for Master Kenneth?"

"No, ma'am, she cares for him. She may see him more as a friend than a master if that's what's bothering you."

"What makes you so sure?" Reece asked with knit eyebrows.

"I've never heard her speak of him in any romantic way. She's always quick to serve him like Mrs. Wilma or Master Plecker."

"Did she ever mention going out to the patio at night with him when they were just a bit older than you?"

Riza shrugged. "No, ma'am. This is the first time I've heard this."

"I want you to report to me if you ever see anything between them that looks like more than friendship. You tell me what I need to know, and I promise to make life a lot easier for you. Maybe even setting you free to New York to whatever is left of your family."

"My family?"

"Not to give you hope…from what I know your momma is nothing but ashes now. Do you have siblings?" Riza's mouth opened but she paused. "Whether you do or don't…it doesn't matter to me. If they survived, I'm sure they're running around in the streets. Now that we have understanding…what do you know?"

She shook her head. "I swear there isn't nothing between them."

"The fact you can even say there's a friendship between them is disturbing and beneath him. Befriending a slave is sickening in any way or form. If I could I would have that hazel-eyed snake sent away."

"She has always tried to serve you, Mrs. Reece."

Reece began to laugh hysterically the moment she sat up in the tub. "Get me my towel." She gave Reece her towel, and she began to dry herself off. "I'm no fool. A woman knows when she has stepped into the house of another. She has disliked me from the first day we met and I won't tolerate a slave unable to keep her eyes off my husband."

She began to help Reece dress. "I know it's considered wrong socially but isn't it good Dorothy cares about him."

"Considered wrong? Riza, you test me in ways that make me question my tolerance of you. It's wrong in every form, and you'll tell me anything I want to know. Is that clear?"

"Very clear, ma'am."

"Tell me. Do you have feelings for either of those two half-breeds?"

Riza gulped. "As friends I do."

Reece grinned. "My…so quick to answer me on that one."

"I would rather tell you the truth than to act like I don't care when you know I do. What's the purpose of a game when you've been watching me?"

"Don't play with me, Riza. Your father played and it cost him his life and gave you chains. I promise I will make you feel hell if you don't report things to me, and I'll enjoy it…like you should've enjoyed ripping the flesh off Pearl's back." Reece scoffed. "Hmph, tricking that dumb nigger into almost raping you and trying to justify it. You should've cut her tongue out." She helped her finish dressing, and Reece began to look at herself in a mirror. "Remember, God rewards good slaves, and good wives bear children like I'm going to. Hmm, you may get as tall as me." Reece picked at a small pimple on her chin. "You will be my eyes and ears. Is it understood?"

"Yes, ma'am."

"Good. Go make me a sandwich. I've grown hungry tolerating your answers."

She left the bedroom and made a silent scream. "I hope that woman never has a child." Her dominance was a cancer to Riza, and her accusations made her rethink everything she had seen between Dorothy and Kenneth, but she chose to remain silent. It was never a secret Dorothy didn't like Reece. Riza decided not to give in to Reece's demands. *She'll do whatever she can to break Dorothy. No matter what I tell her.*" she thought. Things remained unchanged in Caledonia, but in Tahlequah, the talk of war increased as division among the Cherokee and the other tribes increased.

———◆———

On October 9, 1861, Stella made acknowledging Joseph's birthday important. Susie was also able to sneak into her house to spend time with him. His birthday made him wonder even more about his family.

During this time in Tahlequah, David sat by the old redbud tree while he looked at a small bison herd passing by. As he stared at the herd, he heard someone approaching him. "You should come inside soon. We'll be starting supper soon," Lizzie said in Cherokee.

"Are you thinking about him, Auntie?" he asked in Cherokee.

"I am, but I'm hopeful more than I have been. This will be the last birthday your brother will miss. We know where he is and when your father returns, we'll bring him home."

He replied with a discouraged tone, "We should've left for him a long time ago. Those White men could be doing anything to him right now."

She placed her hand on his shoulder and looked at him. "Where would we get the supplies to make it that far?" He looked away from her. "You have the same problem that I have."

"What is that?"

"You don't have patience and you lack faith in the Father protecting him. When I was your age, I was much worse. I'd lose control when talking to people. Don't follow my path...be better, promise me."

"I promise," he murmured in Cherokee.

She punched him in the shoulder. "What did you say?"

"I said promise. I promise to be patient, Auntie."

He began to rub his shoulder while she rubbed his hair. "That's good to hear."

"Where are the other herds?"

She frowned. "I've heard many talks when I walk past the courthouse. What I know is the White men are killing them all."

"But how can they eat that much?" He asked with a skewed frown.

"The White men aren't eating them. They're killing them for fun and taking their hide." He looked at her, he jaw slightly dropped. "That's what I know. Come, we're having rabbit for supper to honor Joseph. Rain was proud to catch him."

David began to follow Lizzie. "Rain caught a rabbit?"

"Yes she did. Her and Jannie tried their best when they went with me this afternoon. Remember to congratulate your sister. She's always looking for your blessing."

He smiled. "I will."

"Also, enough growing! You're almost as tall as your father." He chuckled as they continued to go to the family house with her patting him on his back.

Throughout the day, the Lightning-Strongman family celebrated Joseph's birthday the best they could. George prayed over the food and prayed for his safety. Even though the family knew where he was, there was great discomfort in not knowing his well-being. For Annabelle, the fear of her children being threatened remained real. Even though she did her best to focus on Jonathan, she found herself waking up randomly at night to check on the twins and Jonathan. Annabelle remained hopeful for the day to arrive when she would not have to fear for her children.

As days passed on the Plecker plantation, Joseph realized he had become completely desensitized by the sound of men commanding the slaves, the sound of a whip cracking, and the long hours of labor. He was amazed to see Ronald had survived his injuries. However, he was now crippled and covered with burn scars on his legs, stomach, and lower arms. He was forced to cook alongside Alicia an older slave too fragile for the fields. It was the first time Joseph had ever seen a man with his spirit broken. He decided he would pray for him every night because his mother had taught him you're never powerless to help someone.

In mid-October 1861, Joseph noticed how much harder Bo was working. He was talented at fixing numerous things from animal pens, to wagons, to blacksmithing. Joseph viewed Bo as the peacekeeper. While Joseph and Tom were placing the cotton baskets in the barn for Mary, Joseph noticed him welding to fix another wagon.

"Why are you working so hard, Bo?" Joseph asked.

"I trying to make sure Master Wade is pleased when he see the wagon," he said. "I know he'll see my work and be pleased."

"Why do you care?"

"We do good and the Lord will bless us. I have to do what I can to keep Stella and my baby safe. One day when God give you children you understand."

"What?"

He chuckled. "Well…what I mean is if I keep doing good, I got more hope that Master Plecker won't sell them away. I got none of my family left. You know that. I keep Master Plecker and Master Wade happy. I got more hope I win."

"I understand you want to protect them. I hope they never get sold."

He sighed. "So do I, but that the life of a Negro. Now go on hurry back before old Louis start whining."

Joseph smiled at him and went to the wagon. "What was that about?" Tom asked.

He answered, "Wisdom from a working man." Tom looked at Bo who continued working on the wagon. "I'll tell you while we go to the fields."

"Y'all grass niggers move too slow," Louis snarled.

"Be careful Louis, or we tell Master Rice you be sleep while we carry the cotton baskets." Louis sneered at the boys and remained silent. The wagon rode back to the cotton fields while Joseph told Tom about the conversation he had with Bo. As the boys continued to talk, he came to a discouraging conclusion that he may eventually have a family of his own that are enslaved. The Plecker plantation was his dark reality though he refused to lose faith.

On October 24, 1861, Joseph and Tom were carrying sacks

of corn and grain to feed the horses and cattle when they saw Bo bringing out a large brown horse named Gallant. The horse reminded him of Big Boy. The horse was large and kind to him, which made Gallant one of Joseph's favorite horses on the Plecker plantation. "Why are you bringing out Gallant in the morning, Bo?" Tom asked.

"Master Kenneth told me to," he said. "He leaving for the war this afternoon."

Joseph replied, "I never thought he would leave."

He replied, "From what I know he say he leaving to protect his home. I never thought I see when White men tired of White men. Dorothy tell me even some of the Indians fighting it too."

"Which tribes are fighting?" Tom asked.

He answered, "I don't know. I know it bad. This President Lincoln, he tough one. Go on now, so Master Rice can't yell at y'all."

The boys quickly went to task to avoid Master Rice's wrath. "Tell us more later," Tom shouted. At this point, Joseph didn't only fear for his safety, he feared for the safety of those Master Plecker knew he cared about. Susie's beating still haunted him. As the boys were finishing caring for the animals, he carried out a sack and placed it on the ground by Gallant. He noticed Master Plecker watching them.

As the boys were about to go to the storage shed, Master Plecker called, "Joseph, come here boy." He nervously strolled over while he brushed hay off his brown trousers. "Go inside now and get Master Kenneth's sacks. He's saying his goodbyes before he goes and fights for us."

"Yes sir, Master Plecker," he said. He quickly went up to the white mansion, slowly opened the front door, and saw Reece pleading with Kenneth and Wilma frowning as she swayed. "I'm to get Master Kenneth's sacks, Mrs. Wilma," he said.

"They're right there by the stairs, Joseph," Kenneth said. "Take them out to Gallant and I'll be out there in a moment."

"Yes, sir," he said. He picked up the blue sacks and began to go toward the door. He noticed Reece was sniffing and wiping her face as her and Kenneth continued to talk. He was curious about their conversation, but refused to get into trouble so he stepped out to Gallant.

"Kenneth, I don't want you to go," Reece pleaded. "Let the other men finish the fighting for us. I know we're going to win against those Yankees, so please stay home with me."

He replied, "The war is getting worse each month. I feel like less of a man if I don't go out there and fight for what I believe. I don't plan on being out there long."

"But what if you don't come home? I'm terrified with the idea of you being out there fighting those backward thinking Yankees. Are the rumors true that those Indians, and free Negroes are fighting too?"

He exhaled and looked her. "I will return home. I need you to respect my decision on this and see that I'm doing this for you and the rest of the family. I don't do this with ease. Don't make this harder on me."

She looked at him with her reluctant blue eyes and hugged him. "You come back to me, Kenneth Plecker."

"I will and you better give me the same hug when I do."

"Kenneth," Wilma said with a saddened tone.

"Momma, I promise I'll come back," he said.

"I believe that, but you be careful fighting those Yankees. The good Lord will protect you. I know this."

He grunted. "I need to go upstairs. I forgot my Bible. I guess I'm a little nervous to forget my Bible." Kenneth quickly walked upstairs leaving Wilma and Reece. Kenneth entered his bedroom, and saw Dorothy sitting on the bed holding his Bible to her chest. "Dorothy."

She looked over at him and he could see her bloodshot eyes. "Kenneth, I wasn't sure if I was going to get a chance to say goodbye," she said with a weak tone. "Mrs. Reece told me to clean upstairs until you left. I respected her."

"I forgot my Bible," Kenneth calmly said.

Kenneth walked up to Dorothy and held out his hand.

"Please don't go. I'm scared this is going to be the last time I see you. Let them fight."

"I can't do that. I don't feel like a man standing here watching over slaves and being fed. I need to help fight for what I believe."

Dorothy stood up and embraced him while she held his Bible. He slowly wrapped his arms around her as she held him tight. "I know I can't stop you, but please return to me...return to our girls." She looked up at Kenneth and softly kissed him.

The two slowly let go of each other and as they did, she handed his Bible to him. The moment he was about to take the Bible, a tear fell on the book. "Dorothy, I...I need to leave now."

"I'm sorry. I don't mean to make this worse. Let me wipe that off."

Kenneth shook his head. "No, it will give me more reason to come home. I will think of you while I'm gone."

"And I will pray for you every day." He smiled at her and slowly walked away as she watched. "Lord Jesus, please protect him," she whispered. She exited the room and consoled herself.

He quickly moved downstairs as Reece and Wilma watched. The other house slaves had already been summoned to give him a fair well. "What took you so long?" Reece asked.

He anxiously replied, "I misplaced my Bible. Dorothy helped me find it."

Reece apathetically replied, "She did? How nice of her. I'll be sure to thank her later as she massages my feet."

"Don't start with me. I have to go now." Kenneth walked up to Wilma and gave her a hug and a kiss. "Love you, Momma."

"I love you too, my baby boy. Be careful and make us proud," Wilma said with a worried tone. "You and your brother stick together now."

He approached Reece, and she gave him a kiss. "You come back and tell me all your stories about teaching those Yankees a lesson. I love you."

"I love you too." He looked at the house slaves and gave them all a smile. "I look forward to telling all of you about my battles, especially you two, Doris and Daisy. Listen to your momma."

"We will, Master Kenneth," Doris said.

Kenneth stared at the girls and lovingly went up to them. "You want to give me a hug, don't you?" he asked. Daisy shyly shook her head yes, and he gave her a tight hug. He also gave Doris a tight hug. "You be good. Everyone take care of yourselves."

He began to go to the door, and as he did he saw Reece's eyes were wide. She followed him out of the mansion. "Why did you hug them?"

He stopped walking and replied, "They're little girls and wanted a hug, so I gave them that. I would expect you to know compassion."

"Well of course I do, but not to mulatto slaves," Reece bickered. "I understand it I...you're a complicated man, Kenneth Plecker. I do love you for that."

He smiled at her and marched to Gallant while Joseph made sure his sacks were secure on the horse. "Well done, Joseph. You keep this up and I'll have a talk with Master Plecker about giving you a position over the others like Bo."

"Thank you, Master Kenneth," he said.

"You worked with horses before, didn't you?"

"Yes sir, Master Kenneth. My Pa is good with them, and my cousin Lisa. We have four horses."

"That's not too bad for some Indians." Kenneth got onto Gallant and waved at Reece, Wilma, and the house slaves. "Behave yourself, Joseph. You'll go far here if you do."

Gallant slowly trotted away. As he watched him leave, he felt a slight sadness. He was the nicest White man on the plantation, and with him gone, Joseph and the others were at the mercy of the other overseers. Master Plecker went up to Kenneth while he rode the horse and spoke with him as Joseph watched. Their conversation made Joseph wonder what a father would say to his son when his son went off to war. *I should pray for him*, he thought.

CHAPTER 7
The Eyes of a Mother

In Tahlequah, on October 29, 1861, Annabelle, Lisa, and Lizzie worked the supply store. Lizzie finished helping an elderly woman put her supplies on her wagon. She saw Paul slowly riding a horse toward the supply store from the corner of her eye, but walked inside the supply store. Paul entered the supply store and kept one hand slightly behind his back as he looked at Lizzie. "Good afternoon Miss Lizzie," Paul said with a cheerful tone.

She replied, "What do you want, Paul?"

He pulled out a list from his pocket and looked at it. "Well…I know I need a sack of flour and corn mill."

"Wow, still getting supplies for Nancy, I see. Thought you would stop that by now."

"Well, it's my job and I get paid for it now. It's not like the old days no more you know that."

She gave him a smirk. "Right…I'll bring out her sacks." Lizzie went into the supply room and exited carrying the two sacks. She placed the sacks on the counter. "Here you go."

He came up to the counter and calmly took his hand from behind his back to present a blue flower to Lizzie. "Here you go." She struggled to contain her smile when she took the flower from Paul. "I learned you like the blue ones more, and the seasons is changing. So I know I better give to you while I can."

She slightly leaned over the counter as she looked at the blue flower. "Thank you. You always think of me."

"That was so sweet of you Paul," Lisa said. Lizzie quickly stood straight up when Lisa walked to the counter. "Who are you trying to fool?" Lisa playfully swatted Lizzie's long braid. Lizzie rolled her eyes at her. "How are you, Paul?" Lisa cheerfully asked.

"I doing well, Miss Lisa," he answered. "Getting some supplies for Mrs. Nancy."

"I'm glad that's working well for you. She likes the flowers, by the way." Lizzie squinted slightly at Lisa and she pressed her lips.

"Don't tell my business to him," she barked in Cherokee.

"I believed she did," Paul cheerfully said. He gave Lisa the money for the two sacks. "Well, I happy to see you both doing good, and my prayers to Jesus being Joseph comes back soon. I was happy to hear y'all found him."

"Who told you that?" Lizzie asked.

"It was Tsula. She told me last week. Told me not to tell nobody else including Mrs. Nancy and I keep my word. I ain't told nobody."

"Thank you for keeping your word. You're a good man. Stay that way."

"I promise you." He picked up the two sacks, smiled at the two women, and left.

Lisa looked at Lizzie and grinned. "You should spend more time with him," she said.

Lizzie replied in Cherokee, "I don't need to spend more time with him. Why would I?"

She chuckled as she looked at her. "Who are you trying to trick? I've been watching you, Lizzie Lightning. You should give him more time. You need to stop hiding how you feel. It's not fun seeing you struggling to hide how you feel."

She huffed. "I'm giving him time."

"He always approaching you isn't giving him time. If you're worried it won't work, that's understandable, but it takes the work of two for anything special to happen. Try harder if you really want to give him a chance. I don't mean to pressure you."

She looked at the door while she bit her lip, and looked at Lisa. "You always find the good in life. Even after what you suffered, you stand a fighter…I'll try harder."

Lisa playfully twisted Lizzie's braid. "Okay."

Three days later, John, Eli, and Samuel returned to Tahlequah. The exhausted men were disappointed they hadn't brought Joseph home. John entered the family house with Eli and Samuel walking behind him. Rain came out of the kitchen, and a large smile appeared on her face. "Papa!" Rain shouted. She ran to John and gave him a hug. John picked her up as he gave her a kiss on the cheek. "Auntie Tsula, they're home!"

The kitchen door slowly opened as Tsula came out holding Katelyn as she cooed. Tsula walked closer, but noticed their silence. "Well…all of three of you look like losers," Tsula said. "Sit so I can feed y'all. I know none of you can cook."

The men sat at the table ashamed they were unable to bring Joseph home a second time. "Papa, are you happy to see me?" Rain asked.

John nearly frowned, but forced a smile the moment he looked at her. Eli placed his hand on John's back to help calm him. "I'm happy to see my sun," John said. "Now where is my moon?"

Rain replied with a smile, "She's with Momma and Auntie Grace."

"How about we play a game when they get home? How does that sound?"

She giggled. "Good, Papa. Uncle Eli, Samuel, are y'all going to play too?"

Eli replied in Cherokee, "I would be happy to play."

Samuel replied, "I will too. I want to see how badly you beat Michael." She laughed and the men chuckled with her.

Afterward, Tsula brought out some stew for the men. "Did y'all run into any serious problems? Tsula asked.

"No, we were able to stay well hidden," John said. "It was sad seeing some of the things we saw. A few children were obviously Indian."

"A number of them were house slaves," Eli said.

"Really," Tsula said.

"Yeah, it slowed us down. We had to wait and see where all of them were working and sleeping."

"We have to find him this next time," John said.

The corners of Tsula's mouth arched into a big grin, and she said, "They found him."

The men's jaws dropped, and their eyes enlarged. "Tsula?"

"I'm serious. The husbands of Annabelle's friends came here at the end of August. We had to wait for you to return."

"Where's Annabelle?"

"She's at the store." John stood and immediately went to the front door. "I'll keep this food warm for y'all."

"I'm coming too," Eli said.

Tsula and Samuel smiled at each other. "I miss you," Tsula said.

"I miss you too," Samuel said. The twins reached across the table and held each other's hands.

They released each other's hands. Tsula leered. "I honestly can't tell what makes me happier. Seeing you or knowing I have a new babysitter." The smile on Samuel's face dropped while Tsula quickly went into the kitchen. She came out of the kitchen holding Katelyn, but Samuel stood up to leave. "Don't you dare." Samuel froze, and Tsula gave Katelyn to him. "You haven't seen her, and I need alone time." Tsula kissed Katelyn and went back to the kitchen humming.

Samuel looked at his niece and kissed her forehead. "Don't be like your momma."

"I heard that!" Tsula bellowed. Samuel's eyes widened, and he carried Katelyn outside to the porch.

John and Eli arrived at the supply store and got off the horses. John hurried into the store and saw Grace at the counter. She smiled and said, "Y'all made it home."

She walked around the counter and hugged John. Eli entered after John, and she hugged and kissed him. "Where's Annabelle?" John asked.

"She—"

Annabelle came out of the storage room and put down a jar. The corners of her mouth lifted into a smile. She ran from around the counter and hugged John tightly. "I miss you so much," she said.

"Tsula said they found him," John asked.

Annabelle's eyes welled up. "It's true."

John wept as he pressed his cheek against Annabelle's. "We're bringing him home. I swear it."

Tears covered Annabelle's cheeks. "I know you will." Annabelle wiped away her tears. "Oh, Jannie is outside. Jannie, come in here."

Jannie entered the store through the backdoor. Her eyes shot open, and a big grin etched on her face. "Papa!" she yelled. She ran and jumped onto John.

"Oh my moon," John said.

Annabelle stepped aside and gave Eli a hug. "Welcome home," she said.

"Thank you, Annabelle," he said. "I'm happy to hear the news."

The women closed the store early, and the family went home. John gave Jannie a piggyback ride the entire way home and listened to his daughter tell him about the past months. John and Eli greeted David, George, Jacob, and Michael as they worked the fields. John and Eli explained they had already been told about Joseph's whereabouts and were anxious to bring him home.

During supper, George said the prayer over the food and joked that John, Eli, and Samuel went into the house first to avoid telling the other men they didn't find Joseph. The family laughed and began to eat. As the family ate, Annabelle felt the strongest feelings of home she had felt in a long time. However, as the family interacted, she could see frustration in David building as he played with his food. "John, did you see the White men fighting?" Lizzie asked in Cherokee.

The table went silent while John put down his fork and looked at Eli. "On our way back, we came across traveling families going to smaller towns," John said. "It was surprising to see all of them. We could see the smoke rising in the air from the distance, so we went around. Samuel asked one man where they were coming from. The man told them Springfield, Missouri. We were told a lot of men died in there. I think it was October 25 or 26, but we tried our best to stay away from the area."

"This war is growing every year," Eli said. "It's no longer the United States. Not until the fighting stops."

"Stand Watie continues to try to persuade many of the men to fight for the Confederates," Grace said. "Many of us that are more traditional are standing with Chief Ross, but the ones mixed with White are heavily on Stand's side. They believe the Confederates will respect us and make fair deals with us."

"They're nothing but fools," George said. "It doesn't matter, Confederate or Union the White man is the White man. One wants to end slavery, the other wants it to reign with an iron fist, but both will still cheat us in every agreement. None of them have a reason to keep their word to us and never have kept their word."

"Some of the men are calling us traitors now for not agreeing with them," Michael said. "Will we be forced to fight our own people?"

"If it comes to that then it comes to that," Lizzie said in Cherokee.

Michael replied, "How can you say that so calmly?"

Lizzie somewhat frowned. "I don't say that calmly. I'm thinking about the future. Not how many lives we could lose or how much money our people that are slave owners could lose. If slave owners win, it will continue to sicken our people's views on Negroes and half-breeds and we'll still be under the White man's control."

George replied, "Don't be so strong in your words, Lizzie. We're not under the White man's control."

Lizzie sharply replied, "How can you say that? Look around us. Our people haven't been in control for over a hundred years. We now live in this lie because we understand that in their politics, we're free. But we're not free. That's why we're unable to stay out of this war. I think Chief Ross was lying to himself… believing we could stay out of it."

George remained silent. He folded his hands and shifted his gaze to the table. "We have to make things better for the children," Maria said. "I agree with Lizzie. I'm worried that too many of people in Indian Territory don't see the whole picture. These White men don't know how to give, only how to take."

"Does it look like the battles will reach this far out, Eli?" Lisa asked.

He replied, "I'm afraid some might after seeing what happened in Missouri."

"Then we should make a plan to move if we have to or at least be careful with who we can trust now. We've been through enough losses. The Creek and Seminole seem to have already voiced their position, and are with the Union. Their decision has already created conflict between them and the Chickasaw."

Tsula replied, "I agree, sister, and as the most beautiful, only matched by my Katelyn, I vote that we enjoy this meal and make a plan. None of the men can cook, so let them enjoy some real food."

Tsula's demeanor caused laughter, breaking the seriousness at the supper table. As the family ate and talked about other things, David continued to slowly eat his food. He put down his fork. "Father, can we leave tomorrow to bring Joseph home?" He asked in Cherokee. "He's been away for over a year."

John stopped eating and placed his hand on his shoulder. "David, Momma has told me you've been struggling to be patient. Now that we know where he is," John said, "I understand your feelings, but we wouldn't be able to make the journey. The weather has already begun to change, and we're low on supplies. We may have enough to get to Mississippi, but not enough to return."

"Why not ask one of our neighbors for help?" David asked with a frustrated tone.

John sharply replied, "We can't because they also need what they have. Most families are no better or even worse off than we are. We can't be selfish. I know it hurts, but I need you to continue to be strong."

"Did you see the White men fighting?" He asked.

John frowned. "No, only what was left after they were done fighting. I doubt this war will end by next year with so much hate between them."

"I hate them. They're savages."

John abruptly slapped him. The entire table went silent while John angrily stared at David. "No son of mine will speak like that! We won't continue to grow their circle of hate. I refuse that for my children." Annabelle could see the anger in David's eyes. John placed his hand on his shoulder. "I love you, son, and I want to see you stay on the right path. Don't make that mistake and let hate have any place in your heart."

"I'll do better. I'm sorry."

"No need to apologize. Protect the family that's all I ask of you. Trust Jesus, ask for guidance, and protect the family. You're more important than you know right now." David nodded and went back to eating. Rain got out of her seat and gave him a kiss on the cheek. He picked up Rain and placed her on his lap.

"I need to start writing memoirs for this family," Tsula said in Cherokee. The family laughed as Lisa playfully hit Tsula on her arm. "Little David, don't forget your words matter. Be patient, sweetie."

Later in the night, Annabelle and John prepared for bed. Annabelle sat in the bed with her right hand on her left shoulder. "What are you thinking about?" He asked in Cherokee.

"I'm thinking about these scars on my back," She said in Cherokee. "I can't even tell the difference between the scars, and the rest of me. Do you think that's weird?"

"No, I don't think it is. Those scars healed really well when you were young, but what's really on your mind?"

She slightly frowned. "I'm bothered with how those White

men have harmed our family. Not only did they take Joseph from us, but they managed to change David. I mean, all of us have changed, but he has changed the most. It scares me."

John sighed. "Maybe I should allow him to come with us next time. I think part of this is my fault. I should show him more that I do trust him."

"John, do you think it's wise with this war going on?"

"I think it'll help keep him from doing anything foolish. I'm trying to understand him more, but what do you think?"

"I think he has a good heart, and he can't accept the pain Joseph may be experiencing. I think he is afraid we'll find Joseph when it's too late."

John began to rub Annabelle's back. "He was too young to fully understand Camille's passing. I think he is afraid Joseph's kidnapping will lead to his murder. Elder Joyce's passing was the first death he's experienced while being old enough to understand it. I think it's time to allow him to grow into becoming more of a man."

"If David goes, who will stay behind?"

"I think Eli should stay behind, especially with Gabriel being so young. He should spend more time with his son."

"When do you want to tell David that he's going with you the next time?"

"After we get the fields prepared to plant the crops." John kissed Annabelle on her cheek, and she smiled. "Are the twins staying with Lizzie?"

"Yeah, its girls' night as far as they're concerned…half the time I feel like she's going to keep those two for good."

John playfully whispered, "Well, I have missed you."

She turned around on the bed with a smirk. "I've missed you more."

"Oh, I don't know about that." They kissed and she giggled.

"Careful or you'll end up with baby number six." Annabelle and John spent the night together enjoying a childless night. As they slept, she held onto him tightly and was grateful for his safe return. Even more hope filled her heart as she felt they had created a solution to keep David safe and from developing more hatred in his heart.

Two days later, the twins followed Grace and Lizzie out to their practice range. While Grace and Lizzie talked to each other, Rain strutted over to Jannie with an arrow. "I bet I can hit one of the targets before you can," she said in Cherokee.

"You know you're not better than me," Jannie confidently said in their language. "Auntie Lizzie said we're even right now and said Rosita is as good as us."

She scoffed. "You're scared to accept my challenge."

Jannie arrogantly replied, "I'm not scared of any challenge you can make. I can make a challenge too. I think I can twist my hair around the arrow tighter than you can."

"You're bad at braiding, and you know it."

Jannie took the arrow from her. "Braiding is different than twisting hair." Jannie took down one of her braids and twisted the arrowhead into her hair. "See, I bet you can't do it tighter than that."

She pouted. "I know I can do it better than you. Give me the arrow!"

Jannie side-eyed and smacked her lips. "You wish you could." She began to untwist her hair when there was the sound of the arrowhead cutting her hair. Both of the girls gasped as the arrow fell to the ground. "Oh no! It cut my hair."

"What are the two of you doing?" Grace asked in Cherokee.

"Nothing," the twins said in unison.

"Then why did the two of you make that sound?" Lizzie asked.

Rain answered, "We dropped the arrow, that's all, Auntie Lizzie. We're going to see if Auntie Lisa started to prepare some soup."

Rain picked up the arrow and pushed Jannie to start walking.

"Wait a moment…Jannie, turn so I can see your cheek," Grace said in their native language.

Jannie's eyes widened when she turned around, showing

her hair on that side was almost cut in half. Grace and Lizzie gasped. Jannie began to shake.

"The two of you are going to give me gray hair before your auntie." Lizzie then side-eyed Grace. "Go on, we'll see how long you can hide that from your momma."

The girls gulped and ran to the family house.

"Well, at least they didn't almost shave their heads like Tsula," Lizzie said in Cherokee.

When the twins got to the family house, Rain stopped in front of the door. "What are you doing? We need to hide from Momma," Jannie said.

"Give me your other braid," Rain said. "I'll cut it so it's even with the other side, and Momma won't notice the difference."

"Do you think it'll work?"

"I think it will. We can have another girls' night with Auntie Lizzie and your hair will grow back by then."

"Rain, I don't think hair grows back that fast."

Rain grunted. "We have to try or Momma is going to be really mad."

Jannie shrugged. "Okay, cut it."

Rain cut Jannie's hair with the arrowhead and braided it so her hair looked more even. "There, it's done. We can do this."

The day went on as the girls helped Lisa prepare lunch. They were having such a good time they had forgotten about Jannie's hair being cut. Annabelle and Maria came inside the house with Jonathan and Sky holding their hands.

Rain exited the kitchen and yelled, "Welcome home, Momma!"

"Hi, Rain, what have you been doing…helping your aunties?" Annabelle said in Cherokee.

Rain replied in her native tongue, "Yes."

A minute later, Jannie left the kitchen with a smile. "Hi, Momma. Hi, Auntie Maria," Jannie said in Cherokee.

"Hi, Jannie," Maria said in Cherokee.

Annabelle looked at Jannie, and before she could respond her smile disappeared. She slowly approached Jannie. "Jannie… you cut your hair?" Annabelle said. Brow furrowed, Annabelle raised her voice, "You cut your hair! Who said you could cut your hair!" She grabbed Jannie by her arm and raised her hand to spank her, but Rain bolted out the front door. Annabelle turned around and ran after her. "Rain, you get back here!" Annabelle's voice echoed.

Annabelle managed to barely catch up to her when she reached the front door of their home. "Momma please!" Rain cried in Cherokee as she forced the door open. She ran past one of the rocking chairs and knocked it down to block Annabelle's path. She sprinted into her room and slammed the door. She then crawled under her bed.

Annabelle angrily opened the bedroom door. "You come from under that bed!"

"Momma please! It was an accident! Jannie cut it first!"

Annabelle reached under the bed and struggled to pull Rain out from underneath. "I know you had something to do with it!" Annabelle pulled her from under the bed, and gave her four whacks on her butt. "Don't you ever cut your sister's hair without my permission!"

Annabelle was about to give her another whack when John entered the bedroom. "What is this about?" John asked.

"Those two little troublemakers…Jannie's hair has been cut!" Annabelle yelled, breathing heavily. "She cut her sister's hair!"

"Jannie did it first, Papa," Rain cried.

"Nobody asked you to speak," Annabelle growled.

"Annabelle, calm down," John said. "Rain, did your sister cut her hair too?"

"Yes, Papa," she said.

John huffed. "Come here." She moved past Annabelle avoiding eye contact with her mother. "Don't do things without asking me or your momma, is that understood?"

"Yes, Papa."

"Good now go back to your sister, little girl." She sprinted out of the log cabin. "I could hear you all the way in the fields."

"Those girls…I should've given birth to them first," Annabelle said in Cherokee. "How many times I wish they were calmer like their brothers. It's supposed to be the boys that do crazy things."

John replied, "The boys have done some crazy things."

She shook her head. "Not like those two. I feel like I need to take a nap. That girl can move."

He laughed. "But you can move too. You caught her from the looks of it. Is the haircut that bad?"

She suddenly began to sob. "No, it isn't, but that isn't the point. I need them to do as they're told. When people see the girls, they don't think they have a Negro mother, and I want it that way. I can't stand the thought of something happening to them because they're half-bloods. They've experienced enough. It's in their best interests that strangers remain ignorant about who they are."

"But things are changing. Elder Joyce has always spoken about change happening, and when this war ends, it will benefit us. I have faith it will be an end to slavery and the children can do things freely."

"Even if that war ends in our favor, those White men will make it their business to make Negroes lives harder. I don't trust them."

John hugged Annabelle. "Let's do what we can to prepare the children for that. If you want the girls to keep their hair long, I won't disagree with you."

"Good." She let go of him and walked out of the room. "I see you put the chair back up. Your clever daughter knocked it over to slow me down."

"Where are you going?"

"To deal with the other one. I won't have my daughters creating an argument over who is more favored because one didn't a whooping." He sighed and followed her out of the house, and began to go to the fields. "So you're going to go walk back to the crops, and I look like the mean parent?"

He raised his hands. "I have to help the others finish."

She smacked her lips. "Right...I'll see you at supper. Those girls rule you."

"They are my sun and moon," he chuckled. She looked back at him and rolled her eyes to fight her smile.

Annabelle entered the family house, and gave Jannie the same punishment and speech she gave Rain. Afterward, she gave the twins hugs and told them to behave. She thought, *I can't tell what bothers me more...them reminding me of my younger self or not being able to tell them right now why they can't cut their hair. I think them holding to their Cherokee culture is the best way to protect them from being seen as Negro children. I have to do what I can for them.*

The next morning, Annabelle fixed the girls grits for breakfast. She walked out of the kitchen carrying two small bowls. Lizzie followed a few steps behind her carrying her own bowl and Annabelle's bowl. Her eyes first locked onto two-year old Jonathan who was playing with Lisa and Sky. She placed the bowls down in front of the girls, and both looked up at her pouting. "Momma, can I please have some butter in my grits?" Jannie asked.

Annabelle's eyes narrowed. "Absolutely not. Not after what the two of you did. Neither of you are having anything with butter for the entire week!"

The twins' mouths dropped in unison with their widened eyes.

"But, Momma," Rain griped.

"Don't you 'but Momma' me nothing," Annabelle sternly said with her hands now resting on her hips.

Lizzie placed Annabelle's bowl down and sat at the table eyeing the twins. "Auntie," Rain cried.

"You heard your momma," Lizzie said. "I agree with her." Rain's face crinkled. She folded her arms and turned away from Lizzie. "I suggest you drop that ugly face, little girl, or I'll be the one to give you a whooping."

Rain's face straightened out. "I'm sorry, Auntie Lizzie."

"The two of you eat up," Annabelle said. "I and your auntie are walking y'all to school this morning." Annabelle glanced at Lizzie who had begun to eat her grits which were mixed with salt and butter. She sighed and sat at the table in front her bowl. "I never thought my children would like butter so much."

Lizzie pointed her spoon at her. "Now, we're not going to sit here and talk about how butter doesn't have that much taste. I never thought I'd meet someone that didn't like butter that much. It's great for cooking. I think the girls might become a better cook than you if you don't stop talking so bad about it."

The girls turned their heads toward Lizzie and bit their lips attempting to hide their smiles. Annabelle side-eyed the twins but then smiled. "Don't get my daughters into more trouble," she joked. "It doesn't have that much taste. No different than I don't like mixing my food up. It all belongs in its own section." After having breakfast with the rest of the family, Annabelle and Lizzie walked the girls to school with thoughts of Joseph deep in her mind.

November 1861 arrived in Caledonia as the harvesting of the remaining cotton continued and the preparations for winter had already begun. During this time, Joseph had learned to focus more on positives that were at the plantation. The friendships he had established were enough for him to thank God. They helped him push away the sadness he experienced every day. The conversations in the morning helped him. Bo seemed to be able to create his own form of joy every morning. His positive leadership would often help Joseph forget about the hardships half the time and reminded him of Michael.

The early morning chill of November 11, 1861, was felt in the wind despite the sunrays piercing through the white clouds. Joseph worked with Tom to bring more firewood to the storage shed. "I used to like carrying firewood," he said.

"At least it got warmer," Tom replied. "I guess now we gotta go over to that broken wagon and help Bo. I—"

"Joseph," Susie said. The boys turned around and saw her standing behind them. "Mrs. Wilma has summoned you."

"Why me?" he asked as his brows drew together.

"Mrs. Judy Mays is here and has requested to see you."

"Okay." He followed her to the mansion.

"She seemed like she was in a good mood. I wouldn't worry about seeing her."

"Do you think she knows my momma?"

"Riza said she's not sure. It would be crazy if she did know your momma."

Well...my momma is from Missouri. She has White friends there."

"Riza said to only answer what is asked of you."

"Oh, okay. I'll do that."

The two children arrived at the large mansion, and Susie entered through the front door. She stood in the foyer as Joseph took his shoes off outside and then quickly stepped inside.

"Ugh, my feet are so cold."

"They have the fire burning in the study hall. It is warmer there."

He followed her through the mansion with the sunrays illuminating their way. He could hear the cheerful echoing voices of Judy Mays, Reece, and Wilma. His hands suddenly became clammy, and he rubbed his hands on his beige pants. The children entered the study hall and saw Wilma sitting down on the crème-colored couch with Reece sitting to her left. Judy Mays sat in a Victorian chair with one hand resting on top of the other. The warmness of the room was quickly overshadowed by the stares of the women. Joseph's gaze moved to the coffee table which had teacups and a book placed onto it. He immediately stopped walking when Susie stood still.

"Joseph, I've heard you've had an incident," Judy Mays stated. "It's why Susie is missing more than half of her hair. Is that true?"

"Yes, ma'am," he answered. "I try very hard to do everything right."

"I'm sure you do. It doesn't change what happened."

His voiced raised, "I didn't mean to make Master Plecker mad!"

Judy Mays's eyes narrowed. "Watch your tone with me, little boy!"

"It's that Indian blood," Wilma grumbled.

"It's no matter. He will learn self-control."

He replied, "I—"

Brows furrowed, Judy Mays interrupted, "I'm not done

speaking, and you will learn. You remin—" Judy Mays bit her lip and took a deep breath. His gaze went to his hands. "I imagine that's how you were raised. Look at me."

He gulped, his eyes fixed on Judy Mays's now calm blue eyes, and felt his neck and shoulders relax.

"Do you have understanding that your actions affect others?" Judy Mays asked her tone now softening.

Joseph could feel his throat tightening again. "Yes, ma'am."

"Despite this little incident, you've been quite productive here. I can tell you're still learning, though."

"At least this one doesn't smell as bad as the others," Reece said. Both of Judy Mays's eyes slightly twitched as she forced herself to grin.

Wilma chuckled, "Now, Reece, you know he's just a boy. Once he gets of age, I'm sure he'll struggle to prevent manly odors. Though I doubt it'll be as bad as a full-blood Negro."

"Yes, well, there are some things we can't change," Judy Mays said. "All men can have an odor if they're not clean. I certainly remember some of Kenneth's smelly moments."

A hysterical laughter escaped Wilma's mouth as she covered it with her hand. "This is quite true, my poor baby! He certainly struggled with the concept of taking a bath." Reece inhaled as her cheeks puffed and she forced herself to smile, and Judy Mays shrugged, responding with a fake smile.

Judy Mays turned to Joseph. "Anyhow, I'm glad to hear that you're doing well here, despite the past. And being told why Little Susie had her beautiful hair cut off."

"Beautiful," Reece mocked.

Judy Mays kept her gaze on him.

"I agree, despite his minor setback, there has been strong improvement," Wilma said. "And well done, Little Susie. Now bring us that platter of treats we had talked about earlier."

"Yes, ma'am," Susie replied. The eyes of the children locked before she left the mansion.

"Step closer, Joseph," Judy Mays calmly said. He took a few steps forward, his steps on beat with the ticking of the grandfather clock. "I imagine you must be surprised to be inside this mansion."

"Yes, ma'am," he answered.

"As am I," Reece remarked.

Judy Mays exhaled and brushed a blonde bang away from her eyebrow. "Do you think I had you brought in here to hurt you?" she asked.

"I don't know, Mrs. Judy Mays," he answered quietly.

"Hmm, I imagine you have a lot of questions about me. Well, I only want you comfortable here. I think you'll become a positive influence here. However…what if I told you I now own you?"

Joseph's eyes enlarged. He looked at Wilma and quickly looked back at Judy Mays. "I…I…"

"Does that scare you? I'm sure my own children would be thrilled to have someone around their age."

"I want to be f—"

"Boy, this isn't about what you want," Wilma sternly said. "There will never be any negotiations in this room. You forget your place so easily, little boy. You are here due to her request, not favor."

"Yes, Mrs. Wilma," he replied.

Wilma picked up her teacup. "I told you, Judy Mays. Riza certainly has influence."

"Yes, I can see that," she said. "It doesn't change my mind."

A leer drew across Reece's face. "Because you like your rebellious little pet, like this little creature."

Judy Mays's tone deepened, causing him to freeze. "I don't need to explain myself to you nor do I like your assumptions. There is a difference between admiring and liking."

"That is true," Wilma said as she took a sip of her tea.

"Joseph, pick up the book."

He jolted and picked up the book.

"No need to worry, dear."

Reece scoffed. "Not yet."

Judy Mays tapped her fingers on the armrest of the chair. "What's the title of the book?"

"The Holy Bible," he answered.

Reece's eyes widened. "That little nigger can read."

"Yes, this little boy can," Judy Mays said with irritation coating her tone. "Now, Joseph, start reading Psalm 27."

He took a deep breath, turned the pages, and began to read, "The Lord is my light and my salvation; whom shall I fear? The Lord is the strength of my life; of whom shall I be afraid? When the wicked, even mine enemies and my foes, came upon me to eat up my flesh, they stumbled and fell."

Judy Mays took a sip of her tea, her eyes shifting onto the other two women whose mouths were agape as they listened to him read the scriptures. Her face relaxed as she heard his voice. The crackling of the fireplace and the ticking of the grandfather clock were the only background noise as he continued to read. More sunlight pierced through the windows as the clouds moved, brightening the room. She could feel her left eye begin to become watery. She thought, *The way he makes sure he pronounces his words…he's just like—*

"Mrs. Wilma, I have the cookies," Susie said with a smile.

Joseph stopped reading, and Wilma slightly shook her head as if mesmerized by his reading. "Ah, yes, very good," she said. "Set them down."

Susie put the silver platter on the coffee table. The platter contained rows of butter and sugar cookies.

"And bring us some more tea," Reece said.

She replied, "Yes, ma'am."

Judy Mays stared at her split ends caused by the jagged cutting of her hair. "Please hurry back, Little Susie," she calmly said.

She nodded and immediately went to the cookhouse.

"Whoever said you could stop reading, Joseph?" He gasped, his eyes wide and his mouth curved downward into a frown. He immediately put the book up to his face to read.

"It's no problem, Joseph."

"I actually enjoyed this half-breed's reading, Judy Mays," Wilma said. "Perhaps that'll be a new role for him. I never imagined he'd read so well."

"Your momma must've put a lot of time into you," Judy Mays said.

"My…momma?" Joseph said.

Judy Mays picked up a few cookies from the platter, saying, "That is who taught you how to read, am I right?"

"Yes, ma'am."

"You did such an excellent job reading the Lord's word. Come closer." He nervously stepped up to Judy Mays. "You followed instructions so well. I want you to eat some cookies with me. What will it be, butter cookies or sugar cookies?"

Joseph's eyes widened as his face went blank. "I get to choose?"

She smirked. "Of course you can."

"Can I please have a sugar cookie?"

"Why, yes, you can." She handed him a sugar cookie, and he took a bite. "It seems you have a preference, Joseph."

"I don't really like butter," he replied as he chewed his food.

She tilted her head, continuing to smile. "You don't say. You know I'm not a big fan of butter either…it doesn't have much taste."

"Yeah, it doesn't," he boldly said.

"See, I knew we would agree on something." She leaned forward and held another cookie in front of him. "Go on, have another."

He slowly took the cookie and began to eat it. He noticed Judy Mays also had butter cookies in her hand. "I thought you didn't like butter."

"I'm not a big lover of the butter cookies, but I had to know which ones you'd pick. After all, we're just getting to know each other."

He squinted. "Okay."

"I'll tell you more about me. I don't like a messy plate. It amazes me how people mix up their food. It's very unsophisticated. It ruins the rest of the food. I bet you don't like to mix up your food either."

His eyes widened. "How did you know?"

"Well, you have superior taste, Joseph." She dismissively waved her hand. "Everyone else is weird," she joked.

He giggled, revealing his smile. "I think so too."

"See, we're just learning more about each other." Her eyes anchored onto his smile. *There it is…your momma's smile*, she thought. *Annabelle, we will have a lot to talk about.* She looked at Wilma. "I imagine you want to continue our conversation."

"Well of course, dear," Wilma replied. "When Susie returns, he'll go back to work. It also seems you were right, but we will talk about it later."

"Have some more, Joseph," Judy Mays calmly said as she handed him two more cookies. He ate the cookies and kept his eyes on her. *He's still very nervous*, she thought. *If I ask him about his family, I'm sure Riza will voice her concern. It'll sabotage my efforts.* She wiped her mouth with a handkerchief. "What's your favorite color, Joseph?"

"It's green," Joseph answered.

Judy Mays's eyes widened. "Is that so? It's such a strong color. No wonder you like it."

"What's yours?"

"Well…I haven't been asked that in so long. At one time, it was red. Now it's blue." Susie then entered the room with a kettle of tea. "And there she is." She placed the tea down on the coffee table.

"Great timing, Little Susie," Wilma said. "Now, take Joseph back to the front door. He's to return to the fields. Afterward, have Riza return from helping Dorothy. I want her presence here."

"Yes, Mrs. Wilma," Susie replied.

"Go on, Joseph," Judy Mays said. "I will be watching you. I'm sure we have more to talk about. Listen to what you are told. You never know, I might just take you myself."

"Yes, Mrs. Judy Mays," Joseph replied. "Have a good day, Mrs. Wilma and Mrs. Reece."

"You are a well-mannered half-breed," Wilma said.

He then followed Susie out of the room and into the foyer.

The two friends gave each other a hug and he returned to the fields while Susie went to find Riza.

"Before Riza returns, what's your verdict Judy Mays...is he Annabelle's son?" Wilma asked.

Judy Mays stared at the two women for a brief moment. She thought, *He's so much like her.* She cleared her throat. "I'll need a little more time with the boy. He is a rarity. Did you hear how well he pronounced as he read?"

Wilma's eyes widened. "Yes, it is quite worrisome. Well, take as much time as you need to decide, dear. You know none of those children are going anywhere."

"Clearly, this child has been taught, and from what I know of your precious Annabelle, was well versed," Reece said.

Judy Mays's nose crinkled. "And as I said, I just need more time with the boy to get the full truth. It's a reason Riza was sent with Dorothy. She can get him to be silent and that's not what I need."

"You choose to do things the hard way. All you need to do is take a switch to that boy, and he'll talk. Why do you show him so much kindness?"

"It's a game, Reece. If you had a brain..."

"Judy Mays!" Wilma griped as she slapped the couch seat.

She replied, "She would understand fear will set back my goals..."

"You fear Riza," Reece bickered.

"I respect the Mohawk, you'd be wise to do so," Judy Mays said, pointing her finger at Reece. "She's not like those Negros in the fields...she's always thinking. Now, as I said, I need more time with the boy."

Wilma smiled. "I have no problem with it, and perhaps even now may be the time to tell your father."

"I will tell him when I am certain."

"Very well, it's good we finished this before Riza's return. It's wise to listen to Judy Mays, Reece. She's right about that girl."

Riza arrived a few minutes later, and the women continued with different conversations.

Judy Mays forced herself to smile and interact. I can't let them know that I know the truth, especially Papa, she thought.

On November 12, 1861, Joseph and Tom were feeding the cattle. Bo entered the barn, panting. "All right, now after y'all get done feeding them, sharp them knives," Bo said. "We got a lot of cutting to do today."

"Which ones are we butchering?" Tom asked.

"That old brown bull and that brown and white one there."

Tom frowned. "I like that cow. Do we have to kill that one? Why not kill the other bull?"

Bo sighed. "Look here, Tom. I told y'all not to let your hearts hold to these animals now. We cutting them up 'cause we only got one working bull. That old brown bull can barely stand now so he not making no baby cattle."

"Can I sit here? I don't want to kill the brown and white cow."

"Tom, you ain't killing nothing you cutting them up after. The only option you got is helping me or going out with Louis to start chopping wood."

"We gone help you, Bo," Joseph said.

"That what I thought," Bo said. He left the barn.

Joseph replied, "We do as we always do. We pray for them, and Bo kills them. My Auntie Lizzie said we always thank the spirit of the animal to show respect and thank the Creator."

"Yeah, I was taught that too," Tom said. "I just think this cow is the nicest one we've had."

"You didn't give her a name, did you?"

Tom pouted. "No, I'm glad I didn't. It would hurt a lot more if I did give her a name."

"Yeah, it would." Suddenly Riza entered the barn, and Joseph's eyebrows lifted. "Riza, what are you doing here?"

"Well, good morning to you too," Riza said. "Mrs. Reece made me come here to see if y'all had started to butcher the meat. She has guests coming over this afternoon."

"No, we haven't. We have to sharpen the knives and tell Bo when we're ready."

Riza grumbled, "Well, don't take so long. Mrs. Reece has been short-tempered ever since Master Kenneth left for the war. I swear she wants all of us unhappy. So hurry it up."

Riza left the barn. "I guess we don't have a choice but to hurry up," Joseph said. "If we take too long. Mrs. Reece might come after us."

Tom replied, "Yeah, you're right. I think she's crazy. Do you see how she looks at Dorothy? It scares me thinking about it."

The boys quickly hurried to sharpen the knives and informed Bo when they were done. The cattle were butchered, and Bo instructed the boys to bring the meat to the cookhouse. When the boys arrived at the cookhouse, Dorothy instructed them where to put the meat. As Joseph was placing one of the slabs of meat, Reece entered the cookhouse in her pink-trimmed orange Victorian dress.

"Ah, Joseph and Tom, I see you two are the reason why Dorothy hasn't heard my calling," Reece bickered. "Dorothy, when you're done here, remake my bed. I don't like it sloppy like Master Kenneth."

"Yes, Mrs. Reece," she said.

Reece slightly sniffed the air and looked at Joseph. "It must make you boys proud not to have to work next to those field niggers today," Reece said. "All I can smell is meat and not animals. I knew it was the stench of slaves the last time I asked you, Joseph. I suggest you boys continue to work so you spend less time in the cotton fields with the animals. It should make your skin crawl to smell like them since you're half-breeds. Does it disgust you to smell like an animal?"

Joseph passively replied, "I think it would bother any person, Mrs. Reece."

Reece smirked. "Joseph, a Negro doesn't know the difference. That redskin blood is the only thing that helps you understand what I mean. It's amusing how you continue to try to defend them when one sold you out to Mr. Rice. Riza's plan was ruined by a nigger." Reece looked at her with her instigative blue eyes. "Hurry these boys up. I want my bed corrected before I take a nap."

"As you wish, Mrs. Reece," she said.

Reece began to leave the kitchen and looked back at her as the boys finished placing the meat. "Make me some tea while you're in here, Dorothy." Reece, with her cruel demeanor, exited the kitchen.

She took a deep breath while Joseph and Tom continued to work. "All right, boys put the last pieces over there and go get back to work," she said with a slightly agitated tone. While Joseph and Tom placed the last pieces of meat, she prepared the tea. The boys said their goodbyes to her as she finished making the tea. When they left, Dorothy spat in the tea.

Dorothy went up to Kenneth's and Reece's bedroom. When she entered the sunlight room with the tea on a silver platter, Reece entered the room from the balcony. "Go on, place my tea down, and fix this bed," Reece commanded. She placed the silver platter down on a dresser and redid the bed while she sadistically grinned and watched as she held a teacup. When Dorothy finished, she strutted around the bed with her hand gliding across the bed. She sat down on the bed. "Ah, now see, was it that hard?"

"No, ma'am," Dorothy said.

"I can tell that you miss him too." Reece stared at her with her conniving eyes as she stood by the tea set. "Pour me more of my tea, mulatto." She picked up the pitcher and poured the tea into Reece's teacup as she held it. She took two sips of the tea. "I find your favor toward Kenneth disturbing, and I find it even more disturbing that he keeps finding a way to protect you. I imagine you have little to no respect for me."

She shook her head. "That isn't true, Mrs. Reece."

Reece laughed and took another sip of the tea. "The bed is proof enough. Even though I did tell you two times already, you must think I'm a fool. You're listening a little too much to Judy Mays. I see it so clearly now. Kenneth doesn't see you as a slave. His mother excuses this behavior. I won't. So what is it? Is this a…we're friends to the end childish game, or did something more happen between the two of you when you were younger?"

Her gaze went downward. "He has always treated me good, that's all."

Reece lightly chuckled, but her smile dropped from her face. She flung the remaining tea in the cup into Dorothy's face. She gasped and groaned in pain. She quickly wiped the hot tea off of her face. "I will say this once." Reece's voice elevated, "I want the truth, and your ability to hide your feelings sickens me! I've grown tired of you giving me looks like I came into your home! When this is my home! Now again, why does he care so much?"

"Because we are friends!" she shouted. "You prideful White witch!"

Reece dropped the teacup and aggressively stepped toward her. She smacked Dorothy, causing an echo. "If you ever speak to me like that again, I'll have you whipped! I'll make sure to have you whipped so bad that those pretty hazel eyes wouldn't be able to sway the ugliest man! Is that all, or is there more to this sickening story?"

She growled, "There isn't nothing more to it."

Reece's cocked her head and pointed her finger in her face. "I expect the truth out of you. Not that tone in your voice. I suggest you be careful. Were you involved with Kenneth when you were younger...around my age?"

"No, Mrs. Reece. We were good friends when we were younger."

"'Were good friends' is a lie that he, to this day, has defended your behavior. You're still friends, and I bet that's what took him so long." Reece continued to point at her. "It was you." Reece's eyes glided up and down her body with a conceited leer. "Were you his practice doll?!"

Her left eye twitched, and her brows began to furrow before she could keep her face blank.

Reece covered her mouth with her fingers, her tone now dripping with sarcasm. "Oh, did I offend you? I wonder...you certainly have a fire in you, like Riza. Do you have Indian blood? It would certainly make sense."

"I don't know, ma'am. Both my parents were mulatto. I know

my momma's daddy was White, and my grandma was mulatto too."

"Maybe that's what it is…you're a savage. Certainly, nigger blood pollutes all races, but the backbone to raise your voice to me. You must have that blood to be crazy enough to do that. Maybe that's why Riza feels so bold. She can tell you're one of them." Reece scoffed. "Anyway, back to what really matters… this sickening favor. You see, he certainly knew a woman's body when he had me for the first time."

Dorothy slightly bit her lip. "He's never had my body."

"You're telling me the only man that's touched you was that slave Geoffrey? You grew no sympathy for none of those nappy-headed niggers out there in those fields?"

"No, ma'am, I didn't…some are friends."

"Why do my instincts tell me otherwise? I think you'd let him have you if he wanted to." She locked eyes with her and clutched her hands into fists. "You'll forever be a thorn in my side, and it sickens me. Do you feel the same way about me?"

Dorothy took a deep breath. "I don't."

Reece sneered. "You raised your voice to me. I thought we'd gotten somewhat past telling lies here. I hate the favor my husband holds for you…my husband. But I love him too much to take you away. Now again, for my entertainment, do you feel the same about me?"

She sighed. "I do feel the same sometimes."

"Well, at least we agree on something, but you understand your well-being will never come before mine." Reece put her pointer finger on Dorothy's forehead. "You're nothing but a slave, and you'll never be nothing more than a slave! I own you and that pretty face. I should have you placed with the ugliest nigger! Now get out of my room, you hazel-eyed Delilah before I'm tempted to hit you like a man."

She narrowed her dilated eyes. "My pleasure, Miss Reece."

She started to leave but Reece aggressively grabbed her arm. "That's Mrs. Reece," she growled. She snatched her arm away. Reece's jaw unhinged and she smacked her. "If you ever do that again…" The two women's furious eyes remained locked as their breathing became deeper. "Get out of my sight." Dorothy backed up and stormed out of the bedroom. Reece put her hands on her hips and deeply exhaled with her face twisting. "Kenneth, you have no idea how much I love you."

Dorothy marched down the stairs leading to the library. As she walked down the stairs she quietly shrieked, "I can't stand that woman! I hope she falls down the stairs." Riza happened to hear her rant as she was going toward the living room hallway, but decided not to let her know she heard her.

Meanwhile, in Tahlequah, the Lightning-Strongman family focused on keeping their voices heard against those Cherokee siding with the Confederacy. The Creek and the Seminole also strongly stood against the Confederates. While the Choctaw remained divided like the Cherokee, the Chickasaw almost entirely sided with the Confederates. John became concerned with the growing tensions, and it was decided it was best for Annabelle to stay home. She agreed especially with the growing presence of the Confederates outside of Indian Territory. Reality of the division was made clear when Colonel Douglas H. Cooper led an attack with Choctaw and Chickasaw Confederates against the Creek and Seminole that had sided with the Union. Fear and hatred spread throughout Indian Territory like a wild fire as old tribal rivalries helped feed the division. On the afternoon of November 17, 1861, the sound of Annabelle's front door could be heard opening. Lizzie stepped into the home with the winter sun outlining her body. Her long braid swayed as she closed to door. "Hi Lizzie," Annabelle said in Cherokee.

Lizzie's brown eyes anchored onto Annabelle who was braiding Rain's long, wavy hair. She noticed the small frown etched onto her niece's face. "What's wrong?" she asked.

"Rain has been feeling very sad. She wanted to talk about Joseph."

Lizzie approached her, saying, "I miss him too."

Tears suddenly trickled from her eyes, and her eyebrows

slanted upward. "What if he never returns?" she asked. "What if they kill him?" She began to sob and she wiped away her tears.

Annabelle let go of her daughter's braid, and leaned over to give her a kiss on the cheek. She then placed her cheek against Rain's cheek and embraced her daughter. "You are not meant to think of such evil things. We're bringing your brother home." She wept harder and Annabelle began to sway her body as she continued to hold her. She put her small hands into Annabelle's hands as her tears fell.

Lizzie's left eye welled as she watched Annabelle console her niece. She turned her head away from her family. Her hands gripped onto the sides of her skirt, and she took deep breaths. Rain's wailing pulled on her spirit as she fought to control her own anger and sadness. Lizzie turned her head back to her family, and calmly walked up to them. She knelt down next to them as Annabelle continued to sway with Rain in her arms. "We must hold onto faith. There is no shame in you missing your brother," Lizzie said.

Rain turned her head toward Lizzie with her cheek still pressed against Annabelle's cheek, saying, "I'm so scared, Auntie Lizzie. I want to be strong like you and Momma."

Lizzie calmly wiped away the tears on Rain's exposed cheek. "I've experienced many evil things in my life, and I've done evil things. But having these experiences never takes away the pain. You only learn to cover how you feel."

"I want to help find Joseph."

"Oh, sweetie, that's too dangerous," Annabelle replied. "The best thing you and your sister and Rosita can do is to follow the rules. Knowing that you're safe is helping the family."

Rain sighed, and her eyes shifted downward to her hands.

"Your momma is right," Lizzie said. Rain's almond-shaped eyes lifted and anchored on Lizzie, but tears still coated her eyes. "When I was a child, we were forced here at gunpoint," she continued. "It was very cold. I lost all of my grandparents, our family friend Kay, and our cousin William and I lost seven of my friends who were children. Soon after we got here, we lost your grandma, and not long after that, your grandpa and Auntie Shay.

"Did you cry a lot? Rain asked.

"Not as much as you would think. I think I was too tired to cry. All of it seemed like a nightmare, and it kept getting worse and worse. I used to have a friend named Lucia, but we don't talk anymore."

Rain's eyebrows drew together. "Why not?"

"After your grandpa walked on, I was very sad. It was hard for me to be happy. When I was fourteen, Lucia saw me praying with my old cross in my hand. She said I was a fool to be praying to the White man's God. She said I was a weak-minded savage."

Rain gasped as her eyes widened.

"I know! But I kindly corrected her…but she said one of the most hurtful things to me. She said I was no different than the other Cherokee who gave up our land for Bibles. Had the nerve to say, that I was no longer Cherokee. Your auntie may have lost her temper, but Lucia is alive."

"I still feel scared that we won't see him again, and that Elder Joyce was wrong."

"How about we pray for your brother right now? Would you want to do that now?" Rain nodded yes. "Then I will grab some sage from the kitchen." Lizzie left the small house and returned with the sage, which was placed in a small iron bowl. "Do you remember how to smudge, my Sunshine?"

"Yes."

"Good, we will pray for your brother."

Lizzie took a small branch and took fire from the fireplace, and put a little on the sage. "Sit next to me, sweetie," Annabelle calmly said. Rain sat down next to Annabelle.

Lizzie looked at Rain as a wall of smoke arose from the slowly burning sage. "Remember that we never gave up our land. It was stolen from us, but through Jesus, we will rise above what they did to us. As in the old ways, we still pray to the Heavens in our way." The sage smoke continued to rise, and Lizzie reached for Rain's hand. She held her hand and then stuck her hand out for Annabelle's hand. Annabelle held Lizzie's hand. "When we pray, we think of good things…to you we pray, Father, as you are the Great Spirit, the Creator, and there is no one greater. Fill us with your love, and strengthen hearts and minds. Rain, remember to rub your hands in the smoke like you're washing your hands. Then bring the smoke to your mouth to speak good things, smudge your eyes to see good things, your ears to hear good things, smudge your hair, smudge your legs so you walk in a good way, smudge the rest of your body, and you smudge your heart to feel good things. We smudge to release bad spiritual thoughts or things we may have picked up, and we go to the Father, for his grace is more than enough to help us through our pain."

Annabelle rubbed Rain's shoulder, saying, "Go on and pray for your brother, sweetie."

Rain then did as Lizzie instructed and prayed for Joseph as she smudged herself. Annabelle and Lizzie smudged themselves after Rain.

When Lizzie finished through the walls of sage smoke she could see Rain's eyes glistening with tears as the fire reflected off of them. "You did well, Sunshine. Elder Joyce would be so proud of you." The tears broke away from her eyes as she cried and Annabelle held her. Lizzie scooted over and rubbed her back. "Rain, remember, we walk by faith and not by sight. Now say it with me."

"We walk by faith, not by sight," Rain said in unison with Lizzie. The two women continued to console the scared and saddened little girl until she calmed down. Soon after, all three walked to the family house with the winter sunlight warming them and reflecting off the remaining snow. Before entering the house, Lizzie slightly glimpsed up to the sky and thought, *Jesus, I know we cannot avoid wrongs, but please spare us from any more pain.* She then went into the house after Annabelle and Rain.

CHAPTER 8
Confrontation and Reflection

ON NOVEMBER 19, 1861, THE Battle of Round Mountain occurred, led by Opothleyahola, a Creek chief. The Union Indians lost their battle and continued up north to Kansas for Union support. Annabelle's family heard of the battles, and it concerned them that the Confederate forces were continuing to grow. It was the beginning of the Indian wars and a painful realization the tribes were truly divided. In Kentucky, Kenneth met up with his older brother Cornelius and joined the Confederate's 52nd Virginia Infantry. Many of the men hailed from Virginia and welcomed the brothers into the company. Unlike Kenneth, Cornelius had a less stocky build than his younger brother. The blond-haired man also had a beard. Cornelius and Kenneth pitched their tent and looked around as the other soldiers prepared for battle. Hundreds of white tents covered the campgrounds and campfires were set up to help keep the campsite warm. "Look at all this," Cornelius said. "You ever seen us so united against those backward Yankees."

"No, never seen this many men together, brother," Kenneth said. "Cornelius, you think we going to win?"

"What kind of question is that? We going to make them Yankees bow on their knees and lick the dirt off our boots. I'm tired of them Yankees trying to tell me how to run my land and saying slavery is wrong. That's why God put niggers on this Earth. To have a nigger not work and challenge they small minds is to go against what they made for."

"I heard we've lost some battles already, but I say let's keep that from happening here."

Cornelius smiled at Kenneth and patted him on his back. "We got to win this. We got wives to go home to. How are things going with you and Reece? I enjoyed y'all wedding."

Kenneth replied, "Things are good, real good. She's a good wife with a temper."

The corner of Cornelius's mouth pinched. "You sound like you complaining. I know you always like them women that have some kick to them. Not a lot of White women like that."

Kenneth huffed. "Yeah, you can say that again. How are Betsy and the boys doing?"

"They're good, the boys are growing fast and I'm gone be a real proud man when they get old enough for me to buy them some land."

"None of them are even ten years old yet, and you talking about doing all that for them already."

"When you get you some children, you'll understand, brother. Those children change your whole world. You want nothing but what's best for them. And winning this war is what's best for my boys and the children Reece gone give you." Kenneth's eyes slightly widened when he thought about Doris and Daisy. "What's wrong with you?"

Kenneth shrugged. "Nothing, I guess I never did think of things in that way. You're a good father, but I would like to see my nephews more often."

"You sound like Momma now." The two men laughed as they strolled toward the command center of the base. Kenneth was slightly overwhelmed with the training drills but wanted to be strong enough to defend what he believed in. However, as the day went on, he struggled to keep his mind focused and kept having flashbacks of giving Doris and Daisy hugs. For the first time, he felt ashamed the girls didn't know he was their father. At nightfall, Kenneth sat with Cornelius and some other men in the company by the campfire while eating stew, but his mind was on his daughters.

While some of the men started to go to bed. Cornelius noticed Kenneth's unusually quiet nature. "What's on your mind, brother? You haven't said much since this afternoon."

Kenneth looked at Cornelius with pursed lips and a downward gaze. "Come with me to our tent. I have to tell you something important."

"All right, but you don't have to look so serious about it. That's not a good look for you. Remember, you're the good-looking one."

A half-moon guided the two brothers to their tent in the cold night, and they sat in their tent while a fire pit burned outside it. "When you told me that when I become a father, I would understand because you're planning all this stuff for the boys…the truth is I'm already a father."

"Ah, you and Reece are having a baby! Good for you, brother," Cornelius cheerfully said.

He shook his head. "No, it wasn't her…this was before her."

"What is wrong with you? Why haven't you married this woman?" Cornelius groaned. "She's not one of those harlots, is she?"

He sneered. "No, she isn't, not even close."

"Oh well, good. You had me worried. Who is she? I must know her."

He blurted, "Dorothy."

Cornelius leaned forward. "Lies…don't play with me."

"I'm telling you the truth."

"I don't understand which one is yours?"

"Both of them are mine."

He cocked his head. "Please tell me this is a lie. What about Geoffrey? He was with her."

Kenneth stared at the ground. "It was all a lie. She was never with him. The girls are my girls."

"Does Reece know?"

He huffed. "No, she doesn't, and I don't know if I'll ever tell her."

"I think it's best you not tell her...ever. Have her give you children to inherit our property, and keep it quiet on those two girls. Do the girls know you they daddy?"

"No, that was part of me and Dorothy's agreement."

"Yeah, Pa told me you made a promise to her. He was real mad about it, but now it makes a lot of sense. All these years and you been keeping secrets like that. Boy, I outta beat you right now. Momma would pass out if she heard this. How long this been going on?"

"Since I was seventeen, I've been seeing her, and it never stopped."

"She got you, a mulatto girl got you. I blame myself. All those times I took you out to that old slave house they used to stay in, and we would look at the girls through one of them cracks. Hell, I can be honest, she always had a nice body, but you gone fell for the girl. So you're messing with her and Reece?"

"No! It's not like that at all...I mean I...I really have been trying to honor my marriage to Reece. But it hurts Dorothy. I'm struggling, and I know the good Lord says to not commit adultery, but I also see I'm the cause of the problem."

Cornelius shook his head. "You so deep in the hole you need to dig a tunnel to get out. Why don't you drop her...keep her in her place? You know she fertile, ain't nothing but trouble coming from that. Have Reece give you some White babies and leave it at that."

He rubbed his forehead. "I don't know how. She has done so much for me...for our family. She's always been loyal to us. You know that, and she's a good mother. I have a hard time wronging her."

With his blue eyes, Cornelius analyzed his furrowed brow, but a leer appeared on his face. "I know what it is." He looked up and saw the leer on his brother's face. "She's wild, ain't she? That's what it is. No wonder how you got her pregnant twice when you not trying!" Cornelius began to cackle as he glared at his brother with a frown. "Ha, tell me, whose better, Dorothy or Reece?"

He squinted as he pulled his head back. "I'm not answering that."

Cornelius continued to laugh louder while he looked at his embarrassed expression. "Come on now, you know I'm not gonna tell. But tell me that much. You know I'm loyal to Betsy, but you got two. So who's better?"

"I'm a Christian man, and so are you. I'm not answering that."

"But you did, brother; one of them is better. So is it Dorothy?" He grabbed his heavy blankets and slid under them to cover his head. Cornelius laughed as he patted his brother on the back. "I knew it, boy, you in so much trouble! Well, at least she "s not a nigger. I bet it's those hazel eyes too. I bet they suck you right in." He pushed Cornelius and pulled the blankets back over his head while he laughed. "All right, all right I guess that's enough, but we gone talk about this some more in the morning." He exhaled with regret while he lay down with the blankets over his head. The brothers slept under the cold night sky.

Several days later, in Tahlequah, a snow storm arrived forcing some of the Cherokee to stay home. The day after, on December 10, 1861, John and Michael strolled through Tahlequah to the supply store to give supplies to any customers that arrived. As they talked to each other, the store's door opened. Brock entered wearing his black frock coat. "Good morning, I'm pleased to see even in these weather conditions you Cherokee work," Brock said.

"What do you want, Mr. Jackson?" John calmly asked.

"Two bags of flour and a chicken."

John folded his hands. "We're not selling anymore chickens for the rest of the year, Mr. Jackson."

"Hmph ain't that something. So what am I supposed eat, just bread? Is that all that you feeding your family? It's one less of you so I would imagine it's not that hard anymore."

John folded his arms. "Be careful with what you say about my son."

"Still a bit sore over that unfortunate event I see. Well, my apologies."

"Michael, go get the flour so he can leave." He angrily glared at Brock and entered the supply room.

Brock sighed. "These are some hard times, especially with this war going on. Those Yankees don't know what's coming for them."

John's brow furrowed. "Why haven't you left to fight? I can see you want the Confederates to win."

He leered. "I already know who's going to win, and the North is going to crack like an egg. Every abolitionist including Reverend Hills will either be fined or taken care of. Once that's done, order will be restored and every nigger from the north to the south to the east and the west will be in their place. Besides, I like my money and I'm still getting paid to keep your people in order."

"I think you're scared. You're letting other men fight for what you want."

He rubbed his trimmed beard and looked at John. "I can already say I know what side you on with your nigger wife. Only thing you did was dirty your bloodline. Only good you got from it is those twins girls. By the grace of God they look nothing like they momma…lucky them."

John's voiced raised, "Don't ever talk about my family like that again, or they'll have to send out another White dog to watch us. I know what you did to Lisa. Lizzie isn't the only one that'll send you on your way to hell."

He chuckled. "I like you John. Such an honest Indian. I'll keep that in mind." Michael came out of the supply room with two bags of flour, and placed them on the counter. "I guess I'll take these and be on my way."

"Well don't forget to pay, Mr. Jackson."

"I thought this time of year y'all gave out supplies for free?"

John grinned. "As you said, you're getting paid to keep the order."

Brock gave them an amused smirk. "Well, here yah go." He tossed a three dollar piece onto the counter. He picked up the two sacks of flour, opened the door, and stopped in the doorway. "Tell my daughter Daddy says hi. I'll be seeing her soon."

"Be careful with your words," Michael said.

He turned around sneering. "Boy, when this war is over and the South wins I will have my daughter, and she'll be raised properly. Not like a redskin." He exited the store.

"If he does that, he'll see a war," Michael boldly said. John patted him on his shoulder. The men later closed the store and went home.

As days passed, Kenneth and Cornelius talked about his predicament. Cornelius now criticized his brother for having feelings for Dorothy. A slight rift grew between the brothers. Cornelius suggested Dorothy be sold to him so he would stop being tempted by her, but also the girls would be able to see her once in a while. He felt this was the only idea that made any sense. He ignored Cornelius's idea, arguing even if Dorothy hadn't given him children, Dorothy had always been loyal to them and deserved better. The brothers remained silent to clear their minds while they patrolled and practiced drills with their rifle-muskets. Even at night, the brothers were only telling each other goodnight to avoid an argument.

On December 13, 1861, while the 52nd Virginia Infantry began to eat breakfast, a soldier shouted, "The Yankees are here, they're coming! The men scattered and grabbed their weapons as the sound of gunfire echoed through the cold winter air. Cornelius and Kenneth ran together with other men to hillside fields.

"Come on, Kenneth, this is what we came here for, brother," Cornelius shouted.

"I'm with you, brother," he shouted. The fighting continued throughout the morning as they fought together on the right side flank. The men tried using the trees as shields as shots were fired, and both sides experienced casualties. Suddenly, artillery opened fire on the Confederate men in the area, tearing down some of the trees. Two men went down in the carnage as

Kenneth watched in terror. "Fall back!" he shouted. The men began to fall back while the artillery continued to fire, supporting the Union troops. "Cornelius, we have to go!"

He screamed and took a shot at a Union soldier grazing the man in the shoulder. "You Yankees will never win!"

"Cornelius, we have to fall back!" He turned around to run when a Union soldier took aim, and shot him in his leg. He fell to the ground and began to crawl when Kenneth took aim, and shot the Union soldier killing the man. A sudden feeling of regret fell upon him as he saw the man fall down to the ground. He grabbed him and began to help him hop away as the sound of rifles, and artillery fire echoed. While the brothers were escaping the artillery fire, two trees fell, barely missing them, causing Kenneth to lose his grip on Cornelius.

He began to crawl on the ground toward Cornelius in an effort to dodge enemy fire. "Forget me, Kenneth. Run, get out of here. I won't have your blood on my hands."

"Don't say things like that. I would never leave you." He put Cornelius's arm around his shoulders as the other Confederate men opened fire to support them, and other troops were caught in the artillery's fire. Suddenly, artillery hit another section of the trees, causing bark to explode off the trees violently. Pieces of sharp wood wounded nearby soldiers. Kenneth felt extreme pain shoot through his arm while pieces of wood pierced his triceps, and it forced him to lose his grip on Cornelius again. "Ah, I'm sorry, brother, curse that artillery... ow, my arm." He pulled the pieces of wood out of his arm and looked over at Cornelius only to see that two large pieces of wood had pierced his back. He looked over at him and could see his brother shaking. "Cornelius!"

He slightly turned his head as he looked at Kenneth. "Hey brother, I'm here," he said with a struggling voice.

"We gone get you help, you hold on now."

He put his hand on Kenneth's shoulder. "No, it's too late. I can't even feel my legs now, and it hurts to breathe."

Kenneth yelled, "Don't say that! We fight like you said we fight."

"I'm sorry. I should've listened to what you were trying to tell me. You're a good Christian man, and I'm happy to call you my brother."

"No, stop talking like that." He grabbed Cornelius by his shoulders and began to drag him as the fighting continued.

"Kenneth…Kenneth, stop." He stopped dragging Cornelius as more men moved up and continued to fight against the Union soldiers. "My boys…take care of them. Tell them the truth about your girls. They should know they got more cousins, even if they mulattos. We supposed to love our family." Tears began to go down Kenneth's face while he looked at Cornelius. "I'm sorry about what I said about Dorothy. I know how you really feel," he said with a labored voice. "You love her, but I still don't know what you should do…pray, follow your heart. You always had a good heart. At least I did see my beautiful nieces. At least they knew their Uncle Cornelius…the good side of me."

"Cornelius…Cornelius?" His half-open eyes appeared lifeless. Kenneth began to shake him desperately, ignoring the background of gunshots and yelling men. He hugged him and wept. As he held his brother, blood-soaked ground. "No! Cornelius!" Kenneth panicked and pulled his body closer to the commanding base as the fighting continued. Kenneth saw the medics approach him while he dragged his body.

"Let's check him," a medic said. The medic shook his head. "He's gone. Son, let us take his body and clean it up."

"I want time with my brother. I just want time with my brother," Kenneth said.

"All right, son, but after some time, we have to fix your arm or you could lose it. I don't think your brother would've wanted you to lose an arm." The medic returned to the medical tents while Kenneth cried, holding Cornelius's body. "God, what are we fighting for?"

The Battle of Camp Allegheny later ended in a draw with both sides taking losses.

The wounded and dead were gathered with Colonel Edward Johnson examining the battleground and shouting, "We will give them nothing!"

Kenneth later went up to Cornelius's dead body with a bandaged arm and stared at his brother. "I'll do what you asked of me," he whispered. "Thank you, brother." During the night, he held Cornelius's blanket unable to sleep, and was unsure of how his family would take the news.

The next day, he fought through depression as he patrolled the area with other men. As he returned to the tents, he saw Colonel Johnson approaching him. "You there, your name is Kenneth Plecker, correct?" Colonel Johnson asked.

He quickly replied, "Yes, sir, it is."

"I heard one of those men was your brother. I'm sorry for your loss, but these are times of war. I heard you continued to fight bravely against the Union. That says a lot about you. Most of the men here are from Virginia, but y'all are from Mississippi. You and your brother are good men to join this company."

He frowned. "What are we fighting for?"

Colonel Johnson's eye widened when he heard his question. "We are fighting to not be bullied by a nigger loving president. We are fighting for our way of life...our rights, and no nigger lover, no Indian lover has the right to take that from us. Stay strong boy, we will win. Avenge your brother and go home a hero."

"Yes, sir." Colonel Johnson walked away as Kenneth watched. "I think we on the wrong side of the fight," he murmured. "God help us."

Several days later, Joseph and Tom were tasked with bringing firewood into the mansion. The cold air motivated the boys to try to work quickly as Bo supervised them. While the boys were entering the mansion with more wood, Joseph heard two men arrive on horseback. He looked back while he stood in the mansion and saw one of the men who looked like a preacher. He walked down the living room hall following Tom. When the boys finished putting down the wood, they went back toward the main entrance and heard Wilma crying.

The boys stopped walking. Bo frowned as Master Plecker embraced Wilma. "No, please God, no, not my baby boy," she cried. The boys slowly stepped into the foyer while they watched her cry in Master Plecker's arms. "I can't...I can't. I need to rest." Master Plecker let go of Wilma, and she ran upstairs wailing.

Dorothy came out of the cookhouse passage and looked at Master Plecker. "Master Plecker," Dorothy sorrowfully said.

Master Plecker turned around, holding a death notification in his hand. "Those Yankees killed my boy," he grievously said. Dorothy's eyes widened as she placed her hands over her heart and began to walk closer to him. "Them damn Yankees killed Cornelius!"

Dorothy slightly exhaled while her eyes shifted from Master Plecker. "Master Plecker, is there anything you want me to do?"

"Bring me some ham slices and bread. I need something to go with my scotch."

"Yes, sir, I do it right now." She immediately returned to the kitchen. Master Plecker moved past the boys while they remained silent. Joseph was shocked by the news and felt bad for the family. Cornelius was not as nice as Kenneth, but he at least knew that if he followed his commands, he would be thanked by the man.

The boys went outside to get more firewood from the wagon and walked past Bo. "Bo, does this mean Master Kenneth is coming home?" Tom asked.

"I don't know. This White man war is ugly...he might keep fighting for Master Cornelius," Bo said. "I never seen Master Plecker look so sad. Y'all be on y'all best behavior. I don't want to see nobody get whipped no more." The boys nodded at Bo and continued to quickly finish their task. The news spread quickly of Cornelius's death, and the slaves were told to setup three large fire pits. The fire pits were made large so they burned throughout the night to represent his love for his three sons. The mourning of Cornelius made Joseph think of his family even more.

Days passed with the war, and Kenneth decided to keep fighting. In Caledonia, the slave tasks dominated the day while Joseph and Tom spent time with Bo repairing farming tools and wagons. The only joy Joseph had was feeding the animals, which reminded him of home. Susie's hair had grown back a little with it reaching the base of her neck. Joseph and Susie continued to talk to each other in Cherokee secretly. When Christmas Day arrived, there was little celebration as the Pleckers' children all arrived at the white mansion. It was a hard time for them with Kenneth off fighting the war and Cornelius's untimely death. Wilma struggled to cope and held Katie's and Sydney's hands half the time they sat at the dining table.

On January 17, 1862, in Tahlequah, the Lightning-Strongman family sat around the supper table eating, with Tsula and Samuel leading the conversations. As the family conversed, Lisa grinned as she looked at Grace. "I'm having another baby," Lisa said in Cherokee.

The family stopped eating and cheered with excitement. "How many months are you?" Tsula asked.

"I think it has been two or three months," Lisa said.

Tsula amusingly replied, "Well, that's not surprising the two of you can't keep your hands off each other."

Lisa and Jacob blushed while the family laughed. Lisa nudged Tsula. "That wasn't funny…saying that in front of the children."

"Don't be so serious. Show your pretty smile." Lisa playfully hit Tsula on her arm again as the family laughed. "I'm sure the baby will be as beautiful as Sunni, but y'all know my Katelyn is the most beautiful, next to her momma," Tsula comically said.

"You would say that," Lizzie snobbishly replied in their language.

Tsula arrogantly replied, "You have no children. You have no say in this."

Lizzie's tone sharpened. "I will have children and even though I don't have any right now, I'll say what I want to say. Go shave your head again!"

The family cackled while Tsula pouted. "I was five years old you short-tempered, wildcat!"

"Enough," Grace humorously said in Cherokee. "Eat! The

two of you can argue about it later. This is Lisa's time. I'm sure more blessings will come to our family." The family went back to talking to each other as George stood up to give Lisa a kiss on the cheek. During the rest of the evening, the family spent time with each other and told stories.

Lisa noticed John was quiet as the children played with each other. She stood up from a rocking chair and approached him. "You look like a lot is on your mind," she said.

"I'm thinking of many things, but I'm happy," he said. "I'm happy for you and Jacob."

Lisa sat down next to him and placed her hand on his shoulder. "Soon we'll be a complete family again. The next time, you'll bring Joseph home and we can move past this terrible time." She rubbed John's shoulder. "Have faith in that. I know that I do."

He looked at her with a half-smile. "It's hard being patient and having faith. I preach it to David, but I'm struggling too. I'm a hypocrite."

"I know you're struggling, but you're not a hypocrite. If we do this right, it'll bring us peace. Look at me, a healed woman filled with life and love." She showed off her dimpled smile. "Through faith, we please the Father."

"Thanks for saying that…the smile does help." Lisa chuckled and playfully hit John on the shoulder. The two cousins continued to talk to each other throughout the night bringing more hope into the situation.

Over a month passed as life on the Plecker plantation seemed to have returned to normal. Wilma had mostly broken free of her season of mourning for Cornelius, and would often read a letter sent from Kenneth. Mr. Plecker started to visit the city hall more often, and became adamant to obtain information on each battle. Joseph and Tom became even more careful to stay on Mr. Plecker's good side as his temperament had worsened. Keeping track of the war was the only way Mr. Plecker was coping with Cornelius's death and Kenneth's absence.

On February 24, 1862, Stella went into labor. Bo paced outside the slave house while Dorothy, and other slave women helped her through the labor. Joseph and Tom continued with their tasks. When the boys returned to the slave houses with firewood, they saw Dorothy speaking with Bo. He anxiously entered the house. The boys walked up to Dorothy and she smiled at them. "Stella is doing well and so is the baby," she said. "They now have a healthy baby boy."

"Can we go inside?" Joseph asked.

"Yes, but make sure you close the door quickly to keep that cold air out."

He replied smiling, "We will." She returned to the mansion to report on the birth of the baby.

Joseph and Tom entered the slave house and saw Stella holding the small baby in blankets. "Y'all can come closer," she said.

They walked closer and looked at the baby while he rested. "He's so small," Tom said.

She smiled. "Well, he won't stay that way for long."

"Do you have a name for him?"

"We gone wait and see what Master Plecker say," Bo said. "I know it be a good name." Joseph looked at Bo as he looked at his son. *I wonder if Bo is okay with Master Plecker naming the baby*, he thought. Though he had no interest in children, he believed the parents or an elder would be the ones to name the child. Not the slave master. It was a painful reminder to him that even at birth, no Negro was free. He thought, *I hope this doesn't make him sad.* Joseph remembered Riza had told him he was being paired with her or Susie.

"What you thinking about Joseph?" she asked.

Joseph smiled at her. "I guess I was surprised it took so long for the baby to come out," he said. "The sun will be going down soon."

"I better start making this stew so we can have some food," Bo said. "Celebrate my good wife, my new son, and good friends. We family here."

Clint entered the slave house. "Well, look at that. Ain't he the tiniest thing," Clint said. "He look like you Bo. I bet he gone think like you too." Bo looked back at him and smiled.

Mary later came inside the slave house excited to see her little cousin. Mary walked up to the baby boy and touched his small hand. "Hi baby. I'm yo big cousin, Mary." Joseph had never seen Mary make such a big smile. It reminded him of when Jonathan was born. When Bo finished making the stew, Master Plecker suddenly came into the slave house.

He greeted everyone and looked at the newborn baby. "Well, good job having a healthy baby boy, Stella," Master Plecker said. "Now…this boy's name will be Saul. He will be a hard worker like his parents, and as a good master, I will bless him as he grows. Well, go ahead and eat. I need you strong tomorrow, Bo."

"Yes sir, Master Plecker. I be ready tomorrow," Bo said. Master Plecker left the slave house, and he brought over the stew so everyone could eat.

While Bo and Clint ate and talked, Joseph noticed a slight frown on Stella's face. *I wonder if she liked the name, or is she scared about him being a slave*, he thought. The questioning gave him even more reason to hope that Riza had devised a new plan so they could escape. He knew he couldn't do it alone, and she was the best at learning about the White men.

On March 13, 1862, spring could be felt in the air with the rising temperatures. Grace, Lisa, and Lizzie went to the supply store to reorganize. Grace and Lisa went outside to check the chicken coops while Lizzie began to reorganize the supply room. Lizzie heard the door open so she walked out of the supply room to see Nancy standing at the counter.

"What do you want, Nancy?" Lizzie asked.

"I see the winter still hasn't tamed your attitude," she bickered.

Lizzie reached for her braid and began to play with it while she approached. "Was that rude of me? I should act like we're in church," Lizzie sarcastically replied. "How are you, Nancy?"

She pursed her lips. "I'm fine."

Lizzie huffed. "You're a terrible liar. It's easy to see you're angry. Let me guess, you couldn't get Paul to come here for you."

She grunted. "Curse this stupid war. The only thing this war has done so far is give my husband a reason to leave and fight."

Lizzie sarcastically replied, "Buck had a choice. He could've stayed home and worked on the farm. I'll agree it is a stupid war."

"Why are you trying to be nice to me? You know we're not on the same side. You are so blinded by love because you have a family with Negro blood. You fail to understand the importance of us winning the war."

Lizzie side-eyed Nancy, "By us, who do you mean? What White man has ever kept their word to us?"

"Slavery is our way of life. Several of our people would be terribly hurt if Lincoln and abolitionists have their way. They'll destroy all that we have for some Negroes." Nancy's head tilted slightly. "I suggest you remember Negroes like Annabelle are uncommon."

"Careful with your mouth…if those White people down South only knew who you really are."

Nancy's voice rose, "How dare you say such a thing! Why is it so hard to understand how much it would hurt my family? They need to mind their own business, and that includes any Cherokee that supports those stupid abolitionists"

Lizzie's mouth curved downward a little forming a frown. "You embarrass me…you and every Cherokee that supports slavery. You're doing nothing but supporting the White man's way." She raised her voice, "My nephew is somewhere out there alone, bound in chains because of White men who stole him from my family! Don't ever question what I understand! Maybe you should return to your White cousins."

Nancy's blazing eyes narrowed. "Maybe John should've thought about that before marrying a nigger!"

Lizzie abruptly slapped Nancy. The echo of the slap was drowned out by the sound of her head hitting the counter. "I'm so tired of you…you hypocrite!" Lizzie quickly moved around the counter, her long braid swaying and her hands tightening into fists. Nancy crawled on the ground. However, Lizzie stopped when she saw the fear in her widened eyes and raised eyebrows. She exhaled and calmly approached her as she covered her head.

"Please stop, Lizzie. I swear I'm sorry. It was evil of them to take Joseph, it wasn't right." She began to cry as she moved her shaking hands over her face.

"Enough, Nancy, I'm sorry too. I shouldn't have done that. We're divided in what we believe, but we are Christian women." Lizzie stuck out her hand and helped her stand up. "I learned from Elder Joyce that it's good for us to have opinions, but we should recognize evil for what it is. Are you able to see the evil slavery is or have you placed your faith into the profits they bring you?"

Nancy was speechless as Lizzie sympathetically looked at her. She walked into the supply room, and came out with two bags of flour. Nancy humbly approached the counter, but stayed out of her strike range.

"I should be a more faithful woman." she half-shrugged. "But what am I to do with Buck? He believes strongly in slavery."

"We change people through love. I know that makes me a hypocrite. I lost my temper, but I'm a better person than I was. It takes time...my anger has always come from pain."

Nancy pulled out her reticule. "How much, Lizzie?"

"Nothing Nancy, I'll carry these to your wagon. I know you can't carry both of them." She grimaced, and she followed her outside. Lizzie placed the sacks on the wagon.

Nancy's driver helped her up the wagon. "I really am sorry about Joseph. He was a sweet boy. I know Annabelle is in a lot of pain. Let's go, Theodore." The wagon slowly rode away, and the women half-smiled at each other.

Lizzie entered the store and took a deep exhale. "Father, I apologize for losing control, but you know she challenges me. I'll try to do better next time." She returned to the storage room. She thought, *A few years ago, I would've killed her. I guess I have improved.*

On March 15, 1862, Joseph sat behind the cookhouse and waited for Susie. She had gotten to hold Saul in Stella's slave house last night but had to return to the slave house to avoid being seen. She snuck over to the cookhouse through the old weeping willows. Joseph saw her come from around one of the large trees. Once she got to him, the two friends gave each other a hug. "I don't have much time. What did you want to tell me?" She said in Cherokee.

He replied in Cherokee, "I had a dream two days ago. We were riding away on horses."

Her eyebrows knit together. "What do you think it meant? Was there more?"

He shook his head. "I heard someone whisper my name. The next thing I remembered was a fire and Riza smiling at me while we rode away on horses. I think Jesus was showing me the future."

"Do you think this will happen soon?"

"I don't know. I couldn't tell how old I was."

"I'll pray on this, and you should too. Heaven has heard us. We will return home."

"Susie, does your momma remember having to go to Indian Territory and leaving Georgia?"

She suddenly frowned while she looked at him. "She's spoken little of it to me. I think it's because it brings her so much pain. My family is small because we lost almost everyone. My grandma, my two uncles, and my momma...they were the only ones to survive it. My momma, lose all of her cousins, her uncles, and her two younger sisters. Did your family lose many?"

"My papa's grandparents all died, his cousin William, and when they stopped, my grandma passed when he was a child. I hate thinking about it to be honest."

"Me too, well I better leave and tell Riza the dream."

"Okay, we will see each other again."

She smiled. "We will see each other again." Excitement began to build up in him even more believing the dream would lead to them figuring out a way to escape. He began to pray more hoping to receive instruction. Susie later told Riza about the dream.

On the early morning of March 16, 1862, Riza awakened, covered in sweat with her hands shaking. She hugged herself and wept silently. *I had another nightmare of him,* she thought. *Jesus please don't let him hurt me.*

While preparing breakfast for the Pleckers, she hid one of the knives in her apron and tried her best not to be alone. She took leftover bread to feed the chickens. She suddenly noticed Rice watching her as he sat on his horse. She could see him smirking, and immediately turned around to return to the mansion. "That man will never touch me," she murmured.

As she stormed into the mansion, Master Kit slowly rode up to Master Rice on his horse. "Now, what you doing Rice?" Kit asked.

Master Rice replied, "Nothing Mr. Kit, a little tired."

Kit shook his head while he looked at him. "Now, you need to keep your eyes away from that girl. See, I can't tell if it's because she makes you mad or because you like the way she walks."

"I'm not thinking about Riza. She ain't important."

"I know you still mad at her because she not scared of you. She always gone be that way. You know it."

"Riza is a grass nigger slave that needs another lesson. Girl is missing one of her fingers, and still talks to me like I'm her equal. I'm tired of the looks she gives me…she isn't nothing."

"You need to think about other things. Keep talking about Miss Tiffany. The last gathering y'all seem to really like each other. It would do you good."

"She could be good for me and give me a son."

Kit looked around to make sure the slaves continued to work, but noticed Rice's blank stare. "Remember what I told you about that girl. Them Indian girls will fight you. They not like White women. She'll leave a mark or more on you. You getting vengeful and I know it."

"I know you seen what I seen. She walks like a woman, got

shape like a woman, and she talk like a crazy one. She needs another reminder of what her role is."

Kit cackled. "See now...boy you letting her walk get to you. She still a girl and you need to think about Tiffany like I think about Theresa. After that, you be fine."

"You know them Indian girls grow faster than White girls. They built that way. I bet Riza could pop out a baby right now if she had been with a man."

"You keep it up and Riza gone get you. You know redskin blood runs strong in her...Kenneth said to leave her be so leave her be. Come on. Let's make sure these niggers work the other fields right. Keep your eyes on what you really want, not that grass nigger."

"I only want break her soul." Master Rice spit on the ground and followed Kit to the other fields to patrol the cotton fields. As they patrolled, Rice kept taking glances at the white mansion.

Later in the day, Riza stood outside while Wilma entertained herself with Judy Mays. She kept her eyes on the overseers. *You all have a schedule*, she thought. *I'll remember it.*

When Wilma walked up to Dorothy requesting more treats, Judy Mays turned to Riza, asking, "Riza, what do you have your eyes on?"

"Nothing, Mrs. Judy Mays," she said.

Judy Mays slightly squinted and the corner of her mouth arched upward. "Okay. If you say so."

She looked at Wilma as she continued her conversation with Dorothy. Riza lightly tapped her foot. *She's smarter than Wilma*, she thought. *I want to believe her.* "I'm jealous of the birds."

"Why is that?"

"Because the Creator provides for them even though they don't farm the land, and they are free."

"I see. We will certainly talk more."

"I look forward to it, Mrs. Judy Mays."

The corner of Judy Mays's mouth slightly lifted as she held back her grin.

Wilma sat down next to Judy Mays and continued their previous conversation.

Riza thought, *I want to trust her, but...I don't know*. That evening, she began to build up the other native children's spirits and, as the days passed, sent messages through Susie. They all understood the next attempt to run away would have to work or it could cost them their lives.

CHAPTER 9
Showdown

On March 19, 1862, the spring winds arrived strongly in Tahlequah, Oklahoma. Annabelle noticed the plant life had bloomed early, and it seemed to have put Lizzie in a good mood. The women decided to close the supply store early and go home to enjoy the weather. While walking, Lizzie sighed and closed her eyes before saying in her native tongue, "I forgot my reticule in the store. I'll catch up."

"Okay, well, hurry up," Grace calmly replied in Cherokee. "If you can time it, we can have rabbit instead of chicken."

"You're right. I can pull off a quick hunt." She hurried to the supply store.

"I'm not sure what makes her happier, the hunt or something else besides chicken," Annabelle said in Cherokee.

"None of us do," Lisa said with a light chuckle.

Lizzie greeted townspeople on her way to the store. From the corner of her eye, she noticed Brock slowly riding down the street but ignored him. After retrieving her reticule, she jogged to catch up with her family. "Miss Lizzie Lightning," he said. She kept walking forward. "Don't be rude now or do you need to be accompanied to speak with me."

She stopped, slowly turned her head, and side-eyed him. "You're a waste of my time," she boldly said. "Do you need to know anything else, Mr. Jackson?"

His jaw unhinged a little. "You still have this inability to show respect."

"Respect is earned and you've killed any possible chance of gaining mine."

"I see all the women of your family have been married off except you. Would you like to know why?"

She scoffed. "Mr. Jackson, you're not one to give relationship advice. And you accuse me of being rude."

His forehead creased. "Your inability to be a lady is one of the reasons you'll never get married."

"Never is a strong word, Mr. Jackson."

"Well, I didn't say a man has never touched you. A few are suicidal. I'm sure there have been a number of redskins in your life. Lisa, certainly knew a man's touch."

Her eyes dilated. "You're a sick man! One of the reasons you'll never see your daughter. I'd send you to hell right now if you didn't have the US government protecting you!"

"We'll have our time, and I'll tame you like I tamed your cousin."

She could feel her heart rate picking up. "You wouldn't be the first man I put into the dirt."

"I'm sure I wouldn't be. You have a confession?"

She cackled. "Confession…to a sinner like you? No thanks, I'm going to enjoy my hunting. We have nothing else to discuss."

His grip tightened on his horse's reigns. "This is the last time you'll speak back to me in this matter! Woman! I'll make sure you know your place in this world. If a man is brave enough to marry you, he'll be in my debt for taming the savage in you."

Lizzie's voice deepened. "We're done here."

She spun on her heel, causing her green cotton dress along with her long braid to sway, and marched away from Brock. "I didn't say we were done." She kept walking past businesses, and he slowly followed her. "Did you hear me?" He yelled. Some of the townspeople started to stare at him, and it forced him to back off. He clenched his teeth while she went down a trail he couldn't follow on horse. "You won't win today. I'll make sure of it."

She arrived at home smiling, retrieved her bow and quiver, and went to the practice grounds. Arriving at the practice grounds, she saw Annabelle and Grace with the girls. "How was school, my little wolf pups," she said in Cherokee. The girls ran to her and she gave all three of them a kiss on the cheek. She watched Annabelle hit a target with an arrow. "You've gotten better, Annabelle."

"Thank you," Annabelle said in Cherokee.

"I'm going to hunt."

Annabelle retrieved the arrow. "Be careful."

"Remember not to take too long," Grace said.

"I won't," Lizzie said. She went down a trail to hunt for dinner. Several minutes went by and she crossed a dirt road to continue her hunt. She looked up at the sun and sighed. "It's been an hour." She moved quickly through the sparse forest and kept an eye out for other predators. Lizzie stomped her foot and began to return home. A few minutes, later a rabbit caught her eye, and she slowly moved toward it. She moved to stay down wind and had her bow half drawn. She turned to aim at the rabbit but she caught an image in her left eye. She felt her heart jump and stopped. *What did I see?* she thought. *I can't lose the rabbit. If he goes down the hill, I won't catch him.* She slowly moved forward using the trees to hide her body. Lizzie took aim but the rabbit ran away. She heard someone pushing through the tallgrass. She quickly looked from the behind the tree, her eyes dilated as she gasped, and she ducked behind the tree. A gunshot was followed by birds scattering from the tallgrass.

"I said you're gonna learn today, Lizzie Lightning," Brock yelled.

"You coward," she yelled.

"How am I a coward? It's you and me. This is what you wanted, isn't it? No worries the shot wasn't meant to hit you…a fair warning. Now come out with your hands up. I will no longer tolerate your disrespect, woman!"

"I'll kill you!"

"Come out! Or I'll take you the hard way."

She ran from one tree to the next. He took low aim, and shot at her foot. She drew her bow and listened. She heard him take a step. She quickly poked from behind the tree, and released the arrow.

His eyes widened. He stepped back to hide behind a tree, but the arrow nipped his nose. "Argh, you redskin squaw!" He took low aim and shot at the tree Lizzie was hiding behind.

"You should've known. I'm not Lisa."

"I'll chain you up." Brock ran to another tree and she took another shot at him barely missing him with the arrow impaling the tree. "You only have so many arrows."

"You only have so many bullets."

A few minutes passed with each daring the other to move. "You know I'm not here to kill you, but you will learn your place today."

"Sounds like you have a lot of anger. I see why your wife keeps leaving you."

He growled and kicked the tree he was hiding behind. Some of the bark fell off, and he looked down at the large pieces of bark. He picked up a piece. "I'll show you anger." He looked at three small logs and sneered. He crunched up the bark in his hand, and picked a log. He threw one log and hit the tree she was hiding behind. He picked up the other log then flung it over the tree. The log came down hitting several branches forcing Lizzie to move while Brock ran to the tree.

Her eyes widened when she heard him running. She moved back to avoid getting hit by the log, slanted her body, and saw he was now within a few feet of her. She released the arrow as he threw the log at her. The log hit her shoulder, and pieces of the bark flew into her face. Simultaneously, she heard her arrow hit him and he fell. He groaned in pain as she hopped back in panic. "Curse you!"

He rolled on his back with the arrow in his upper arm. "I swear I'll make you suffer." He stood up as blood oozed down his arm, pulled out the arrow, and charged Lizzie with his rifle in his other hand.

She panicked and rubbed the tiny pieces of bark out of her eyes. She gasped when her vision cleared and Brock was swinging the stock of his rifle at her head. She lifted her bow and blocked the swing. "You won't win."

"We'll see, woman." He grabbed her arm and hit her back with the rifle's stock. She growled, pulled her arm breaking his grip on her, and hit him in the face with her bow. Blood gushed out of his nose. "Damn you!" He attempted to hit Lizzie again with the rifle, but she stopped it with her bow. He gave her a quick backhand causing her to lose her balance and step back. He aimed his rifle at her arm and fired. The bullet broke the upper body of Lizzie's bow and grazed her shoulder. He gritted his teeth and lowered the rifle at her calf. He pulled the trigger and it clicked. He gasped as his eyes enlarged.

Lizzie lunged at Brock and punched him causing him to fall. "I hate you!" she bellowed. She pulled the rifle away and jumped on top of the fallen man delivering another punch to his face. They rolled around on the forest floor with him trying to overpower her and pin her. Lizzie aggressively kneed him in his stomach, and got back on top of him again. She followed up with several more punches to the tall man's face. He punched her face but she was barely fazed as she punched him in his jaw. He attempted to grab her collar but missed as she stepped back. Her green dress was now speckled with his blood and dirt. Breathing heavily, she picked up her broken bow. "Look at that. You can get color on that skin."

He breathed heavily, his face slowly beginning to swell. "Once I'm done with you, me and Lisa will have a long talk."

Lizzie spit blood on the ground. "Why won't you leave her alone?"

"I never wanted her, but I won't tolerate disrespect, especially from a prairie nigger woman that soiled my pure White bloodline! The only way to correct it is by making sure the girl doesn't grow up a savage, like you."

She shook her head. "You're an abomination."

Brock rubbed his swollen jaw while blood dripped from his lip. "You hit like a man. When this and the war is over, I'll be sure to make you my trophy slave. The niggers won't be the only ones to be dealt with once it's over. You'll be on your knees like a woman should."

"I'll die before I serve you."

His brow lowered as his bloody nose scrunched. "I won't give you the option." She quickly reached back to her quiver for her tomahawk, but he pulled out his revolver from his side holster. He groaned as his arm shook while blood dripped from his wounded arm onto the forest floor. "Now we're going to play a new game." He slowly approached her, and she released the tomahawk's handle. "Still looking at me with rebellion, knowing I can kill you right now. Drop the bow."

Lizzie smacked her lips and reluctantly dropped the bow. "You're like your ancestors…a coward that lies and cheats his way to win. No honor."

He rubbed his busted lip, his eyes filling with more rage. "Go follow your rabbit." He backhanded her with the revolver and she fell back down the small hill with her quiver. She rolled down to the bottom of the hill and landed on her back. She moaned while she held her head. He maliciously approached her with his revolver aimed at her with his other hand pressing on his bleeding shoulder. "I haven't felt this good in some time. I had good times with Lisa but this…is beautiful." He stopped in front of her, and knelt down with the revolver aimed at her chest. "You've lost, Miss Lizzie Lightning."

"You're arrogant…you've won nothing."

"You're a dangerous, sweet trophy. Now, you're going to lay there because that's my command. Today you learn, Miss Lizzie Lightning." He climbed on top of her but she pushed back. He growled, "You fight me and those two girls will be next!"

She squinted. "You're lower than any animal. You're the savage."

He slapped her. "Now your lesson begins, and you'll call me Master." With a leer drawing on his face, he reached up her dress and started to pull down her undergarments. She kept her eyes on the revolver. He finished pulling down her undergarments and put his hand on her breast. "I'll take my time." He looked down to pull down his trousers, but Lizzie quickly grabbed the revolver's barrel and pushed it up.

His eyebrows raised as his eyes bulged. The revolver fired. "Damn you," he yelled. She grabbed his upper throat and held onto barrel of the revolver. The revolver fired again as she turned the barrel sideways. Brock then grabbed the revolver with both hands. Abruptly, an arrow grazed his cheek splitting it wide open.

She turned her head while struggling with the gun. "Annabelle!"

Lizzie tightened her grip on his neck and he gagged. He took his right hand off the revolver and punched her in her eye causing her to lose grip on his throat. Gasping, he barely turned the revolver with Lizzie holding its barrel and shot at Annabelle. She ducked behind a small tree.

"You're not a man!" A bloody-faced Brock looked back at Lizzie. She kneed him in between his legs. He whimpered in pain. She turned the revolver up in the air and it fired again. With her free arm, she elbowed him in the chin, knocking him off her. With one eye throbbing, it partially blurred her vision. She quickly sat up on her knees and pulled her tomahawk out of the quiver. His eyes widened as the sun reflected off of the weapon's blade. Off balance, he tried to quickly stand, but Lizzie swung her tomahawk slicing his backhand. His hand jolted and he dropped the revolver. She roared with rage echoing from her voice and took another swing with her tomahawk.

His jaw unhinged, his eyes widened as he lifted his bloody hands. "No!" She sliced his lower right abdomen and oblique.

"Argh!" he yelped. He and fell back holding onto his side as blood began to coat his torn shirt. His body began to quiver with his vision fixed on a kneeling Lizzie with the now bloody weapon in her right hand. Continuing to hold his wound, he hurried to stand with a loud painful groan.

Squinting with one eye, Lizzie quickly took a step forward but her downed undergarments made her stumble. Brock coughed and tried to run when an arrow abruptly hit the ground barely missing him. He quickly looked up at Annabelle and turned to run away again. "Where do you think you're going?" Lizzie roared as she struggled to pull up her undergarments. "Damn these stupid clothes! Kill him, Annabelle!" Breathing heavily with sweat pouring down his face, he ran up the other side of the hill through the vegetation holding his bleeding side.

Annabelle took another shot while Brock hurried up the hill but missed. Now scowling, she pulled out another arrow from her quiver. She took a deep breath and quickly released it, hitting him on his upper leg. He groaned and fell to the ground "I hit him," Annabelle yelled.

He aggressively pulled the arrow out as he screamed in agony and limped away. "Damn you, nigger!"

Annabelle reached for another arrow but saw she only had one left and grunted.

"Wait for me! I'm coming." Lizzie ripped off her undergarments and forced herself up the hill with one eye still squinting and blood dripping from her lower lip. Breathing heavily, she ran up to Annabelle. "Come on, Annabelle, we can't let him leave," she yelled in Cherokee.

Annabelle pointed through the trees. "He went that way."

"He's going for his horse. He didn't walk out here." Holding her tomahawk, her right hand began to shake. While the women searched for him, Lizzie thought, *I can feel my blood rushing through my body*. "Everything is growing back early. It's making it harder to find him."

"I'm sorry I didn't get a better hit."

"Don't worry about it. Follow my lead in case he has another gun." A few minutes later, the women found his blood trail. They began to move through the forest when they heard branches breaking. Brock's horse suddenly ran onto a dirt trail on their left. "You coward!" The horse quickly galloped down the trail. Lizzie took aim with her tomahawk and threw it. The swooshing axe cut him on his shoulder, but it kept moving through the air. He whimpered, and Lizzie stomped her foot. "Argh! I'll kill you!"

"Where do you think he's going?"

"Back to his rat hole." Lizzie wiped more blood off her swollen face and went to retrieve her tomahawk with Annabelle following. She picked up her weapon and the women went down a trail to their home. "Why did you come out here?"

"I was only going to come out this far. I told Grace I'd take a quick look because you were taking a long time. Lizzie, you're leaving your undergarments." Annabelle's brow lowered. "Was I too late? Lizzie…did he—," Annabelle asked with hesitant tone.

Tears started to trickle down her cheeks. "No." She began to cry with anger etched in her voice. "He tried. He has to die. No more of this."

"Lizzie I—" Annabelle tried to calmly put her hand on her shoulder but she put her hand up to stop Annabelle.

Continuing to walk, she wiped the tears from her face. "You have nothing to apologize for. You and Lisa are really strong to endure what happened to y'all."

"I think you're strong. Not many women can fight off a man like you."

She began to laugh hysterically while she cried. "I really tried to control myself, but…he dies tonight."

"Lizzie."

"No!" Lizzie's aggressive voice echoed, causing a small group of birds to fly away.

The women arrived at home, and Grace was standing on the porch. Her eyes widened seeing Lizzie's reddish eye and the drying blood on her face. Her footsteps embodied her anger as her blooded and dirty dress swayed with her movement. She ran to the two women. "Oh my God, what happened?" Grace asked, frowning.

She broke down in tears. "That animal tried to rape me," she cried.

Grace tried to hug her, but she pushed her back. "Don't hug me!"

Grace's eyes began to well up, and they shifted to Annabelle. "Are you okay, Annabelle?"

Annabelle nodded, saying, "I think so. Lizzie is alive. We hurt him badly."

"Where is Lisa?" Lizzie asked.

"She's in the house," Grace answered.

"I'm taking her bow after we cook supper."

"Wait, Lizzie—"

"No, I'm not negotiating with anyone! He dies today!" Her grip tightened on her tomahawk. "His blood will soak the dirt!" She barged into the house and went into her room.

"We need to tell the others what happened now," Annabelle said.

The women jogged to the fields and told John and the others what happened. The men stopped working and went to the main house to check on Lizzie. Annabelle could feel her heart pacing when they entered the house. Annabelle knocked on her door.

"Lizzie, can we come inside?" Annabelle asked in Cherokee. The silence made her heart drop. She opened the door and Lizzie was gone. "She's not here. Oh Jesus, please." She ran through the kitchen door, followed by John and the others. They went through the backdoor and saw Lizzie cleaning herself off at the well. She deeply exhaled.

John embraced her from behind and kissed her on the cheek. "We'll talk with her," he said in his Cherokee tongue.

The men calmly approached her while she washed the blood off her. "Lizzie, we're sorry about what happened."

Her eyes narrowed, and she took a step forward in her soaked dress. "I'm alive, I'm untouched, that's what matters," she replied. "Isn't it?"

"Come on back to the house," George calmly said in Cherokee.

She let out a sarcastic giggle. "For what?" she said.

"Lizzie," Jacob said.

"I'm killing him," she boldly said while shaking her head. "I'm not negotiating this. He doesn't get away this time."

"We need to make a plan," John said.

She scowled. "I don't believe you."

"Listen to us. He's already hurt Lisa, and we know he was involved in Joseph's kidnapping. It stops now. Let's go together."

"Fine, I'm changing out of these wet clothes." She walked around the men. Annabelle stood beside Grace while she watched her approach the house. "I'm changing my clothes."

She gave Annabelle a kiss on the cheek. "Thank you, sister." She then gave Grace a kiss on the cheek and went inside.

Annabelle looked at John and knit her eyebrows together. "What did y'all say to her?"

His lips pressed. "We're going after him."

Annabelle's eyes widened, and her voice raised. "You're what?"

He put his hands up to his chest. "Calm down."

"John, you weren't there! He almost raped her!"

"We have to go. If we don't we have to tie her down, or she goes on her own. She won't stop."

Annabelle frowned. "Please tell me you're not going to kill him. I hate that man. I know he's involved with Joseph's kidnapping, but killing him will bring us more problems."

John held Annabelle's hands. "We won't kill him," he whispered. "But we have to catch him and bring him to the courts. Lizzie is a Cherokee woman. This is different than Joseph's situation. He won't escape this. We're going after him." The couple embraced each other, and everyone went inside. Lisa became infuriated when she learned about Brock's assault, but being pregnant forced her to remain at home. The family ate supper with the serious silence only being broken by the children. Lizzie ate one plate of food and went into her room.

She came out of her room with her tomahawk and Lisa's bow. "I'm ready," she said in her native language.

"Okay, Lizzie," Eli replied in Cherokee. "Give us a moment to get the horses."

Annabelle felt her chest tighten while Lizzie sat on the porch. A few minutes later, the men got up from the table. "Please be careful," Annabelle said in Cherokee.

"Where are you going, Papa?" Jannie asked.

"To do something important," John answered. "Listen to your Momma. I love you." John gave the twins and Rosita a hug, followed by the other men. The men marched out of the house and got the horses ready.

Eli, George, John, Jacob, and Lizzie rode to Brock's home with the sunset in the background. The closer they got to his home, she could feel her blood boiling over. Within a few hundred yards, they stopped the horses. They scanned the land and saw the horse pen empty. "He may not have come here," Jacob said in Cherokee. "What if he went to the council?"

"We have to check inside," she replied in Cherokee.

John sighed and said, "She's right." Armed, they slowly approached the house and kept scanning the landscape. John carefully looked into the window and turned from it, his brow lowering.

"What is it, John?" Lizzie whispered.

"I don't know." With his rifle, John crept alongside the house, and the others followed. He then crept up to the front door avoiding the one window in the front with George behind him. He suddenly saw drops of blood leading inside the house. He pressed his lips and looked through the front window. He then knocked the glass out of the window with his rifle's stock.

"John, what are you doing?" George said.

John pointed his rifle through the window. "He was here but not anymore," he said. He climbed through the window and opened the front door. Lizzie came around to the front door with the others. "Lizzie, I need you to remain calm."

Her brows furrowed. "Why?" she asked. She quickly marched up to John and stood on her tippy toes, attempting to see over his shoulder. Her eyes widened, and she aggressively brushed past John to enter the house. She began to breathe heavily, her brown eyes scanning the cleaned-out log cabin. "He ran…" Her voice rose to a shriek. "He ran!"

She took her tomahawk out of her quiver. She slowly moved through the empty house, which only had a cast iron stove and a table occupying it. Her grip tightened on her tomahawk as she followed the light blood trail leading to the bedroom. She entered the room and saw all of the drawers of the dresser pulled out, a bed without sheets, and a lamp on a wooden desk. She walked out of the bedroom and stood in the doorpost.

"You demon!" she shrieked. She swung her tomahawk at the

door. She yelled and continued her assault on the door, eventually cutting it in half.

Eli, George, Jacob, and John watched as she let out her frustration.

She approached her family with her eyes now shimmering with tears. "I'm burning it to the ground."

"Lizzie," Jacob said. Her burning gaze shifted on him. Jacob cleared his throat when he noticed her hand slightly swinging the tomahawk. "I'll see if we can find something we can set on fire."

"Wait," George said with a stern tone. "Come here, Lizzie."

She walked out onto the porch and up to her uncle continuing to hold back tears.

"What he tried to do to you was evil. Once your father walked on, you and Grace were no longer my nieces, but my daughters." He placed his hand on her shoulder. "I will not stop you from releasing your anger here, but after this you can't seek revenge. The protection of the family will come first. Is it understood?"

A tear escaped her eye, and she wiped it away. "It is understood, Uncle." She turned around and marched back inside the house. "He left a lamp. I'll use the oil out of it."

George sighed. "Be careful," he said.

Lizzie marched to the bedroom, each of her footsteps echoing anger. The men walked out of the house and continued to cautiously look around. She poured the oil around the house while Eli made a small fire. She exited the house and went to the small fire. Jacob gave her a burning stick, and she returned to the house. She stood in the doorway and tossed the burning wood onto the oil soaked floor. The oil burned and she watched the house catch on fire.

"He can only run so far," John said.

"I hope a cougar catches him," Lizzie said. "I hope it's a slow death." The fire reflected off her eyes while the house burned. "Thank you." She turned around and gave Eli and Jacob a hug. She then walked to Queen, and the men followed her to the other horses. They rode back home while Brock's home burned to the ground. Arriving home, Lizzie saw Annabelle sitting on the porch in a chair. The family put up the horses, and she quickly approached the main house alone. She kept her eyes forward and went by Annabelle without saying a word. She immediately went into her room, closed the door, and locked it. Tears fell from her eyes while she sat on her bed. "I tried Elder Joyce," she cried. Jesus, I really tried. I feel so much hate and anger because of him. I want a hug." She placed her face into her pillow and continued to wail.

At this moment, Annabelle approached the men with a slight frown. "John, please tell me she didn't," Annabelle said in Cherokee.

"Don't worry," he replied. "He ran before we arrived. No food or clothes were left in the house. Where's Grace?"

"She went to Mr. Gross's home to tell him Mr. Jackson tried to rape Lizzie. So he's gone?"

"I don't know, but he won't be returning there."

"Will y'all return later to see if he's returned?"

"He'll have nothing to return to," Jacob said in Cherokee. "She burned his house to the ground. There's nothing but ashes there now."

Annabelle sighed while rubbing her forehead. "We have to keep our eyes on her."

"We will and it'll be better for her to keep working at the store," George said. "The girls are in school and the babies can be watched by Tsula and Maria. There's no reason for her to be alone."

"I agree," John said. "Let's go inside."

The family went inside the main house. Lizzie remained in her room unresponsive to anyone's attempts. Grace later arrived home and told the family Mr. Gross was infuriated with the news. He immediately went to the council to inform them of the incident. He was adamant about the removal of Brock Jackson as the Indian Agent. Annabelle thought, *Finally, we're getting some justice, but will he try to attack us? If he comes onto our land, he'll be killed. He's caused us so much pain. Lord Jesus, please protect and guide us.* Later that night, an irritable Lizzie finally came out of her room. Annabelle had the twins sleep in her room, hoping to nullify her rage. She stayed up half the night replaying in her mind the times Mr. Brown raped her. *I agree with Lizzie. I hope a cougar mauls him. Father, forgive me, but that man deserves no quick death.* Annabelle finally fell asleep with John's arm around her.

On March 24, 1862, Annabelle celebrated her thirty-fourth birthday. For her, it was special because she believed it would be the last birthday she would celebrate without Joseph. She tried her hardest to keep her spirits high. The family was still nervous after Brock's attempted rape of Lizzie. Annabelle noticed David's silence and forced smiles while picking at his food. She also noticed his lack of interest in playing card games which was his favorite. She approached her son and sat next to him at the dinner table. "Are you going to play with them?" Annabelle asked.

"I'm sorry I—" David said.

"There's nothing to be sorry about. It's okay if you don't feel like playing with the girls. What's on your mind, little warrior?"

He half-smiled. "I don't know."

"Yes, you do."

"I'm scared, Momma, and I feel angry. Pa and Uncle George made us plant crops this week instead of going after Joseph. It's warmer now."

"First, we need the crops. Second, be patient. Things are being prepared to bring him home. Everyday your father talks about Joseph. He's uncomfortable too."

"Why doesn't he show it like you?"

"He's trying to keep you and the rest of the family calm, especially with what happened to your auntie. I'm uncomfortable too. I want all of my boys here with me. Please be patient."

"Okay."

"I love you."

"I love you too."

Annabelle kissed him on the cheek. "My little warrior isn't so little anymore. You're almost as tall as your father." She kissed him on the forehead and calmly rubbed the back of his head. "I promise we're going after your brother. Now go make your sisters mad and beat them in cards."

He stood up from the table and entered the living room to play cards with the others. She leaned forward on the table to watch them. Her finger began to lightly tap on the table. "Things will be fine," John said.

She turned her head, and John was standing in the kitchen doorway. "I can feel his impatience, but his anger scares me," she said.

He sat down next to her and put his arm around her. "I'll let David go with us. We'll need some eyes out there while we free Joseph."

"That doesn't bring me comfort."

"Don't worry. Like I said, I'll let him be our eyes. He won't go onto the plantation. That'll be too dangerous. We've had enough excitement."

She sighed. "Okay. Jesus, let this be the end to a nightmare."

John placed his hand on top of Annabelle's hand. "It will be." The couple cheekily hugged and watched the children play.

CHAPTER 10
His Momma's Shadow

SUNRAYS OUTLINED AND WARMED THE Mississippi land on March 30, 1862. A few sparrows flew over a carriage as it went down a road. Judy Mays's blue eyes followed the birds until they were out of sight. The carriage stopped in front of the Pleckers' white mansion, and she exited the carriage. She scanned the cotton field and then walked up to the front door. Dorothy opened the front door, saying, "Welcome, Mrs. Judy Mays."

"Good afternoon, Dorothy," she replied. "It seems we're going to have a warm year. It feels like it's May today."

"Yes, ma'am, it is warm for this time of year."

"Well, let's not keep Wilma waiting. I am a bit late." The two young women walked through the mansion and entered the study. "Oh, she's not here."

"I will go look for her immediately, Mrs. Judy Mays."

"Okay, well, I will take a seat. She must be close and with Riza." Judy Mays sat down on the couch and saw the Bible she had Joseph read still sitting on the coffee table. A few minutes went by with the ticking of the grandfather clock removing the silence from the room. *God, why do I feel conflicted in my heart,* she thought. *All these years later, I struggle with what she did... but if I'm honest with myself.* Her brows lowered as the edges of her mouth curved downward, forming a tiny frown. *I've been struggling with knowing the tru—"*

"Judy Mays!" Wilma said with a welcoming smile.

Her head slightly jerked and she forced a smile. "Hey there! I'm sorry I wasn't able to come yesterday with Daphne. Breanna had a terrible cough."

Wilma dismissively waved her hand. "No worries, dear, your messenger was clear. You're a good momma. I'm happy to have you. She's feeling better?"

"Yes, she is full of energy today."

Riza put down a silver tray carrying a tea kettle and teacups. "Even Riza seemed to have a greater urgency to have things prepared."

Judy Mays looked at her. "Your efforts are appreciated, Riza."

"Thank you, Mrs. Judy Mays," she said.

"Where's Reece?"

Wilma sat down next to Judy Mays, saying, "Oh, she's taking a nap. This whole war has her as worried as I am about Kenneth. She's just calming her nerves. I'm sure she'll be down later." The two women began to converse as Riza stood at attention next to the grandfather clock. Over an hour passed with Judy Mays convincing Wilma to have Riza sit down so she could better serve.

"Besides Riza and Susie, how are those half-breeds doing?" Judy Mays asked.

"They are doing well from what I hear and have been quite obedient. It's impressive how children can even set an example for adults. Of course, we're talking about adult Negros. Those boys are far beyond them, even at their young ages. I even had Joseph brush my horse, Triton."

"Sounds like Joseph has been respectful."

"If it hadn't been for the past incidents, I would've suggested Calvin start training the boy to be a slave driver. However, as you said…he is a rare chil—"

"Well, look who's here," a brown-grayish-haired man said.

Judy Mays froze and felt her heart drop. "Why Mr. Ethan

Brown!" Wilma said slowly, standing up with a large grin. "Sir, you missed my baby boy's wedding."

Mr. Brown replied, "I did, and me and Regina regret it. Speaking of babies, hello, sweetheart."

She now breathed heavily as she looked at her father. "Why in the world are you here?" she blurted.

"Judy Mays!" Wilma said with her eyebrows raising.

"I mean…hello, Papa. I'm so sorry." Judy Mays quickly stood up, walked around the coffee table, and gave her father a hug.

"Oh, there's my sweetheart," Mr. Brown said, giving her a kiss on the cheek. "She's just surprised to see her papa here. It's been far too long since I have spent time with Calvin. He wanted me to come out and said he has something to discuss with me."

"Yes, I did, sir," Mr. Plecker said as he casually walked into the room. "It might be more proper for Judy Mays to tell you, though."

She glared at Wilma with piercing blue eyes, and she struggled to keep a straight face. She let out a weak chuckle and smiled. "Why, Mr. Plecker, you certainly are a man of surprises," she said.

"Why, thank you, Judy Mays, I…" Mr. Plecker's eyes anchored on Riza. "Now Riza, who said you could sit in that chair! What is this—?"

"Calvin, I told her she could," Wilma said.

"Yes, she did and she has served me very well today," Judy Mays said. "Papa, have a seat." She took her father's hand and had him follow her around the coffee table. The father and daughter sat down next to each other on the couch. Smiling, Wilma walked around Mr. Plecker and sat down next to Judy Mays on the couch. "Let's…have a good talk, Papa, before I tell you what Mr. Plecker thought you should know."

"You know I'm always open ears to my little girl," Mr. Brown said.

"Riza, go get my scotch and two shot glasses," he said. "I want to have a nice toast with Mr. Brown before I forget. His presence here is a celebration." Mr. Plecker sat down in a chair and joined in on the conversation Judy Mays was having with her father. The men soon began to talk about hunting. She used the opportunity to ask Wilma to show her the new renovations.

As Wilma began explaining the new renovations, she stopped walking and looked at Riza. "Stay right there, Riza," she said with a stern tone.

Wilma's brows drew together. "Why did you tell her that?"

She answered, "Please walk with me." She marched upstairs with Wilma following her. She stopped at the top of the stairs. "Did you know my daddy was going to be here?"

"Why no, this…this was entirely Calvin's doing. I apologize, Judy Mays. It seems to have you upset."

She put her hands on her hips. "Of course, I'm upset I…I don't need more pressure in terms of Joseph."

"Judy Mays, I understand you're still uncertain if Annabelle is his mother, but what harm is there in you telling your daddy?"

"I feel better knowing without a doubt that Joseph is her son. My daddy will jump without a second thought. He will ruin my chances of bringing Annabelle back here."

"You should trust him."

"I do…but I want Joseph to trust me. My daddy's impulses would ruin my efforts."

"Well, that's all you had to say dear. I mean, you know men… they go with action first and then they think about it. My only question is, how much more proof do you need?"

"A bit more time is needed."

"As I said before, I have no problem with it. You know Calvin is very loyal to your father. I should've known that any new clue of Annabelle Brown would open up his ears."

"As I said, I need my daddy to stay out of it."

"Understood. Making sure Riza doesn't hear this makes it clear you're worried what information would get back to the boy."

"Yes, well…speaking of Riza, I'd rather not increase her interests by being up here and talking in secret." She quickly marched downstairs.

"Judy Mays, I can't go down the stairs that quickly." Wilma slowly began to follow her. Once she got to the bottom step, she calmly walked up to Riza. "I appreciate your obedience, Riza. I want you to do something"

"Of course, Mrs. Judy Mays," she said.

"Bring Joseph to me." Riza raised an eyebrow. "I'm sure by the time this day is over, you'll have questions for me."

. "Judy Mays, it always amazes me how you can still move up and down these stairs like a young child, Wilma huffed.

"Go on, Riza, and be quick about it," Judy Mays said.

"Wait, what is she doing?"

"She's bringing Joseph to me."

Wilma's brows lowered. "Are you sure? Especially considering what you want."

"Please trust in what I'm doing."

"Of course, I trust you, dear. Riza, go get the boy quickly."

Riza rushed out of the mansion to the cotton fields. Judy Mays and Wilma stayed in the foyer. Judy Mays slowly paced the floor as the minutes went by. Riza entered the foyer with Joseph behind her. He began to take off his shoes. "Keep your shoes on, Joseph," she commanded. She looked at Riza as she quickly approached Joseph. "Thank you, Riza. Joseph, you're to walk with me."

"Judy Mays," Wilma said with panic trickling in her voice.

"Please, a moment." She put her hand on Joseph's back, coaxing him to her carriage. "Get in the carriage."

"Mrs. Judy Mays, I—" Joseph said.

"Do as you are told. I know your momma raised you to do as you're told!" Joseph got into the carriage and sat down. Judy Mays was about to close the door.

"Judy Mays," Mr. Brown said with an echo.

Her eyes shot open. Time seemed to have stopped as her father's voice echoed in her head. Her eyes then anchored onto Joseph. She saw fear building in his brown eyes. "Don't move... don't say a word," she whispered. She closed the carriage door and turned around to see her father approaching her. "Hey, Papa."

"Were you about to leave?"

She forced a smile and playfully cocked her head. "No, no I...I just thought I left something in my carriage." Her eyes quickly drifted to Wilma, who was watching on the porch, and back to her father. "You wanted to speak with me."

He looked over his daughter's head. "Is there someone in the carriage?"

Her eyebrows raised. "No."

His brows drew together. "What's going on with you? It feels like you want to say something, but you keep avoiding it."

"Papa, I—"

"If it's about Edgar not going to war…I understand, but I do expect him to continue to uphold our laws. He can't be passive on this."

"Papa, it's been so much on my mind." He took a step forward around her. She immediately stepped in front of him. "Papa, please."

"You've always been a clever girl. Calvin says there was a discovery that I should discuss with you. He hinted it had to do with runaway slaves."

She gulped as her face went blank. "Can you please walk with me?"

"Of course, like I said, I know I was harsh on Edgar, but you're my little girl. What did you want to talk about?"

"I want to show you over here." Judy Mays grabbed her father's hand and marched over to the main dirt road leading to the cotton fields. She could still feel her heart beat heavily as she pointed out to the fields. "I've been observing the Pleckers' structure of slave ranks, and I believe this has prevented them from having any recent runaways."

"With the exception of that crazy fire Riza set. You know, I would've had her beat within an inch of her life, but I do agree with Calvin. Killing her would signal weakness and be the loss of a valuable slave. I was told Riza and Susie were the only full-bloods, and the other two were half-breeds. I want to see them."

She scoffed and looked away from her father. "There's no reason for you to see them both, and you know what the half-breeds look like."

"However, that's what Calvin said you wanted to talk with

me about. That's what the discovery was, especially one of the boys."

"Papa—"

"I like the idea he's planning to bring to fruition. Training them to be the slave drivers of those field niggers. In turn, he creates loyalty while maintaining authority. Do you disagree with this?"

She looked at him and said, "Well, no…but there's no need to see them both. I mean…oh, there's Tom." She pointed at Tom as he walked to a wagon. "Now the other one looks just like him. That I swear to you."

Mr. Brown crossed his arms. "Why do you feel the need to swear to me?"

"I…well, I know you're looking to improve things and prevent another tragedy, I—"

"You mean Annabelle." He shook his head. "We will find her, and I will teach her a lesson!"

Her eyes dilated as her nose flared. She bellowed, "No!"

He uncrossed his arms, and his brows lowered. "Judy Mays, she—"

"I don't care anymore. I only want her back here alive. It's all that matters…not her being punished…not her being made an example."

Mr. Brown's voice raised, "Judy Mays, I will not tolerate her actions! She will—"

Her voice rumbled, "She is mine!" She pointed at him. "If anyone should be angry at her, it's me! I cared for her! I begged you to have her brought back to the mansion! She was special to me, and she ran!" She pounded her open hand on her chest. "I am a momma! She has no idea that I'm a momma, and she's missing! So, no! I don't want anything done that will cause her to run again! I already have Ruthanne to thank for helping her run. Don't you dare put yourself on that list because she embarrassed you."

Mr. Brown looked down at her. "You've always had fire in you, but you best remember your place in this. I know you want

Annabelle back, as do I. I've already sent out a detective to hunt her down in Missouri. We will see what comes of it."

"You what?"

"Out of love for you, I will spare her, but when she's brought back here, she stays with me."

Judy Mays's jaw unhinged. "Papa."

"I will not have the voices of women in my ear on this."

"But, Papa—"

"There is no discussion here. I will not hear it from you or your sisters. Maybe I will give her to you as I promised years ago, but she's not escaping this." She pouted, crossed her arms, and looked away from her father. His thin lips tightened. "I see it now…Riza reminds you of Annabelle, doesn't she?" She deeply exhaled, continuing to look away from her father. "You know better than to let a prairie nigger too close to your heart. Somehow you keep allowing yourself to grow attached to the lesser."

Judy Mays side-eyed her father. "Whoever said I did."

"I know my little girl. You can become quite vicious protecting the ones you like. You've simply learned how to hide it better. However, I do appreciate you bringing up how they do things here. Can I give my little girl a hug, or do I have to wait for me to leave?"

Judy Mays glanced at her carriage and frowned. She cleared her face and turned to her father with open arms. "I love you, Papa."

Mr. Brown hugged her, "I love you too, sweetheart." She continued to talk with him and returned inside the mansion with him. Over an hour later, he left the plantation with Mr. Plecker.

While Wilma went out to the patio with Dorothy, Riza went with Judy Mays. "Riza, I want you to wait here," she said.

"Yes, Mrs. Judy Mays," Riza said.

She approached her carriage and calmly opened the door. "Hello, Joseph," she said.

"Hi, Mrs. Judy Mays," Joseph quietly said.

She looked at her driver. "Leroy, please help me up."

"Yes, ma'am," he said and helped her step inside the carriage.

"We won't be going anywhere. We're having some time alone."

He nodded. "Yes, ma'am."

Judy Mays looked at a frowning Joseph. "I know you're probably confused, but I want you to know you're not in any trouble. I had you sit here because…an angry man came here. This angry man doesn't like children your age."

"Is that why you didn't have Tom sit here too?" he asked.

She smirked. "Why yes, it is. You're very smart for asking me that."

"Is the angry man your papa?"

She leaned back. "No. He's…he's a man I don't know. A man I never want to know. I did want to make you feel better about being alone." She pulled out four sugar cookies from her dress pocket. "These are for you."

His eyes widened. "Really?"

"I think you'll find I'm not a liar, Joseph. I may hold back information, but I'm not a liar." She handed the cookies to him, and he smiled.

"Thank you, Mrs. Judy Mays!" He began to eat one of the cookies and continued to smile.

She stared at his smile and she felt her brow lower. *Every time I see you, I see her*, she thought. *Jesus, why do you challenge my heart?* She smiled back at him, saying, "My goodness, don't eat so fast. I'm sure your momma taught you better." He paused and began to chew more slowly. "You're going to continue to be obedient here, aren't you?"

"Yes, ma'am. I promise."

"Joseph, I know you miss your family, but this is why I tell you to be obedient. So you do have the chance of seeing them again."

"Mrs. Judy Mays, have you been away from a family member? Or away from someone you love?"

She felt her left eye become watery. "You remind of…you remind me of my younger self in some ways even though you're not White. I do know how it feels to love someone and not know how they are doing. Sometimes the pain and sadness can turn into anger. I know it's painful, but I know you're strong enough to endure it."

"Endure means to be patient?"

"You're so smart, Joseph. It does mean to be patient, but be patient while suffering or being uncomfortable because this is only one chapter of your life. You have a whole book to write. Never forget that."

Joseph grinned. "I won't." He finished eating the cookies as she watched. "Mrs. Judy Mays, can I pray with you?"

Her brows drew together. "Pray about what?"

"Is the person you love still away?"

She sighed. "The person is."

"Okay, I can pray for your person to return, and you can pray for my family."

She put her hand out. "Okay, I'll do that for you." He held her hand, and he prayed for her, and then she prayed for him. *What am I going to do with you*, she thought. Judy Mays then let Joseph out of the carriage, and he went back to work.

She walked up to the mansion toward Riza. "You're interesting, Mrs. Judy Mays," she stated.

She side-eyed Riza, replying, "I've had enough excitement for the day. Come on before Wilma starts complaining."

"Can I ask what you talked about with Joseph?"

"Riza, surely there is something else on your mind."

"I'm not sure if your answer has changed."

Judy Mays stopped walking and glared at the bold teenager. "I will speak with Wilma about your momma. You do deserve to know the truth."

Riza's face began to scrunch up. "And what about him?"

Her nose crinkled. "It's not that simple and you know why?"

"If you had the power, would you free him? Or any of us?"

"You test me, Riza. Come on." She began to storm off.

Riza's brows furrowed as her tone deepened, "Mrs. Judy Mays."

She turned around, scowling. "You be careful with your tone, Riza. He doesn't deserve to be a slave. That's my answer. Now come on." Riza huffed and followed her outside to the patio. She spoke with Wilma for a little bit of time before she went home, thinking of the different choices she needed to make.

CHAPTER 11
Dangerous Pride

THUNDER SHOOK THE SKIES, AND strong rain covered the land on April 01, 1862, in Tahlequah. While David watched the storm, he had flashbacks of him and Joseph playing in the warm rain. He heard the girls laughing and walked into the living room. He saw the twins and Rosita braiding each other's hair. The innocence of the girls made David smile as he watched them interact. His smile dropped as he thought, *What if they had kidnapped one of the girls?* His brows furrowed. *I promise to protect everyone. I'm tired of waiting.* He marched out to Annabelle's house in the rain. When he entered the house, he saw Annabelle, John, and Eli sitting at the supper table talking. "Pa, when are you planning to leave Tahlequah?" he asked in Cherokee as he approached the table.

"We're planning to leave in a few days," John said. "Calm down, son. We're making plans right now with the map we have. We have to make sure we're avoiding the war too. Things are different now."

"I think this is taking too long," he bickered. "What promise do we have they haven't broken his spirit? I'm afraid he won't be the same if we wait any longer."

"David, your brother will never be the same," Annabelle said with a worrisome tone. "It will take time for your brother to heal. Some people take a long time. Come here." He moved around the supper table and stood before her. She held David's hand while he looked at her. "I feel your anger, and I understand it, but please trust your father's judgment. He's not enjoying this... he wants your brother home too."

"David, we'll talk about this some more tomorrow," John said with a stern tone. "We need to finish making plans to make it to Caledonia. I'm sorry if I appear not to be worried." He calmly let go of Annabelle's hand and left the house in the rain.

"Time is testing him," Eli said in Cherokee. "I think it's good for him to come with us. Luke and the others can protect our home if Mr. Jackson tries something."

"John, you didn't tell him that you want him to come with you two?" Annabelle asked.

"David must learn patience so he can learn his anger won't bring him the answers he wants," John answered. "We're leaving tomorrow. He can survive for one more day." She stared at him, her eyes narrowing. "I promise I'll wake him in the morning, and that will be the first thing I tell him."

"I don't like this," She said with agitation etched in her voice. "Did you see the look in his eyes? He wants to fight."

"He may get his chance when we arrive in Caledonia."

Annabelle grunted, stood up from the wooden table, stormed into their bedroom, and slammed the door behind her.

Eli looked over at John and sighed. "I guess you're sleeping in the rocking chair tonight," Eli said.

He replied in their language, "No, I'm sleeping in the twins' room."

Eli grimaced. "You know she'll kick you out of their room. You know you're sleeping in a rocking chair tonight." He exhaled and took a sip of water from his cup as Eli lightly chuckled.

Later in the night, a frustrated David went into his room and listened to the girls talk to Tsula and Lisa. As he sat in his room, his eyes shifted to the tiny rectangular wooden box. *For a month,*

I thought about what I needed to leave, he thought. He pulled out a sheet of paper from the box. *It's good I thought about making a copy of the map. I'm coming, Joseph. It's a good thing I broke into Mr. Jackson's home for ammunition when he was patrolling. I know I can bring him home.*

David later took a short nap and woke up when his family had fallen asleep. He put on his clothes and quietly rushed out of the family house after leaving a note on the dinner table. He hurried to the barn, where he placed supplies on Big Boy and placed his rifle on the horse. He put on his quiver and marched out to the practice fields with the light of the full moon lighting his path. He reached behind the loose bark of one of the large trees and pulled out extra arrows he had made in his spare time. He put the arrows in the quiver and went to Annabelle's house. When he slowly opened the door, his eyes bulged when he saw John sleeping in one of the rocking chairs. He crouched and crawled on the floor to the twins' room, where they and Jonathan slept. He softly touched Jonathan's forehead and gave Jannie and Rain a kiss on the cheek.

He took Joseph's bow and quiver that were sitting next to the stove, and quietly left the house. When the door quietly closed, John was startled by the wind. He quickly went to check on Annabelle and went to the twins' room. "I think I'm losing my mind," John said.

He walked out of the twins' room and went past his bedroom. "John," Annabelle moaned. He slightly opened their bedroom door and looked at Annabelle as she lay in the bed with her eyes closed. "Come to bed. I hear you walking around." He groggily entered the room and got into their bed. She gave John a kiss on the cheek, and the two went to sleep.

During this time, David returned to the barn where Big Boy was waiting. He approached the large horse and placed his head on the horse's head. "We're bringing Joseph home, Big Boy," David said in Cherokee. He rode off into the night with moonlight casting over the landscape.

The next morning, Lizzie awoke and stretched as she left her room. Slightly dazed, she stood in her doorway and was about to enter the kitchen when she saw the letter on the supper table. She picked up the letter and read it. She panicked and first ran to the barn. "David!" She shouted. "David, where are you?"

Lizzie's echoing voice awakened most of the family. John ran outside and saw her looking around and following the horse tracks. "What's going on?" he asked in Cherokee.

She ran to him with the letter in her hand and shouted, "David left! He's gone after Joseph!" His heart dropped as she placed the letter on his chest. "We have to go after him now!"

John rushed inside his house, and as he did, he saw a few small tracks of mud leading to the twins' room. John ran past his bedroom and opened the twins' door. He looked down at the ground and saw a small trace of mud. He looked at the girls and Jonathan while they slept. "He came in here to see them last night," he murmured in Cherokee.

Annabelle left their bedroom. "John, what is it?" she asked.

"David left early this morning to go after Joseph."

Annabelle gasped.

"I have to leave now. There's no telling how much time he has on us. The moon was full that means he could ride through the night." He walked past Annabelle and began to put on his clothes. He then rushed over to Eli and Grace's home riding Ray and told them the critical situation. Eli got onto Ray with John and rode to Victoria's home to get another horse. They rode back to the Lightning-Strongman farm, where Lisa had already gathered Queen and Cari.

The men got off the horses and approached Lisa. "We only need Queen, Lisa," John said in Cherokee.

"No, I'm going with you," Lizzie said. He turned around and saw she had put on a brown blouse and brown trousers. She put her hair into one braid and had her new bow and quiver with her.

"Lizzie—," Eli said.

Her voice roared, "I'm not arguing with either one of you! I'm going!" Lizzie got onto Queen and looked at the men with a blank stare. "I have no children and I want my nephews home. If I don't return, I've left no one behind." John sighed as she rode the horse to Grace's house.

The men put the two horses on the carriage quickly and made sure they had their supplies. At this time, Lizzie took extra arrows from Grace's quiver to make sure she had enough adding her count to fifty arrows. "We have everything. Let's go," Eli said.

John went up to Annabelle. The twins stood next to her. "Papa has to go, but I will return with your brothers," he said. The twins gave him a hug while Lizzie slowly rode up on Queen. She got off the horse and the twins ran to her and gave her a hug. "I'm sorry I didn't listen to you."

A tear went down Annabelle's face, but she wiped it away. "Bring home my boys," Annabelle said in Cherokee. "The past is the past. Bring them home." She kissed and hugged him. "I wish I could go with you."

"I won't fail. This is the last time." He got onto the carriage with Eli and Lizzie got back onto Queen.

"I will catch up. I have to do something important," Lizzie said. John nodded and the men rode off. Annabelle's eyebrows slanted upward and she frowned. She slowly rode up to Annabelle. "I do want you to come, but it'd be stupid," Lizzie said. "The White men wouldn't care if you were born a slave or not."

Annabelle replied, "Yeah, you're right."

"Have the girls make more arrows in case there are problems while we're gone. There are only twenty arrows left right now."

Lizzie rode off down a different path than John and Eli. She arrived at the Scott plantation. Nancy heard Lizzie arrive and came out of her home nervously. "What do you want, Lizzie," Nancy humbly asked.

Lizzie answered, "I need to speak to Paul right now."

"I just saw him. Paul, please come out here," Nancy yelled.

He came from around the house and approached the women, carrying a small black bucket. "What can I do for you, Mrs. Nancy?" Paul asked.

Nancy replied, "Lizzie wishes to speak with you quickly."

"Good morning, Miss Lizzie," he cheerfully said.

She replied, "Hi, Paul. David left the family last night to go after Joseph, so I'm leaving with John and Eli right now."

"I can go with you."

"No, you would bring us more unwanted attention because you're mulatto."

Paul's brows lowered, and his mouth curved downward. "You right."

She sighed with a low growl. "It's you're right." She could see the embarrassment in his eyes and quietly exhaled. She stepped up to him and locked eyes with him. "I've often found it difficult to open myself to people. I find it easier to push people away. I've gone through so much, but I'm ready to leave the past in the past. You scare me, Paul…your kindness and good heart scare me because it makes you easy to trust."

"I'm sorry if I did something disrespectful to you, Miss Lizzie," he calmly said.

"You've always been respectful to me. You always try to make me smile. Always try to make sure I don't feel alone. Maybe one day I'll make you smile." She gave him a hug, and he hugged her back. She stood up on her tippy toes and gave him a quick kiss on the cheek. Paul's eyes shot open, and Nancy's jaw unhinged and her eyes bulged. "Now you know how I feel. If I don't return, you don't have to question how I feel about you. We will see each other again," she said in Cherokee.

Lizzie quickly mounted Queen. "Bye Nancy." She rode off to catch up with John and Eli.

"What did you do for her to like you?" Nancy asked.

"I did what the good Lord said to do," he said. "Love people, even the ones that don't want to be loved." Nancy patted Paul on the back and walked back into her home.

Lizzie caught up with John and Eli. "You said what you needed to say," Eli asked in Cherokee.

Lizzie replied in their tongue, "Yes." She reached into one of her sacks and pulled out two pieces of cornbread. "Here, eat so we have energy." Lizzie gave the two pieces to John and Eli.

A week passed while the Cherokee made their journey to Mississippi. Lizzie would ride ahead and scout because of the carriage's limited speed. However, it seemed to not be enough to catch up with David. On their way to Mississippi, they came across horse tracks going in the same direction, but they couldn't determine if they were Big Boy's tracks, forcing them to move on faith.

David rode through the countryside, determined to reach Joseph. One day he stopped in a small forest surrounded by tallgrass. He rested against a large elm tree in a wooded area while Big Boy ate. He ate a piece of jerked chicken and watched the clouds slowly move. He frowned and thought, *Was I selfish to leave like that? I can't return home without Joseph.* He then scanned the land for Confederates. *I can't win against a platoon,* he thought. *I have to keep my eyes open.* Everywhere he rode, he kept his quiver on his back and his bow and rifle within quick reach on the side of Big Boy. When he arrived in Arkansas, a powerful storm arrived. He pitched a tent with three arrows. He stuck the three arrows into the trunk of a large tree and stretched out buck hide over the three arrows to keep himself and Big Boy mostly dry. Impressive lightning bolts lit up the sky, and he sulked. He looked at Big Boy and said, "Maybe I should've kept asking Papa to let me join him." Big Boy nickered, and he petted him. He knelt down and prayed, "Jesus, please guide me. I only want my family to be reunited and free." The next day, David continued his journey. However, as the days passed, he started to doubt his abilities because the search for him was taking longer than he expected.

On April 10, 1862, in Caledonia, Dorothy cleaned Kenneth's room. She opened up the closet and stared at one of his shirts. She exhaled, walked to the balcony window, opened it, and looked at the birds. *I remember when we were younger, we'd watch the birds out here together,* she thought. *I hope we get to watch them again.*

"What are you doing?" Reece asked.

Dorothy pouted but straightened her face before turning around. "Mrs. Reece, I was looking at the birds," she said. "I'm done here now and on my way to the other rooms."

She was about to walk past Reece, but she placed her hand on the doorpost blocking Dorothy's path. Her tone dripped with suspicion. "You looked like you were doing more than watching birds. What else were you doing?"

Her nose slightly crinkled. "Nothing, Mrs. Reece."

She glared at Dorothy and lowered her arm. "Do you miss my husband?"

"Yes, ma'am, I do miss him. Do you miss him?"

"You'd be wise not to test me today. I already have to deal with Judy Mays later today." Her voice deepened, "Those hazel eyes still can't hide your intolerance of me. Get out!"

Dorothy strolled past her and began to walk to the other bedrooms. "You look good for having two children."

She stopped walking and slightly turned around.

"I can admit it. I hope I look as good, if not better than you when I give Kenneth children…and yes, I do miss him. Now get back to work."

Dorothy's lips tightened, and she quickly went to work in the other bedrooms.

Later in the afternoon, Judy Mays and Daphne arrived at the Plecker plantation. The women met with Reece and Wilma and sat on the patio. While the women talked, one of the main topics of their conversations was the war. Daphne had already lost two of her brothers, and Judy Mays's older sister Genevieve lost her husband. She was adamant the war could have been prevented. Riza listened intently as she voiced her opinion. Reece quickly rose against her stance claiming the only non-Whites that showed any constructive intelligence were some Indians, half-blood Indians, and mulattos. Reece vented her frustrations about Dorothy believing she was too close to Kenneth. Wilma spoke to defend Kenneth's treatment of her increasing Reece's frustration. She grinned as she listened to Reece's frustration and jealousy. "I've seen this before and I find it entertaining," Judy Mays said.

"Judy Mays," Wilma barked.

She replied, "I will say this…Kenneth is a good man, and it should make you proud that he would even keep his word to a mulatto. Those are the actions of a Christian man. Now if there's something or was something more between them you certainly won't learn it from Dorothy. She's like Riza." She glanced at Riza with a slight smirk. "Her mind can't be controlled like the rest of these slaves and it bothers you."

"I don't want to talk of this anymore," Reece whined and slapped her thigh.

"Calm down, dear. Judy Mays, what do you truly mean about there being something more between my son and Dorothy?" Wilma asked.

"What Reece fears, of course, is that they were more than friends," she unapologetically said. "It's no secret some White men like caramel."

Daphne's and Wilma's jaws dropped.

"We simply ignore it." Reece stared at her with her furious blue eyes and grimaced like she had bitten into a lime.

Wilma pointed at Judy Mays. "I know my son and he's a good boy. He's never touched that mulatto girl or any of these niggers. Dorothy is a good slave and those two girls she produced were from that weasel Geoffrey having his way with her. I'll have nothing more of this!"

Judy Mays slightly frowned. "My apologies Wilma, I didn't mean to upset you."

"Your apology is accepted, dear. Now, Reece, their friendship is a reflection of my mistake. Dorothy worked hard when she was a child to help Kenneth fight his sickness. The girl worked without being told steps, and I must admit, I was impressed. I can't change the friendship created in that moment in life. It will only change when Kenneth is ready to assume more command over Dorothy. I doubt that means he'll never show her favor."

Reece pouted while she listened to the women's advice. Water started to build up in her eyes. "Wilma, even though we won't be leaving for a while, I would like see Joseph before we go," Judy Mays said.

"Of course, the boy has been doing a good job from what I hear. Calvin is certainly thinking of the possibility of making him a slave driver. The boy is good with the animals and is learning how to fix things quite well. Riza, go tell Dorothy to come out here while you go and get Joseph from the fields."

"Yes, ma'am," Riza said as she left to get him.

"Are you sure it's good to let her go on her own?" Daphne asked.

"I'm timing her right now. She's been quite well behaved the past few weeks," Wilma said. "Have some faith, Daphne."

Dorothy quickly went out on the patio and served the women their crackers. She stood at attention while the other women talked. Judy Mays noticed the obvious tension between Dorothy and Reece when she served them. A warm wind slightly picked up causing Dorothy's soft frizzy hair to blow with the wind. The shining sun also made it easier to see her hazel eyes. Judy Mays leered and said, "You must have the prettiest eyes I've ever seen on a mulatto Dorothy."

Dorothy blushed, saying, "Thank you, Mrs. Judy Mays."

"You're welcome. I enjoyed your daughters' cheerful welcome. They must bring you a lot of joy."

"They do, ma'am."

Judy Mays slightly looked over at Reece who was staring at Dorothy while scowling. "Well, as a mother, I always say the children are the reflection of the parents. You've done well. I think Mrs. Wilma has been right to speak so highly of you." Wilma smiled at Judy Mays.

Suddenly, Riza came into view toward the patio with Joseph. "Ah, there they are and in proper time," Wilma said. "Dorothy, you're dismissed."

She replied, "Yes, Mrs. Wilma."

She went past the women when Reece quickly stuck her foot out tripping Dorothy. "Yes, a cute face, but clumsy," Reece snobbishly said. Reece leered at her with a raised eyebrow. Dorothy stood and wiped off her blue cotton dress.

"Do be careful, Dorothy," Wilma said. "I'd hate to explain to Master Plecker you're unable to work because of a fall."

"I'm sorry, Mrs. Wilma," she said. She briefly narrowed her eyes at Reece, and walked back to the white mansion.

"Here they are," Judy Mays said. "I see you've grown an inch or two, Joseph."

"Yes, I have, Mrs. Judy Mays," he said.

"I wasn't surprised to see Riza had grown a few more inches because of her age, but I guess it's to be expected for you too. I hear you've been well behaved since our last talk."

"Yes, ma'am, I have."

She grinned. "Is there anything more you would like to tell me about your family before you came here?"

Daphne scoffed, "Why do you even bother, Judy Mays."

"One day they'll bring me home," he said.

"You still believe that," Judy Mays said, her brows lowering. "How interesting…do you get that spirit of hope from your momma? I guess her smile isn't the only thing she gave you." Joseph's eyes widened and he gulped. "I suppose the good Lord has a way of giving children the good characteristics of their parents to them."

"I see nothing good. Just a half-breed slave," Daphne bickered.

"Quiet Daphne! You won't put your sorrows onto this slave," Judy Mays said with an authoritative tone. "We're all saddened by your loss, but you won't take it out on this child." Daphne remained silent and sipped her tea as Joseph and Riza stood next to each other. "I expect great things out of you. Do we have an understanding?"

"Yes, ma'am."

"Perhaps…another talk over some sugar cookies." Judy Mays dismissively waved her hand playfully. "We have no need for butter cookies. Blah." He nearly cracked a smile. "You see, nothing to fear, little Joseph. Well I'm satisfied with this Wilma. Riza can take him back to work, if you wish."

"Yes, well this is a busy time of year," Wilma said. "Joseph, go back to work."

He replied, "Yes, Mrs. Wilma. Goodbye, Mrs. Judy Mays."

"Try to have a good day, Joseph. We will talk soon." He nodded at Judy Mays, and the others before returning to work with Riza escorting him.

"Hmph, Riza likes the boy," Reece said.

"They like each other…well, this was interesting," Judy Mays said. "It seems he fits in quite well here, Wilma."

She cheerfully replied, "As I told you, he's become valuable here. I wish we had more half-breeds like him or a few more Indian children. I'm honestly quite fearful of going outside of my home one day and seeing nothing but empty fields. We must keep things the same or it'll ruin the South."

Judy Mays sipped her tea. "Yes, I think change would be quite the shock to many families." *I can't get her smile out of my head*, she thought. *A final decision needs to be made on Joseph soon. Who knows what will happen if Papa visits here again.*

Later in the afternoon, Daphne and Reece had Riza and Susie walk around with them carrying small woven baskets while they collected the wildflowers that bloomed.

Judy Mays remained with Wilma. "Today truly is a good day. I did want to receive clarity on something."

Wilma's brow raised. "Clarity on what?"

Judy Mays sighed and folded her hands while Wilma sipped more tea. "Riza's momma…I want to know more."

Wilma's green eyes shot open, and she put down her teacup. "I see. Well, if there is more to that story. A brutal story it is."

"I'm all ears."

In the late afternoon, Wilma gave her goodbyes with a large grin as Daphne and Judy Mays rode away to Columbus. Joseph watched thinking about what Judy Mays said about his mother. He was almost tempted to ask Judy Mays what his mother was like as a child, but knew he couldn't.

On April 12, 1862, David passed Memphis, Tennessee and stopped in the wilderness of southwest Tennessee to rest and eat. The moment David was about to untie the reins from a tree, he heard a branch break. Three White men walked from behind one of the large trees. David recognized that none of the men were Confederate soldiers, but remained cautious of them. "What you doing out here boy?" a beardless man asked.

"I'm on my way home," David said.

"Who's horse is that?" a short man asked.

He boldly replied, "He's mine."

"A horse like that…who you trying to fool boy?" a blue-eyed man asked. "Now, where did you get the horse?"

"He is my horse," David bickered. "He's been in my family since I was a small child."

"You best watch your mouth boy. Like you said, you not at home," the beardless man said. "What you think, Obadiah?"

"Obadiah replied, "I think we got ourselves a horse thief, Jesse." Obadiah pulled out his revolver, and David quickly pulled his rifle off of Big Boy. Obadiah took a shot, missing him as he slid behind a tree. Big Boy stood up on his back legs and neighed while the White men stood back. "Gilbert, keep them blue eyes open. You know what we do to horse thieves, boy? We hang 'em."

David yelled, "He's my horse, you crazy White man."

Obadiah shouted, "I know you Indians ain't got no good horses like that unless y'all steal 'em, so give up the horse or get put in your place. Gilbert, you go to the left, and Jesse, you watch my back. Come on out, boy."

David shouted, "I don't want to fight. I want to go home."

The men cackled as they stayed in their positions. "Should of thought about that before, boy," Gilbert said. "I've been looking to take a few shots at you grass niggers anyway." Gilbert aimed and shot at David, but it hit the tree. "You one of them Indians helping that Union army?"

"I couldn't care less about your stupid war!" David growled.

Gilbert bickered, "Stupid? Did he say the war is stupid?"

Jesse replied, "He one of them nigger lovers, I know it."

"Boy, if you not with us, you for them nigger lovers," Gilbert yelled. "Obadiah, do you see him?" Gilbert whispered. Obadiah shook his head no. Gilbert began to slowly approach. "So you on our side, or are you a nigger lover?"

David took a quick shot at Gilbert causing him to fall down. David ran through the trees as Jesse shouted, "Woo-wee look at that Indian! He can run! Gilbert, you all right there?"

"Yeah, he missed me. Let's get that redskin. Nobody shoots at me like that." The men shouted and ran after David through the forest. He ran in a circle to keep himself from getting too far away from Big Boy. Jesse and Obadiah took aim and fired shots at him, hitting the trees. He took cover and the men slowed down once they were unable to see him.

David slowly moved through the forest brush while the men tried to track him. As he crept alongside a large log, Jesse opened fire on him. "I see him over there!" he yelled. Jesse took another shot as Gilbert and Obadiah approached the log.

David quickly sprung up with his rifle, aimed and fired, hitting Jesse in his lower neck. Jesse fell to the ground, gagging. Gilbert and Obadiah turned around to see what happened to Jesse. "Jesse, I'm coming to help," Obadiah said. "Gilbert, get that savage!"

Gilbert searched for him in the brush. He turned around just as David took a swing at him with the stock of his rifle, knocking Gilbert down a slope. He rolled down the slope, and David gave chase, separating them from Obadiah. David was about to take another swing at Gilbert with his rifle as Gilbert slid down the slope. However, he quickly took aim with his revolver and shot David in his left shoulder. The impact caused him to fall back next to a large boulder and drop his rifle as Gilbert stopped sliding down the slope. He took aim to fire another shot, but David forced himself to stand up and run alongside the large boulder. He took two shots but missed. Gilbert took another shot, but his revolver clicked, revealing that he was out of ammo. David charged him while the man attempted to stand up, knocking him down again. He punched Gilbert, causing his nose to bleed. He tried to push David off of him, but he continued to punch him. Gilbert grabbed David's wounded shoulder as he was about to punch him again. He screamed in pain and immediately pushed Gilbert's hand off his shoulder. He punched David off of him and pulled out his hunting knife. While David held onto his shoulder, he charged at him with the knife and attempted to stab David. He dodged Gilbert's first strike. "You going to die, prairie nigger," Gilbert growled.

He took another swing with the knife cutting David on his left arm. He then lunged himself at David again, attempting to stab him in the chest, but he grabbed Gilbert's wrist, stopping him. Gilbert tried to press the knife into him by using both hands, but he quickly used both of his hands to stop the knife. The pain in his left shoulder grew, and he felt himself become weaker as he bled from the wound. He kneed Gilbert in his stomach, causing him to back up and gag. He grabbed a broken thick branch and began to hit Gilbert with it. "I'm not dying here," David yelled. He continued to try to stab David, but he struck him on his side with the branch. He began to swing wildly at David.

David began to breathe heavily from beating Gilbert, and he struggled to deal with the pain. His body shook. Gilbert stared at David with his cold dark brown eyes. "When this over, I be sure to hang you from a tree where you belong," he snarled. He charged at David, but he sidestepped him and struck him in the face with the branch. Gilbert fell down from the blow and landed on his knife. He rolled over, gasping with the knife sticking out of his lower chest.

David stared at him with a scrunched face and then limbed away while Gilbert struggled to breathe. He cautiously looked through the forest to see where Obadiah was and saw he was still with Jesse's body. "Gilbert, did you get that redskin?" he yelled. "Gilbert, you hurry up and get back here. Jesse is gone… wait until we get back into town. We gone tell everyone and every Indian town in Mississippi is going to burn to the ground! You hear me, you dirty savage!" David's heart dropped when he heard what Obadiah was planning to do. He clenched his teeth as his brows furrowed. After a few minutes, Obadiah left Jesse's dead body to search for Gilbert. He searched through the forest and found their tracks. He followed the tracks and saw Gilbert lying down on the forest floor with the knife sticking out of him. "Gilbert!" Obadiah yelled. Gilbert could only wheeze as Obadiah approached him. "He gone done it now, first Jesse now you…I'm gone carry you home."

Abruptly, an arrow hit Obadiah in the back, and he fell over. David stepped up to the two men with another arrow drawn. "I didn't come to fight, but you attacked me and call me a horse thief!" he yelled. "I'm tired of you people and your hate!" He spit on the ground. "I won't let you destroy the Indian towns because you failed to kill me."

"Now, wait just a minute, boy. I was lying, I swear I was," Obadiah said while he coughed. "I was only saying that so you would get more scared and run away. You the one that killed a man, so what does that make you? How about we leave all this be and forget we saw you? We not gone touch them Indians in Mississippi. I swear we not gone tell nobody we saw you."

David looked at Obadiah but saw his right hand slightly move to his revolver. "You're a liar. You're just like the man that took my little brother."

"Well, no real difference between a grass nigger and a nigger. One likes feathers, and the other works the fields." Obadiah tried to pull out his revolver, but David released his arrow, striking Obadiah in the chest and killing him instantly.

David approached Gilbert as he continued to wheeze. "Don't worry, I'll let the Devil take you."

"No, I'm a Christian man," Gilbert wheezed.

"Then I'll let Jesus take you. I'm not like you. I don't enjoy killing." David walked over to his rifle and picked it up as Gilbert remained unable to move. David hobbled away leaving Gilbert alone while he continued to struggle to breathe.

David untied Big Boy, and the large horse rubbed his head against David's. He lay against the large tree and began treating his wounds by pouring water on his cut, drying it off, and wrapping his left arm with a cut cloth. He made a small fire and heated up his knife. He took the heated knife and cut into his upper shoulder. He screamed in agony and popped the metal ball out. He heated the knife again as his shoulder bled and placed the heated blade on his shoulder, cauterizing the wound. He squeezed on the bark of the tree when he forced the hot knife onto his shoulder. He then passed out.

David awoke with the sunrays piercing through the leaves. Sore from his wounds, he stood up, walked over to Jesse's body, and began to dig a shallow grave using a sharp rock. He groaned as he was forced to use one arm. He pushed Jesse's body into the shallow grave and kicked leaf litter over Jesse's body. He went over to Gilbert and Obadiah to do the same with their bodies. After burying the men, he wearily approached Big Boy and noticed he had left a blood spot on the smooth bark of the tree. He shook his head and frowned. He then rode off, determined to get as far away as he could.

The incident set David back two days forcing him to focus on recovering. His pride submitted when riding on Big Boy aggravating his injured shoulder. On the morning of the second day, he rested on a ledge that overlooked a river. "Jesus was I wrong to go after my brother this way," He prayed in Cherokee. "Please guide me and give me wisdom in this journey. I'm afraid I'll fail. I do need your help." He spent the rest of the day meditating and going over scriptures he had memorized to help reassure himself.

On April 15, 1862, Riza turned fifteen years old but showed little excitement. She was now as tall as Dorothy and Reece. Dorothy and the other house slaves tried to cheer up her while they ate breakfast, but the frown on her face remained. The gloomy sky increased her depression as she walked into the white mansion. Later in the day, she went out to the pigs' pen carrying a tray with the leftover breakfast from the Pleckers. She dumped the food into the pen while she ate an uneaten biscuit.

"I hope your birthday is okay, Riza," Joseph said.

Riza turned around and smiled. "I'm trying to enjoy it," she said. Riza saw Rice approaching to feed the dogs. "Joseph, go back to work. Here comes Master Rice."

"Okay."

He left her to finish his duties, and she marched toward the mansion as Rice continued to walk in their direction. "Joseph, you better stay where you supposed to be," he yelled. "Riza, you stay right there!" She reluctantly stood in her place while she held the silver tray. Scowling, Rice approached her. "Now I know you know the rules, Riza. You're not to go to the slave's houses at all, and you not supposed to talk to Joseph or Tom alone. If I see it again, I will have you beat!" She took a step forward, and Rice grabbed her arm. "Did I say you could leave?"

"No, Master Rice," she calmly said.

"You must believe I'm stupid or that you special in some way." She looked at him with a blank stare. "Well? What is it? That was a question."

"I don't believe you would be pleased with my answer."

Rice slapped her. "You will follow the rules of this plantation and respect me. Do you hear me, grass nigger?"

"Yes, sir, I do. Now may I leave before Mrs. Wilma starts looking for me, or do you want to explain to her why I'm missing?" Master Rice let go of her arm as he gritted his teeth. She moved past Rice, side-eyeing him.

Master Rice gave her a malicious smirk. "Happy birthday, Riza. You becoming more and more of a woman each day. Best remember you're not no little girl anymore."

Riza spit on the ground and stared at Rice with her narrowed eyes the second she walked away. "I will die before you touch me," she snarled. "I'm not Pearl. I'll tell everyone!"

"Who's gone listen to a redskin that tried to burn down a house? Wait till we win this war. You can say goodbye to any plans your savage mind can think of to escape."

"I'll make you regret me, and to answer your question, I do think you're stupid!" She growled. She sprinted to the mansion as he started to chase her. She ran through the large front door and slammed it while Rice ran after her.

Rice stopped at the wooden door, turned around, and kicked

one of the pillars. "I'll be sure to let Mr. Plecker know about that smart mouth of yours, Riza! You not getting away from me, you crazy redskin nigger." He stormed off as he grumbled.

Joseph and Tom watched Rice go to the dog houses while they cleaned the animal pens. "Why is Master Plecker always going after Riza?" Tom asked.

Joseph replied, "I think it's because she leads us and because he hates her. Without her, we might not get away from here."

The rest of the day she felt nervous and avoided being alone. She felt the only person she could express her feelings to was Dorothy. Riza didn't want to scare the minds of her friends, especially since sex hadn't been explained to them. She spoke with Dorothy in the covered walkway when she was instructed to bring Wilma lunch. "He scares me. He keeps telling me how he's going to rape me," she said with a worrisome tone.

"I wish Master Kenneth was here," Dorothy said. "I'd be able to talk to him."

"What can I do?"

"You stay close to Mrs. Wilma and Mrs. Reece. I know you hate them, but he wouldn't dare touch you in front of them. Even better when Mrs. Judy Mays visits."

"There's nothing else I can do."

"Don't show him fear, and you fight. You give him hell if he ever gets you alone. Scratch out his eyes if you can."

"Is that what you wish you did against Geoffrey?"

Dorothy's eyes somewhat widened. "I love my babies, but if I could've had them in a better life, I would. I'll do my best to make sure you're not alone too."

She hugged Dorothy. "Thank you."

Dorothy hugged her back. "I'm sorry we can't do more. Now go on and give Mrs. Wilma her lunch."

She went into the cookhouse, and Dorothy frowned while Riza gathered food. She prayed every night for protection and tried her best to mask her fear.

A few days later, John, Eli, and Lizzie passed through the forests of southwest Tennessee. Lizzie continued to scout and rode back to John and Eli while they drove the carriage down the used trail. The three setup camp to eat and rest. When they were eating, Eli noticed something odd sticking out the ground. Eli stood up and walked closer to it as John and Lizzie watched. "There's a body here," Eli said.

"Are you sure?" Lizzie asked in Cherokee.

"Yeah I'm sure of it." John and Lizzie drew their weapons and followed Eli. He removed some of the leaf litter, and saw Jesse's body. Lizzie covered her nose when the foul stench rose from the grave. "Gunshot wound to the neck. He didn't live long after that. No sign of a struggle so it must've been a ranged shot." Eli slightly squinted and stood up looking into the distance.

John and Lizzie looked the same direction. "What do you see?"

"I think I see an arrow in a tree."

Lizzie began to go forward looking up into the branches of the trees as she held her bow. She suddenly began to move faster. "I see it, it's an arrow!" She yelled. John and Eli ran toward her as she approached the large tree. Lizzie jumped and pulled out the arrow. "No...this is one of our arrows."

"How do you know that?" John asked in Cherokee.

"There's a group of arrows the girls marked for fun." "See, look at it." Lizzie showed John the arrow. On the arrow were the letters J, R, and R. "David was here, or he still is here." She noticed the old, dried blood spot on the smooth bark of the tree. "John, this is blood!" She screamed for David.

The three Cherokee searched the area for clues for over an hour when John found David's foot track behind the log he was using as a shield. John and the others continued searching when they found the disturbed leaf litter going down the slope. They went down the slope and saw some of the tracks from David and Gilbert's fight. The group then noticed the unevenness of the leaf litter. Lizzie thought, *These are graves*. Her hand began to shake while she held her bow. John calmly held her hand and looked at Eli. He nodded at him as she continued to look straight forward at the graves.

Eli began to remove the leaf litter from one grave. "Another White man," he said. He uncovered the other grave and sighed. "Same here…he has arrow wounds."

She let out a big exhale and said, "Those men must've attacked him. He would never attack first. We need to go back and check for Big Boy's tracks."

The three Cherokee headed back to the blood-stained tree and searched for tracks, only to find one set of Big Boy's faded tracks. It was enough for them to have faith David was able to escape with his life. They followed the direction of the tracks the best they could. "If those bodies get found, we'll have to go another way so we don't catch any of these White people's attention," John said.

"I say forget that…I'm tired of lowering myself," she griped.

"When we reach the plantation, I doubt it will be a peaceful meeting. You can let all your anger out there."

"I will, and you should too, brother." She pulled out her sharpened tomahawk that had been fitted onto a new haft. "We will end one war while they continue to fight their own." The three Cherokee rode after David.

Maybe we can beat him to the Plecker plantation, Lizzie thought.

CHAPTER 12
Blood Brothers

David arrived in Mississippi but rested to help his shoulder heal. On April 18, 1862, his shoulder felt better, so he hurried to Caledonia. He looked at the map and cautiously rode down the dirt roads. As he continued down a road when a carriage was approaching in the distance. He went into the bare forests and waited while the carriage rode by. He watched as the carriage drove by the trees. Judy Mays saw a glimpse of Big Boy's hindquarters. She looked back as much as she could but sat back down in her seat. "What was so interesting for you to look that long?" Daphne asked.

"It was nothing," she said.

Daphne scoffed, "Please don't lie to me. What was it?"

"It was a cute little chickadee cleaning another. I thought it was cute."

"You always had a soft spot for the creatures of this world."

"Well, I find all of God's creations interesting. Talking about this makes me wonder how many birds are in the world."

Daphne giggled. "Only you would think of that question. Why not just focus on your children and not the outside world or those books? You're the only woman I know that reads as much as a man."

Judy Mays grinned. "Well, there were some good habits my

father did pass down to me. I always did have a little bit of a rebellious side. I guess some parts of us are not meant to change."

Once the carriage was gone, David carefully went down the dirt road and looked at the scenery of Caledonia. In the distance, he could see field slaves working the land and decided to carefully go down a dirt road leading to the plantation. While he went down the dirt road, he saw a middle-aged man sitting underneath a large maple tree with a jug next to him. The man had a grayish-brown beard, wore a blue vest that covered a brown cotton shirt, and wore brown trousers. David got off of Big Boy and asked, "Excuse me, sir. I was trying to find the Plecker plantation. Can you tell me the right way to get there?"

The man slowly raised his head and hiccupped as he looked at David with his bloodshot brown eyes. "Well…another Indian. I guess we better tell Andrew Jackson y'all still here," the man slurred. "You so tall."

"Sir, can you tell me where the Plecker plantation is?"

"The Pleckers' home. Yeah, I know where it is…yeah, I know where it is. Why you want to be there?"

"I have business there."

"You fighting in the war?"

"No, I won't fight in the war."

The man laughed and took a drink from the jug. "I like you, boy…you like me. The Pleckers are three or four miles down the road. You gone pass one estate, and the next one is the Pleckers with a pretty large white house. What's your name?"

"Don't worry about my name. Thank you."

"Well…I guess it was no reason for me to ask your name. I won't remember it. My mind don't hold on to stuff." The man took another drink and looked at David. "You Indians something else. That's why I like you people…fearless."

He smiled at the older man, got onto Big Boy, and rode away. As he rode down the road, he saw a plantation with overseers watching the slaves. David's grip tightened on the reins as he scowled. He surveyed the land carefully while he went by the plantation. He continued through the woods to avoid being seen. Looking at the map, he confirmed what the man told him and located the Plecker estate. He took Big Boy through the sparse forest. His eyebrows shot up, and his eyes widened while looking at the massive fields of cotton. He saw Kit and Rice patrolling the cotton fields. From a distance, he could hear the men shouting. He vigorously scanned the fields for Joseph.

David signaled for Big Boy to rest so the horse laid down, and he gave Big Boy some grains to treat his obedience. He tied Big Boy's reigns to a tree, and he traveled through the sparse forest on foot with his weapons. Carefully moving through the forest, he saw the animal housing but saw no one outside of the buildings, so he kept moving. He then saw the patio with Wilma sitting there eating her crackers. David saw Riza and mumbled, "She's not a Negro girl. Did the numbers on Pa's map mean something? Were they Indian children? I should've written them down." He continued to scout the Plecker plantation carefully, and to his frustration couldn't find Joseph. He returned to Big Boy and sat next to the large horse while he petted him. He watched patiently throughout the day. A wagon began to pass by the cotton fields. He leaned forward and saw Joseph jump from the wagon. David gasped and clutched the ground when he saw his brother carry the cotton baskets. Tears started to fill his eyes as he took a deep breath. "We found him, Big Boy…we found him." He carefully watched and waited for the arrival of sunset.

At nightfall, David snuck onto the Pleckers' plantation by circling the estate. He moved through the old willow trees to the slave house he saw Joseph go to. He watched the slaves talk to each other and moved to avoid being seen. He suddenly heard Joseph speaking inside Stella's slave house. "Little brother, I'm here," he said in Cherokee.

He heard a tin cup hit the floor of the house, and the door abruptly opened. He moved around to the side of the house and saw Joseph standing and looking around. He turned around and saw David and sprinted to him with tears running down his face. He clung to David. "David, is this real?" he asked in Cherokee.

"All of this is real. I'm here," he whispered in their language with a sorrowful tone. The brothers tightly held each other as if time stood still for them. "I'm sorry we didn't find you sooner."

"Who else is here?"

"Father and Uncle Eli are coming. I left a little before they did, but I should've waited." David felt the scars on Joseph's back, and he grimaced. "What did they do to you?"

"I got into trouble and was beaten."

He snarled in Cherokee, "I should give them a beating!"

"Joseph, who that boy?" Bo said.

He abruptly pulled out his knife and charged Bo when Joseph grabbed his arm. "No, David, he has been good to me," he said.

"Look, I'm a good man. Please put the knife down," Bo said with his hands up.

"I've experienced many things," he said. "I'm sorry for scaring you."

"Who you is and how you know Joseph?" Bo asked.

"This is my brother David I was telling you about," he cheerfully said.

"How you find him?" Bo asked.

He answered, "Our momma's friend knew someone who could get information so we could find him. I'm taking him home now. Do you have a problem with that?"

Bo shook his head. "I have no problem. I have a wife and a new baby boy. I understand why you want to take him home. I want my family to stay together too."

"Thank you for taking care of my brother. Joseph, let's go."

"We can't," Joseph humbly said.

"What are you talking about?" David agitatedly asked.

"We have to take the others with us. The other Indian children."

"I didn't come here with enough to take all of them." Joseph frowned. "How many are here?"

"There are three others, and Susie is Cherokee. We'd be wrong to leave her."

"Another Cherokee here…take me to her."

"First, you need to meet Tom. He's inside. He's from the Natchez."

"Okay, but we have to do this quickly."

Bo looked around and saw only a few slaves outside their houses talking to each other. "It good now, not many out here. We can get you in without the wrong people seeing you," Bo said. They quickly followed Bo and went into Stella's slave house.

Stella, while holding Saul, stood up with her brows lowered. "Who this?" she asked.

Joseph grinned and said, "This is my big brother, David."

"I never met no full-bloods besides Riza and Susie. It nice to meet you."

"You too," he said. Joseph quickly introduced David to Clint, Mary, and Tom. He listened to Tom's story and agreed to rescue him.

They went outside and snuck through the old weeping willow trees. David immediately grabbed Joseph's arm and hid them behind one of the trees. Wade strolled down the path with his rifle and whip. "That's Wade. He's a bad man," Joseph said in Cherokee. "He's the next one in power when Master Plecker is gone, and because Master Kenneth is fighting the war." The brothers waited for Wade to continue to patrol. The brothers ran to the slave house. Joseph knocked on the door. "Susie, it's Joseph."

"Joseph, why are you coming here?" Dorothy said through the door. "You know you're not supposed to come here."

"Please open the door Dorothy, it's important," he begged.

Dorothy opened the door and saw David standing next to Joseph. "Who this?"

"This is my older brother David. He's come to take me home, and Riza and Susie. He wanted to meet them."

The other house slaves turned to the door. Riza came up behind her. "Dorothy, please let them in," she said. She stepped back, allowing the brothers to come inside, and closed the door behind them.

Susie walked up to David with a smile. "You're Susie?" David asked in Cherokee.

She replied in Cherokee, "Yes."

"You must be Riza. My brother has spoken strongly of you," David said.

She replied, "Joseph has spoken a lot about you. It's nice to meet you."

"We need to leave before sunrise."

"How many horses do you have?"

"I have one horse, but he is large and can easily carry two people. We can keep switching back and forth so nobody is too tired from walking and meet up with my Pa."

Riza sighed. "It won't work. They will have two dogs on us in no time and find us. They'll kill you and probably me, then take Joseph and the others back to be punished."

"How are you sure of this?" David asked.

"I've been watching them for a long time. We'll need three horses and time to keep the distance between us great when they realize we're gone. We'll also need to keep them from releasing the dogs."

"How will we do that?"

Riza smirked. "We take away the key that opens up the dog's gate. It's the only way to make it harder for them to find us."

"No, Riza," Dorothy said. "I know what you're thinking, but there has to be another way."

"What do you know?" David asked.

Dorothy shook her head. "Master Rice is the one with the key to the dog houses, but he's also after Riza, like a drunk man after a woman. It's too dangerous. He'll hurt her if he learns what she is trying to do."

"Master Rice is patrolling at night tomorrow, and I'm the only one besides Pearl that can hold his attention," Riza said.

"I don't want you to experience what Pearl does," Dorothy anxiously said. "Children, step outside for a moment. That includes you too, Joseph and Susie." Dorothy looked at the other house slaves. "Y'all too, except Emma." Jude and two women followed the children outside. "They have open mouths. Riza, the first time I was with a man, I was sixteen years old, but I loved him. I've never been raped, but I've seen what it does to women. I've seen Pearl change so much because of that man, and I'm afraid it will change you too. Please don't go that way to get the key. There must be another way."

"I know there's another way, but I also want to get away from here so he can never control me like he does Pearl." Riza's eyebrow rose. "And what are you talking about? I thought Geoffrey raped you."

Dorothy exhaled, "I will tell you something that isn't to leave this house." She whispered in Riza's ear, "I didn't lie to you now when I said I was in love when I was with a man. That man is the girls' father. I hope he returns to give them another hug."

Riza's eyes bulged, and she blurted, "Jesus, Master Kenneth!"

"We fell in love when I was supposed to be nothing more than a slave."

"Lord, if Mrs. Reece find out, she's gone put you on the cutting board," Emma said.

"That's why this doesn't leave this house," Dorothy said. "The girls don't know. Do I have everyone's word?"

"I will say nothing," Riza said with a smile.

"You have my word," David said.

"I keeping my mouth closed, but now I get to laugh. Mrs. Reece, she been number two all this time," Emma said.

They laughed while Dorothy shook her head. "That's enough," she bickered. "Please try a different way, Riza."

She replied, "I will."

"Okay. Everyone come inside."

Joseph and the others reentered the house, and David closed the door. "One of these days, y'all going to let us be around for all the talks," Joseph said. "I hate being left out."

"Well, you didn't miss what we're going to plan, so don't complain," Riza said. "Well, come sit so we can do this quickly. David needs to find another place to hide so Master Wade doesn't see him." Joseph and Susie sat down next to Riza, and a plan was forged. David left back into the woods after making sure Joseph made it back to Stella's safely.

David was impressed with Riza's analytical skills, and it gave him confidence he could get them all home. He prayed, "I understand now, Jesus. You wanted Joseph to meet them so they would be found and taken home. I'm sorry I didn't wait for Pa. We would've been able to leave tonight if I had waited."

During the night, Riza dreamed she was riding a horse and breathing heavily. She could feel herself trembling, and her heartbeat increased. "Get her!" men shouted.

"What am I doing?" she said. Suddenly she heard a gunshot. "Lean to your left, Riza," a peaceful voice said. Her eyes widened. She leaned to the left, then heard a horse give a terrifying neigh, and awakened. She looked around with her hand on her chest. "Holy Spirit, what was that? Why do I feel so much fear," she whispered.

Deeply, she heard the Holy Spirit say in a soothing tone, "A warning. So you know what to do. Trust the Father with every step." Riza lay down, took deep breaths, and fell back asleep.

On April 19, 1862, the sunrise felt different for Joseph and Tom. Excitement and nervousness filled their hearts, knowing they were going to get their chance to go home. The boys worked as normal but left the horse barn door open. While the boys worked the cotton fields and carried heavy cotton baskets, old Louis gave them grief. Joseph lost his temper with Louis's degrading comments. "I should kick you off the wagon," Joseph snarled. "You aren't better than us, you lazy old man."

"Look here, nigger. I get to drive the wagon 'cause you niggers too dumb to do it," Louis bickered. "Now hurry up, half-breeds."

"I'm happy to be a half-breed than to look as ugly as you," Joseph bickered.

Louis griped, "Keep on talking half-breed. You still a nigger."

"I can't wait until I don't have to look at his ugly face anymore," Tom said.

Joseph replied, "Same here." Louis looked away from the boys and murmured while he continued to drive the wagon around the plantation. Louis remained one of the slaves Joseph didn't trust. Louis's allegiance was to himself.

During the day, Riza was sent to polish the furniture while Wilma took a nap. She hummed as she cleaned. "Why are you so happy?" Reece asked.

Riza was startled by her and turned around. "I'm trying my hardest, Mrs. Reece," she said.

Reece stared at her, despising her mannerisms. "I want you to make me some roasted chicken after you get done cleaning the furniture and make sure that chicken has the seasonings I want, including onions. Is that clear, Riza?"

She forcefully smiled. "Yes, Mrs. Reece." She walked away, and Riza's smile quickly faded. "She knows good and well I hate onions. Ugh…I hope she chokes on that chicken."

Reece suddenly reentered the room. "Did you say something about the chicken?"

Riza forced a smile. "No, I didn't, ma'am."

She stared at her, examining her facial expression. "Be careful not to test me. Also, has Dorothy mentioned anything to you about Kenneth?"

"No, ma'am, she hasn't spoken a word of him."

Reece continued to stare at Riza with her lips pursed. "You better remember my words. Hurry up, so I'm not waiting long for my chicken."

"Yes, Mrs. Reece." Reece left, and Riza continued to clean the furniture. "I'll make sure I cook that chicken real good for you… real good, Mrs. Number Two." She continued her day giving Reece fake smiles, and pleasing her. Later in the day, she reluctantly took out the leftover food to the pigs. She saw Rice in the cotton fields heckling the slaves. She waited for Rice to see her by the pig pen. After waiting several minutes, Riza purposely knocked over a few metal buckets stacked next to the pen. She looked over at the cotton fields and saw Rice and Kit looking at her.

Riza kicked one of the buckets and Rice rode toward her past the slaves while Kit yelled at him. She quickly put the buckets back in place. When she turned around, Rice jumped of his horse. "What was that, Riza?" Master Rice yelled. "You think you walking away from what you did?"

"No, Master Rice. I'm sorry but I was only trying to get your attention," she said. "I was thinking about what you said and I wanted to say, I'm sorry." she gulped. "Also would you allow me to visit you tonight? It'll be some time before Master Plecker decides if I'm to be with Joseph or Tom."

Riza could saw Rice's eyebrow lift and his jaw unhinge before his face contorted. "What you saying, girl?"

Half-smiling, she seductively replied, "Master Rice, I thought you said I wasn't a girl no more. If it's okay, I can come to your shed tonight? I promise I'll never disrespect you again. I'd be something different than Pearl."

"You must've hit your head on something. This ain't you."

Her half-smile fell from her face. "I'm fine, Master Rice. I know you're right. I see the way some of them niggers out there are looking at me." She started to sniff and made her eyes well up. "You know what Clint tried to do to me. I'm scared one them niggers will try for me again. Please let me have one choice. I thought you said you liked my body."

Sweat went down his neck and her brown eyes could follow his eyes gliding up and down her maturing body. "I...I think we can do something quiet, but you gone behave yourself. Understand I don't want you...only servitude. You're mine when I say, until you given to Joseph or Tom...I'll keep any nigger away you say is bothering you." Rice put his hand on her lower back and it slid down, groping Riza's butt. She balled her right hand into a fist as she closed her eyes. "You're so firm...I think tonight is a good night. Now get back to Mrs. Wilma. I don't feel like hearing that woman's mouth today."

"Yes, sir." She left and took a deep breath.

"Riza, don't disappointment me by not showing up." She turned around and looked at him. "You have until nine o'clock tonight to get to my house. If you not there by that time, I promise when I catch you alone, I'll make you suffer."

"I won't break my word, Master Rice." Riza quickly left and mumbled, "I promise it'll be a day you'll never forget." As she was serving the Plecker family, she went back into the kitchen carrying a tray, but quickly ran outside through the kitchen door toward the willow trees making sure she wasn't seen and met up with David. "The plan is set. Tonight we leave."

"I agree with Dorothy. I don't like the idea of you doing this," he said.

"It's the only way to get the keys, and you'll be waiting outside of Rice's house. When I trick him, you can tie Rice up, and we can leave. There's no way they would catch up to us in time."

David bit his lip. "We should've went with the plan for me to knock him out and take the keys."

"You know that would not work. These White men are stupid, but they work together well. They'd know something was wrong if he was gone for too long. Tonight is the night. I'll see you at Stella's." Riza quickly ran back to the mansion. She served the Plecker family, hoping this was the last time she would see the inside of the mansion.

While she slaved for Reece and Wilma in the distance, she heard Rice yelling at a slave. He began to whip the slave. She deeply exhaled and thought, *I can't risk anything around that crazy man.*

Riza begged Wilma to go use the outhouse and was excused. The moment she went to the outhouse, she quickly ran into the mansion. She quietly moved through the house as she listened for the other slaves and slowly opened the cookhouse door. She entered the kitchen when she realized nobody was there and grabbed a knife from a drawer. She went outside and quickly scanned the land, seeing all of the overseers near the fields and the barns. She sprinted toward the overseers' houses that were to the left of the apple and walnut trees. Over the years, she'd seen Rice leave his small house several times. She entered the house and began to heavily breathe. She put the knife underneath a pillow on the bed and ran out of the small house toward the outhouse.

Riza stopped in front of the outhouse, breathing heavily as sweat dripped from her forehead.

"Riza!" Dorothy bickered. "I was sent out here to find you… thank God you were where you're supposed to be."

She started to approach Dorothy quickly and said, "I'm coming. I'm sorry I really had to use the outhouse."

"It's all right, but Mrs. Wilma was worried. Come on." Dorothy returned with Riza to Reece and Wilma. "Here she is, Mrs. Wilma. I walked up to the outhouse as soon as she walked out."

"Oh good, you had me worried, Riza," Wilma said.

"No need for worry, Mrs. Wilma. I'm sorry it took me a while," she said.

"She does have an odor to her," Reece snobbishly said.

Riza slightly squinted while she gripped her blue dress. "Well, all right, take these dishes back, Riza, and bring us some tea."

"Yes, ma'am," she said. She took the dishes and soon brought out the tea for the women, hoping this was her last day of serving.

Night fell and David met with Joseph and Tom inside Stella's house. David spoke with Bo as he carried Saul in his arms. Bo reminded him very much of Michael because of his positive hope for everyone.

At that moment, Susie and Riza said their goodbyes to Dorothy and Emma but didn't tell the other house slaves. The two girls exited the house with Dorothy following. "At least this time, I get to say goodbye to the two of you," she said.

"I'm sorry we didn't do that the first time," Riza said. You were always a big sister to us."

A tear ran down Dorothy's face. "I hope y'all do make it…God bless you both." Dorothy gave them a hug. She gave them both a kiss on the cheek. "When Doris and Daisy get old enough. I'll tell them everything about you two."

The young girls smiled at Dorothy. "We will see each other again," Susie said in Cherokee.

Dorothy replied in Susie's language, "We will see each other again."

"Goodbye, my good friend," Riza said in Mohawk, wiping away a few tears.

Dorothy wiped away her tears, replying in Riza's language, "Goodbye, my good friend." The girls quickly went to Stella's house. Soon afterward, Stella's front door slowly opened as Susie and Riza walked inside. "Sorry, we took so long. We had to make sure the other slaves didn't see us. I feel so excited to finally escape," Susie said. She looked at Stella and the others and frowned. "I'm sorry we cannot bring you."

"Susie, girl, don't feel sorry," Bo said. "Truth is, we got enough horses here for all us to leave, but we be easier to find. Stella don't know how to use a horse, and Clint and Mary don't. It better this way."

She continued to frown. "I feel so bad leaving all of you."

"Maybe the North will win, and we visit you out there with the other Indians," Stella said. "The good Lord sees it important you go home. Makes me sad, but this is our home. I a slave my whole life. Not you. If the White people don't change things…you fight to change things." Susie gave her a hug and gave Saul a kiss on the cheek while he slept in Stella's arms.

Joseph stepped up to her and gave her a hug. "Thank you, Stella," Joseph said.

Tom did the same and turned to Bo. "You're a smart man Bo. Don't listen to Master Rice or Master Kit," Tom said.

"Thank you, Tom, that mean a lot," Bo said.

"Stella, Bo, thank you for your kindness, and Mary, I will miss you," Riza said.

Mary walked up to Riza and gave her a hug. "I will miss you too, Riza, and you, Susie, and you, Joseph, and you, Tom," Mary said as she hugged them.

"Clint…maybe in the future we will see each other again," Riza said. "I forgive you, and I know when the time is right, the

Creator will guide you to the right woman. We are friends." Riza smiled at Clint.

Clint sniffed while he wiped away his tears. "Thank you, Riza, and maybe when we see each other again," Clint said. "I be a better man when you do."

Tears started to build in Riza's eyes, but she took a big exhale to stop them. "I do hope we see each other later. Let's go, David. I have to keep my promise for the last time." David and Riza snuck out of the slave house and traveled through the weeping willow trees pathway.

The two cautiously approached Rice's cabin and made sure not to be seen by Wade or Kit. They each had a cabin a few hundred feet away from Rice's cabin. "Remember to be careful," David said.

"I know that better than anyone right now," Riza whispered.

David sat down on the side of the cabin as she approached the door. She knocked on the door, and it slowly opened. "Well, come in," Rice said. She entered, and he quietly closed the door as he scanned the area. "I'm glad you kept your word. For that, I can keep my word."

"Thank you, Master Rice," she said.

"I must say. That dress Mrs. Wilma has you wear fits you well. You filling out like Dorothy." He approached Riza and ran his fingers down her face. "Take your hair out of that bun." She took her wavy hair out of the bun, and the hair dropped to the middle of her back. "My…did most of your hair grow back?"

"All of it, Master Rice."

"All of it. Well, I guess that was a lesson for you to learn that day." He rubbed her shoulder and touched the top of her breast next to her scar. Riza felt a chill go down her spine. "You Indian women sure is tough. I was surprised how you took that gunshot. I know that must've changed your whole world."

"It hurt for a long time."

"Well, no need to worry now. I'm about to change your world some more, but for the good. Go on and lie down in the bed." She walked over to the bed. Her body started to tremble, but she tightened her muscles to stop shaking. "Take off your undergarments too, while you sit on that bed." She tried her hardest to keep a straight face and pulled down her undergarments while she kept her dress on. "Oh…you nervous, Riza?"

"A little."

Rice boldly stepped up to her and ran his hand through her hair. "Well, no need for that. I'll keep my word. Now lie down on the bed." She froze as she took a breath. "Now, Riza, I being nice here. So you lay down on that bed, or we change things here."

"Forgive me, Master Rice. I'm sorry. I'm nervous."

"Well, now lie down." He kneeled down before Riza and put his hand on her left thigh. Leering, his hand slid up her thigh. His eyes widened when he flinched, pulled his hand away, and looked at his finger. Abruptly, she pulled out a knife from her apron, but he grabbed her arm. "I should've known you, little redskin devil!" They struggled with the knife on the bed as she tried to put it into her other hand, but Rice managed to make her drop the knife.

He pressed Riza down on the bed and forced her wrists together. He then used one hand to hold both of her wrists. "Let go of me!"

As his other hand struggled to hold Riza's wrists, Rice punched her in the eye. "You sneaky little prairie nigger!" He slapped her, bloodying her lower lip. "I swear I'll make you suffer…you think you're so smart." He tried to slap her again, but lost his grip on one of her wrists. She swung and scratched his eye. "Argh!" Rice grabbed her wrist and pressed her down harder on the bed. She began to try to kick him. "After this night I'll make you mine every night you disrespectful grass nigger!" He held her wrists together with one hand. Rice attempted to slap her again, but she kicked him in the chest. Growling, he began to pull down his trousers with one hand as the other hand struggled to hold Riza's wrists. Suddenly, there was a thud on the door. Rice looked back. "Who was that? Was that one of them half-breeds…you tricked them half breed niggers to help you?" Rice slapped Riza again.

"I don't know who it is, ugly!"

"Argh! You gone remember this day, Riza Plecker." Rice

slapped Riza again while he tried to keep her wrists from moving as she attempted to kick him again.

She leaned up and bit his free hand, causing a crunching sound. Blood oozed down Rice's hand and onto Riza's face as he screamed. He let go of her wrists, and she spit out his hand.

He yelled at his bleeding hand. "You whore!"

Another thud was made on the door. Rice grabbed Riza's throat with his uninjured hand. He looked back at the door, scowling. At this moment Riza reached underneath his pillow. He looked back at her, and she jabbed the knife into the side of his neck. His blood spilled onto her blue dress as she held onto the knife.

"I will remember this day! As Riza Moon, a Mohawk!" She yelled as she looked into his bulging eyes. She spit in his face the moment she let go of the knife.

Rice held onto the handle of the knife as he backed away from Riza. He gasped while he coughed up blood and stumbled, knocking down an argand lamp. The oil from the lamp immediately caught on fire and lit Rice's shirt on fire. While holding her eye, Riza immediately jumped off the bed. He jumped up and howled in pain. She quickly picked up the other knife, backed up from the bed as the fire spread on Rice, and watched him collapse on the floor. The fire continued to spread along with his blood. Riza immediately reached into his pockets and pulled out the keys. She ran to the front door and opened it.

"Riza, what did you do?" David whispered. Riza looked at David and his eyes shot open. "You're covered in blood and your face is starting to swell."

"Most of it isn't my blood," Riza said.

"Okay, let's go!"

David and Riza ran toward the animal pens while the fire inside Rice's cabin grew.

Wade opened his door and saw Rice's cabin on fire. In the distance, he saw David and Riza running down the dirt trail. "Rice!" he yelled.

Kit ran out of his cabin, which was a few hundred feet north from Wade's. "That crazy Injun girl done set Rice's cabin on fire! Get your clothes on! We going after her!"

During this time, David and Riza arrived at the horse barn with Joseph, Susie, and Tom waiting. "We have them saddled," Joseph said.

David replied, "Good job. Riza, can you ride?"

"Yes, I'm not that hurt," Riza said.

"What happened?" Tom asked.

Riza replied, "We'll talk later. Get on a horse." Joseph quickly came out with three horses and they all got onto the horses. David and Joseph shared a horse, while Riza shared one with Susie, and Tom had his own.

"What y'all think y'all doing?" Louis said.

David and the others looked back, and saw Louis sitting up in a wagon he had fallen asleep in. Riza sharply replied, "What you can't!" Quickly, Riza and Tom followed David's lead as they rode off of the estate.

Louis grunted and ran to the Plecker plantation yelling, "Master Plecker, them crazy Indian children gone run away again! It was Riza! It was Riza, Master Plecker!" Louis loudly knocked on the mansion door. "Master Plecker, Mrs. Wilma, them half-breed niggers stole some horses!" Louis jogged back to the horse pen and he looked inside to see the horses. He turned to return to the mansion. A wooden plank hit him over the head, and he fell unconscious.

Out of the shadows, Bo walked up to Louis. "You gone said enough," he whispered. He released the remaining horses out of the barn, letting them run as far as they wanted. He quickly ran through the cotton fields to Stella's house. While he ran, he saw Wade and Kit arrive at the mansion as the lamps in the mansion lit up. He entered the house and kissed Stella on the lips. "It is done. What happen now is in the Lord's hands."

Stella looked down at Saul as she held him and smiled at Bo.

Abruptly, Mr. Plecker could be heard screaming and shouting.

At this time, David and the others quickly arrived at Big Boy's hidden location. David got onto Big Boy and gave Joseph his bow and a few arrows. The group rode down the dirt road with the light of the moon guiding them. David knew they needed to get several miles down the road to be safe, and continue running in the morning. The group rode for over an hour and settled on the outskirts of a forest. They huddled together with a few blankets that were placed on Big Boy, and slept until sunrise. When the sun rose, Riza's wounds were clearly visible.

At the Plecker plantation, the smell of smoke filled the morning air. "In all my years, I've never been so challenged," Mr. Plecker said while he stood before Rice's burnt body. He looked at the destroyed cabin, and kicked a piece of burnt wood. "I want all three of them back here, and whoever it was that helped them! I want Riza back alive! That redskin prairie nigger will suffer... death is too easy of a solution for her!"

"She took the keys," Kit said with his shoulders shaking the moment Mr. Plecker looked at him. "See, we can't get the dogs without them."

Mr. Plecker growled, "You take a pipe and knock that lock off, or you take a rifle and shoot it off! I won't be outsmarted by a savage! Go!"

Kit jumped and ran to the dog kennel. "Old Louis don't know who hit him," Wade said. "So it could have been whoever was helping them, or it was one of the slaves here."

"Let's focus on getting those half-breeds back here. They stole three horses and will be moving. Lucky for us the horses they released didn't run too far away. I want you to ride to Sydney's immediately and meet me at the road that will take us to the Tennessee woods. I think we gone need support bringing them back this time."

"Are you sure? I can bring them back."

"I trust you Wade, but I'd rather not risk it, especially not knowing who helped them escape. No telling that person's skills."

"Who you do you think it was?"

"Hard to say, but it could be one of Riza's kin after all this time or maybe one of Joseph's kin. That little nigger was always talking about them coming for him. Either way, they gone learn once we find them."

"Okay, I'll see y'all on the road." Wade got on his horse and rode off to Sydney's mansion in Columbus to get help. He arrived at Sydney's mansion and explained the situation to her. She was shocked to hear of Rice's death, and had three of her overseers accompany Wade to chase down Joseph and the others.

During this time, Joseph and the others rode down the dirt trails. David kept his eyes open for anyone that may be a threat. After a long ride, the group took a break to his disliking. The group ate while he watched worrisomely. "David, you should eat with us," Joseph said.

"I was looking to make sure we've gotten far enough," David said.

"We won't get far enough until we reach Indian Territory," Riza said. "I know Mr. Plecker. He will he hunt us down. He wants nothing but to control of us."

"Plecker was the one that shot you right?"

"Yes."

"Then we should hurry so we don't have any more problems. I think they'll shoot to kill." He noticed the Joseph's slight frown. "Relax, Joseph, we'll keep moving, and meet up with Pa."

"Does he still look the same?" Joseph asked.

David's eyes slightly widened and frowned. "He looks the same. He'll be surprised when he sees you because you've grown." Joseph smiled at him and went back to eating. After the group ate, they continued to ride through Mississippi.

However, Riza's eye had swollen more overnight. It kept forcing her to stop temporarily. "I'm sorry. I can't fully see out of my eye yet," Riza said with a frustrated tone.

"We can take cover in the forest for now, and stay away from the road," David said. The group went into a thick forest outlining the dirt road. He scouted before they moved forward, and left the others in the forest. He rode through the tallgrass area, and went on top of a small hill. His heart dropped as he looked down the hill at a Confederate campsite which had hundreds of soldiers. He could also see the dirt road further down, and saw soldiers sitting by the road.

He rode back to the others constantly looking back. He approached the others his brow now furrowed and his lips pressed. "What is it?" Riza asked.

"We can't take the road. We have to go through the swamps," he said. "The Confederates have moved a base out here, and there's no way we won't be seen on the road."

"Are you sure we have to go through the swamps?" Tom asked.

He answered, "Yes, I'm sure. We'll have to take our time but we will make it out of this state. If we're lucky when they come looking for us, they'll stay on the road."

"How will we run into Papa?" Joseph asked.

"He'll see the soldiers on the road far before the soldiers can approach him," he said. "He'll also travel through the trees to be safe." The group later continued through the forests once Riza felt a little better.

Meanwhile, at the Plecker plantation, Wilma had gone into a state of rage with the escape of the children. Doris and Daisy had been assigned to do whatever Wilma wanted keeping the two girls away from Reece to Dorothy's delight. As Dorothy finished cleaning one of the bedrooms, she went through the hallway to go to another room. "Dorothy," Reece said. She stood still while Reece slowly and confidently approached her. "Did you know nothing about Riza's plan?"

Dorothy replied, "I told Master Plecker all that I know which is nothing." "She planned it again without telling me a word."

Reece narrowed her eyes. "So you mean to tell me some Indian shows up, she kills Mr. Rice, and then they escape."

"I believe that's all there is to the story."

"Well, whether you knew anything or not, I will personally make sure she suffers when she is captured. She'll only get so far. A slave is a slave. It's best you remember that yourself."

Dorothy gave a slight side-eye. "Yes, ma'am."

Reece's nose crinkled. "Please show your disapproval of me again." She tilted her head slightly. "What? Nothing?"

"I don't—"

"What…know what I'm talking about? Please, Dorothy. Woman to woman, I know that look. I know it well, slave."

"Is there anything you want of me, ma'am?"

Reece leered and shook her head. "I want to hit you like a man. When Riza returns, I'll save it for her. Me and the Mohawk have more to discuss. Go on and finish cleaning. Afterward, make me some lemonade." Reece crossed her arms. "You hazel-eyed Delilah."

"Yes, ma'am." She walked away from Reece and entered the guest room. "I'll make it just for you…you blue-eyed crazy woman," she murmured.

CHAPTER 13
Mysterious Ways

News of Joseph's escape spread like wildfire through Caledonia and Columbus. Judy Mays was shocked about the escape, and felt in her heart there was more to the escape. She put on a fake smile while she marched through her mansion. Her abrupt responses made her servants nervous to approach her. "Momma, can you come with me to the flowers so we can see which butterflies come today?" a young girl asked.

Judy Mays turned around and looked at her daughter's beautiful blue eyes that reminded her of her younger self. "Breanna, I...I will join you outside shortly. Momma has much to think about," she said.

Breanna jumped with joy. "Okay, Momma. Can I ask Miss Patty to make me some apple slices for lunch?"

"Only if you share them with her and your brother." Breanna ran down the stairs in her light blue dress straight to the kitchen. She calmly followed her daughter downstairs but stayed back as she stood on the bottom steps. She watched her daughter's interactions with the young Negro woman and smiled, listening to her daughter respectfully speak to Miss Patty. She went back upstairs to think a little more about Joseph's escape before she went outside to spend time with Breanna. "God, can I do something? I thought I had more time with the boy. Please guide me, Lord. I almost have her." She then went outside to keep her word to her daughter.

During the night, Judy Mays struggled to sleep. When she finally fell asleep, she realized she was a child. She looked over to her left and Annabelle was standing there, but it began to rain as she grabbed Judy Mays's hand. She looked down at their hands and looked back at Annabelle, surprised to see a teenage Annabelle. She saw sadness in her eyes even though she was smiling. She felt tears go down her face and cried, "I'm sorry. I'm so sorry, Annabelle. I wish I could do more." Suddenly, a thunderclap echoed while it rained. "What can I do? God, show me what I can do." Annabelle calmly let go of her hand, and Joseph stepped up from behind Annabelle and held his mother's hand.

"Where the old bear lived," an echoing voice said.

Judy Mays turned around and saw the shallow creek and saw the old black bear sitting by the creek. "Who is there?" she asked. She felt drawn to the black bear as it sat by the creek calmly. She slowly approached the bear. As she stood several feet from it, she heard men yelling and gunshots. The large bear aggressively stood up and roared over her head causing her to place her hands over her ears. "Please don't hurt me!" The bear aggressively charged around her. When she felt the massive power of the charge, she awoke. She sat up in her bed and looked over at her daughter, Breanna. She looked up at the ceiling, whispering, "Bear Creek." For several minutes, she leaned against the bedpost, looking at her daughter as her chin rested on her folded hands. She remained unable to sleep with Annabelle and Joseph on her mind.

At this time, John also dreamed. He was standing in a forest and felt the wind pick up. "John," a calm voice said. He turned around and saw two paths, one leading down a dirt road and the other going into the woods. He saw a man with a gold aura coming off his body. "This way, John." He followed the man through the forest and into a swamp. While he followed the man through the swamp, he saw a shallow creek. "Here is where you need to be." He heard a gunshot and awoke.

He looked around the carriage as Eli and Lizzie slept. He rubbed his forehead and sighed. "Jesus, was that your answer to me?" he whispered. "Please protect my boys. I know your will be done, but please let their protection be your will." He tried to go back to sleep.

In the morning, Judy Mays's brother-in-law Austin came over to her home, a normality since Edgar was away on business. Wearing a white-trimmed, brown Victorian dress, Judy Mays welcomed him inside as he was greeted by the children. Wearing black trousers and a blue vest that covered a white high-collar shirt, the average-built man took his time to acknowledge each child. He had a well-trimmed brown beard and curly brown hair. After coaxing the children away to eat breakfast, Judy Mays turned to Austin. "You've heard of the Indian slave children that escaped Mr. Pleckers' plantation?" she asked.

"News of it has spread. He wants those children back quickly," he replied.

"I think I know where they are."

Austin's brown eyes shot open. "Really?"

"But I need to be the one to bring them back."

"Judy Mays, now you know you're overstepping on this."

"I know what I'm saying, but I can't explain it. I know I can bring all of them back without any serious consequences."

"This is Riza's doing. There is no way there's not going to be consequences."

"If I can bring her back peacefully, I know I can speak to Wilma about it. I need you to escort me to Bear Creek. It may take a whole day."

"Bear Creek, Judy Mays, that is no ride for a lady, especially with this war going on. And why are you talking about a whole day?"

"Austin! There is no time for this, please take me out there."

"I'm not taking you to hunt down some slave children. I'll go tell Mr. Plecker, and they will be brought back alive."

Judy Mays's brows furrowed, and her voice boomed, "No! I will not have that man ruin the chances of me finding Annabelle."

He crossed his arms. "That's what this is about."

"Joseph is her son. I need him, so please, Austin." He looked away from Judy Mays. "Brother, please do this for me."

"I won't endanger you, Judy Mays."

"There is no danger, they're children."

"They're Indian children! Who's to say they won't turn on you!"

"I know they won't. If there's one White person they'd expect help from, it'd be me. Now, we've wasted enough time arguing. Please, take me to Bear Creek."

"I'm not taking you."

Her eyes dilated. "I will tell Edgar how you lost the deal."

His brows lowered. "What deal?"

"I know you cost you and Edgar the Peterson Deal. You were mouthing off to Brittney Warner about the deal and capitalizing on it. You let your eyes for her get the better of you because you clearly forgot she is Jedidiah Hayes's little cousin. He made a better offer, and that's why y'all lost the Peterson Deal."

Austin pouted, saying, "How did you know that?"

Judy Mays cocked her head. "As I said, Brittney is a talker. Now you take me to Bear Creek, or I tell Edgar you cost us tens of thousands of dollars. Take your pick."

Austin stomped his foot. "You bitter woman! Tell them to get that stupid horse."

She marched past him with her head held high and went outside to the horse barn. A few minutes later, one of her workers put a side saddle on her horse and brought the horse to the front of the house. She went back inside the mansion, changed her dress, grabbed a rifle from Edgar's gun case, and went to the front door.

Austin mounted his black horse, and Judy Mays exited the house with the weapon, wearing a blue cotton dress. "What do you need that rifle for?"

"What else…for safety."

"Now, Judy Mays, you don't need to be handling a man's weapon."

She narrowed her eyes. "Do I need to talk to Brittney?"

He bit his lip. "Let's get this over with before the sun goes down. This shouldn't take a whole day."

"I need to say bye to my babies." She reentered the house as her former slave, Patty, was escorting the children into the dining hall. Judy Mays kissed all of her children and spoke with them as they ate breakfast. When she was about to leave, her daughter Hannah, tugged her dress. "Momma, are you sure you will only be gone for one day?" she asked.

She smiled as she rubbed her daughter's brown hair. "I will be gone no more than a day with Uncle Austin, and I might have someone special with me when I return," she said. "Now, all of you behave and do as Miss Patty and the others say. Breanna… that especially means you, young lady."

"I love you, Momma," her son said.

"I love you too, Alexander."

Judy Mays walked through the foyer with Patty a few steps behind her. She put on her leather gauntlets, and Patty handed her a sack with prepared meals. "Mrs. Judy Mays, is you sure this is the right thing to do with Mr. Reynolds gone?" Patty asked. No woman is supposed to be out alone."

"Austin Reynolds will be escorting me. So no worries there. He's reliable."

"What we supposed to say to Mr. Reynolds?"

"Patty, if my husband returns before me, you tell him what I told you, and if he has a problem with it, I promise that you'll face no form of punishment," she said. "Watch my children."

"Yes, ma'am, I make sure they get to bed on time too."

The two women walked outside and a worker helped Judy Mays mount her horse. She smiled at Patty and secured the sack of goods. "Thank you, Patty. I'm off to Bear Creek."

"May the good Lord protect y'all."

They rode off with Austin leading the way.

During this time, John awoke and saw Lizzie had left the carriage. He awakened Eli and exited the carriage, anxious to find her. The men looked around but didn't see her. "Lizzie?" John yelled.

"I'm here," she said in Cherokee.

John and Eli turned around and saw her sitting on a large boulder, braiding her hair. John exhaled with relief as he watched at his sister tightly braid her hair. John replied, "We were looking for you."

Lizzie smacked her lips and sighed. "And you just now called for me. It's been at least ten minutes."

"You haven't changed your hair like that in a very long time."

"If we fight today, it will be harder to grab my hair, and it will honor Kay. I've been up for a few hours. I'm done, let's leave."

The Cherokee traveled and came across two trails. John remembered his dream when they looked at the two trails. "We're more likely to reach the plantation quicker following the road," Eli said in Cherokee.

"We should take the path through the swamps I had a dream last night about this," John said. "I was told to take the path through the swamps."

"Are you certain?"

John confidently replied, "Yes."

Eli smirked. "Then we'll need to put the carriage in between those trees and hope it's there when we return." They took the horses off the carriage and hid it behind a few trees. The trio rode through the swamp determined to find the boys.

Meanwhile, Joseph and the others traveled through the swamp on the horses. While they were traveling, they went by a stream and Tom stopped his horse. "Hey, I need to get some water," he said.

"Hurry up. It's bad enough we were forced to stop for a day," David said. He got down from his horse and began to fill his waterskin. The horses casually approached a pooled area of the stream to drink water. As Tom stood up, he saw a large log moving toward the horse. When Joseph got off his horse, David also noticed the log, but it oddly submerged under the water. He quickly jumped off of Big Boy, pushed Joseph back to his horse, and sprinted to the other horse. "Get away from the water, Tom!"

Abruptly, an alligator exploded out of the water, narrowly missing the horse's neck. The horse jumped onto its hind limbs and neighed. Tom screamed, "I've never seen one that big!" The horse ran into swamp while the large dark-gray alligator growled and looked at the others.

Sitting on their horse behind a tree, Susie and Riza embraced each other as they stared at the large reptile. "Tom walk around...this is his water," David said.

He looked at David while he struggled to not shiver. "Do you think he'll chase us?"

"As long as we stay away from the water, we'll be fine. He's claimed this as his own we'll respect his claim." Tom moved around the trees to the others while watching the gator follow his movements.

"Should we go get the horse?" Riza asked.

David answered, "The horse will keep running for some time after being scared like that. Chasing the horse could put us right into the path of those White men. Tom, ride with Joseph. We should try to get out of the swamps and into the forest before sunset."

"What a greedy and mean animal," Susie said. She stuck her tongue out at the alligator. The gator let out a low hiss, causing Susie to hold a little tighter to Riza. "Can we leave now?"

"Let's go," David said. The group continued through the swamp with their hearts racing.

As they went through the swamp, Susie lightly tapped Riza on her shoulder. "What is it, Susie?" she asked.

"What did it feel like to kill Master Rice?" Susie asked.

"I never planned to kill him." Her mouth curved downward. "Not as good as I thought. I thought I'd feel happy, but I feel only free of him. I feel sad that I thought I'd enjoy it."

Susie smiled. "It's because you have a good heart."

Riza sighed. "Maybe you're right…"

While continuing through the swamp the group was forced to make change in their course because the ground was too wet and unstable. David didn't want to risk them losing another horse. During the late afternoon they entered into a more forested area with a field. "We can rest here for a moment and eat," David said.

"Do you think we'll run into your Pa?" Riza asked.

"I think we still can. We're going in the right direction now."

Riza nodded. "The more ground we cover, the better. Do you mind if Susie rides with you on the big horse?"

"She can ride with me."

The group gathered, and David helped Susie get onto Big Boy. "He is so big," Susie said.

"He's an old horse with a good strong spirit," David said. "I can teach you later how to ride him. I'm sure he'd be happy to have a new person on his back." When the group went through the tall grass, David looked over to his right and noticed a dirt path through the trees. A few hundred meters ahead of them was a creek. "This can't be the same path." Abruptly, the group heard howling and barking as four dogs came rushing off the road. "Ride fast," David yelled.

The group rode through the sparse forest while the dogs chased them. "I see them," a man yelled. The children continued to ride as the dogs gave chase and tried to nip at the horse's legs. David continuously looked back trying to think of a plan while trying to make sure nobody was left behind. When he looked back again, he saw Mr. Plecker and the others furiously riding on their horses. During the chase, one of the dogs nipped the lower leg of Riza's horse. The horse kicked one of the dogs with its hind leg, severely injuring the animal. Another dog jumped attempting to bite Riza. Simultaneously, she pulled out the knife she had and sliced the dog's ear.

She looked back and saw Master Plecker and the other men coming closer. She signaled the horse with the reins to run faster. David stopped Big Boy and pulled out his rifle. "Joseph,

Tom keep riding, we will catch up," he yelled. The boys kept riding as the men behind them shouted.

"I want her alive!" Mr. Plecker bellowed. "Kill the horse!" The men began to shoot at Riza as she raced toward David. The bullets hit the trees surrounding her while she attempted to race the horse in a cross pattern.

As Riza got closer to David, Wade took aim at her. "This is for Rice, you redskin Delilah!" Wade yelled. He fired his rifle. The sound echoed through the woods and Riza's heart dropped. The sound that was identical to the sound she heard in her dream. She quickly sloped over to her left and the bullet struck the horse in the back of its neck. The horse squealed in pain and it violently collapsed to the ground causing her to lose grip of the reins, and roll across the forest floor, ripping her dress.

Riza struggled to balance herself. As she struggled to get up, David fired shots from his rifle striking one of Sydney's overseers in the shoulder knocking him off his horse. "Take some cover!" Master Plecker yelled. The men spread out and took cover behind the trees while they shot at David. Master Plecker quickly hid behind a large boulder.

David had Susie jump off Big Boy and run toward a creek. "Get up, Riza," David yelled when he took another shot. As she struggled, she heard something charging her. She turned around and saw the brown dog she had beaten with a rock over a year ago. Struggling to move forward, her eyes widened, but as the dog charged her, an arrow hit the dog killing it. It slid on the forest floor next to Riza. Joseph and Tom ran up to her to help her run behind a tree.

"Go get them, boys," one of Sydney's men yelled. Two dogs charged the children as David was forced to take cover behind another tree with Big Boy.

"Run through the trees to the creek," David yelled. The children moved the quickest they could with Riza as the dogs chased them. David attempted to shoot one of the dogs, but Plecker's men shot at him, forcing him to take cover behind the tree again. When the dogs got closer, Joseph let go of Riza to take aim with his bow. He took one shot grazing one of the dogs in the shoulder, causing it to back down. Joseph quickly drew his arrow again, but as he shot, he missed the dog. The dog lunged at Joseph knocking him down, but Joseph managed to block the dog's bite by using his bow.

David attempted to take aim at the dog, but Mr. Plecker and his men took more shots at him. "I suggest you pay more attention to us than that nappy-headed half-breed!" Mr. Plecker yelled. "We want them alive, but we'll take you either way, grass nigger."

"You're cowards," David yelled while he took another shot.

Joseph desperately tried to reach for another arrow as he struggled to push the dog back as his heart raced. The dog aggressively attempted to bite him again. Unexpectedly, Tom hit the dog on the head with a log, shattering the wood and knocking the dog unconscious. "Thank you Tom," he said.

The children ran toward the trees by the creek when one of Sydney's overseers ran to the other side of the forest. David saw the man and jumped off Big Boy to get behind another tree. Gunshots from Mr. Plecker and the others shot through. "Joseph, Tom, get down!" David yelled. The boys immediately ducked to the ground as the man took aim at them.

As the second the man lowered his aim to the boys' legs, an arrow struck the man in the head. David's eyes widened and he gasped when he saw Lizzie sliding down from a ledge the creek flowed by. "Now who is that?" Mr. Plecker yelled.

Lizzie, with her tightly braided hair, ran up to Joseph with her bow draw. "Joseph, get behind the trees and you stay there, you too boy!" she commanded. The boys quickly got up and ran toward Riza and Susie while the men opened fire. Using the trees as a shield, she approached David. "David you should've waited!" She growled.

"I'm sorry, Auntie Lizzie," he whined.

Lizzie yelled in Cherokee, "We'll talk after this. How many more men are left?"

He answered in Cherokee, "Five!"

"John, Eli they're here!" She fired more arrows and David took a few shots. A minute later, John and Eli charged through the creek. "There are five of them and the children are behind the trees."

John looked back, and saw his son. He nodded at Joseph and he smiled. "We're taking my son home," he yelled while he and Eli took cover behind the trees.

"You're not taking any of them Indian children! I own them!" Master Plecker yelled. "You have no rights here, Indian." The men stopped firing their weapons as John and Eli drew their rifles.

"All we want is to take our children home, and we can all leave in peace."

"The name is Mr. Plecker, and I don't make deals with Indians. Just like I don't make deals with Negroes. So you give us them children back, or we're gone have a bigger problem."

"We already have a problem." John took a shot from behind the large tree grazing Mr. Plecker in the shoulder.

"Kill them and take the children alive," Mr. Plecker growled while holding his shoulder.

Lizzie backed up and used the trees as shields. She ran past John and Eli with her bow drawn. She used the trees to shield her to get to the left side of the forest. John and the others quickly separated behind different trees on the right side. The Cherokee continued to exchange fire with Mr. Plecker and his men for several minutes with John and Eli trying to create crossfire. One of Sydney's overseers had David trapped behind one of the trees. John noticed he wasn't firing back. "David, did you run out of ammunition," John asked in Cherokee.

He replied in Cherokee, "Yes. I didn't have time to grab my bow off of Big Boy."

"Run over to us son."

David ran to them but he staggered when a bullet grazed his arm. Sydney's overseer leered while John pulled David to him. The man tried to take another shot with his revolver, but Lizzie quickly took a shot, propelling an arrow into the man's shoulder. The man fell to the ground howling in pain.

"Is David okay," she asked in Cherokee, a crease now forming between her brows.

"He's fine," Eli replied in Cherokee.

"I'm taking the woman!" Wade yelled.

Lizzie slightly poked her head out from behind the tree. He fired a shot and she hid back behind the tree as the shot hit the tree. "I see she's wanting to test me," he bickered. He ran at a diagonal to avoid John's and Eli's aim while he got to the left side of the forest. Wade's movements forced her to move further back so he couldn't get an angle or her.

"Be careful Lizzie," John said in Cherokee.

"Come on out and play," Wade said. "You want to fight like a man? I'll show you how men play!"

"I'm here for my nephew!" She shouted.

"The boy belongs to Mr. Plecker now. I think you better pay more attention to me. You better understand what you've done now. You killed one White man and hurt another. That pretty face won't save you from answering for what you did."

"Well he was about to shoot a child. He deserved to die." She shot an arrow hitting the tree Wade was hiding behind. He took another shot with his revolver missing Lizzie as she hid behind a tree.

Kit charged from behind his tree to try to support Wade against Lizzie when Eli shot him in his leg. He fell to the ground, howling in pain. He tried to reach for his rifle when Eli took another shot, hitting his wrist. He held his wrist and cried in pain. He rolled on the ground again and crawled behind a tree.

"Kit, you all right," Wade yelled.

"I can't move my hand. That Indian shot my wrist. My fingers hurt to move."

Lizzie noticed the last of Sydney's overseers trying to aim at her, but his wounded shoulder handicapped him. She refocused on Wade and took a shot with her bow narrowly missing him. He glanced at the tree's ruined bark indicating Lizzie's accuracy.

He clenched his teeth and yelled as he took another shot at Lizzie. The lead ball grazed the tree causing pieces of wood to go into her left eye. She grunted while she struggled to quickly get the wood dust out of her eye. She panicked to clean her eye. She heard Wade open up his revolver to put in lead balls. She rushed from behind the tree with her bow drawn. She quickly turned to her right and released the arrow.

The arrow struck the last of Sydney's overseers in the chest as he was trying to take aim at her again. The revolver fired straight into the air and the man fell over lifeless. Wade cocked his revolver while he squinted. "Curse you…redskin whore!" He yelled. "You ain't nothing!" He took another shot at her, hitting the tree she was hiding behind.

She tried to take another shot at him, but he was waiting for her. It forced her to retreat behind the tree. She felt the lead ball hit the tree. She rubbed her eye and tried to take another shot but he continued to hide. She noticed his left foot was slightly poking out from behind the tree. Her brows furrowed. She took quick aim, and shot Wade's foot with the arrow. He screamed in pain as he knelt to the ground. He quickly tried to pull the arrow out, but when he looked up, she had run up to him with her tomahawk pulled out. He took aim at Lizzie with his revolver, but she hit the revolver from his hand. She swung again barely missing him as he dodged the swing.

The tomahawk sliced into the tree. Before Lizzie could pull it out, he tackled her, knocking most of the arrows out of her quiver. "Get off of me," she snarled.

Wade punched her in face. "Lizzie!" John yelled.

John was about to run over to help his sister, however, Eli quickly pulled him back as Mr. Plecker took a shot. The shot hit a nearby tree. Mr. Plecker shouted, "Your fight is with me, redskin!" He fired another shot trying to discourage them from helping Lizzie.

Wade continued punching her while he choked her. "You hear that, you murdering grass nigger. It's you and me now," he maliciously said.

As Wade was about to hit her again, she quickly punched

him in the nose, and punched his chin knocking him off her. "I'm not afraid of you," she coughed.

He wiped the blood from his nose while he looked at her. "You a God fearing woman?"

"Every day I pray."

"I suggest you say some prayers. Normally, I don't believe in hitting women but you and that little savage Riza hiding in them trees. Y'all are different breed that needs taming."

"I always had problems being told what to do, and you're sure not gonna break me."

"I'll break you first, and then Riza." He took a swing at Lizzie missing her, and she took a swing barely missing him. They continued to size each other up as he looked into her brown eyes, seeing no fear. He tried to take his time against her. Abruptly, she changed her strategy by charging Wade, taking two punches with one hitting him in the chest. Her aggressiveness forced him to step back as he breathed heavily. He tried the same strategy, with her boldly taking two hits to the face and shoulder. She jumped back to give herself more room when Wade tried to tackle her again.

She misstepped and hit her head on a branch. Wade took advantage of her mistake and rammed her into the tree. He grabbed her by the throat. She violently lashed out hitting him in his eye, and punched him in his lower jaw, loosening his tooth. He growled as he let go and pulled out a small knife from his side, violently swinging it. The knife cut Lizzie on her lower arm, and he slowly began to move closer to her. She held her bleeding arm. She pulled out one of the few arrows she had in the quiver while she backed away from him. "You're coward."

"You ain't no lady and there are no rules out here. Now, you can give up and we take you and them children back alive, or we can end this here." She quickly looked around but couldn't see John or Eli. "So you want things to go this way? You have no bow and can only do so much with that arrow."

Blood ran down Lizzie's arm soaking her brown blouse's sleeve. "I already told you, I never wanted to fight. All I want to do is to bring my nephew home."

"And I already gave you my answer. That pretty little face of yours would work on most men, but not me. I'm about the win." She sprinted through the forest back to where they first started to fight. He chased her. "You can only run so far!"

Wade struggled to keep up with Lizzie. As she ran, she could also hear Mr. Plecker yelling at John and Eli as he shot at them. She slowed down and threw the arrow at Wade. He gasped and instinctively lifted up both arms, the arrow lodging into his left arm. "I guess I don't need a bow!" He stopped, moaned in pain, and pulled the arrow out of his arm.

He looked around but saw nothing while he moved through the forest cautiously. "You know what? Killing you out here won't do me justice! First, I'm gone hold you down and see how much of a woman you are. Then I'm going to tie you down and whip the skin off your back! Then I'm going to make you watch as we whip the skin off them Indian children and brand your nephew with a poker until he passes out! When all of this is over, you'll wish you stayed home with some children where you belong!" He continued through the forest, tightly holding the knife. "You can only hide for so long. You keep this up and I'll go for the children."

"You won't touch my nephew."

Wade whipped around, finding Lizzie standing behind him, holding her tomahawk. He raised his knife to her, leering.

"Now, I'm giving you a chance to leave."

He chuckled. "Me leave? Woman, you is one of the crazy ones, ain't you? Does that make you feel strong now? Thinking you can tell me what to do when you haven't won. Your nephew is Joseph, isn't he?" Wade circled around Lizzie while she lifted her tomahawk. "He always said his family was going to come for him. I always thought that half-breed was losing his mind."

"All you have to do is walk away, and we'll forget all of this."

Wade leered. "I enjoyed killing his spirit, hearing his cries, but you should be proud of him. He held on longer than those field niggers. Now, I'm going to set you in your place like the rest of them."

He faked a charge, and Lizzie took a swing with her tomahawk. The two continued circling each other. "I will tear you down like the cougar," she said.

"Please try your best, redskin. After this, I'll enjoy every moment inside you while I hold you down."

Lizzie's nose crinkled. She charged Wade, screaming, and took a swing at him with her tomahawk. Wade moved to the side to dodge her swing and attempted to stab her. However, Lizzie changed the motion of her swing as she inverted the tomahawk, cutting off his hand. She then sliced into his lower back. He howled in pain. She pulled out the tomahawk and plunged it into his lower back again, then pulled out the blood-soaked blade.

Wade's eyes bulged as he collapsed.

"I wonder if Jesus will have this counted as a sin," she said while staring into his brown eyes. "I meant what I said…I didn't want to end your life."

He grumbled, "I hate you. Your people are meant for nothing but to be our servants. You'll die one day by the hands of a White man for what you did today."

"I don't hate you. I feel sorry for you. I suggest you forgive me and be grateful. The wounds I gave you leave you with time to pray for forgiveness. That's the only reason I didn't kill you faster."

"What kind of woman are you?"

"I'm a Cherokee woman…a woman who now understands her faults. I love Jesus and my family." She spit blood on the ground and limped over to her bow. "I always find it interesting. White people claim to be Christians, but you hate us. Only live by the scriptures you like. I've met few White people that show their Christian beliefs through action."

"So this is your Christian way? Leaving me here to die?"

"There's nothing I can do for you. Those two wounds on your back will kill you. I know you understand what it takes to reach the gates of Heaven. To be honest, I don't believe you deserve to see any part of Heaven but to see Hell in its full glory. I also deserve such a fate for things I've done."

Lizzie began to walk away while Wade watched, trying to

compress the wounds on his back with his left hand. "Wait...you can't leave me like this."

"For if ye forgive men their trespasses, your Heavenly Father will also forgive you. But if ye forgive not men their trespasses, neither will your Father forgive your trespasses. It took me a long time to accept that truth because I'm a prideful person... like you. That's all that I have to say to you." Lizzie limped back to John and Eli.

Wade began to weep as he felt his body grow weaker. He began to shake and couldn't feel the sun blazing through the leaves. His consciousness began to fade as he raised his hand to the sun, tears streaming down his face. "She was right about me." Wade died looking into the sun's rays.

Mr. Plecker continued his fight against John and Eli. When he hid again behind the boulder to reload his revolver, Eli quickly moved over through the trees. John shot at the boulder to provoke Mr. Plecker, who then shot at John again.

Calmly, Eli pointed his rifle at his head. "You lose, Mr. Plecker," he said.

He turned his head and saw Eli pointing the rifle at his head. "Now, hold on, boy," he said. "You best think before you pull that trigger."

"Mr. Plecker, believe it or not, I don't want to kill you. Now drop your gun."

He dropped his revolver and began to walk from around the boulder.

John stepped from around the tree, and David stood up, holding his arm. "All of this fighting when you could've given me my son back," John said. He approached Mr. Plecker while Eli held the rifle to his back. "You could've also killed my other son."

John punched Mr. Plecker, knocking him down. "Wade... Wade, where are you?" he yelled. He looked over as Kit slumped against one of the trees. "Kit?"

"Your friend, Wade, won't be able to help you," Lizzie said as she stumbled out of the woods.

John hurried toward her, noticing her blood-soaked arm.

"I'm fine. Don't worry about me."

As she approached them, John noticed the abrasions on her neck and cut on her right cheek.

"Where is he?" Mr. Plecker asked while sitting up.

She replied, "Not far from here, but he'll be dead soon."

"He gave you a real fight," Eli said. "We need to fix that arm."

She replied, "I'm fine."

"You Indians ain't nothing but savages," Mr. Plecker said. "By law, that boy and all of them children are mine. I'll have all of y'all hanged and beaten."

John kneeled down and looked at Mr. Plecker. "I'm tempted to kill you," he said. "Be grateful I'm a Christian man, but my sister is different."

Lizzie stepped forward, and Mr. Plecker gawked at her bloody arm and tomahawk. "Now wait a moment. We can make a deal," he pleaded. "I can make a deal…a fair deal."

Aiming his revolver, Kit yelled, "Now!"

Everyone's eyes widened as a gunshot echoed through the forest.

"See…" he grunted. Blood suddenly began to soak Mr. Kit's beige shirt, his eyes bulged and he fell over dead.

John and the others turned around and saw Judy Mays standing on the ledge by the creek with her rifle. John and Eli raised their rifles as Lizzie placed her tomahawk to Mr. Plecker's neck.

Austin suddenly stepped in front of Judy Mays with his revolver drawn. "Please, nobody shoot!"

"Judy Mays, have you lost your mind!" Austin yelled with his eyes locked on the Cherokee.

"Y'all are Cherokee, I assume," she said while she lowered her rifle.

"Judy Mays, what have you done?" Mr. Plecker yelled.

"I was only trying to stop Mr. Kit," she answered.

Austin looked at the dead man and sighed. "This is why women shouldn't have guns. Now we outnumbered, Judy Mays."

"Go get help," Mr. Plecker yelled.

"Quiet," Lizzie growled.

"I want to talk to y'all," Judy Mays said. "Austin, lower your gun."

Austin scowled. "Judy Mays."

"Like you said, we're outnumbered, so let's play this safe."

Austin lowered his revolver, grumbling, "You have created a mess, Judy Mays." She took a step down the ledge toward the Cherokee. "Where are you going?"

"I need to do this."

"You will stay right here. Are you blind to the blood they spilled on this land?"

Judy Mays's brow furrowed. "I have to know." She slowly approached them with her hands up.

John lowered his rifle, "Are you Judy Mays Brown?" he asked.

"Yes, I am…now Judy Mays Reynolds and I know Joseph is Annabelle's son. I was told about his escape and felt that somehow he would come across this old Bear Creek."

"I know the law, ma'am, but I'm taking my son home. I'm John Lightning."

She smirked. "So, you're the man my Annabelle fell in love with. How interesting. I'm not here to create problems. If I truly wanted to make my claim on Joseph, I would've done so a long time ago."

"Then why have y'all come out this way?" Eli asked.

Judy Mays answered, "I've grown quite fond of Joseph. He reminds me of his momma. He has her smile."

"I see," John said, his brows drawn together. He pointed to a tree sitting several feet in front of the shallow creek. "We'll talk there, but tell your husband to drop his revolver."

She nodded, replying, "He is my brother-in-law, Austin." She looked at him who had now stepped down from the ledge holding his revolver. "Austin, I need you to put down your revolver."

"You need me to what?" he said with a crinkled nose.

"As you said, we're outnumbered. There is no more need for bloodshed. They just want to speak with me."

"Have you lost your mind? These savages can't be trusted."

"Austin, please. I'm asking you to trust me."

"Women ain't got no strong judgment." Judy Mays scowled and put her hands on her hips. Austin scoffed and put his revolver on the swamp floor. "Thank you."

Lizzie nodded to Eli, and he stepped up to Mr. Plecker to guard him. Judy Mays nervously walked to the tree with the Lightning siblings walking beside her. "Don't you savages touch her," Mr. Plecker said.

"Quiet," Lizzie commanded as she turned around.

Judy Mays stopped in front of the tree, saying, "In all honesty, I miss Annabelle greatly. I was hoping he'd eventually lead me to her. I know that may sound strange."

Lizzie's eyes narrowed. "Annabelle is a runaway slave. Why would we risk the chance of Annabelle becoming enslaved again?"

"I know there's fire in her and if pushed, she'd risk it. I know her, because I did what no White girl was supposed to do. I grew a strong friendship with a Negro girl," Judy Mays said. "I love her so much. I can admit I was very angry at her, but she is a sister to me. I'm so sorry for what Joseph has experienced. But I couldn't claim him. It's complicated and with this war, there was no way I could take him to Indian Territory."

"Why didn't you claim Joseph?" John asked.

Judy Mays sighed. "Because my papa is alive and he did terrible things before Annabelle ran away. He would've beaten Joseph to near death to find out where she was. My papa would be too dangerous around him."

Joseph came out from behind the trees and went to Judy Mays. "Thank you, Mrs. Judy Mays," he said.

A tear escaped her right eye and she gave Joseph a hug. "Tell your momma, I miss her so much and maybe after this war, we can see each other again," Judy Mays said.

"I will."

The other Indian children came from behind the trees and approached her. "I believe after this war would be a wise time for you to see Annabelle again," John said. Lizzie looked up at her, saying, "Whichever way this war ends, I think we will welcome you in Tahlequah."

"Thank you. I'm sorry, what's your name?"

"I'm Lizzie, his sister and that man over there is our brother-in-law, Eli."

Judy Mays looked at Lizzie and saw her blood-soaked arm. "How nice…well, I think it's wise that I stay in place. You seem slightly short-tempered at the moment."

John grinned. "She can be nice most times. We need to decide what to do with Mr. Plecker."

Judy Mays replied, "Send the grumpy man home. I'm friends with his wife. You've won today. He won't be able to find you, especially with this war going on."

"Eli, get one of the horses, and make sure Mr. Plecker isn't armed," John said.

"I'll do that fast," Eli said.

"Judy Mays, you killed Kit!" Mr. Plecker yelled. "You reckless woman! Look at the position you put us in!"

Her nose scrunched as she approached him. "Mr. Plecker, I clearly misfired and killed him accidently. I'm not proud of it, but…I've watched you for years sadistically rule your slaves," Judy Mays said standing a few feet before him. "I used to believe my father was one of the worst in the state, but year after year you proved me wrong. I'll gladly inform authorities myself and Austin encountered this incident, and I tried to help. As far as they will be concerned, my actions were accidental. At this point, the children should be set free. I see no other way to resolve this."

"So you on their side now? After all these years, and being raised by a good family, you gone turn against your roots?"

"I'm outnumbered, Mr. Plecker. Further, my concern is how my children grow up. I want them to grow up into people far better than myself. This requires them to look beyond a person's skin color. Again, to be honest, I didn't mean to kill Mr. Kit. I'm sorry."

Mr. Plecker growled, "Your lack of empathy says otherwise."

"I never cared for Mr. Kit. Though I must admit I'm in shock."

"I'll be happy to inform your parents and the authorities of this transgression. Austin is a witness."

"Actually, Mr. Plecker, given the circumstances, I'm with Judy Mays," he said.

Mr. Plecker's eyes bulged. "You're what!"

"This was an accident, Mr. Plecker."

Judy Mays sighed. "By all means, tell them. I apologize for Mr. Kit. I know he has his wife, but I'm not standing with this sick culture anymore."

Mr. Plecker scoffed. "The boy, he belongs to your family, doesn't he? Think, all the effort you gave to find Annabelle, and by God's great hand you find her son. Take what is yours and bring that runaway back to where she belongs. Bring honor to your family. I know you cared about that slave. Your papa spoke so much about how sad you were when she escaped."

Abruptly, Lizzie walked past Judy Mays startling her. She pressed her tomahawk against Mr. Plecker's throat and snarled, "That's enough from you." Eli brought a horse to them. "Get on the horse." He stood up and towered over Lizzie. "Is there a problem, Mr. Plecker?"

"I'm gone remember you and when I get settled, I'm coming after all of y'all," he bickered.

"Goodbye, Mr. Plecker." Lizzie said.

Mr. Plecker's face began to turn red. "Judy Mays, you helping these prairie niggers?"

"To be honest, she doesn't have a choice. Don't be fooled by my nephew hugging her. She's a prisoner. She leaves after you and Mr. Austin. If you come back, I'll kill her."

Austin took a step forward, replying, "If you touch her—"

She side-eyed Austin. "Don't make me change my mind. I'll end you and then her."

Mr. Plecker's brows lowered. "We're being held hostage by a squaw. Judy Mays, I'll have to consider you ever being welcomed onto my property after this. Your father will hear of this!"

"I'm sure he will," she said.

"Don't be scared, I'll keep my word," Lizzie said. "Unlike your people."

Holding his rifle, Eli stepped up to Austin. "It's time for you to get your horse."

"I'm not leaving her," he said. "I could never do something so cowardly."

Eli's brow lowered. "What should we do with this one, John?"

Mr. Plecker bellowed, "You grass niggers will be hanged! And Annabelle will be brought right here where that nigger belongs."

Lizzie abruptly kicked Mr. Plecker's back knee, and he fell. "Lizzie," John sternly said.

"Get up, old man and get on this horse," she said with irritation in her voice.

"Do as they say, Judy Mays," Mr. Plecker said as he slowly stood up. He then mounted the horse.

"It's time to leave, Mr. Plecker," John commanded.

He huffed, signaled the horse, and rode off. In the distance, he shouted, "We will find you!"

"Tie Mr. Austin to that tree over there," John said, pointing to a young elm tree standing over fifteen feet in height. Eli and Lizzie tied him to the tree so he was facing away from John and Judy Mays.

Judy Mays sighed. "I know all of you have to leave now," she said.

"Yes, it's wise we leave now, and get the rest of these children back to Indian Territory," John said.

They finished tying Austin to the tree and walked up to John and Judy Mays. "John, it's time to go," Eli said. "He won't hear us from this distance, but the clock is against us, even though it will take Mr. Plecker time to get help."

John replied, "That's true." He turned toward the four children whom were standing by the tree where he had spoken with Judy Mays. "Children we're leaving."

Judy Mays approached the children, "Riza, how are you going to return to your family?"

Riza answered, "I was going to stay with them for a while,

and return to New York. I can't think of another way to return to my family."

"I can make sure you return safely to New York, and they wouldn't be able to find you."

"Why would you?"

"As a Christian woman, I've grown to question many things in our country. I never lied when I said I enjoyed your company, and to be honest, you remind me of Annabelle and myself. More importantly, I know your momma is alive, Riza."

Her eyes widened and she shook her head. "Please, don't lie to me, Mrs. Judy Mays."

"It's no lie. She did fight for you. Sadly, she couldn't get you back, but I'm certain she is alive. Please allow me to do what I couldn't do at the Plecker estate and send you to your family. No one would question me while I take you back up north."

Riza's eyes shimmered with tears. "You're telling the truth."

"Yes, I am."

She took deep breaths attempting to stop herself from crying. She wiped away the tears escaping her eyes, replying, "Thank you, Mrs. Judy Mays."

She smiled. "There is no need to say that. I believe returning you home is long overdue."

"How can we be sure you'll take this girl back home?" Eli asked.

"I know she will," Riza said. "She's known me for years since I was a scared seven-year-old girl. She was the only one to show me kindness and call me my real name. She had no reason to do such a thing. I understand her now."

"Judy Mays, how did you know we were here?" John asked.

She answered, "It's embarrassing to say, but I had a dream about a bear being here. I'm familiar with this area because my father used to bring me here. We used to see an old black bear that would lay down next to the creek, and sleep in the sun. I felt it was God sending me a message."

"I also had a dream that helped us get here. The Father works in mysterious ways. I'm glad you listened."

"So am I."

Lizzie brought over one of the men's horses and gave the reins to Riza. "I can tell you're a fighter like me," she said. "Never lose that kind of heart."

Riza replied, "Thank you, Miss Lizzie Lightning."

She beamed. "See, even a good listener. I didn't tell you my name." Riza smiled back at her.

Lizzie walked over to the creek and washed off the blood on her right arm. "I think it's wise that you and Riza go a different path than Mr. Plecker," Eli said.

Judy Mays replied, "We'll take the dirt road that I came on. The road will take us straight to Columbus. I can hide her in a small patch of forest that's right next to a bridge. The few Confederate men we may come across won't question me. I can then grab her at sunset. I can't leave Austin out here, so I'll have to drop Riza off first and then come back for him. It'll be the safest way."

"Good, it was nice to meet you, Judy Mays," John said.

"Yes, it was a pleasure to meet all of you," she said. "I wish this was under far better circumstances."

Lizzie moved past Judy Mays and John while she wrapped her wound. She approached David and smiled at him. Abruptly, Lizzie slapped him, and the sound echoed through the forest. "You idiot! You come out here alone!" Lizzie roared. "Look at you, you've been shot twice, and is that a cut on your arm? I should shoot you myself!"

John cleared his throat, grumbling, "Lizzie—"

She angrily replied, "I'm not done! Just wait for us to get home, and you explain to your momma what you did!" Her voice slightly broke with concern. "You should have waited for us. We were going to take you with us!"

David frowned as he stood before his aunt. "I'm sorry, Auntie Lizzie," he said. Please forgive me...I missed Joseph so much."

Lizzie gave him a hug and kissed him on the cheek. "Next time, you wait." She approached Joseph and tightly embraced her nephew. "Look how much you've grown! My little warrior."

He suddenly began to cry as Lizzie held him. "I never stopped praying, Auntie Lizzie," Joseph cried in their native tongue.

"You did good. It's time for us to go." She continued calmly in English, "Judy Mays, it was nice to meet you. I heard many good things about you."

"Thank you," she said. "After all of this chaos ends, I will visit Tahlequah."

Lizzie smiled and walked to the other children with her arm around Joseph. "Now who are these children?" she asked.

Judy Mays watched while Joseph introduced Susie and Tom to Lizzie and turned to David. She huffed. "So you're Annabelle's son too…wow, I've missed a lot."

"Momma spoke a lot about you," he said.

She grinned, "At least I know she misses me. Well, Riza I agree it's time we go. My horse is over here."

"I'll walk you to the horse," John said.

"Wait," Joseph said. He ran up to Riza and gave her a hug. "Bye, Riza."

She smiled and said, "Bye, Joseph. Grow up to be strong. Maybe we will see each other again."

He smiled. "I hope so."

Susie and Tom also came up to Riza to say their goodbyes.

"Thank you for being our strength," Tom said with watery eyes.

"Thank you for your kindness. It made life easier," Riza said as she gave Tom a hug. Susie and Riza then hugged each other and began to cry. "I know we'll see each other again," Susie said wiping away her tears.

"It'll be a happy day," Riza said.

Out of Austin's sight, John, Joseph, Judy Mays, and Riza walked up to Judy Mays's horse hidden in the forest with the horse Lizzie gave Riza. Judy Mays and Riza got onto the horses. She smiled at the Cherokee. "Hopefully this war ends soon," she said. "Take care, John and Joseph."

"The both of you take care too," John said.

"Bye," Joseph said.
"Bye," Riza said.

Judy Mays and Riza rode off as John and Joseph watched. John looked at Joseph and gave his son a hug. "I've missed you so much, son. Your momma will be so happy to see you," John said.

"I missed you too, Papa," Joseph said. "Can we have cornbread when we get home?"

John replied with a smile, "We brought some with us. You know your auntie wasn't going to go anywhere without it."

"It doesn't have butter on it, does it?"

"Nope, no butter, son." Joseph smiled, and the two walked back to the others. Lizzie took care of David's wounds, and they rode off to the carriage.

Once they reached the carriage, they rode back to Tahlequah. During their ride back to Tahlequah, Joseph and Lizzie sat next to each other the majority of the way to let her arm heal. Eli took Queen, and David rode Big Boy while John steered the carriage. The ride to Tahlequah was exciting for Susie as she had more than one person now to speak Cherokee to. "I can't wait to see my momma," Tom said. "She was the last person I saw before I was taken." Tears fell down his face. "I was starting to forget what she sounded like."

Joseph frowned, "You never said anything like that before."

"I was scared. I didn't want it to mean I didn't love her."

"I wonder if Riza experienced the same thing."

"Forgetting the sound of someone's voice doesn't mean you don't love them," Lizzie said. "Forgetting memories on purpose means you're trying to forget them."

"I would never do that," Tom said.

Lizzie half-smiled. "Then that means you never stopped loving them. I'm sure your momma will never let you out of her sight. You've grown since your kidnapping, I'm guessing."

He slightly frowned. "Yes, ma'am, I did."

"It'll give your family more reason to celebrate your return."

"Is it really over?"

"We've gained too much distance. It's over, but I'm not sure about the war. Hopefully it ends soon so the three of you can grow up in peace." Lizzie rubbed Joseph's head. "I think the three of you deserve some real peace."

"I hope I can see Dorothy again," Susie said.

"Pray to the Father to help make it possible. I know you children had a rough time, but it doesn't mean your prayers go unanswered. It means there is something more important to the story. If we'd found Joseph sooner, we wouldn't have freed you two or Riza. Never let anger take over your heart, and always believe in your heart Jesus is for you. I wish getting older made life easier, but it doesn't."

"Auntie Lizzie, did you get married?" Joseph asked.

Her eyes bulged. "What makes you ask that?"

"You sound like Auntie Grace."

She lightly chuckled. "Careful now, other arm isn't hurt." She lightly tickled Joseph causing him to giggle. She hugged him and kissed him on his forehead. "I guess you can say Elder Joyce had some final words for me."

Joseph smiled. "I can't wait to see her. She makes the best three sisters soup."

Lizzie's gaze shifted off Joseph and frowned. "Yeah, let's get all of you home."

At this time, Judy Mays had led Riza to the wooden bridge, which had large trees on both sides shading it as the sun moved. "Riza, you stay here, and I promise to return," Judy Mays said. I have to go get Austin, and once I'm able to get him and return home with him, I should have no time returning here by sunset."

"What if you don't return?" she asked.

"I promise you I will return." Judy Mays handed her the sack of prepared food Patty had given her. "It took us two hours to come out this far. If I don't get back to you by sunset, I will come here in the night."

She grinned. "My momma is alive."

Judy Mays put her hand on her shoulder. "Yes, she is. Now, just be patient and I will return to you."

She gave her a hug. "Okay."

Judy Mays mounted her horse and had the other horse walk alongside them. Once she got to Bear Creek, she let the horse go wander off, and untied Austin. He was furious with what the Cherokee had done, but was happy to see they kept their word and she was unharmed. He immediately took Judy Mays home. Once they arrived at home, he left to report the incident. Judy Mays beamed as she greeted her children with hugs and kisses. She thought, *I couldn't imagine how you're going to feel once you see Joseph, Annabelle. I'm sorry I couldn't do more.* Moments later, Judy Mays instructed her carriage driver to get the carriage prepared. She sat on her porch for an hour with the thought of Austin returning and entertained her children. The sunrays began to cut the land as the sunset began. She approached LeRoy, "It's time. We're going to the wooden bridge that's about half an hour away from Bear Creek."

"We gone be pushing it close, Mrs. Judy Mays," LeRoy said.

"I know, but if Austin does come back, I have you with me, and as far as I'm concerned, I needed to take a calm ride after all the excitement today."

He nodded. "Yes, ma'am." He then helped Judy Mays into the carriage, and they rode off. A few hours later, the sun had nearly set, and the sounds of insects filled the air. The bridge had come into sight in front of them. "Mrs. Judy Mays, we here, just a few minutes away."

She scanned the land as her fingers drummed on her thighs. "Do you see anyone?"

"No, ma'am."

"Good, stop right in front of the bridge."

"Yes, ma'am."

He stopped the carriage in front of the bridge and helped Judy Mays get off. "Riza, come on, girl," she shouted. A few minutes passed, and there was no response. "Riza?" She began to march toward the trees, her eyes rapidly scanning the land.

"I'm here, Mrs. Judy Mays," Riza said. She exhaled and looked up to the sky. "I was squatting, I think I drank too much water."

Judy Mays waved her toward her. "Well come, we don't have much time. We can't let anyone see us." Riza quickly hurried to her and they walked to the carriage.

LeRoy's eyes widened. "Why, Mrs. Judy Mays, that's Riza. Ain't she a runaway now?"

"LeRoy, you will say nothing of this or we will have a problem, is that understood?" She said with a stern tone.

He helped Riza into the carriage, saying, "I saw nothing, ma'am."

"That's what I like to hear." He then helped Judy Mays into the carriage and drove them back to her mansion. They arrived at the mansion with a half-moon shining light onto the dark land. Once inside the mansion, she introduced Riza to her children, and had her stay in one of her guest rooms upstairs.

CHAPTER 14
Chosen Paths and Reunions

A FEW DAYS LATER, THE CARRIAGE arrived in Tahlequah. The sight of the town caused Joseph and Susie to become filled with joy seeing the Cherokee town. The carriage arrived at the Lightning-Strongman farm. "Joseph, we're home," David said.

He anxiously got out of the carriage and slowly walked to the family house. John began to tremble as he wiped tears from his face. David put his arm around his brother's shoulders and walked with him. Abruptly, Joseph shouted, "Momma!"

As the brothers approached the house, the door quickly opened, and Annabelle came out. She screamed, "My boys…my baby boy!" She ran to David and Joseph giving both of them a hug. She gave David a kiss on the cheek and embraced Joseph as she cried while giving her son kisses. "My baby boy, I knew Jesus would make a way for us to bring you home. Look how much you've grown, my baby boy." Annabelle continued to hug her son, but frowned as she felt the scars on Joseph's back.

Tsula and Maria came out of the house with Gabriel, Jonathan, Katelyn, Sky, and Sunni. The two women brought the toddlers to Joseph and greeted him with hugs and kisses. For the first time, he saw his younger cousins, Gabriel and Katelyn. He gave a big smile while he interacted with his younger cousins and Jonathan. Jacob heard the commotion while working in the fields and strolled around the barn to see Joseph crowded by the others. "They found him! Joseph is home!" Jacob yelled in Cherokee. George, Michael, and Samuel dropped what they were doing and followed Jacob while he ran to Joseph. Susie and Tom were also welcomed and were immediately sat down at the supper table to be fed lunch. During this time, Jacob rode the carriage to the supply store and told Grace and Lisa the great news. The two women immediately ran out of the supply store leaving the door open, and Jacob drove them to their home. Annabelle saw Grace and Lisa entered the house. The corners of her mouth curved into a big smile. The two women entered the living room and saw Joseph. Immediately, they approached him and gave him hugs and kisses.

"Auntie Lisa, you're having another baby!" He excitedly said in Cherokee.

"And you'll be here to welcome the baby," Lisa tearfully said. A few hours later, the twins and Rosita were being escorted home by a teacher, and screamed once they saw Joseph standing on the porch. The girls sprinted to him and gave him hugs while they cried with joy. Annabelle wiped tears from her face while she watched the children love each other.

A few minutes later, Grace came out of the house with Susie. "Joseph, it's time for us to take her home," Grace said in Cherokee.

Speaking Cherokee, she said, "I already spoke with Tom." "Being here with your family makes me more excited to see mine."

Joseph embraced her, and she hugged him back. "I'm going to miss you so much," he said in their native tongue. "Thank you. You protected me."

"You tried to protect me too."

As the two friends let go of each other, Susie gave him a kiss on the cheek, and he blushed. "Ooo," the girls said.

"Girls," Grace sternly said.

"We will see each other again," Susie said.

"We will see each other again," Joseph said.

"I'll let you know where she lives later," Grace said. "Let's get you home, Susie." She followed Grace closely. Grace reassuringly patted her on her back. The two stopped in front of the carriage. She felt her heart pound heavier.

"Let's get you home," John said. John and Grace took Susie to her family. She fidgeted with her fingers while she spoke with Grace. The carriage stopped in front of a brown house half the side of the Lightning-Strongman family's house. A well was a few hundred feet to the left of the house. Two small red barns were to the right of the house and a medium-sized field was placed behind the barns. Susie got out of the carriage and stepped on the green grass. She took a step forward to the house and her body began to tremble. "Momma," she bellowed in her native tongue. Tears fell from her eyes as she breathed heavily.

The front door quickly opened, and a brown-skinned woman with her hair in a bun and Annabelle's height came out. The wide-eyed woman put her hands to her chest. "Susie!" she yelled. She ran to her mother and the two embraced each other tightly while they cried and kissed each other. "My Susie, look at you," she said in Cherokee. "You've grown, my baby you've grown." She looked up at Grace and John as they approached. "Thank you, thank you so much. How did you find her?"

"My son was kidnapped and taken to the same plantation," John said in their language. "I'm John Lightning."

"I'm Grace Five Killer, John is my brother. We live on the outskirts of Tahlequah."

"May Jesus bless you all of your days. I'm Lena Coleman. My baby was stolen four years ago. Thank you for what you did."

"I understand your pain," John said. "We should get together later on to celebrate their freedom."

Lena smiled. "I'd like that."

"Sounds like a plan," Grace said. "We will see each other again, Susie."

She grinned and wiped away her tears, saying, "We will see each other again, Miss Grace, Mr. Lightning."

John smiled and nodded, saying, "We'll return soon to make plans for a celebration."

"We'll be looking for you. My husband Eddie will be pleased to meet you. We will see each other again," Lena said.

"We will see each other again," John said. He and Grace left the Coleman farm for their family house smiling and delivered the good news to Joseph.

At supper, the family celebrated Joseph and David's safe return. The family sat down at supper with chicken stew, cornbread, beans, squash, and a freshly cooked turkey. George prayed over the food with his voice slightly breaking. He looked at Joseph with watery eyes and smiled at him, saying, "Today, we are complete and the Heavens have blessed us beyond what we asked. Welcome home, Joseph." He sat next to David, and Tom sat to his right. The atmosphere at supper was the same as Joseph remembered it. Tsula created a humorous conversation while she fed Katelyn in her lap. Grace and Lisa kept Lizzie in check when she was provoked by Tsula.

Tears began to hit Joseph's plate and his arms began to shake. The others at the supper table frowned seeing him breakdown. "Joseph…it's okay," David said.

"I missed everyone so much," Joseph said as he wiped tears from his face. "I love all of you."

"We love you too, Joseph," Rain said with a smile on her face.

David then put his arm around his brother. "It's like what Uncle George said. Now we're complete," he said.

Joseph replied, "I miss good cornbread."

The family laughed, and Lizzie put another piece on Joseph's plate. "That's my nephew," she said smiling. He wiped the tears from his face, and he kept smiling the entire night. The family spent the rest of the night together, catching up and keeping Tom encouraged since his journey home would begin tomorrow. Later in the night, Tom slept in the boys' room with Joseph and David, anxious to see his own family.

At this time, Annabelle was lying in bed with John. Their room was illuminated by a lamp sitting on a wooden stand next to Annabelle's Bible. She rolled over in bed and looked at John. "You're an amazing man," she said. "I want you to know that I never believed you failed us. Not once did I feel that way."

"Please don't say that," John said.

"Too late…what's this tear I see on your face?" He wiped away the tear and caressed Annabelle's cheek. "I'm worried about Joseph. It wasn't like him to start crying like that."

He frowned. "I know."

"Did you feel the scars on his back?"

He sighed. "I didn't want to make him relive what happened to him. He's safe…that's what matters to me."

"We know it was Brock Jackson. What are we going to do about him?"

"We'll do what we have been. Keep the children close. Capture him, if Lizzie or Lisa doesn't kill him first and have him shipped back east where he belongs."

"I know the Lord says, vengeance is mine, but I've never been tested like this. Not after what he did to my baby."

"He won't escape what's coming to him whether it's a bullet, an arrow, or a noose. My personal favorite would be lightning."

"I guess we have to leave it to the Father."

"There's no better hand to handle it. We'll do our best to move forward."

Annabelle half-smiled. "I still can't believe y'all met Judy Mays. I was still struggling with the fact she encountered Joseph. What was it like seeing her?"

"She seemed a little desperate but kind…like Molly. It's rare to meet White women like that."

"I imagine she still looks the same."

"Yeah, looked young with pretty blonde hair. Are you going to grow blonde hair now?"

Annabelle laughed and playfully hit John on his chest. "That isn't one of God's gifts to me. She wants to visit after the war. It'll be good to see her."

"The two of you have a lot to talk about."

"Yeah, we do. I'll have to make sure Joseph is okay first. Who knows what my baby witnessed." She exhaled.

John kissed her. "Everything will be okay."

She kissed John and laid her head on his chest. "I hope so."

The next morning, the women prepared breakfast for the family. Joseph sat at the supper table with Tom and the other children enjoying the food. Annabelle came out of the kitchen with another big bowl of grits. She put down the bowl on the table and smiled while she watched Joseph talk to the others. Lizzie approached her with Sky in her arms. "Momma, after this, can I go see Elder Joyce?" he asked.

Annabelle felt her heart drop as the table went silent. She glanced at Lizzie and saw the frown on her face. "Joseph, sweetie, come here," she said. He got up from the table and came to her. She caressed his cheek. "Not too long ago, Elder Joyce walked on in her sleep. Lea found her. I'm so sorry, baby."

"She's gone?"

Annabelle shook her head yes. "Yes, but she prophesied we'd find you." Joseph began to weep, and she embraced her son. David and the children watched frowning. Lizzie approached Joseph, who had his head embedded into Annabelle's belly and lovingly rubbed his head. Tears started to fall down her face. She grunted, annoyingly wiped the tears away, and went into her room with Sky. "We'll take you to her grave so you can say your thanks to her. Okay?" He nodded yes. Annabelle took Joseph and sat him back down at the table.

"Was it only her?"

Annabelle rubbed Joseph's back. "Nobody else has passed since you were gone." She kissed him on the cheek. "I promise."

Later in the afternoon, Luke and Lizzie prepared the wagon for a short trip to the Natchez Nation. Tom said his goodbyes to everyone and then walked to the wagon where Joseph was waiting for him. He looked at Lizzie and smiled, saying, "Thank you for rescuing me."

Lizzie replied with a smile, "You're welcome, Tom."

Tom looked at Joseph. "If your family didn't come for you, we might still be slaves," Tom said. "I owe you."

"You owe me nothing, Tom," he said. "We're friends."

"Yes, we are. Hopefully, over time, we'll hear from Riza."

"I think Mrs. Judy Mays will keep her word."

"I think so too. I will miss you."

"I will miss you too. When we get older, maybe we can visit each other."

"I think we will. Bye, Joseph."

"Bye, Tom." He grinned at Joseph and got into the wagon.

"We'll be back by supper time, Joseph," Luke said. The wagon rode off while Joseph waved bye. Annabelle smiled as her son said goodbye to his friend. Lizzie, Luke, and Tom arrived in the Natchez territory. Tom directed them to a small brown house with two chicken pens next to it. A brown-skinned, curly-haired man was seen going to a shed. He turned around and his brown eyes widened. Tom got down from the wagon and ran to the man. "Papa," he yelled.

Tom's father ran to him and hugged him. Lizzie and Luke approached the man. "I'm Larry Clearwater," he said. "You found my boy. Thank you."

"You're welcome. I'm Luke Fields. He'd been kidnapped to the same plantation as our nephew."

"I'm Lizzie Lightning."

"Nice to meet you both," Larry said. "My wife, Theresa, is at the supply store right now. She's going to be so happy. God bless you both."

"We'll return later on with Joseph. We're coming from Tahlequah."

"Wow, you have a nice ride home."

"Yes, we do. Tom, keep being brave."

"Thank you, Miss Lizzie," he said.

"We'll see you again, Tom," Luke said.

"Bye Marshall Luke," Tom replied.

"Y'all take care," Larry said.

"You too," Lizzie and Luke said. The Cherokee got back into the wagon and rode away. While driving away they saw Tom be greeted by his siblings. Lizzie smiled. When they arrived home, Annabelle had already started to write letters for Mercy, Missouri. She was excited for her friends to know of Joseph's return home.

Meanwhile in Mississippi, tempers flared as Mr. Plecker had gone to the courts accusing Judy Mays of impeding their efforts to recapture the Indian children and recounted her disrespectful conversation. He also had her intentions questioned in regarding Mr. Sean Kit's death. However, Judy Mays claimed she was on her way to the creek with Austin to enjoy memories of her childhood. She stated the Cherokee outnumbered them so she complied. She claimed she has no strong rifle skills and tearfully apologized for Sean Kit's death. She further claimed Mr. Plecker was simply furious the Cherokee spared her life because she knew Joseph's mother. She stated to the courts that Mr. Plecker hated her kindness toward the children, and she felt greatly insulted by Mr. Plecker's accusations. She continued stating her family's reputation, and apologized for leaving her residence. She continued to cry stating she believed her life was in danger and she had failed her family by not discovering Annabelle's location in Indian Territory. She further apologized for insulting Mr. Plecker, and said she was upset with Joseph's escape. Austin supported her claim in that there was no way they could've known they'd ran into such a dangerous situation. The courts later dismissed Mr. Plecker's accusations because of the lack of evidence and their belief in Austin's claims of the incident.

Edgar and Judy Mays later arrived home and entered their mansion. "We have a lot to apologize for over time," he said.

She sighed. "Yes, I know. Again, I'm sorry, dear."

"I know you. You're not a bad shot. I don't believe you meant to kill him, but you have to admit, you've put us in quite the predicament."

"I never thought her son would stand before me first. I always believed it'd be her. By God's grace, her family found Joseph. How could I stand in their way?"

"There was nothing you could've done. You were outnumbered. Even if it was one Cherokee, I know you would've let them go. You've always loved Annabelle."

"Why do I feel like I didn't do enough?"

"You did everything you could. There was a good reason you didn't claim him."

She deeply exhaled. "I'm going to check on our guest."

He kissed her on her forehead. "Okay. I look forward to hearing more of her wit."

Judy Mays smiled and went upstairs. She greeted her children and then approached a guest room. She opened the door and saw Riza sitting in a chair with a book on her lap. "You look worried," she said.

"Are they looking for me?" she asked.

"Yes, they are. The courts believe the Cherokee took you, though."

Riza closed the book. "It's going to be a while before I go back to New York, isn't it?"

"Mr. Plecker is more than upset with me. I'm sure I'll have more unannounced visits, so yes. We have to let the attention on me quiet down. I promise we'll leave in a few weeks at least."

Riza half-smiled. "I believe you. Is it crazy almost forgot what it feels like to sleep in a real bed. I used to lie down on a bed for a minute before cleaning but to actually sleep on one. Thank you, Mrs. Judy Mays."

"No need to thank me. Your freedom was long overdue. I've watched you almost completely grow up. I guess you can say it makes me feel guiltier, but I'm more than happy to get you home. I'll have lunch brought up to you, and afterward, we can play another guessing game."

Riza grinned. "Okay." She left the room and had lunch brought to her. She and her children later spent time with Riza.

Weeks later, Edgar and Judy Mays made arrangements to make a trip up to New York City with Riza, Patty, and their children. The carriage rode across the states, avoiding the war-torn parts of the country. Once passing through Kentucky, they reached Pennsylvania and took a train from there to New York. Once in New York, they took a ferry to New York City and rented a hotel for a night. During the night, Riza stared out of the hotel window.

Judy Mays calmly walked up to Riza. "Nervous?" she asked.

Riza answered, "I think so, that and excited. I haven't been here in eight years. I've been away from my family for eight years. They won't know me."

"Mommas never forget. I promise the moment your momma sees you, she won't be able to control herself. Try to rest so when we go through the city, you'll be rested, and there will be nothing holding you back."

"Thank you, Mrs. Judy Mays. If it wasn't for you and Mr. Reynolds's kindness, it would've taken me longer to get here."

She smiled at Riza. "When I said you remind me of me...I actually see much more that reminds me of Annabelle when she was your age. And as a momma, I couldn't imagine the pain yours has suffered all these years. My only regret was not finding a way to do this sooner."

Judy Mays went to bed, followed by Riza. She sat up in her bed, continuing to look out of the window. Riza thought, *I can't believe how much the city has changed*. The next morning, Edgar and Judy Mays took Riza around the city to find her family. As they traveled through the city, she recognized a supply store she always went to as a child. She immediately went a few blocks down and recognized the neighborhood. She took the lead while Edgar and Judy Mays followed her to a tan-bricked house. She knocked on the door. Someone could be heard walking to the door.

The door opened, and a caramel-skinned woman stood at it. "Hi, Mommy," Riza said.

The woman gasped and slowly put her hand to her face, and touched her hair. "How...all these years. I thought they killed you," Riza's mother said as she began to cry. "I thought we were never going to see you again." Her mother embraced her as she cried, "Thank you, Jesus!" Riza's mother looked at Edgar and Judy Mays. "Who are they?"

Riza replied, "That's Mr. Reynolds and Mrs. Judy Mays."

"Hello, ma'am, there's much you need to know," she said. "You have an incredible daughter."

"I'm Violet Moon, please come in." Judy Mays and Edgar entered Riza's home and stayed down in the living room. The wooden floored living room had white walls, a brown couch, three tall windows allowing in sunlight, and a few old pictures on a wall and a lampstand. Here, Judy Mays explained how Riza had been put into slavery. The news was shocking for Violet. She wept when she felt the scars on Riza's back and noticed her injured pinky finger. Her shock quickly changed to gratitude for her efforts. Violet was so overcome with joy she insisted that Edgar and Judy Mays stay for lunch. It was hard to ignore her eagerness to bless them. The Reynolds enjoyed seeing Riza's interactions with her younger siblings who could barely remember her.

While Riza reunited with her two brothers. Violet got up from a chair and went into her bedroom. Returning to the living room, her long, straight, dark brown hair bounced while she smiled. She handed ten pictures to Judy Mays. The pictures were of Riza when she was a little girl. After a few hours, the Reynolds had to leave. They left the home as Riza stood next to her mother. "Thank you, Mrs. Judy Mays. I'll miss you and you too, Mr. Reynolds," she said.

Judy Mays smiled and turned around to take one more look at Riza. "I'll miss you too, Riza," she said. "Please write me."

"It's been a pleasure, Riza," Edgar said. "God bless you."

'Thank you again for bringing her back to us," Violet said. Tears streamed down her face. "You have no idea how the Father has used you."

Continuing to smile, Judy Mays replied, "It was an honor

to bring her home." They walked away back to the hotel. On their way back, Judy Mays began to feel she had accomplished what God had put into her heart. She was now focused on preparing herself to deal with her family. The couple arrived at the hotel and were greeted by their children and Patty. Later in the day, the family caught a train to travel back to Columbus, Mississippi. The children were happy for Riza. Judy Mays looked out of the train window as it passed through a forest. She began to lightly tap her finger on her thigh, and her mouth curved into a slight frown. *I can no longer remain silent, I don't have a choice*, she thought.

CHAPTER 15
The Unapologetic Truth

ON MAY 3, 1862, a few days after Judy Mays returned home, there was a knock at the Reynolds mansion. She opened the door and sighed while she looked her father. "Hi, Papa," she said.

"May I come in to see my daughter and grandchildren?" Mr. Brown asked.

"Come in, Papa." He came inside the mansion and was greeted by the children. She escorted her father into the living room. A burgundy rug with white flowers covered most of the room's floor. The room had a fireplace, family pictures on a coffee table, and two burgundy couches. A large window behind the two couches allowed the sunlight to shine into the room. After the children spent time with their grandfather, Judy Mays called for Patty to take the children upstairs. She sat down next to her father on a couch.

Mr. Brown chuckled. "Them children are growing fast. They remind me of you."

"What are you here for, Papa?"

He wiped his forehead. "You worry me greatly. You lied to the courts, and more importantly, you withheld the truth from me. You figured out that boy was Annabelle's, but you didn't tell me. How disrespectful is that?"

"I didn't mean to disrespect you. I wanted to learn more about him."

"What can you even tell me about him? Besides the fact he was involved in Riza's crazy revolt."

"He has her smile. He's smart like her, speaks good English like her."

Mr. Brown's brows lowered, and he exhaled. "I question if you helped that boy escape. Annabelle belongs back here in Mississippi, and every single child she has produced, that's the law."

"I'm sorry, Papa. I couldn't help Mr. Plecker, I was outnumbered. I also saw how much effort Joseph's family put into finding him. I kept thinking to myself about how the mothers of those children felt. Not being able to kiss their children before bed, or cook a meal for them. I can't be a part of this slave culture anymore."

Mr. Brown squinted and pouted. "So you gone turn your backs on us? You favor Annabelle over the law of this land, the very laws we survive on. So you're going to raise them children to be nigger lovers now?"

"Don't say that in my house, Papa. I love you and the family, but I can't teach my children to hate. I grew up that way, and it took me years to break free of that thinking. I won't curse my children with the same problems!"

"You have let your feelings for her mess up your head. I expect every one of my slaves to show me respect. I expect them to do the same with my grandchildren. Where is Annabelle?"

Judy Mays gave a blank stare. "I don't know."

He huffed and shook his head. "You've always been too smart for your own good." His voice raised with each word. "First, Ruthanne's rebellious spirit encounters her and aids in her escape! Now you're sitting here lying to me! All these years searching for that girl and you find out but refuse to tell me. Well, I know she's out there with them Cherokee now."

"They would kill you before you got the chance to take her away."

Mr. Brown's voice rose again. "Is that a threat? Are you threatening me?"

She raised her voice. "No, Papa! I'm telling you that because I love you. I want all of this to end, and I want the good times back. Why do you want her back so badly?"

"She belongs to us. She's family. I can accept that you see Annabelle as more than a slave. You and your sisters have always given her favor. Why leave her out there with them redskins?"

"They are her family now. If I care about her so much, why would I tear her away from them?"

"We take the children too. Teach them their role in this world like it should be, and put things back in order."

Judy Mays gave a cynical chuckle. "How can things go back when you sold her mother and little brother? How will she react when she finds out that her papa died years ago?" Her nose crinkled. "I hate that you make me question if you're a Christian. It breaks my heart."

"Stop making this unnecessarily hard. What did those Yankees do to my little girl?"

She pouted. "Those Yankees...Papa it has nothing to do with what those abolitionists had to say. I've been feeling God pull on my heart about the darkness of slavery before the children were born. The most hurtful part of this was learning the truth." Her eyebrows slanted upward, then furrowed, and she frowned. "I know what you did to Annabelle."

"I treated her good her entire life. Better than any slave deserves to be treated, but here you're talking about what I did to Annabelle! I kept her in her place as she needed to be."

Judy Mays stared at her father, tears filled her eyes, and she suddenly began to sob. "You raped her! You raped my best friend and I was too naive to see the signs. There was a day when she was cleaning and had rolled up her sleeves. I went into the room and saw the bruise on her arm, but she said she had fallen... that was a lie. Then there was her constant fear of you. The day after she ran away, Claire tried to tell me, but she was terrified to say the words. I figured it out because I came home the day before she ran away. I heard you in her room raping her. I heard you raping my best friend, but I was in denial. I told myself it was with another slave she liked, that she was nervous to tell me she had fallen in love, but the truth is, she was trapped."

"Judy Mays…I…it's not what you think."

She wiped away her tears with a handkerchief while they constantly poured down her face. "How can you sit here and lie to me about it? I was sitting on the porch when you came outside, but before that…I went to all the bedrooms, the cookhouse, the living room, your study, and I looked outside by the barns. When I came back and sat on the porch, you walked out of the house." Judy Mays body began to tremble. "You raped her while I was in the house and when Momma was away. I had five minutes with Annabelle that day because I couldn't handle it…I couldn't. I asked her if she was having a good day when I knew she wasn't. She looked at me with that fake smile and told me she was. It took me years to forgive you. Even speaking of this makes me question who you are."

Mr. Brown reached to console her.

"Don't touch me!"

He pulled his hand back. "I'm sorry I hurt you. I was going through so much with your momma. You was never supposed to know."

She shook her head. "I trusted you, Papa. Do you even know how many times you raped her?"

"Look, sweetie, I know this is upsetting."

Judy Mays slammed her hands on her lap. "What about Annabelle? Or does it not matter because she's Negro?"

He looked at his daughter with lowered eyes.

Judy Mays continued to cry. "You're a monster. I was raised by a monster."

"Judy Mays."

"Get out! If you can't even gather the words to say you're sorry for what you did to her, get out!"

Mr. Brown frowned. "Judy Mays."

"No, you scared her away! It was you! It was bad enough she

was a slave, but you did what you did to her! Do you have no regret?"

"Who else knows?"

Judy Mays side-eyed and pursed her lips. "Scarlett knows. It's why she hasn't invited you over the past two months. We're telling Genevieve and Sue Ellen later. Your daughters will know the truth."

"Does your momma know?"

Judy Mays's jaw dropped and she shook her head. "Would you even apologize to her if she did?" Judy Mays placed her hand on heart. "I trusted you. Get out. I don't want you here for the rest of the month. I won't torture myself with attempting to get you to see the evil you did."

Mr. Brown stood up and stepped away from the couch. He looked back at Judy Mays and looked at her blue eyes. "Did you purposely kill Sean Kit?" She crossed her arms and unremorsefully scrunched her face. "Well, if they ask me again…as far as I know my little girl wouldn't pull a trigger to save a slave child." Mr. Brown opened the front and his eyebrows lifted when he saw Scarlett. His eyes bulged while his jaw dropped. "Scarlett."

The blue-eyed Scarlett's jaw dropped and her gaze shifted to a tearful Judy Mays. Her voiced boomed with anger, "I have no words for you!" She aggressively walked pass her father and into the mansion. "I'll be upstairs, Judy Mays."

Mr. Brown turned around, he mouth curving downward. "Scarlett! Sweetie!" She kept walking toward the staircase unappeased by her father's calls. "I see I have created my own storm. I love you, sweetheart." He left Judy Mays's home with his hands in his pockets.

Judy Mays went back into the living room and grabbed another handkerchief. She cleaned her face, and deeply exhaled. She and Scarlett later told their sisters the truth. The rift between Judy Mays and Mr. Brown lasted for months, with Judy Mays's mother, Regina, continuously trying to convince her to speak to her father. She continued to keep Annabelle's rape a secret from her mother.

Over time, the American Civil War continued with great brutality. Three months after Joseph's return home, Kenneth returned to the Plecker plantation. He comforted Reece, who was concerned the Indians would return. The next day, Kenneth sat at the grand piano but kept faltering as he played. After Cornelius's death, Kenneth found himself praying for guidance and truth. *Have we been wrong the whole time,* he thought.

Dorothy climbed down the stairs and stared at him, then turned around to go upstairs.

Kenneth stood up. "Dorothy, please come here," he said.

She walked down the stairs and stood before the piano.

"If I'm to be honest, I've missed you greatly."

Dorothy smiled. "I missed you too," she said. "I'm very sorry about Master Cornelius. He was a good man."

"Thank you, it...it was hard, it's still hard. I told him the truth about us...about the girls. The funny part was that he blamed himself for me becoming involved with you."

Dorothy's eyebrows drew together. "Why was that?"

"It was a childish reason, but he made me think of many things. He apologized for what he first said. He thinks the boys should know the girls are their cousins. What do you think of that?"

"What would that mean? I don't want them to know if it put the girls in danger."

"I would never do that. I see those girls, and I realize how blessed I am." He felt his throat tighten. "I've seen so much. So many men that won't return home. I've been questioning if I've been on the wrong side all this time. I'm a man. I shouldn't be confused."

"You're a good man, and good men question what they do."

"Right now, all I want to do is spend time with the girls. I want to spend time with you, but I know I must spend time with Reece." Dorothy exhaled and slightly looked away from Kenneth. "I have to do what I believe is right."

"I'll make you some lemonade to help calm you. You deserve

that much." Dorothy turned around to walk toward the kitchen when Kenneth lightly held her arm. She turned around and smiled. She leaned toward him, and they kissed. "I miss you so much. I'm glad you're home." She gave him a kiss on the cheek and happily walked toward the cookhouse. As Kenneth watched Dorothy leave, he took a deep breath as he put his hands in his pockets, and stared at the piano.

Kenneth spent the rest of the week at the Plecker plantation and spied on his daughters. However, he became distant from Reece, but tried to show his love for her so she wouldn't feel abandoned. After the week passed, he went to Cornelius's estate to keep his word to his brother. He could see his nephews greatly missed their father and vowed to be there for them after the war ended. Mr. Plecker made regular trips to ensure the estate remained stable. Kenneth decided he would move in after the war. Two days after spending time with his nephews and his sister-in-law, Betsy, Kenneth returned to his father's plantation. Later in the day, he entered the living room and sat on the crème-colored couch. While watching his daughters dust the shelves, he drank cider while tapping his finger. "Doris, what's your favorite color?" he asked.

Doris smiled, replying, "Yellow, Master Kenneth."

Kenneth smiled. "Is that right? I imagine you'd like a yellow dress." Doris shyly smiled. "What about you, Daisy?"

The corners of Daisy's mouth curved into a big grin. "Purple and light blue," she confidently said.

Kenneth playfully widened his eyes. "Is that right? You have two favorite colors?"

"Yes."

"I imagine you'd like a dress that's purple and light blue."

"And pearls."

Kenneth laughed. "And pearls! Woo-wee, you're an expensive one." The girls giggled. "Well I think the two of you may get your wish one day. Have y'all been obedient to Mrs. Wilma and your momma?"

"Yes, Master Kenneth," the girls said.

"Well, y'all keep it up. Come here." The girls walked up to

Kenneth, and stood before him. "Y'all is as pretty as your momma. I'm proud of both of you." Daisy gave him a hug. "Oh, you miss me? I miss you too. I miss the both of you." He smiled at Doris and signaled for her to come to him. "You get a hug too. You're growing so fast." Doris gave him a hug. "Okay, now go on and finish up." The girls went back to cleaning and Kenneth went outside to the patio. He deeply exhaled. "How can I do better?" He stayed home for the next two weeks spending time with his family, and took in all the memories he could.

The day before Kenneth had to depart, he spent time with Dorothy in one of the guest rooms while Reece was on the patio with Wilma. The two girls now replaced Riza and spent most of their time with Wilma. After Kenneth spent time with Dorothy, he kissed her on the cheek, and went downstairs to be alone. He wandered outside by the apple and walnut trees. He sat underneath one of the walnut trees and prayed for help. He could no longer deny his feelings for Dorothy were stronger than his feelings for Reece, but he loved both women.

Kenneth later walked out to the cotton gin barn and saw Bo replacing wood on the barn. "Good afternoon, Bo," he said.

"Master Kenneth, good afternoon, sir," he said.

"I know my Pa has questioned you countless times already about them children, but I have a question. How many times do you think Riza met with the others before they escaped?"

Bo put down the hammer he was using, nervously replying, "I wouldn't know, Master Kenneth."

Kenneth stepped closer to him and put his hands into his pockets. "Riza is a planner. All of that chaos that night wasn't done overnight, but that Indian that helped them. I think he helped her make that final decision."

"Why you say that, Master Kenneth?"

"Mr. Rice's door was damaged from someone kicking it or ramming into it. The door never got damaged by the fire. I bet he thought she was going to be an easy girl to take. He thought wrong."

"I sorry for Master Rice's death. I never thought Riza could do it."

"He reaped what he sowed." Bo's eyes widened as he gazed downward. "You didn't hear that from me."

"Yes sir, Master Kenneth."

"Stay a good man, Bo. It goes a long way in the world."

"I will, sir." He walked away as Bo exhaled. He would later tell Stella about his talk with Kenneth surprising her.

Later in the day, when nobody was looking, Kenneth gave Daisy and Doris hugs before he went outside. "The both of you listen to your momma and continue to be good," he said. "I'm proud of you both."

"We will, Master Kenneth," the girls said. He smiled at the girls and left, but while he walked away his mouth slowly curved into a frown. He said goodbye to his parents, Dorothy, and Reece. Reece showed aversion that Dorothy was present to say goodbye even though she remained silent, and had no physical contact with Kenneth. He rode off with the blessings of his family to fight in a war he now greatly questioned.

On July 12, 1862, Lisa gave birth to a girl named Maggie. The beautiful copper-skinned baby girl had Lisa's almond-shaped brown eyes, dimpled smile, and her hair was slightly curly. Sunni was quick to adore her baby sister. "She so pretty mommy, she looks like you," Sunni said in Cherokee.

"She's as beautiful as you are," Lisa replied in their native language. Sunni smiled and held Maggie's tiny hand. Lisa looked at Jacob with a big dimpled smile. She felt Jesus had wiped away her tears. She had Joseph be the first cousin to hold Maggie. The family was thrilled Lisa had a safe delivery.

The war tore through the United States and Indian Territory with the Cherokee remaining divided over the war. A letter from Rebecca and Ruthanne informed Annabelle that Allen and Daniel joined the Union army. Annabelle kept her friends in her prayers. The Lightning-Strongman family kept on guard against the possible return of Brock Jackson. Lisa kept a sharp eye on her daughters. The children were never allowed to be alone, even on a walk home from school. On August 24, 1862, Mr. Gross entered the supply store, and greeted two people that were leaving. "What can I get you, Mr. Gross," Grace said in their native language.

Mr. Gross replied in Cherokee, "I have good news for you."

Grace's head tilted slightly. "What would that be?"

"Brock Jackson has been arrested by the Choctaw."

Grace's eyes shot open. "He what! When did this happen?"

"About two weeks ago. I wanted to tell you personally."

"Thank you, Mr. Gross."

"I know he brought a lot of grief to your family. He was caught raping a Choctaw woman and nearly killed. The Choctaw had a messenger sent along with Brock to Washington DC. He's done as an Indian Agent."

"Lisa, did you hear that?"

Lisa came out of the storage with her brows lowered. "Are you sure, Mr. Gross," she asked in Cherokee.

"I'm one hundred percent certain he's gone," Mr. Gross said.

Lisa smiled, and she hugged Grace. "It's over! He'll never find her!" She happily cried.

"I'll leave you two to tell your family. We will see each other again."

"Thank you," the women said. The cousins continued to embrace each other and wipe the tears off each other's faces. The news of Brock's banishment was a relief for Annabelle, but Lizzie seemed to have mixed emotions because he was alive. Soon after, Brock was stripped of his duties but was handed no other punishment for his crimes. Out of rebellion, he joined the Confederate Army's 50th North Carolina Infantry Regiment.

In late August of 1862, Lizzie returned to Nancy's farm. She waited for Paul while she calmly patted Queen. He came out of a barn and approached her with a smile. "Before you say anything, I want to thank you for checking on me and my family," she said.

Paul replied, "You welcome, Miss Lizzie. I know it's been a

little over a year since y'all got Joseph back, but it's different. Children don't heal like grown men."

"That's true. He's still easily startled, but he's sleeping good now. We'll never get the old him back, but I think we'll get a healed version."

"I'm happy to hear he has gotten better. He's a smart boy."

"Yeah, he is."

"I...wanted to know if I can walk you home from the store sometime this week. I know it's been a while, but I didn't want to say nothing because I know Joseph was on your heart. I'm an honest man, and I do think about your kiss."

Lizzie fought to withhold her smile. "Well Paul...I wasn't sure if I was coming back alive. I would've given my life for my nephew." she sighed. "I did come by to talk about the kiss a little. Most men would've said something about it instead of waiting a whole year."

He slightly frowned. "I really was trying to show my respect. Joseph was gone for so long. I'm sorry."

"Paul, don't apologize. I don't want to get your hopes up." Her gaze shifted to the sky and back to him. "I do work at the store tomorrow. Come by tomorrow."

He grinned. "I'll come by tomorrow."

The corner of Lizzie's mouth slightly curved upward. She turned around and got onto Queen. She saw Nancy watching her through the house's front door. "Did you have something to say, Nancy?"

"No, but please don't take up too much of his time."

"I'm leaving. Bye, Paul."

"Bye, Miss Lizzie."

Lizzie was about to signal Queen but paused. "And it's you're welcome, not you welcome."

"I promise I'll work on it."

She smirked. "Good." She snapped Queen's reins and left the property while Paul watched. She arrived at Victoria's home and got off Queen. She calmly approached the brown wooden house, which was slightly larger than Annabelle's house. The property had a small animal pen with two cows and a small garden and chicken coop to its right.

The front door slowly opened, and Victoria stepped out of the house with her dimpled smile etched on her face. Victoria spoke in Cherokee, "I was wondering if you were coming today."

"I visited him today," Lizzie replied.

Victoria's eyebrow rose. "Oh, keep talking."

"Stop smiling."

"What? I'm happy for you."

"Happy for what?"

Victoria crossed her arms. "Keep talking, Lizzie."

She sighed. "I told him he can visit the store tomorrow."

"Okay, remember what we've talked about. It's obvious you want to give him a chance. It's been a year since you gave him the goodbye kiss."

Her brow lowered. "There's a part of me that's disappointed in myself."

Victoria's smile dropped. "What would make you say that?"

"I made myself unavailable. I was so angry at Jacob. I was hoping he'd change his mind, so I didn't allow anyone else a chance."

"We can't hold onto the past. Unlike Lisa, I know that you're still in love with Jacob." Lizzie shook her head slightly, but Victoria soothingly rubbed her shoulder. "It's okay, this didn't start after Lisa's relationship with him. You were talking about Jacob way before it was him and her. Like Annabelle, I won't tell anyone you still love him. You're not perfect…and there's still time for you to become a mother. Look at me. I just got married." Victoria let out a light giggle. "Both of us would be considered to be old brides."

"Sometimes I wonder if this is my punishment."

"If anything Elder Joyce taught us was the Father's forgiveness. I've made mistakes too."

Lizzie frowned. "You haven't killed."

"You defended yourself, and you protected Joseph. I had two men before I married Teddy. Jesus still blessed me with a good man. I wish he was the only man who knew my body…instead of having the memories of those two coyotes too. This is your walk of faith."

"Falling in love with a man that isn't Cherokee."

"He makes you smile, and it scares you."

Lizzie grabbed her braid and began to redo the bottom of it. "I'll try. I'll be patient with him."

"He was the one that gave you the blue flower, wasn't he?"

Lizzie's gaze shifted off of Victoria to hide the tears starting to shimmer in her eyes. "It was the last thing she told me."

"I trust Elder Joyce."

Lizzie fought back her tears. "He's a good man."

"Yeah, he's a sweetheart and a handsome mulatto." Lizzie laughed and wiped away a tear that escaped her eye. "I love you, and I trust Elder Joyce's vision. Do you feel in your spirit he's right?"

"I'm not sure, but what good is getting the right person when you're not ready?"

"Take it slow. Annabelle thinks he'd be a good match for you too."

"Ugh, you backstabber! You've been talking to her about Paul!"

"I had to talk to someone else that wasn't going to talk. She thinks y'all look cute too. Since Annabelle has been brought up, how's Joseph doing? I haven't seen him since church."

"He's doing a lot better. He's sleeping through the night. We took him to see his friends two days ago."

"That's good. It was hard seeing he had grown while with those crazy White folks had him. His little crush on me is amusing." Lizzie rolled her eyes, and Victoria cackled. "Don't be that way. It's cute. He'll grow out of it. Would you prefer it be me or one of these miserable women that'd hurt his feelings."

Lizzie smacked her lips. "You."

"Thank you. So are you coming inside or abandoning me?"

She walked past Victoria into the house. "Move out of my way."

"Wow, rude and cute." She followed Lizzie and the two childhood friends continued their conversation before praying together. An hour later, Lizzie returned home and told Annabelle about the conversation accepting she had to take a leap of faith.

Three months later Lizzie informed her family Paul was courting her. Annabelle was especially excited for her. After finishing supper, the women went into the kitchen to clean up. Annabelle could feel her joy and smiled while she taught the girls how to clean. "Are we going to be having a wedding soon?" Tsula asked.

"We'll see," she said.

Tsula replied in their native language, "We'll see…you're not getting any younger, Lizzie. You're not a man."

"I'll make my own choices."

"I know you will. I'm only giving you a reminder. Even though you still look the same as you did ten years ago."

"I'm glad you do too. I was scared you'd get plump."

"Lizzie," Grace said.

"Aw, why thank you. I'll be sure to give your first baby a bag of flour," Tsula sarcastically replied. "And I know I look good. I'm still the most beautiful."

"Whatever, you were so scared of getting fat you didn't eat for almost a week."

Tsula pouted. "Not all of us can lift like a man. Besides, at least I don't have a body count on my record."

"What do you mean, Auntie Tsula?" Rosita asked.

The women stared at Tsula with pursed lips. Lizzie side-eyed Tsula, grunted, and stormed out of the kitchen. Tsula sighed, saying, "Ignore me, sweetie. I didn't mean nothing by it, okay?

"Okay, Auntie."

"Tsula," Annabelle said.

Tsula replied, "I'll go apologize to her." Tsula exited the kitchen, but Grace followed.

"Tsula, wait," Grace said.

"I'm going to give her a real apology." She whispered, "I know she's not proud of killing people."

"Just ease off of the relationship. You know how she is. The last thing we need is for her to end it because she feels like she's being forced into it."

"She does seem really happy about it."

"Yes, she does," Annabelle said. "I agree with Grace. Otherwise, when we're old, she's moving in with you."

Tsula leered. "Ha, not in my house. Where's Flour Face? I've got a good apology for that short-tempered woman."

Grace grinned and shook her head before returning to the kitchen while Tsula left the house. Tsula approached Lizzie, who was standing by the redbud tree. Annabelle watched the cousins talk and smiled. "Hmph, that's all it took for her to apologize. Those two will forever fight and love each other. That's my family." Over the next five months, Lizzie and Paul spent more time with each other.

On April 3, 1863, with Pastor Bluebird's blessing, Lizzie and Paul married under the eyes of the church because the Cherokee courthouse did not recognize their marriage. Lizzie didn't care about the courthouse's approval. She only cared that their union was acknowledged by her family and the church.

The celebration of their wedding was held on the Lightning-Strongman farm. George approached Lizzie while she was talking to a pregnant Victoria. "Lizzie, I know it's your wedding day, but I want you to check on something," he said in Cherokee. "Victoria can join if that baby isn't coming out yet."

Victoria joked in Cherokee, "If this child was ready to return my body back today, I'd welcome it."

He lightly chuckled.

"Okay, Uncle George," Lizzie said.

"Well, then, let's make this quick," George said. The women followed him and approached a new brown wooden building sitting behind Tsula's home. "Now, I know I didn't allow you to work on the new building. I believed it was best for the others to work on this one."

Because I'm a woman, Lizzie thought.

"But we need some last adjustments to it. It's better you do that by moving in with Paul."

Lizzie gasped and glanced at George. He nodded at her, and she hugged him. He hugged her back. "I know you didn't want to be on Nancy's property."

"Thank you so much, Uncle George."

"You are more than welcome. You're happy, so I'm happy. Now the children have another place to run to." Lizzie smirked. "Paul is a good man. I'm sorry if I was a reason you didn't give him a chance earlier."

Lizzie kissed George on the cheek. "Come on, Victoria. I'll show you the inside." She grabbed Victoria's hand, and they quickly approached the house.

"Okay, Lizzie," she said. "Please remember I'm pregnant." She looked back and smiled at George before she followed Lizzie into the house. After leaving the house, Lizzie gave George another hug and took Paul to the house.

With a grin, Paul explored the house. "This is for us?" he asked.

Smiling, Lizzie replied, "Yes. Do you like it?"

"Yes, I do…I like it very much. But I love you."

"I love you too." Paul walked up to Lizzie and calmly held her hands. The newlywed couple kissed twice and smiled at each other. "There'll be more of that later. Come on before they start looking for us."

"Yes, ma'am." The couple left the house and spent time with the family. Paul thanked George with a firm handshake. On June 25, 1863, all Cherokee slaves were emancipated following a session of the Cherokee National Council on February 19, 1863, led by acting Principal Chief Thomas Pegg. Annabelle's family celebrated the act. Over the next months, the family remained on guard even though Brock Jackson had been taken to the east. Annabelle and Lizzie would go to the school and walk the girls home. Eli would give Joseph a ride home from school in a wagon. Afterward, Joseph would help with the crops while spending time with David. The brothers grew closer with their talks of the future, and welcomed Jonathan on their fishing trips. David remained keen on knowing where everyone was, and remained cautious of the White people that passed through Tahlequah. The only trust the family had was for Reverend Hills and Molly who took great pride in their twins, Malachi and Beatrice.

On August 24, 1864, Lizzie gave birth to a baby girl in her old room. Annabelle put the newborn into Lizzie's hands. Exhausted, Lizzie wiped sweat off her forehead. "What are going to name her?" Lisa asked in Cherokee.

"Sarah," Lizzie said.

Everyone smiled as the baby yawned in her arms. "We talked it over with Grace," Paul said. "If Lizzie was to have a girl first, she'd agree to it. My baby girl, Sarah Hicks."

Lizzie's smile dropped, and she side-eyed Paul. "Sarah Lightning, she won't carry Hicks."

"But—"

Her voice deepened, "None of my babies will carry the last name Hicks. That's the last time I'm saying it, Paul."

Annabelle and Lisa eyed him signaling him to submit. "Yes, ma'am, I'll let you rest."

"Well, come and hold her before you leave." Paul smiled, and Lizzie carefully handed Sarah to him. "Look at her, my little cornbread baby."

"She is a cute little thing," Annabelle said.

Tsula entered the room. "Aw, look at this cute little person," she said. "Oh, it's a girl!"

"Where were you?" Lizzie asked in their language.

Tsula replied in Cherokee, "I wasn't coming in here to commit suicide. I could hear you all the way to the barn. I'm surprised everyone in this room is alive." Lizzie pouted. "Don't give me that look. As strong as you are...a woman's strength doubles in labor. I'm not getting within grabbing distance of you." Lisa lightly giggled.

"She did well for her first time," Annabelle said. "It's a shame Grace went with Maria to visit Maria's family."

"I'll send Luke out to let them know. They're only three hours away, and the afternoon just arrived."

"Well, I'll go back to work and stay out of y'all way," Paul said. He handed Sarah to Lizzie. He then kissed Lizzie on her forehead.

"So now we have a Hicks in the family," Tsula said with a leer.

Paul let out a weak gasp. Lizzie's nose crinkled, and Tsula began to cackle. "I'm sorry. I know we had the talk. I had to say it once." Lisa lightly shoved Tsula. "What? I said I'm sorry. Geez, Sarah Lightning it is, and she's adorable." Paul waved at the women and left the house. The women then tended to Lizzie and Sarah. Soon, the children visited the newborn and Lizzie. "Welcome to motherhood, Lizzie."

"Thanks, Tsula," Lizzie said.

"I'm sure she'll be taller than you."

Lizzie's eyes bulged. "Get out."

Tsula cackled while she leered. "I love you too."

"Uh huh, get out."

"You want some corn?"

Lizzie smacked her lips. "Yeah." Tsula went to the kitchen, and Lizzie looked down at her sleeping daughter. "I'll do the best I can for you."

Four months later, a heavy thunderstorm arrived. The rain drummed on the roof of the family house while Lizzie carried Sarah around. She watched the lightning move through the clouds. Annabelle came out of the kitchen. Her joy could be felt as she held her daughter. "She is such a peaceful baby," Annabelle said in Cherokee.

"I haven't felt this much joy since we brought Joseph home," Lizzie said in Cherokee. "I want to do what I can so she grows strong like the twins."

"I think you're doing a great job. She is such a happy baby, and this is just the beginning—it's only been four months."

"Time feels like it's slowed down. I have a hard time accepting that much time has passed already. Soon, I'll make a bow for her after Tsula makes a new dress for her, and I'll teach her to fish like the twins. My little cornbread baby."

Annabelle couldn't help but smile when she looked at Lizzie

and Sarah. "Yeah, and her hair is growing fast. Just wait until her hair fully grows out, and she can sit down with the others."

"I can already tell it'll be wavy. Crazy how much things have changed...what will come next." Lizzie grinned at Annabelle and continued to watch the thunderstorm.

On March 15, 1865, Kenneth returned home to a bitter Reece and Dorothy. He found himself making a choice he had struggled with for years. He had decided to fully move into his brother's mansion to be a present father figure to his nephews, and so his daughters could develop a relationship with their cousins.

On March 17, 1865, Kenneth sat at the grand piano. Reece walked down the stairs with their two-year-old daughter Alma Jean. "I've been watching you and I can see that you're not the same man that left me here with our daughter," Reece said. "What is bothering you?"

Kenneth looked up at her. His gaze shifted to their daughter. "I regret going back to the battlefield and seeing more and more carnage," he said. "I should've stopped after Cornelius's death. I was foolish to keep going when I felt in my spirit it was wrong. All of it was wrong."

Her eyebrows drew together. "I don't understand. You fought for our honor and our family. There was nothing wrong about it."

"I fought for the wrong side. After Cornelius's death, I felt the urgency to read my Bible more like I should've years ago. It's been so hard making this choice, but I see it now. How evil our culture is. It makes me wonder how I can call myself a Christian man if I support slavery."

"What did they do to you? What's this talk?"

"This talk is the truth. No man or woman should be a slave."

"Doris, you come here!" Reece yelled.

She quickly ran downstairs in her blue dress with her light brown hair bouncing. "Yes, ma'am," she said.

"Take Alma Jean upstairs and keep her company for a moment," Reece said.

"Wow…I wouldn't be much of a man if I denied it," Kenneth murmured under his breath.

"I said go, Doris," she authoritatively said.

Doris picked up her sister and ran upstairs as he watched.

"Did you say something?"

He frowned. "I can't deny it anymore."

"Deny what, Kenneth?"

He sighed. "You want me to say it that badly?" He tapped his fingers on the piano's keyboard. "I'm admitting how much Doris and Alma Jean look alike."

She sternly replied, "Kenneth Plecker, don't you ever say my daughter looks like a mulatto girl. Don't you dare insult me and our daughter like that."

Kenneth looked at the piano, and a tear hit one of the piano keys. He looked back at Reece as he tried to hold back his tears. "I've thought about this for years, and I should've done this a long time ago so it'd be less complicated. I blame myself for being a coward."

Reece gulped. "That half-breed is your daughter, isn't she?"

"Yes, Doris is mine and Dorothy's. I can't lie to my daughter anymore, not to any of them. Daisy is mine too." She leaned against the stairwell post and cried. "I'm sorry, Reece. I should've told you years ago. That's what you do when you love someone. That's what a strong man would've done. Instead, I lied to myself, and you gave me Alma Jean."

She wailed, "I won't accept this, I won't!"

"I won't lie to the girls anymore. I've decided to take Dorothy and the girls to Cornelius's estate. I've talked to my Momma and Pa about it. There will be new help arriving here tomorrow to replace them."

"Did you tell them that Doris and Daisy are your daughters?"

"I'll tell them that when this war ends."

"That could be years from now."

Kenneth shook his head. "No, we're losing. There won't be another year." He walked around the piano toward Reece. "I'm going to go back and forth between here and Cornelius's to watch over my nephews."

Reece's face scrunched. "And to be with that frizzy-haired whore!"

Kenneth lifted his finger to her and raised his voice. "Don't talk about Dorothy like that. She has always been good to me, always! I'm done wronging her. I'm doing what I should've done years ago!"

"You're divorcing me so you can marry that mulatto woman?"

"No, I do deeply love you, but I loved her first for a long time ago. It's the only fair thing I can think of. I don't want any of my children to believe that I love one more than the other."

"Then pack your things and leave me. Take that mulatto woman, those half-breeds, and get out!" Kenneth tried to hug Reece but she pushed him away twice. "No! How can you choose her over me?"

He sighed. "I'm not."

She wiped her tear soaked face. "Leave! I don't want to talk about this anymore today. You take her and go!"

"Alma Jean will know the truth. All I ask is that you don't bad mouth Dorothy or my daughters. You can talk about me all day and night, but you let those children love each other."

Reece tightened her hand into a fist. "They already do love each other. It's like those girls knew who Alma Jean is to them. I hate you! I hate you so much right now that it hurts my body."

He frowned. "Reece."

"Fine! I'll give you that and that's the only thing I'll give you. Alma Jean can see her sisters, but don't you ever expect me to speak well of you, Kenneth Plecker. You're going back and forth between me…and Dorothy…a slave. Have you been with her since we've been married?"

He bit his lip and his went downward away from Reece. "I…—"

She began to cry again. "You unfaithful hound dog. Did you ever consider my feelings? All this time, it wasn't her…it was you. I can't even think of giving you another child. You're breaking my heart." She stormed upstairs while she wept.

Kenneth kicked the lowest step of the stairs and left the

living room to go to the cookhouse. He entered the kitchen and saw Dorothy preparing Wilma's fancy lunch tray.

"What do you need, Master Kenneth?" she asked.

He approached Dorothy and kissed her. "I need you to move in with me to Cornelius's," he said.

"What…what are you talking about?"

"I've already spoken with Momma and Pa about it. Momma wasn't too happy about it, but I convinced them the slaves working on that plantation are beneath what Betsy and the boys need. So they agreed to buy some more slaves and have you and the girls moved to the plantation."

"I see. When will I see you again?"

Kenneth held Dorothy's hands. "I'm coming too. I told Reece the truth. We're staying married and she's staying here. I want the girls to know the truth. No more lies. I'm tired of the lies."

Dorothy frowned. "You still chose her," her voice emitting irritation.

He sighed. "I do love her…but you're always my first choice."

"But you won't let her go."

"No, just like I can't let you go. I'm sorry I didn't take you away."

She quickly hugged him, and tears of joy went down her face. "I love you so much. I thank God every day that you're here." Dorothy took his hand and placed it on her belly. "I didn't know how to tell you, but now I can. I'm sorry if this—"

"No, there's nothing to be sorry about. I take the blame for not being careful. We don't have Geoffrey to blame now. It must be God's timing for me to move you and the girls." Kenneth smiled at Dorothy and they hugged each other again. Later in the day, he had Dorothy and the girls get into a wagon. He rode them off to Cornelius's estate where Betsy and the three boys were waiting. They arrived at the beige-colored plantation with its four large pillars which were surrounded by white flowers, and three large rectangular shaped windows in the front. Two small oak trees were to the right of it, and the fields and slave houses were to the left side of it. The family entered the estate and Kenneth greeted Betsy and the children. He then escorted his family throughout the large house. For the first time in her life, Dorothy had her own room, and the girls were given a large room to share. Betsy objected to them being given rooms, but Kenneth was now head of household. He wouldn't tolerate any mistreatment toward Dorothy or the girls. After supper, Kenneth and Dorothy sat down on a bed with girls.

"Thank you again for giving us rooms, Master Kenneth," Doris said.

Kenneth rubbed his chin and sighed, saying, "You are more than welcome. You're just as beautiful as your momma." Doris beamed.

"Do you want me to tell them?" Dorothy asked.

"No. Girls, to protect both of you, a lie was told. Geoffrey isn't your papa, I'm your papa."

Doris gasped, tears shone in her eyes, and she looked at Dorothy. "Momma?" she asked.

"It's the truth," Dorothy said.

She quickly hugged Kenneth, and cried into his chest. "You were always good to us."

He kissed Doris's forehead. "Y'all my baby girls, always were."

Daisy then hugged him and he kissed her on the cheek. "I always loved you, Papa," Daisy said.

"I've always loved you too," he replied, tears falling from eyes. "I'm sorry I couldn't be man enough from the beginning." Dorothy wiped tears from her face while she smiled.

"So Alma Jean is our sister?"

"Yes, she is. I love all three of you the same. Don't you ever believe someone else's words. You carry my blood. We have to be quiet about it, but I'll always love you girls." The family spent the rest of the evening together while Kenneth thought of ways to keep the peace between Dorothy and Reece.

The Lightning-Strongman family continued to exchange information with Rebecca and the others in Mercy, Missouri. To their shock, Brock Jackson had made a name for himself in the Confederate Army. The family wanted to make sure he stayed out east. On March 21, 1865, Brock fought in the Battle of Bentonville. Brock killed several men as he encouraged the other Confederate soldiers. While getting caught in the crossfire, Brock used a fellow soldier as a shield against artillery fire to save himself. The impact of the artillery left him with a head injury, and the loss of both legs. The Confederate Army lost the battle, and Brock was discharged from the Army after the battle. Informants managed to relay this information to Ruthanne, and she happily had the message relayed to Annabelle's family. A woman named Ethel, who lost her husband during the war, later settled for Brock. Ethel later gave birth to a boy and a girl. Due to his injuries Brock became a paraplegic.

After the American Civil War, Reece kept her word and allowed a relationship between the girls. On May 14, 1865, Reece arrived at Cornelius's estate with Alma Jean by carriage. Kenneth approached them and Alma Jean ran to her father. "Papa," she cheerfully shouted.

"Oh my youngest girl," Kenneth said as he kissed her on the cheek. "Looking as beautiful as your momma."

"Am I really sleeping here tonight?"

"Yes, you are."

Alma Jean cheerfully screamed while she jumped in place. "I can sleep with my sisters?"

"Yes, you can and they're looking for you." Alma Jean ran past him to the large house with a big smile. He turned to Reece and dropped his smile when he saw her face slowly crinkling.

"You have created nothing but chaos," she said.

"Reece."

"No, you're going to start spending more time with me. I'm your wife! I don't care if you loved her first!" The blaze in her eyes increased when she saw a pregnant Dorothy approaching them. "The absolute nerve."

"Kenneth, I—," Dorothy said.

"Are you now blind?" Reece irritably said. "We're having a conversation." Reece stepped up to Dorothy. "Me and my husband, are talking so you can go sit on those stairs until we're done Delilah."

Dorothy squinted and sharply replied, "I only came here to ask him what he wanted for supper."

"You know what he likes on his plate. And behind closed door." Reece's hands slowly began to close into fists. "The absolute nerve to walk around showing off a bastard pregnancy like it's something to be proud of."

"Reece," Kenneth sternly said.

"What? This child will know that its mother is nothing, but an ex-slave, a frizzy-haired husbandless whore."

Dorothy grabbed Reece by her collar, and slapped her. Wide-eyed Reece gasped and Dorothy slapped her again. Kenneth went to break Dorothy's grip when Reece grabbed Dorothy's collar and smacked her back. "I'm so tired of you!" Dorothy yelled. "You bitter gossiper."

"I hate you!" Reece yelled. The women continued to try to slap each other while Kenneth stood in the middle taking their blows and attempting to separate them.

"Enough!" Kenneth bellowed. "I need the two of you to act like ladies. I'm sorry. I know I caused all of this disorder, but for the sake of those girls and this baby."

Reece pouted. "Babies."

"You're pregnant?"

Reece sniffed. "Yes. That's why I want you home more. I'm your wife, not her!"

"Well fine, babies. I need you two to keep the peace. I know y'all don't like each other, but for the children's sake please stop this. I'll keep my time between here and the other estate evenly. As I have been, to keep the households balanced. Now can we please keep it together?"

The two women looked at each other with scrunched faces, dilated-narrowed eyes, and crinkled noses. "Fine, but she apologizes to me!" Reece demanded.

"You first," Dorothy demanded.

"You're an ex-slave, a mulatto."

"You're a jealous—"

"Dorothy," Kenneth bellowed, his voice echoing authority. "Both of you apologize right now so we can go inside and get through this day."

"I'm sorry," the two women growled at each other.

Reece angrily marched to the mansion. While moving, she side-eyed Dorothy and lifted up her left hand so Dorothy could see her ring. She then looked forward at the mansion.

Kenneth put his arm around Dorothy's shoulder to calm her down. "You have no idea how long I've waited to knock the words out of her mouth," she said with a deep agitated tone. She then pushed his arm off of her and marched to the mansion.

Kenneth sighed. "Dorothy, I know what I want for supper."

"We're having fried chicken," she replied with a stern tone.

"Well, fried chicken it is," he mumbled as he followed Dorothy inside the mansion. A few days later, Kenneth told his parents the truth about Dorothy. Mr. Plecker walked away from the table, cursing while Wilma took her time absorbing the truth. Two weeks later, Dorothy gave birth to a boy named Ryan. Six months later, Reece gave birth to a girl named Octavia. Wilma later warmed up to Dorothy's children though it was kept a secret they were her grandchildren. She would often visit them with Alma Jean, spoiling them with crackers and muffins. Over time, he tried his best to raise his nephews, but one of his nephews remained hateful toward Indians and Negroes. He resented his cousins. It broke Kenneth's heart when Willard Plecker left the plantation as a young man, but he continued to pray for his nephew, hoping the spirit of hate would break off of him. The rivalry between Dorothy and Reece remained, but they kept the children out of it. The girls and Kenneth's son would later become the main heirs of the family's fortune because Kenneth was quick to hire Negroes and poor White men to farm the land for cotton, peanuts, and sweet potatoes.

The day after President Abraham Lincoln's assassination on April 15, 1865, Peter gave a passionate sermon. "Yesterday, we lost the life of President Lincoln, and the ugliest form of evil was boldly shown," Peter said. "We've failed our children. Generations allowed an evil division to remain between us and our Indian and Negro brothers and sisters. We've been blind for too long as to who the real enemy is. Scripture in Ephesians six tells us for we wrestle not against flesh and blood, but against principalities, against powers, against the rulers of the darkness of this world, against spiritual wickedness in high places. It breaks my heart that I have to question what kind of world my children will continue to grow into now." Ruthanne watched attentively with a smile. "Being Christian men and women, we should always stand up against evil no matter if we learned evil through our father's whip or through our own transgressions," Peter authoritatively said. "Scripture from First Thessalonians five states pray without ceasing. In everything, give thanks: for this is the will of God in Christ Jesus concerning you. Quench not the Spirit. Despise not prophesyings. Prove all things; hold fast that which is good. Abstain from all appearance of evil. And the very God of peace sanctify you wholly; and I pray God your whole spirit and soul and body be preserved blameless unto the coming of our Lord Jesus Christ. I hope as a congregation we stand strong and be the representors of Christ we are meant to be…maybe by then, we can call ourselves a Christian nation."

Peter continued with his sermon, bringing great joy to Ruthanne's heart. She thought, Look at his transformation from being a passive preacher into a man of God who boldly shows his love for those different than him. I'm proud of him. Peter's boldness began to strongly affect the congregation, with men and women from the church confronting those who threatened the Negroes of the town. Peter lost half of the congregation due to their closed hearts. Allen and Daniel returned to their families in Mercy, Missouri, after the war. They were greeted with open arms. To Marilyn's and the others' shock, Daniel returned with a large scar on his left cheek from a bayonet, and Allen's left arm had been put into a sling to heal. After Allen healed, the mobility in his left arm remained limited, but his spirit remained high. The two men were seen as heroes by only some of the townspeople. Daniel and Marilyn continued to hide their marriage to keep their family safe. Ruthanne could see the grief in the men's eyes when they spoke of the war.

A few days later, John and Samuel returned to Mercy with a letter from Annabelle. Ruthanne and the others were eager to write her back. John and Samuel followed Ruthanne to her home and were greeted by Rebecca when they arrived. The men were seated in the living room. Its two large rectangular windows allowed the sunlight inside, and a large green carpet covered the wooden floor. "I'm so happy y'all decided to visit," Ruthanne said.

"We've been very careful," Samuel said. "Thankfully, the war is over."

"It was sad to hear of President Lincoln's assassination," John said. "Annabelle is afraid we'll see some form of revenge since some Cherokee fought against the Union."

"His assassination wasn't the fault of the Cherokee, though," Ruthanne said.

"Yes, but will the US government take their frustration out on us."

Ruthanne pouted. "I wish I could say they wouldn't. Unfortunately, racism is a lingering disease. I'm glad I was able to give you information on Brock Jackson. Please let us know if y'all need anything."

"Thank you, Ruthanne. It's hard to say what will happen, especially with Stand Watie being the last general to surrender. He's ruined our tribe's name."

That does complicate things." Ruthanne's green eyes brightened slightly. "Annabelle's last letter told me you met Judy Mays."

"Yes, I did."

"How is the blonde?"

"She seemed a bit desperate when we met."

"I'm sure she was afraid of losing her only link to Annabelle. She may still be upset with me for Annabelle's escape."

"She was willing to help my son. I'm sure she must understand now."

Ruthanne half-smiled. "I'm sure she does."

"I'd be happy to meet her," Rebecca said.

"I'm sure you'd get along."

"Does she have your temper?"

"No, but she's a totally different creature when it comes to Annabelle. She put a bullet in an ex-associate of ours years ago over Annabelle."

"Annabelle did mention Judy Mays's wedding before. I'm sure we can arrange a reunion."

The friends continued their conversation not long after Peter entered the house. He was elated to see John and Samuel. The men talked for some time before they had to leave for Tahlequah. Three days later, the men arrived back in Tahlequah. John handed Annabelle another note. The women wanted to set up a reunion, and Annabelle was thrilled with the possibility.

CHAPTER 16
Free and Reunited

In early October of 1865, Ruthanne, Rebecca, Peter, Daniel, and Marilyn made a trip to Indian Territory to visit Annabelle along with their children. It was a true celebration for Annabelle. She now had the freedom to visit them in Mercy when she could. Lizzie and Ruthanne immediately liked each other, and for the first time, Annabelle's children and her friends' children met. Peter and Rebecca later explained the political atmosphere of the United States. Rebecca counted herself blessed because there were many men who didn't return home to their wives. Ruthanne and the others stayed for three days before returning to Mercy, a visit forever etched into Annabelle's heart. The friends planned for another visit in the spring.

On March 30, 1866, a carriage arrived in Tahlequah with two mulatto men casually riding it through the town. Molly walked past the carriage with her twins when it stopped. "Excuse me, ma'am, do you happen to know where the Lightning family farm is?" a woman asked.

Molly answered, "Why yes, it is down that road and is the second farm you will see. It has several houses on the property and a large barn."

"Thank you very much."

"What is your name?" Molly asked.

"Judy Mays Reynolds, and you?"

"Molly Hills, wife of Reverend Hills. It's a pleasure to meet you."

"You as well, thank you for your help." The carriage rode down to the Lightning-Strongman farm. One of Judy Mays's drivers helped her get out of the carriage and she saw the twins sitting down together by the redbud tree. "Thank you, Thaddeus. You and Martin can wait here." Judy Mays casually approached the girls with a smile. "Excuse me, girls, but is this the home of Annabelle Lightning?" Judy Mays asked.

"Yes, that's my momma," Rain said.

"Your momma?" Judy Mays murmured. "Is she here? I would like to speak to her."

"What is your name?"

"Judy Mays...Judy Mays Reynolds." The twins looked at each other and ran to the family house, excitedly laughing. She was taken aback. *They have the same laugh as her*, she thought. She waited by the carriage when the family house door opened, and Lizzie stepped out carrying a one-year-old Sarah. Lizzie smiled and waved at Judy Mays, and Annabelle came outside.

The two women began to walk toward each other, and their steps picked up speed. "How did you find us?" Annabelle said, her voice breaking.

Judy Mays began to cry, and the two women embraced each other. "If you only knew how much I missed you," she cried. "I'm so sorry. I don't blame you for running away. I don't know what else to say."

Annabelle wiped tears from her face. "There was so much I wanted to tell you. I didn't know if you were going to believe me."

"Annabelle, I know."

Annabelle's eye widened. "Wait...what are you saying?"

She frowned. "I know what Papa did to you...I know why you ran away."

Frowning, she let go of her. "How could you...how could you let him?"

Judy Mays put her hand out to her. "No, Annabelle. I found out the day before you ran away. I came over to visit, but I couldn't find him or you. I went to your room and heard it, but I told myself a lie...that it must be someone you liked. You simply weren't ready to tell me yet." More tears escaped Judy Mays's eyes as she wiped her face. "Suddenly, the few times I saw the bruises on your arms made sense. Your fear of him. I'm sorry I failed you. I was so stupid." She cried, "Please forgive me... please forgive me."

Annabelle's lips quivered. "It wasn't a few times."

She put her hand over her mouth. "What?"

Annabelle shook her head. "I couldn't tell you how many times he raped me."

Heaving sobs escaped her mouth. "I never thought saying I'm sorry would mean nothing. I should've known by the way he looked at you."

"It wasn't your fault," Annabelle cried. "It was so hard." She hugged Judy Mays. "It wasn't your fault." The two women let go of each other and held hands. "My parents...Todd, where are they now?"

"I don't know. I'm so sorry. I don't know. Papa sold your Momma and Todd to different men two years after you left. Your papa...he passed years ago."

Annabelle exhaled. "It's okay. I prepared myself a long time ago for the chance I'd never see them again."

"Momma, can we come out now," Breanna yelled.

"Patience is nonexistent in that child," Judy Mays complained as she cleaned up her face. "Yes, all four of you come out now and meet Mrs. Annabelle." Four children came out of the carriage and greeted Annabelle. However, Annabelle's eyes widened when she saw one of the children was a mulatto boy. Annabelle pushed away her questioning and then called for the twins and told them to bring Jonathan, Joseph, and David to her. Annabelle was excited to be introduced to the children. This is Alexander, Breanna, Hannah, and Luther."

"The girls look just like you." Lizzie walked up to Judy Mays and the children with Sarah. It was a refreshing moment for Judy Mays to see a peaceful Lizzie. Judy Mays adored Sarah and was allowed to hold the baby girl that was several months away from turning two. The energetic child had much to say now learning to speak Cherokee and English. The twins arrived with Annabelle's sons. Judy Mays smiled and gave David and Joseph a hug. "This is Jonathan."

"Oh, he's a handsome little man." Jonathan blushed. "And look at you Joseph, fifteen years old and you're almost as tall as me…growing into a handsome young man."

"Thank you, Mrs. Judy Mays," he said.

"And look at you David, a handsome young man as tall as your father."

"Thank you, Mrs. Judy Mays."

The women continued to talk before walking to the family house as the children played outside. The women entered the house and Judy Mays saw Ruthanne sitting at the supper table. The two women locked eyes with each other. "Well would you look at that…the blonde," Ruthanne said.

"The redhead," Judy Mays said.

"Ruthanne, you set this whole thing up," Annabelle said.

She smiled. "I thought of no better reunion. Mr. Brown is no longer a threat with slavery abolished. Judy Mays, this is Rebecca and Marilyn. Marilyn's husband is at the barn."

"Nice to meet you all," she said.

"Nice to meet you," Marilyn and Rebecca said.

"My Ruthanne, you certainly know how to create a show."

"I'm always up for a challenge," she replied.

"Clearly, you managed to keep Annabelle from me," Judy Mays said, her tone sharping.

Her voice rose slightly, "I didn't know your intentions. I was met with Ruben's and Elizabeth's brothers' chains."

"Please, it hasn't even been five minutes," Annabelle said with a frustrated tone.

"I'm sorry," Judy Mays said. "I have no grievance with you, Ruthanne. We're still friends after all. I hope your view is the same."

"We are. You weren't responsible for the upheaval I had with my family. Sit down and enjoy this time."

The women sat down at the supper table. "Are you sure you can leave Sarah with the twins?" Judy Mays asked.

"The twins are mature for their age. They learned faster than the boys," Lizzie casually said. "Is the mulatto boy yours?"

"Lizzie!" Annabelle whined.

"It's okay. I'm surprised you didn't ask me that first, Annabelle," she said.

She replied, "I haven't seen you in so many years. I didn't want to ask anything that might hurt you. I take it things have ended between you and Edgar. I'm sorry."

"No, Edgar and I are still married and he sends his greetings and blessings. He had another untimely business dealing to deal with. That's why Thaddeus and Martin had to bring me. He's actually a great father and I..." She paused and took a deep breath. "I'm sorry. I hate that I get so emotional nowadays. Edgar is a good man, and he spends time with the children as soon as he gets home. Luther is my brother."

The women's mouths dropped. "Wait...your brother?" Lizzie blurted out.

"I don't believe it. I mean...your papa?" Annabelle asked.

Judy Mays answered with slightly upset tone, "Yeah. His only son. After all these years of being married to my momma, this happens."

"How is Mrs. Regina taking it?" Annabelle asked.

"She's not herself. She lost all control once she figured out he was my brother. Luther's mother was a house slave named Ida. Ida was a kind and shy young women...younger than us. One day, my momma became overcome with anger. While Ida was cleaning, she pushed her off one of the balconies, killing her. She then shot Papa in the leg. One of the slave drivers rode to my mansion and told me everything so I hurried over. When I got there, my momma was beating Papa with a rifle. He was barely conscious when I walked inside and pulled my momma back."

Annabelle frowned. "I'm so sorry. I don't know what to say."

"There's not much you or anyone else can say. My papa finally got caught, and it cost an innocent woman her life. That's my world. I won't let his actions ruin that boy."

"Does Luther know what your momma did?" Ruthanne asked.

Judy Mays answered, "No, and it'll stay that way. Some form of peace must return to my family, and I don't want to break his heart. He's three years old, and I'm the closest thing he has to a mother. My sisters are still somewhat in denial that he is our brother. Fortunately, they don't hate him. When he is older, I will tell him his mother passed from sickness. Right now, my children believe he is their cousin. When they become a little older, I'll tell them the truth. This family doesn't need any more secrets."

"What did you decide to do with your momma? I think it's clear Luther will have to be kept away from her," Lizzie said.

"Well, I guess that's the benefit of slavery's abolishment. She has no power to sell him. As of now, and probably until he becomes a man, he will stay within my care. My papa now lives with me until Momma can forgive him. Luther has been in my care for the past year and a half. He'll grow up to be an amazing young man. I can make sure of that."

"It's hard to imagine having a sibling so much younger that you could be their parent," Marilyn said. "I can tell you'll be a great big sister."

"I hope I so. I truly hope so," Judy Mays said. "I'm placed in two roles as a mother and a sister. Right now, I don't have the privilege of treating him like a sibling. He might always see me as his mother, and he may see my sisters as aunts...either way, he needs us. I've met with our pastor to help me prepare for the day more questions will come. At first, it felt like I wouldn't be able to deal with the pain, but I know God has a plan. God can make something good out of this, and think it'll start with my children."

"What do you mean?" Annabelle asked.

"This end of slavery means little, to be honest. Luther will be treated differently and harshly. He's not even a dark skinned mulatto, but I know my brother will be persecuted without hesitation. That's why he needs to be educated and know he's always loved. That's why I brought him with us."

"I understand how you feel. I think the same about Joseph. Even here, he is treated differently. The twins will always be treated differently than Joseph. The truth is they look like Cherokee girls, not mixed children. It hurts me, but I've come to accept that as the truth. As much as I hated your papa, I never wanted this to happen to your family. I hope things improve."

Judy Mays grinned. "Being here is a sign that things already have started to heal. I'm a blessed woman."

"To be honest, I never thought slavery would end when I was young. I always believed my children would be grown up with children of their own. I'm happy I was wrong."

Suddenly, the women heard the front door creak open, and Luther came inside with a pregnant Grace and pregnant Lisa, who were followed by Lisa's three-year-old daughter Maggie. "He said he wanted to be with Judy Mays," Grace said.

"Come here, Luther," she calmly said. "You can sit with us." She picked up the toddler and sat him on her lap. "I'm Judy Mays."

"I'm Grace."

"I'm Lisa."

"You have such a handsome little cousin," Lisa said. "The children said his parents were cousins of yours."

Judy Mays looked at Grace and Lisa with wide eyes and gave an exhaustive smile. "Yes, he's my family; there's no denying that," she said. I'll tell you ladies the full story when this one is asleep, and the children are not around."

Grace replied, "One of those stories."

Judy Mays sighed. "Yes, one of those."

"You're not alone when it comes to stories," Lisa said.

The front door then opened, and Tsula entered the house. "The most beautiful has arrived," Tsula said in Cherokee.

"Shut up. We have a visitor," Lizzie said.

"You don't own me, Lizzie Lightning," Tsula confidently said while pointing at Lizzie. "Who are the new White kids...and another White woman?"

"Hi, I'm Judy Mays and you are?"

A big smile came across Tsula's face. She squealed, "So, the long lost friend, it's nice to meet you! I'm Tsula. I'm so sorry you had to tolerate my Cousin Lizzie's presence. I was told the last time you saw her, she had her tomahawk out."

"Sit down and stop starting stuff," Grace demanded.

Tsula sat down, leering while Annabelle and Lisa lightly chuckled. "I see you've been well taken care of here," Judy Mays said. "God knew what he was doing to bring you here."

"Annabelle has been taking care of us too," Lizzie said. "We're a family, and without her, we're missing a piece. I know you understand what I say."

Judy Mays smiled at Lizzie. "Yes, I do."

She stayed with Annabelle and enjoyed the company of the other women. Afterward, she cooked supper with the other women and ate supper with Annabelle's family. She was shocked to learn Elizabeth had moved to Virginia, and was married. It was the most information Rebecca and Ruthanne could give. She stayed in Tahlequah for four days before she had to return to Mississippi. The time the women spent together strengthened their friendship and created a promised tradition. They promised to return to Tahlequah yearly in April while writing Annabelle to keep in touch with her.

Two months later, Grace gave birth to a girl named Melody, and Lisa gave birth to a boy named James shortly after in June 1866. When Melody turned three months old, Lizzie announced her second pregnancy and continued her reign of refusing to have any of her children carry the name, Hicks. That August of 1866, John, David, and Joseph returned from Mercy with supplies and a letter from Ruthanne. John gave Annabelle the letter while they stood on the family house porch. She smiled, saying, "Thank you, John, how are they doing?"

"They're doing well," John said. "Ruthanne said this is a special letter."

Annabelle looked at the letter and back at John. "It must be something good. I'll see more of you later."

John did a quick scan seeing none of the children around. He gave her a quick pat on the butt. "Yes, you will."

Annabelle cackled and playfully hit John on his shoulder. "I'll make sure the children stay with Lizzie tonight."

John began to walk to the barn and winked at Annabelle. "Good, I need attention."

Annabelle giggled. "Clearly, you do." She opened the letter and was surprised most of it was about Elizabeth. Besides all being well, we finally heard from Elizabeth again. Her husband's name was Steven Chambers but she had lost him in the war. She has three children Martina, Elliot, and Jack. She's raising her children near their father's people. She believes it's the only way she can raise her children and away from her family's racist viewpoints. To my surprise, she did something quite daring. She secretly took her cousin Robin with her. Robin was introduced to a well-off businessman from Pennsylvania and is now married. Elizabeth tells me she couldn't be happier for her. Robin now has four children passing for White. She hopes to be able to visit once her children are older. We love you and look forward to seeing you in April. Ruthanne, Rebecca, & Marilyn. Annabelle felt her heart swell with happiness. She went to her house and stored Ruthanne's letter with the others. For the first time in a long time Annabelle felt comfort. Slavery had been abolished, and Brock Jackson was unable to return to Tahlequah.

On December 02, 1866, Lizzie gave birth to a son she named Joshua. She was exhausted but happy her labor was shorter than the first time. Maria took Sarah out of the room so Lizzie could rest and start nursing Joshua. While she nursed him, she noticed Annabelle smiling with watery eyes. "What is it?" she asked in her native language.

"I'm happy for you," Annabelle replied in Cherokee. "You're a natural mother."

"Thank you. Now wipe your eyes, or you'll make me cry."

Annabelle wiped away her tears. "I'm sorry. I know you hate crying."

Lizzie looked at her nursing caramel-skin-toned son. "I only wish my momma and Elder Joyce could see me now. I never would've thought I'd feel this much happiness."

"Paul seems thrilled he has a son."

Lizzie rolled her eyes. "He thinks I'm going to change my mind about his last name. Give it a few months. He'll ask me again."

Annabelle lightly chuckled. "I'm sure he will."

"You've been happier ever since you saw Judy Mays."

Annabelle's eyes slightly widened. "I guess you're right. I guess it'd be like you being separated from Victoria."

Lizzie's gaze fixed back onto Annabelle. "It would be hard. I'm glad you held on long enough to see her."

"So am I. I want to try to find my Momma and Todd, but I know it's too dangerous right now."

"I wish the stories weren't true of White people killing former slaves. Hopefully, things will calm down soon, so you can try. I wouldn't mind joining you on the adventure."

"I'm sure you'd provide enough protection."

Lizzie smiled. "Don't lower yourself. You're a good warrior. You left a scar on Brock's ugly face." The women quietly giggled. "You deserve to see the rest of your family. If it's the Father's will, it'll be a blessing. If it's not the Father's will, you'll see them again in Heaven, just as I'll see my momma again and tell her about her grandchildren."

"You're right. Jesus is in control even when we don't understand. See, I told you you're a great mother." Lizzie smacked her lips, attempting to hide her smile. The women continued their conversation until Annabelle had to cook supper.

In late April of 1867, all of Annabelle's friends visited her family in Tahlequah, with the exception of Daniel and Marilyn. The couple welcomed another daughter on April 17, 1867, named Lee Ann, who amused Daniel because she looked like his mother. Tsula gave birth to a son named Alex on May 01, 1867. She was thrilled with her chubby baby boy. Later in the year, to Annabelle's shock, she became pregnant again. On August 01,

1868 she gave birth to a healthy baby girl she named Claire to honor her mother. The brown-skinned baby girl looked almost identical to the twins. She had Annabelle's smile, and it was clear to her she was going to rule John like the twins.

On September 05, 1869, nineteen-year-old Joseph saw Annabelle sitting down next to the old redbud tree. He approached his mother, and she turned to him. "Are you avoiding the crops?" she jokingly asked in Cherokee.

Joseph replied in Cherokee, "No, Momma, I'm not. I was only getting some water."

Annabelle smiled. "I know."

"I'm sorry if I interrupted your reading."

"No, you didn't. I was thinking about the family. I'm glad you've healed past what happened to you. Forgiving those White folks freed you."

"It helped having you pray for me and tell me what you went through."

"It was hard hearing what those White people did to you. After coming to Tahlequah, I never in my life would've thought any of my children would experience slavery. But the Father was still faithful. I've met an angel but I still needed Elder Joyce's prophecy. Never underestimate the power of prayer. Jesus is paying attention. No matter what happens, don't forget that."

Joseph's brows lowered. "Is something wrong?"

"No, I want to make sure you don't forget. It's easy to forget our blessings. I know that's why your grandma kept telling everyone about that cougar. She didn't want to become comfortable in the Father's favor."

"I promise I won't forget."

"You and your siblings make me so proud. You've grown into a good young man."

"I had you and Pa."

"And you always will. I love you."

Joseph smiled. "I love you too, Momma."

Annabelle smiled back. "Go on back to the crops before your brothers start looking for you."

Joseph walked to the crops. He thought, *I hope one day my spirit will be as strong as hers*. He heard the twins come out of the family house arguing. He turned around and saw the teenage girls had gone to Annabelle arguing with each other while handing a one-year-old Claire to Annabelle. He smiled and went back to work.

CHAPTER 17
Moving Forward

THROUGH THE YEARS, ANNABELLE AND John didn't have any more children but enjoyed seeing the rest of their family expand. Grace welcomed another daughter two weeks after Claire's first birthday, making her the last of Grace's three children. Lisa and Jacob later welcomed twins, Jesse and Katherine, making them two years younger than Claire. Sunni remained unaware that Jacob wasn't her father. The family kept it a secret. Maria and Samuel's family expanded with a boy named Juan born five months after Lisa's twins. Exactly a year later, Sophia was born, making her the last of Samuel and Maria's four children. Maria called them her twins because they shared the same birthday, September 27. Tsula and Luke's family expanded with Stephen a year after Lisa's twins. Tsula claimed the world wouldn't be able to handle another copy of her. Lizzie and Paul would later welcome two sons, Titus, born on November 09, 1869, and Marcel, born on June 14, 1871. To Lizzie's frustration, she became pregnant again and kicked Paul out of their house. After a month, she let him sleep in their home again, and on July 24, 1872, she gave birth to her last child, Maya. Grace teased Lizzie because Maya was identical to her. Michael later married a young woman named Mimi, and the couple had three sons together. Annabelle would continue to spend time reading the letters she received from Judy Mays,

Ruthanne, Marilyn, and Rebecca. Writing her own letter to her friends was also uplifting as well. However, as the years went by, the bison herds stopped coming, and the pronghorn herds became a rare event. Annabelle later learned that the US government was actively killing the herds.

Joseph and Susie remained good friends over time. The two young adult Cherokee would see Tom occasionally and saw their time together as a blessing. They often wondered how Riza was doing in New York. One day in September of 1872, Joseph received a letter in the mail from Judy Mays. He opened the letter, and his eyebrows lifted. "It's from Riza," he said. He quickly went into the family house. "Momma, I'm going to Susie's. The letter Mrs. Judy Mays sent me was from Riza!"

Annabelle came out of the kitchen, saying, "Oh, your friend from New York. Wow, she managed to keep in touch with Judy Mays. Well, go on. Make sure your Pa knows you're taking a horse."

"Okay."

"And be careful."

Joseph ran out of the house. "It'd be interesting if she came here," Lizzie said. "She almost reminds me of me. Well, let's finish this up before Maya wakes up. I never thought I'd have a baby at forty-four years old."

"You had a good pregnancy with her."

Lizzie's nose scrunched. "So! I'll kill that man if he gets me pregnant again." Annabelle lightly chuckled, and the women went back into the kitchen.

Joseph later arrived at Susie's family farm. He greeted her younger sister, Lacia, and approached Susie. He pulled the letter out of his pocket. "It's a letter from Riza," he said in their native tongue.

Susie's eyes shot open. "Let me see," she said in Cherokee. "I'll read it." Hi Joseph and Susie and hopefully Tom. I know years have passed, but all of you remain on my heart and mind. Judy Mays kept her word, and I'm reunited with my family. I now have two little girls, Alicia, who's three, and Sade, who just turned one. I'm married to Marcellus. He's a handsome mulatto man. He's a good man and a hard worker for one of the construction companies. I took a risk five years ago and wrote Dorothy twice. I'm happy to say she's doing well. She now has three children, but I'll tell y'all the story on that later. She's still in Mississippi. Judy Mays told me that she'd visited Joseph in Tahlequah so I wrote this letter to her first to make sure it made it to Tahlequah. I recently heard from Clint through Dorothy a year ago. He's still in Mississippi and enjoying his freedom. Joseph, tell David I said thank you, and the rest of your family. I love and miss all of you. I'm looking forward to get my first letter from y'all. Maybe one day, y'all can visit New York City or I'll visit first."

"Wow, Riza had children"

Susie handed the letter to Joseph. "We'll write her a letter together. I'm sure Tom will be happy to read her letter."

"When do you want to go to Tom?"

"Let's go tomorrow. If we go now we'll be getting back after sunset. That's too dangerous."

"Okay, we'll go tomorrow."

"Tell Lizzie I'll watch the children this Saturday."

"Why are you telling me now? I'm not leaving."

"I know you're not." She calmly turned Joseph's head toward Lacia. "She's waiting for you." He blushed and Susie playfully pushed him to walk forward. After spending some time with Lacia and later speaking with Susie again, Joseph rode home. The next day, the Cherokee went to Tom's home. He was excited to read Riza's letter. The young adults wrote back to Riza and eight months later Joseph received another letter from Riza. She wrote she'd love to travel by train, and visit the three of them in Indian Territory. She was anxious for them to meet her family, and hoped an arrangement could be made soon. The young adults continued to send letters to each other to make arrangements.

Over time, Annabelle and her friends continued to write to keep their friendship strong, and remained faithful to their April reunions. During the Reconstruction era, great tension remained among the North and the South. Violence was the outcome, first beginning in Louisiana in 1874, and spreading to Mississippi the following year. The incidents were clear that more time was needed for the United States to heal. The Cherokee and the other four civilized tribes also faced great trials once the United States had refocused their attention. All previous treaties made with the government were suspended. Annabelle read in one of Ruthanne's letters of 1874 that Peter had now merged his congregation. The Negro members of the church could now sit where they pleased. The change created outrage among some of his congregation which left the church. However, Peter remained strong in his decision feeling it was God's will. Ruthanne also began a Bible study for women, attended by both Negro and White women. Rebecca and Allen had no more children but became more politically involved attempting to end the inequality and persecution of Indians, Negroes, and women. On July 01, 1875 tensions rose in Mercy as Mr. Hildebrand boldly stood against the couple, and anyone else that sided with them. To Allen and Rebecca's surprise, Mr. Hildebrand suffered a massive heart attack while arguing against Allen inside the courthouse. Rebecca was certain his hate had consumed him, and shortened his lifespan. She was pleased to write Annabelle about the news of Mr. Hildebrand's death stating it was like Mercy received a breath of fresh air.

Marilyn's letter informed Annabelle that Pots' Garments had expanded and remained strong, selling clothing and perfume throughout the years. Marilyn sent Annabelle a bottle of lavender perfume once a year. Daniel had now become greatly interested in photography. On his first trip to Tahlequah, he took a picture of Annabelle's family. Marilyn supported his love for photography. Every six months, she sent pictures of her family to Annabelle. Her profits had expanded greatly and it allowed her to have her children educated so they could run the business when they became older. Marilyn's brother-in-law

Randolph became the face of the business because Marilyn was a woman, but he was a good man that made sure the family was taken care.

On August 18, 1875, Joseph married Susie's little sister, Lacia. Annabelle loved the kind-hearted young woman, who was strong willed enough to speak her mind. The marriage was only recognized by the church, but that didn't stop the celebration. Family and friends celebrated outside of the family house. Sitting in a chair, Annabelle watched Joseph dance with Lacia while the Tate family played music. "Time certainly flies," Grace said.

Annabelle turned to Grace, saying, "Yes, it does. I feel so happy for him."

"Well you're the first of us that's going to be a grandma."

"Ugh, don't remind me. Well, it's been three years since David married Dina. I'm going to be a sharp looking grandma though." The two women giggled.

"I heard that. These three little silver strands don't make me old. I'm so grateful to have had Elder Joyce in my life. As she'd say I gained years. Being old is in the mind."

"Our grandchildren will be ignorant of slavery. I honestly thought I'd be on a cane when that day would come."

"It's a relief, but a sad one. These White people will continue to make laws against us because of the color of our skin. I can see it in those two's eyes. The hope that their children won't experience hate…we'll have to prepare them."

Annabelle's brows slightly lowered. "I wish you were wrong. Joseph has been through so much. Even with slavery gone, this world can still kill their innocence."

"Even so, we did good raising them. They'll be good parents."

"I think you're right." Annabelle and Grace noticed Claire coming from the practice grounds with Lizzie behind her. The long haired girl smiled and waved at them. The women waved back. "That woman has kidnapped all three of my daughters. The girl is only seven years old. And your sister is still lifting like a man."

Grace giggled. "Lizzie is something else."

The women looked back at the rest of the celebrating family. "The Father has blessed me beyond what I hoped for. I pray whatever trial comes next, it'll be nowhere near as hard as the past."

Grace sat down next to Annabelle. "Amen to that."

Annabelle continued to enjoy the wedding reception, then happily wrote about the eventful day to her friends.

In the August of 1881, Victoria's family left the Cherokee Nation for Missouri. The political climate made them fearful of US retaliation against the Cherokee. Annabelle was saddened by Victoria's decision, and she could tell Lizzie was saddened by the choice too. Victoria was quick to write letters once her family was settled near St. Louis. She was very proud of her five children, and often included pictures for Lizzie. On March 1, 1886, George passed away in his sleep at the age of eighty-nine. He had recently fallen ill and with increased tensions between the Cherokee and the United States, he wanted the family to move. He expressed how proud he was of his family. George's passing was hard on Annabelle's family, but knowing his spirit was now free to walk into the gates of Heaven brought them comfort.

In July of 1886, the adults of Annabelle's family met together. The children played outside while they talked. "Me and Maria agree with Pa," Samuel said. "There's no telling what these White people will do because of the Cherokee that fought on the Confederate side."

"Where do you think we should go?" Tsula asked. "I don't want to abandon our people."

"These White men are already trying to control who can leave Indian Territory," Lizzie said. "And they're already pushing these Indian boarding schools even harder now. What do you think is next?"

Tsula frowned.

"We can't move in fear," Grace said.

"I agree but we have to accept the truth," Lisa said. "White men are vengeful. Whatever is coming next, won't be good."

"It's best we decide on an area where the children can grow

up the safest," John said. "I want to stay with our people, but I think Lisa is right. White men retaliate in the most evil way."

"Would going to Missouri be the safest move?" Jacob asked.

"Wherever we go it needs to be away from the Deep South," Maria said. "The violence against Negros and Indians is going unpunished there. We have to do what's best for the children."

"Me and Joseph want to go into business together," David said. "We want to paint for people."

"David, these White men will make it hard for an Indian man to have any property," Annabelle said. "I'm not against you and Joseph doing something for the family. I only want you safe."

"Momma, what about Mr. Keys?"

"What about him?"

"You said he years ago he bought Mr. Boston's store. Can he do it again for us?"

Annabelle slightly sighed. "I'm not sure."

"That would give us an advantage," Eli said. "It'd give us some money without having to beg for one from a White man."

"We can meet with him and ask," Luke said. "It'd be quicker than a letter."

"That's true," Grace said. "It means we'd have to let go of the supply store."

"We've had a lot of good memories in the store," Lisa said. "Momma worked so hard to keep it going. I still remember the day she had you run it yourself, Grace."

"Yeah, we never thought she'd walk on a year later. I think we need to pray on this and see if having Mr. Keys buy us property is the right path."

"The real question is where can we live," Michael said. "Lizzie, what about Victoria? How's her family been doing?"

Lizzie answered in Cherokee, "She said it's day by day. She's working as a cleaning lady, and Teddy is working for a railroad company. The tension is serious, though. They mostly speak to the few Negros living near them, and try to avoid most White people."

"What about Mercy?" Annabelle asked.

"Isn't the town still divided on what happened in the war?" Grace asked.

Annabelle pouted a little. "Yes, they are. We can't ignore that two Negros homes were set on fire last month."

"In that case, I agree with Grace," John said. "We'll pray on this and ask Allen Keys what he thinks about buying property and then us taking it over. Moving the whole family will be a challenge."

The family talked a little more before separating. Annabelle walked outside into the Oklahoma heat and stared at the empty prairies once inhabited by the bison herds. She could feel more sadness building up in her chest. Her brows furrowed. *They did this*, she thought.

"What's on your mind?" John asked.

Annabelle looked at him with a frown, saying, "It's been a whole month, and we've only seen one bison herd. They're murdering them."

John's lips curved downward. "When we heard about the mountain of bones, I didn't believe it. Now we have to hope they don't kill them all."

"If what men put so much effort into killing animals...what will they plan against us?"

"Like Grace said, we'll pray for guidance and make a choice. Don't let worry fill your spirit."

John kissed Annabelle on the cheek, and she put her hand on his cheek. "I love you."

"I love you too." John walked away to their home, but Annabelle's gaze never left the empty prairies. In March 1887, Annabelle's family decided to leave Cherokee territory for Illinois. Allen had agreed to buy property for them in Chicago. John and Eli traveled with him and Daniel to the growing city. The Cherokee gave Allen the money, and he bought the property. In May of 1887, Samuel and Maria's clan were the first to leave at night. Michael and Mimi followed a week later. Two months later, Annabelle's family received a letter from Samuel. They had started construction on a supply store and told the rest of the family to join them. After a family meeting, it was decided for

David and Joseph to leave next with their siblings and families. When Joseph and Lacia returned from Susie's home, Joseph was quiet. His quietness indicated to Annabelle he was uncomfortable with Susie deciding to stay. The next day, Annabelle's children and their young families left. However, Annabelle kept Claire with her. Annabelle felt nervous with most of her children leaving her sight. Struggling to push away anxiety, Annabelle prayed every hour for their safe travel. During this time John, Jacob, and Eli worked with a blacksmith to make another carriage. A month later, Samuel returned with the carriage and with a letter from the family. Annabelle was relieved to read it. Lizzie's and Tsula's families were next to leave. Lizzie at first resisted but agreed to go because Tsula was inexperienced if they were forced to fight. Annabelle, Grace, and Lisa worked to get their supplies in order.

A week after Lizzie's and Tsula's families snuck away, Grace walked into the supply store. She felt an eeriness in the now quiet store. Scanning the store, she started to remember when they were children and learning from Aunt Shay. "Grace, are you okay?" Annabelle asked in Cherokee while entering the store.

Grace replied in Cherokee, "I'm okay. It's a lot of memories here…a lot of good memories. We fought so hard to keep it alive."

"You didn't fail."

"I know, but it's just…hard." Grace sighed. "I know we're making the right choice, but it doesn't take away the pain. I hope Jesus pays these White men back fifty-fold for what they're doing to us. I never thought I'd relive the thought of them massacring us again. Traveling here as a child was genocide. What form of genocide are they planning for us next? Is it with bullets or with a pen?"

"Hopefully, we're wrong."

Grace turned around, her eyes fighting sorrow. "I don't think we'll ever return permanently. It makes it easier for them to target us. Lisa should be returning soon. She's taken the last chickens to Susie. Who'd ever thought we'd give most of our chickens to Joseph's friend."

"The girl can cook."

Grace lightly chuckled. "Yes, she can. I honestly thought she was going to end up with Joseph."

"Yeah, I think she did what a lot of young girls do."

"What's that?"

Annabelle smiled. "Thinking older means more mature."

"Oh yes, that old mistake. Well, in two weeks we'll be gone."

"It's a weird feeling."

"Let's go. I think we'll catch Lisa and Sunni on their way back." The women left the empty store and began to walk home. "We can think of it this way. We won't be seeing Nancy Hicks or Buck anytime soon."

Annabelle smiled. "They're not that bad anymore."

"No, but still…it's a relief."

"Okay, yes, I won't miss them much at all." The two women lightly giggled and ran into an adult and pregnant Sunni and Lisa. Sunni was the spitting image of Lisa with an olive skin tone. The women walked home and enjoyed their last moments in Tahlequah.

Two weeks later, on September 13, 1887, Annabelle's family had everything packed into two carriages. Annabelle walked out of her small house for the last time, holding her Bible and The Three Musketeers. The sunset lit her path. She looked over to her right and stared at the old redbud tree being outlined by the sunset. She heard John approach her, and her gaze fixed on him. "The tree did die this summer," She said in Cherokee.

He stopped and looked at the tree. He replied in his native language, "I think it's more reason for us to walk in faith. That tree witnessed a lot over the years."

"Yeah, let's go. Claire is in the wagon already?"

"Yeah, she's sitting right next to Sunni."

Annabelle hugged John. "This is hard, but I trust the Holy Spirit in this choice."

"Tonight is a full moon. So we'll be able to keep moving at night."

"We have to survive." The couple walked to the carriages holding hands. Annabelle felt a tear run down her face and wiped it away. She got into the carriage and the family left behind the farm. Two weeks later, Annabelle was reunited with the rest of her family. One year later, David and Joseph had their painting company setup making Annabelle proud. On May 13, 1890, Annabelle received a letter from Rebecca informing her that Allen Keys had unexpectedly passed away at the age of seventy-two on May 9th. Annabelle wept when she heard the news. She took a train to Mercy with John, Samuel, Joseph, Grace, Eli, and the twins to give their condolences to Rebecca.

CHAPTER 18
Silent Assassinations

On September 19, 1890, President Benjamin Harrison stopped the leasing of land in the Cherokee Outlet to cattlemen. The lease income was one of the few ways the Cherokee Nation had supported itself and was an effort to prevent further encroachments on tribal lands. In southeastern Kansas, the Cherokee were forced to give up their neutral lands to the government. Like Annabelle's family, some of the Cherokee had already left the territory to find better possibilities in the North. Annabelle's family worried about other laws the government would put over them. The creation of the Dawes Commission changed everything in the Cherokee Nation in 1893. Indian Territory had now been disbanded, and land now had to be allocated to individuals. Years later, White men working for the commission arrived in the Five Civilized Tribes' territories and set up tents to continue the enumeration of the tribes.

The political climate worried Annabelle though she was now in Chicago, but she had the pleasant distraction of Elizabeth's letters. Through Ruthanne's persistence, the women were able to reestablish a connection with her four years before Mr. Keys's passing. On December 02, 1893, Annabelle received another letter from Elizabeth. She entered her and John's wooden floored bedroom with its beige-painted walls and sat down on the queen-sized bed with her reflection in the oval-shaped mirror that sat above the walnut-colored dresser. Two tall rectangular windows allowed the sunshine into the room. She read, Dear Annabelle, your past letters about what you went through truly broke my heart, but I'm so happy with how everything ended. I'm grateful for the pictures you've sent me of your family. Joseph has certainly grown into a handsome man. My only regret is I wasn't there to help you find him. Robin is happily married, he's a great man. Her children are passing for White, which does upset me, but she insists on it. Her children know the truth and that's what matters to her. I thank Jesus every day for you being put into my life. I'm glad you do still look the same except for a few gray hairs. You and Ruthanne seem to have held onto y'all's youth a little longer than me. I hope my wrinkles didn't shock in my picture, but for the most part, I look pretty good if I do say so myself. I'm grateful for Ruthanne's recent visit, and I hope to do the same with you and the others. I do miss you greatly and I love you. Sincerely, Elizabeth. Annabelle inhaled and smiled. Annabelle quickly began to write a letter for Elizabeth, but then she heard the front door open. "Tsula?" Annabelle said.

"Yes, it's me, and I'm actually on time," Tsula joked. "It's time to cook."

Annabelle sighed, put the new letter for Elizabeth on the dresser, and went toward the kitchen.

"Gotta keep these young ones in shape so they can cook… they should be here soon."

"Yes, they should unless your lateness has rubbed off on them."

Tsula put her hand on her chest and sarcastically gasped. "What an incriminating thing to say, Miss Lightning. For that, I'm the food tester."

Annabelle grinned. "You were going to be the food taster anyway."

"I was not. Rain is pregnant again. I was going to let her do it, but I still turn heads." Tsula leered. "I look like I only had one child." The two women began to cackle and waited for Tsula's daughter and Annabelle's daughters to arrive.

I'll have to finish Elizabeth's letter when we finish, Annabelle thought. On December 13, 1896, Elizabeth passed away due to illness. It was a difficult train ride for her to Pennsylvania. She met Ruthanne, Peter, Judy Mays, Edgar, Marilyn, Daniel, and Scarlett at Elizabeth's funeral. She paid her respects to Elizabeth's children with John by her side, and they walked up to Elizabeth's casket. *I wish we'd gotten to see each other one last time, but we will see each other again*, she thought. After saying their goodbyes to everyone, Annabelle and John returned home by train.

Reluctantly in June of 1899, Grace and Eli, Annabelle and John, Lisa and Jacob, Lizzie and Paul, their daughter Sarah, Tsula, David, Rain, Jannie, and Joseph and Lacia returned to Tahlequah. Susie had written that there was concern the government was trying to dictate who belonged to the tribe. Nine districts were created in the Cherokee Nation to enumerate them. The White men of the Dawes Commission were impatient, belligerent, and skeptical of Cherokee accounts. Annabelle was not surprised by the men's insensitivity, and worried that Lizzie would lose her temper with the men. The men only cared about who was related to whom and who to allocate land to. The family returned to the old family house which was given to Susie. At seventy-one years old Annabelle scanned the land as she enjoyed the warm summer breeze and reminisced. She thought, *So many good memories. I wish Doll was around so I could visit her. It's been five years since she walked on.*

"What are you thinking about?" Grace asked in Cherokee.

Annabelle replied in Cherokee, "Doll. Wishing I could say hi to her."

"If we knew where her children were, that'd be a good visit."

"I wonder how many returned for these Dawes Rolls...makes me wonder if they're going to document Negroes too."

"You're still nervous about this too?"

"I am. I know the children are angry at us, but I don't care. They're all grown now. Those are my babies. I'd rather something happen to me than them. I'm too old to be losing any more children."

Grace half-smiled. "I thought we had our talk about age being of the mind."

Annabelle grinned. "I'm not claiming to be old. I'm claiming to be too old for drama. I've had enough."

"I agree. Susie's family has done a good job taking care of the land. Her family applied early to make sure they kept this land. I'd never thought I'd see the day White men would come here and say who's Cherokee and who isn't. I can't get out of my head the ones that won't return. What will happen to their families?"

"All of the Tates left before we left for Illinois. Jacob tried to convenience his nieces and nephews to come, but they don't trust the government. They don't want anyone to have them recorded."

"They all left by what 1878 or 1879. I heard these White men will only go back to the 1880 census we took. We'd have to vouch for them if they returned probably. This is insane. We're experiencing genocide through pieces of paper. With a stroke of a pen, they're saying who are Cherokee. I was talking to Lottie Ward. They made her choose between being Cherokee or Choctaw."

Annabelle's eyebrows drew together. "That's insane. How is she expected to pick one side over the other? What did she do?"

"She enrolled as Choctaw because her mother is Choctaw. Lottie is no longer Cherokee under these new rules. Like I said it's genocide."

"I'm starting to feel like Lizzie. This feels evil."

"This is evil, but I'm moving by faith we need to do this. I feel they're going to use this against future generations like a rifle. Punishing those who are Cherokee but not counted…either way our family will remember they're Cherokee. We don't need a piece of paper to know who we are. Well let's get this over with. The others should be done with breakfast."

The family went to the courthouse and listened to what the commission was doing. Hearing the men determine how much Cherokee blood people had shocked Annabelle. She saw Lizzie's face starting to scowl, representing the tension building up in her. *Please stay calm. I know you don't like this. Lord, I wish she moved like an old woman, Lizzie is still moving like we're in our thirties*, she thought.

A commissioner spoke with a stern tone, "You're next, Indian woman." Lizzie walked up to the man and gave him her information. The man scoffed. "Are you sure you're that old you look like you're forty at most."

"I'm sure of it," Lizzie irritably said.

"You need to watch your tone, woman."

"And you need to show some respect."

The man's jaw unhinged and his eyes bulged. "And who's that next to you?"

"My husband."

"What's your name, boy?"

"Paul Hicks, sir."

Lizzie snapped, "And he's a man."

With his nose crinkling, the commissioner pointed at Lizzie, replying, "Look here, woman. You will speak when spoken to and that's the end of it."

"I'm not one of your White women! I'll speak when I want to! You old—"

"Momma," Sarah called.

Lizzie glanced at her daughter, and her eyes shifted back to the men. "Ugh, fine. Let's continue this." Lizzie and Paul gave their information and registered their children. Lizzie sneered. "Why are all these White men here? It's obvious they're not a part of this commission."

Saturated in irritation, the commissioner replied, "Some of them are citizens of your tribe and others are married to Cherokee women."

"The hell they are! Not that many."

"Lizzie, please," Grace griped.

She looked back at her sister, saying, "I'm serious. You know this many White men don't belong here. Something is wrong." She looked back at the commissioners. "What are they really here for? White men only come here for timber, oil, and coal."

"Look here, Injun, your family is registered now move out of the way," the man yelled.

"Keep talking to me like that and I'll put you in the dirt."

"Lizzie," Paul sternly said.

Grace immediately tugged her arm, escorting her away from the table. Paul followed closely. "There'll be none of that," Grace said.

She pulled her arm away, sharply replying, "Something is off. I think they're putting White men on the rolls. They're giving them our land!"

"We don't have the manpower to stop them." Lizzie's face scrunched and she went to stand in the back of the room, waiting for the others. Sarah, being Tsula's height, stood next to her mother. Paul started to talk to some Cherokee men he knew. As the members of the Dawes Commission determined who was related to who, the men began to determine how much Cherokee blood each family member had. Tsula, David, Grace, John, Eli, Lisa, Lizzie, Luke, and Michael were marked down as full blood. Grace's, Tsula's, and Michael's children were also written down as full blood. Based on Sarah's looks, they assumed even though Paul was a former slave, he had Cherokee blood. As a result, Lizzie's children were written down as three-fourths Cherokee along with Jacob and Lisa's children.

Annabelle watched Rain and Jannie's now forty-five-year-old twins approach another commissioner. The white-bearded White man squinted and put on his glasses. "Some young ones I see," the man said in a raspy Southern accent. The twins gave their information to the man, and he pointed at them. "You're telling me the two of you are forty-five! Mm-mmm y'all look like twenty-five at best."

Rain forcefully smiled, replying, "Thank you, sir."

The man continued to put down their information. "Y'alls momma name is Annabelle? That's a good name for an Indian."

"Our momma isn't a Cherokee woman." Rain pointed at Annabelle. "That's our momma, Annabelle."

"Y'all have a nigger for a momma!"

"Who are you calling a nigger?" Jannie growled. The twins' almond-shaped eyes had narrowed, and their noses crinkled.

"Jannie, calm down," Annabelle commanded. The women looked at her and sighed.

Two of the census takers lightly chuckled. The commissioner's raspy voice echoed, "Y'all best listen to your momma." The twins locked their gazes back onto the old man. "Such an angry breed…I have y'all marked as half though I should put three-fourths with those smart mouths of yours."

Annabelle could feel heat emitting from her twins while she stared at the leering man. *I can't wait for this to be over*, she thought.

"Ma'am," another census taker said.

Speaking calmly, Annabelle replied, "Oh, I'm sorry, sir."

"No problem. I have two grown daughters. No matter how old they get, I still see little girls, so I understand. Clearly, they have some strong Cherokee blood to speak so strongly." Annabelle looked down at the census and saw she had been written down as a freedman.

"A freedmen?"

"You a former slave…whether you have Cherokee blood or not. By looking at you, you've got little in you, if any at all. We're done here."

Annabelle scoffed. "The nerve." She turned to the twins and walked to the back of the room.

The census taker who took the twins information looked at their long, wavy hair bounce while they walked next to Annabelle. He turned to another commissioner who wrote Annabelle's information. "Crazy Injun women," he uttered. He scratched off one-half for Jannie and Rain replacing it with three-fourths.

Standing next to Lacia, Annabelle watched while Joseph and John were being registered. One commissioner with dark brown hair examined Joseph with his glassy brown eyes. "I don't really see any Indian in you, boy," the man said. "I'm sure your momma lied about who your papa was. It's not uncommon for Indian and Negro women to lie about the father." The man began to write down Joseph's name on the freedmen rolls. John's face turned reddish brown when he squinted and yelled, "Joseph is my son! He doesn't belong on the freedman rolls! At least put him down as half!"

"Sir, I don't see a man that's half-Cherokee. I barely believe he has a one-eighth if that," the census man snobbishly said. "Be grateful we are taking notice to him at all."

"You men have no honor. How dare you try to determine who is of blood and who isn't!"

"Sir, is that your wife…the Negro woman, Annabelle."

John angrily replied, "Yes, she is my wife."

"Well, you should've thought about the consequences of touching a nigger." John quickly punched the sitting man knocking him to the ground. People gasped and two census takers stood up from their chairs. Sarah sprinted to the table before Lizzie could grab her.

Annabelle put her hands to her mouth. *Jesus no, this is like Benjamin,* she thought.

The oldest of the commissioners raised his hands with wide eyes while the other John knocked down reached for his revolver. Joseph and John each pulled out revolvers making the man pause. Another census taker was about to pull his revolver when Lizzie's daughter pulled out a knife, and placed it on his neck. The man's eyes bulged and he let go of his revolver.

"John!" Annabelle and Grace called. John looked back and saw the frowns on their faces. He looked to his left and saw a few of the other Cherokee had also drawn their guns.

"Everyone calm down," John said.

The census taker sneered while he stood. He put down his revolver on the table. The other Cherokee lowered their weapons. "I should have you hanged for assaulting a US Official old man," he said.

"Sarah, let the man go," Lizzie commanded. Sarah took the knife away from the shocked man.

The census taker's voice echoed with irritation, "I'm doing my job. Your son is still included with you, Cherokee."

John growled, "Don't speak about my wife like that."

"John, please calm down," Annabelle begged. John exhaled. "Please continue with your job, sir. This is hard for my family."

The census taker replied, "Well, yes, I can see that after taking a fist to my face. You're lucky you're not in Arkansas, boy. Let's finish this."

"I'll take your information sir," the old commissioner said. John went to the older man and gave his information confirming Annabelle was his wife.

Sarah walked up to her mother who was now standing by Annabelle and Grace. "When we left Indian Territory years ago, we should've stayed away," Lizzie bickered. The commission continued their job and kept Joseph on the freedmen rolls. Eli and Michael rushed to pull John back. Joseph's wife, Lacia, was written down as full blood. Two of their sons were put down as one-fourth, while their daughter was written down as half-Cherokee. When Annabelle's family finished with the Dawes Commission, it was a relief and a painful reminder Cherokee sovereignty from the United States no longer existed.

Thank you, Father, for taking Uncle George thirteen years ago so he didn't have to see this, Annabelle thought. The family never mentioned Samuel and Maria's family, which kept them off the Dawes Rolls.

The family returned to the Lightning-Strongman farm one more time. John turned toward Joseph. "I know I've said this before, but I'm proud of son," he said. "You and your brothers have grown into great men."

He smiled. "Thanks, Pa. I had a great man who gave me a foundation."

"Your grandfather was harsher on me than your aunties. I think he was more scared of me becoming like him than I was."

He slightly frowned. "What do you mean?"

"Full of anger, bitter."

"He went through a lot."

"He did, but he allowed it to define him. I almost made the same mistake when Camille passed, but your momma's kindness helped heal me. I know it's difficult but don't be discouraged. You have to trust the Father with what you can't control."

"You've always been there for me."

"That's what fathers are supposed to do. You've become a good father, son."

Joseph lightly bit his lip. "Thanks, Pa, it means a lot from you."

John patted him on his back. "Your old man still has to work on his temper. I swear your auntie's attitude is contagious." The two men chuckled and Lizzie began to rant.

"I'm telling you, we should've rebelled with Redbird Smith and the others," Lizzie complained. "This Dawes Commission is created to kill the old ways, and break our foundation. I don't trust these White men."

"Momma, please calm down," Sarah griped.

"I'm telling y'all, these White men are always planning something evil." While she continued to preach, Annabelle stood in front of the old house which had some of its old wood replaced. She glanced over at the now barren prairies. At this time, Susie's family conversed with Annabelle's family while they got their luggage. Annabelle slowly walked to the small log cabin she'd lived in for so many years. She closed her eyes and then opened them to reminisce of the laughter of her children. "Momma, are you okay?" Rain asked.

Annabelle turned around and half-smiled, saying in Cherokee, "I'm fine, Rain. Some memories are hard to let go of."

Rain bit her lip a little. "Yeah, they are."

"Do you remember the bison?"

"Of course I do."

Annabelle's mouth curved downward slightly. "I never would've believed those White men would kill them all." She shook her head. "Even after all these years, I still don't understand their enjoyment for destruction. It's their curse."

"Maybe some will come back. I heard there are a few left far west."

"It'd be the Lord's blessing if the herds do return." The two women held hands and walked together to a carriage. Annabelle looked at Rain and grinned. "You and your sister have always made me proud."

Rain smiled. "Thank you, Momma. I've done pretty good over the years without cutting any hair."

The two cackled and Annabelle playfully poked Rain. "Lord, that was a day when Jannie's hair got cut. What a day it was. Y'all kept me young." She kissed Rain on the cheek. The women then helped the rest of their family load the carriages.

"Y'all be safe now," Susie said, speaking Cherokee.

"We will, we will see each other again," Lacia replied in their language.

"We will see each other again." The sisters gave each other a kiss on the cheek.

Joseph smiled at Susie and spoke in Cherokee, "We'll visit again before it becomes cold."

Susie calmly replied, "Don't." Lacia raised an eyebrow while Joseph's eyebrows drew together. "We're leaving Tahlequah. We agreed to these Dawes Rolls, but we're scared of what they'll do next."

"Where are y'all moving too?"

"Saint Louis. Some Indians are doing okay out there. It's a lot more White people there, but it's not the Deep South. Tom's family has already left for Texas. We're leaving by August."

"Please mail soon with more information."

Susie smiled. "Don't worry, Joseph. We will. I just sent a letter back to Riza."

"How is she?"

"She's doing well. By the time you return to Chicago you'll have a letter waiting for you from her." Joseph approached Susie and they hugged. "I love you, Joseph."

"Love you too, Susie. Looking like you're twenty."

Susie cackled, hit Joseph on his shoulder, and turned him around to Lacia. "Boy, get out of here with your wife. Y'all write me as soon as y'all get off that train." The Lightning-Strongman family said their goodbyes, and left for the train.

During their ride home on the train, Annabelle sighed as she looked out of the train window. Her mouth curved downward. *Even the pronghorn are gone. They've killed them all and created a lifeless prairie*, she thought. Annabelle and the others arrived in Chicago three days later. The family was greeted by a thirty-one-year old pregnant Claire. Her long, wavy hair blew with the Chicago wind while she gave Annabelle a tight hug. The family returned to their homes and explained what had happened in Oklahoma. News spread that on March 1902 Redbird Smith was arrested in Muskogee and the Dawes Commission forced him to register for allotment. His followers called the Nighthawks, refused to comply, but most were enrolled without their consent. An unknown amount of Cherokee families who never returned to Oklahoma and assimilated in the American culture, were excluded from the Dawes Rolls. Cherokee by blood, but not acknowledged by US or Cherokee government as Cherokee citizens. White men who had married Cherokee women were put on the rolls as intermarried White. However, Lizzie's suspicion was correct as White men who paid the Dawes Commission five dollars underneath the table were put on the Dawes Rolls as Cherokee citizens to get land allotments and benefits. The corruption created a group of White people with no Cherokee blood being put down as having Cherokee bloodline. This group of descendants was called Five Dollar Indians. Annabelle was heartbroken once the Cherokee learned of the corruption with Lizzie cursing the Dawes Commission knowing some who were Cherokee by blood would never be accepted because they were not included on the rolls which meant Samuel and Maria.

Over the years, the Lightning-Strongman family never returned to Oklahoma. On May 01, 1902, there was a knock on Annabelle and John's front door. Annabelle calmly opened the door to see Joseph standing next to a beautiful honey-skin-toned, middle-aged woman who was Tsula's height. "Joseph, who is this woman?" Annabelle asked.

"Momma, this is Riza," he answered.

Annabelle's eyes widened, and a big grin etched on her face. "Oh, you're Riza! Oh, my Lord, you're a beautiful thing. Come on inside. John, come here!"

"Thank you, Mrs. Lightning," she said.

Joseph and Riza walked into the sunlit house. "Please take a seat. After all these years, I finally get to meet you. When did you get to Chicago?"

"I arrived here two days ago."

"Two days? Joseph, why didn't you bring her over here sooner?"

"Auntie Lizzie wanted to see her," he answered.

Annabelle dismissively waved, replying, "She could've waited. I never got to meet the girl who helped my boy escape the Pleckers' plantation."

"It's a pleasure to finally meet you too," she said.

"Girl, you still look like you're thirty. I was just telling Lacia y'all age slowly. How old are you now?"

"I'm fifty-four."

"My, and such a beauty. I heard you have some children of your own by a good mulatto man."

"Yes, I did. Marcellus is actually here visiting a cousin. He should be over shortly."

"Oh good! John! Get in here, stop acting like an old man."

"I am an old man," he said. A silver-haired John walked into the living room and smiled. "There's a face I haven't seen in a long time."

Riza smiled and cheerfully said, "Hi Mr. Lightning."

"Son, you have a habit of bringing in welcomed guests." John sat next to Annabelle. "It's a blessing to see you again, Riza."

"Well, I haven't seen Joseph in decades. I'm grateful for the pictures I did receive. Makes it less of a shock to see him grown, versus the shock of seeing Susie grown. We managed to see each other five times now since she also left Oklahoma. I'm so sorry for how those White folks treated y'all."

Annabelle nodded. "It may be even greater consequences for those that escaped being documented. Well, what about yourself?" she asked.

Riza giggled, saying, "I really haven't changed. I haven't grown an inch since I was fourteen. I do have a few wrinkles on me now."

Annabelle dismissively waved. "No, you're beautiful. You

could pass for someone in their thirties. Not a gray or silver hair on you."

"You look like you could pass for someone around my age."

"I like you even more already." The group laughed.

"Which part of the city are you living in now?" Joseph asked.

Riza answered, "A part of the city called Brooklyn."

"Ah, the Brooklyn Bridge."

"Yeah, the Brooklyn Bridge, and it's a very large bridge."

"Did you meet his children?" Annabelle asked.

Riza replied, "Yes I did. I'm sure they got Lacia's smarts."

"Whatever," Joseph said with a smile.

"How have you healed over the years?" John asked.

Riza sighed, her lips slightly tightened, and she replied, "At first, I couldn't sleep. Mrs. Judy Mays would have to reassure me nobody knew I was in her home. I was too scared to go downstairs. I wasn't sure who would walk into her home. I look in the mirror and still stare at my scars. I know these scars don't belong there, but they do tell a story. The sound of anything sounding like a gunshot still makes me jump."

Annabelle noticed Riza fidget with her injured pinky finger. Her brows lowered and her mouth curved downward forming a slight frown. She said, "I'm so sorry you experienced it."

"Looking back, there was some good that came out of it. I grew closer to the Father and did gain some great friends."

"How is Dorothy?" Joseph asked.

"She's doing well, living in Kentucky right now. All of her children have left Mississippi, and all of them married White. They stay in contact with their siblings and Kenneth. For obvious reasons, Reece has nothing to do with them. All of the property in Mississippi will go to her children."

Joseph shook his head. "That's a shame."

"It is, but from what Dorothy has written, the children of Kenneth Plecker are actually close. Of course, it's a kept secret that they're siblings. The way things are going, who knows what would happen if people in Caledonia learned the truth."

"It's not like they could kick the Plecker family out."

"No, but setting their mansions on fire would certainly force them to leave. I'm just glad I'm not down there anymore. Even though New York has its racists, I still have a home there."

"I hope this new generation can end this foolishness, and we can just love each other," Annabelle said. "I knew the war wasn't going to be enough to end the hate. When men thrive off of tyranny, they become slaves to it...calling evil good and good evil."

Riza exhaled, saying, "It took me a while, but I'm grateful I moved past it. I'm glad I forgave them."

"Forgiveness is a necessary step to heal," John said. "We had an elder who helped me learn that lesson while I was young. Without her, I believe my life would be different today."

"When my mom passed a year ago, at first, I felt nothing but anger because of the years I was away from her. But I'm grateful I was blessed with more years that I did have her."

"That's the best way to go forward," John said.

"I do have a few pictures of my babies though they're not babies anymore," Riza said. She pulled a few pictures out of her reticule and showed them to the others.

"Okay, they all have your eyes," Joseph said.

Riza cackled. "Yes, all of them and Marcellus had the nerve to complain. I was like boy, please, you know you love my eyes." Everyone giggled.

"You sure do have a beautiful family, Riza," Annabelle said.

"Thank you, Mrs. Lightning."

"Fortunately, the girls will be stopping by, so you will at least get to see them. None of them look like me. They all look like their aunties." Annabelle stood up. "I'm going to bring in some iced tea. It's a hot day for May anyway." She went into the kitchen and brought out a pitcher of ice tea. She placed it down and then playfully hit John on the shoulder. "Go on and bring in some glasses."

"All right, couldn't even let an old man enjoy five minutes of sitting down," John said.

"Mm-hmm, play old all you want. You see, the good ones like to be selective on when they're old and when they're not."

John went into the kitchen to get some glasses.

Annabelle continued, "It really is good to finally meet you."

"I'm happy to meet the woman who raised Joseph," Riza said.

"Well, he was a handful but always a good boy. But now, for the good part, tell me what my sister-in-law Lizzie had to say." A large grin etched across Riza's face, and she continued the conversation. Later in the evening, her husband, Marcellus, arrived at the house and met the Lightning family. The rest of Annabelle's children and Grace soon came over and met her. The next day they cooked a large dinner so the whole family could meet Riza and her husband. For Annabelle, it was not only a blessing to meet her but to see that she had healed from her past. She later wrote Judy Mays about Riza's arrival and all that occurred.

On July 20, 1903, Luke passed away due to sickness with Tsula by his side while she sung to him. Tsula was devastated with his passing. He was buried in a cemetery for colored people. Daniel passed away on June 8, 1904 in St. Louis, Missouri, and was followed by Rebecca's passing on September 12th of that year. Annabelle was able to return to Missouri along with John, Grace, and Eli to represent the family. Annabelle comforted Rebecca's children and six grandchildren. She also gave Marilyn a heartfelt hug while she gave her condolences in person. The ride home was difficult for Annabelle with her memories of Daniel and Rebecca running through her mind. In 1906, the entire Cherokee Nation had been completely disbanded by the United States government, and a chief was appointed by the government not the tribal members. The Lightning-Strongman family was heartbroken by the destruction of the Cherokee Nation. Time had taken its toll. On July 21, 1906, Ruthanne walked into the church of Mercy with her red and gray hair bouncing. "Peter, you've gotten caught in your work again," she said. "You missed having lunch with me, dear." She entered the church office and saw him sitting back in his chair with his hand on his Bible. "Peter dear? Peter?" Ruthanne's eyes widened. She rushed to his desk, and put her hand on his chest. She frowned, her eyes welled up, and she calmly closed his eyes with her other hand.

"As long as you went peacefully my love, I will miss you. I'll see you at the gates of Heaven." Ruthanne kissed him and began to weep while she gave him one last hug. She left the office and informed the church staff. She later wrote a letter to Annabelle and the others. For Peter's funeral, Annabelle returned to Mercy with Lizzie, Joseph, and Claire. Peter's funeral was massive as the entire town mourned his passing. A few years later, Samuel passed in his sleep on March 3, 1909 in Illinois. Tsula gave a heart-filled speech about her twin while cracking jokes. "People were always shocked that I was the older twin," Tsula said with tear-filled eyes. "He was always quick to protect me, but we both knew I was the smart one." Family and friends chuckled. "I love you brother, we will see each other again," Tsula said in her native tongue. Annabelle wiped away her tears while she smiled. Annabelle's family continued to celebrate Samuel's life throughout the day.

On May 24, 1910, Annabelle entered Joseph's home on the Southside of Chicago on 24th street. Lacia had decorated the majority of the two-flat house. The wooden floored living room had a set of stairs that led upstairs to the bedrooms and it opened up into the kitchen. Annabelle sat down on the sandy couch. "Momma, did you need some water?" Lacia asked in Cherokee.

Speaking Cherokee, Annabelle replied, "No, dear I've been doing exercises with my water today. I did my stretches and did my jog today. I've got to keep up with Lizzie."

Lacia giggled. "I'm sure it's a challenge."

"Well, I have to thank her. You don't see me needing a cane to move around."

"I'm about to bake some chicken, but I'll go get Joseph. I'm surprised he hasn't come up here yet."

"No, problem, all of my children are grown, though the twins still make me question their age."

Lacia grinned and left the living room. A few minutes later, Joseph came into the living room smiling. "Hi, Momma, I'm sorry I didn't hear your voice," he said. He gave Annabelle a kiss on the cheek and sat down next to her.

"What's going on? You're speaking English."

"I'm sorry, Momma. It's a habit with most of our customers being White men. It's a good thing they still think the Keys own our painting services."

"Allen and Rebecca truly blessed us. You and David…y'all have made me so proud."

Joseph smiled. "Thank you, Momma."

"I know y'all have lost some of your customers to the White painters. Claire told me." Joseph pouted. "Don't be sore with your sister. She's worried about the both of you."

"We'll be fine, Momma."

"I want you to remember to always forgive those White people for what they did to you. I know it was hard on you, and it took a while for the nightmares to stop."

"I promise I forgive them every day."

"When I felt those scars they gave you, it broke my heart. It made me realize we could've lost you, but Jesus is faithful. I used to have nightmares too as an adult." His eyes widened. "Being born a slave doesn't make you strong against trauma. If anything, it brings out rage or passiveness. Both are dangerous. I'm sorry I never told you I had nightmares too. I think I wanted to give you more hope that yours wouldn't last as long."

Joseph placed his hand on top of Annabelle's hand. "Momma, you did everything for me. I wouldn't be the man I am if it wasn't for you and the family."

"I only want you to remember to walk in love. I know it's hard being a colored man. I know people see you differently than your siblings, but don't give it no room to create bitterness."

"I promise I never will, Momma."

"Even after me and your Pa are gone, life will be hard. It'll be a long time before these White men begin to treat us fairly."

"Momma, is something wrong?"

"No, but I want to make sure I say something now. I'm not as strong as Elder Joyce in the spirit. I don't know when the Father will call me home, but I can at least tell you that much."

Little footsteps could be heard running toward Annabelle. A little girl shrieked, "Grandma!"

Annabelle turned to see the frizzy-haired brunette. "Is that my little sweet cake?" Annabelle playfully said. The caramel-skinned girl gave her a strong hug. "Oh, you are so strong for a five-year-old, my little Joyce."

"You're supposed to be taking a nap," Joseph said.

She giggled, saying, "I tricked you! Grandma, Papa isn't hearing good. He doesn't hear like Momma."

Her tone still playful Annabelle replied, "Oh he doesn't! Well, I guess I'll have to wash out his ears." The little girl cackled. "You're my second great-grandbaby. So you can watch and see your grandpa have his ears washed like he was a baby." The little girl continued to laugh. "I see you and Lacia still don't like the idea of being called Grandpa or Grandma."

Joseph sighed. "I'll be turning sixty, Momma. I'm just not ready. David can be called grandpa all day, but I'm still accepting that Arika is married now."

"Oh, still seeing her as your little girl. Well, Joyce looks exactly like her…I know it's hard." Annabelle continued in Cherokee, "You need to leave those snacks alone, boy. You're getting a little chubby." Lacia began to laugh in the kitchen. "Oh you heard that, Lacia."

Joyce's eyes widened and she said, "Oh, Grandma, you said the special words!"

"Why, yes I did. Your Momma hasn't spoken any special words to you today?"

Joyce pouted. "No."

"Well, you sit in my lap and we can say some Cherokee." Annabelle began to teach Joyce. She thought, *We're failing these children. They should be speaking Cherokee and English by now.* Annabelle later left Joseph's home cherishing the time she had with her great-granddaughter.

On August 1, 1911, Annabelle entered her home with Claire. Annabelle thought, *John should be here, why does it feel empty?* "John," she called.

"Daddy," Claire said.

Annabelle saw John's head resting on the arm of their sandy couch. "John?" She felt her heart drop and slowly walked up to the couch. She saw his bronze pocket watch in his hand and realized his body was slumped over to the side. She knelt down and shook him, but his body was lifeless. "John, you stop playing now." She heard Claire approach and looked up at her daughter. A tear streamed down Annabelle's cheek. "Claire, sweetcorn, your daddy has walked on."

Claire put her hand over her mouth. Slowly approaching Annabelle, she began to weep. Annabelle embraced her daughter, and the two women mourned.

Claire took off John's glasses and kissed him on the cheek. "I love you, Daddy," she spoke in Cherokee. "We will see each other again." She quickly left the house to tell the family of John's passing.

Annabelle took his bronze pocket watch and rubbed his shoulder. "Thank you for everything, my love. We will see each other again," she said in Cherokee.

Four days later, they held John's funeral. Many people paid their respects to the hardworking man. The Keys's children all came to pay their respects, along with some of Ruthanne's and Marilyn's families.

During the service, Annabelle went up to the pulpit with David holding her hand. "Many great things can be said about my husband," she said. "He was kind, loving, a pillar of strength, a man that loved Jesus, an amazing father, my rescuer from Mercy, Missouri," she spoke in Cherokee, "My love. We will see each other again."

David escorted her back to her seat and she sat down next to Grace.

After the service concluded, the Lightning-Strongman family went to the cemetery. A woman sung while John's wooden casket was lowered into the ground. Annabelle wiped away the few tears escaping her eyes, while she took a deep breath with the sound of her grandchildren and great-grandchildren sobbing over John.

"Momma, we're here when you're ready," David said.

"I'll be ready soon," she replied.

David nodded and walked back to the rest of the family. Grace could be heard in the background consoling one of their grandchildren while Annabelle took another deep exhale.

"I'm very sorry, Annabelle," Nancy said.

Annabelle's eyes widened and she turned around to a gray-haired Nancy. "It's been a very long time, Nancy."

"Yes, it has been. I don't expect the warmest welcome, but I did want to give my condolences."

"Thank you, Nancy."

"John really was a good man. Many years ago, he tried to open my eyes to racism. I regret not accepting the truth earlier, but I'm grateful to your family for planting a seed of love in me. It kept me from teaching my own children hate. I'm so sorry for everything I did to you."

Annabelle smiled and wiped away a tear. "I forgave you years ago and I forgive you now."

With her eyes welling up, Nancy smiled. "You've always been a stronger woman than me."

"Don't say that."

"It's the truth. I'm grateful I learned as much as I did from your family."

"I think you freeing Paul was one of your strongest steps."

"My father talked about Buck so bad when we freed Paul. You know it's been ten years since Buck passed. God rest his soul. It'll get better over time. You have a close family to keep you company. I'll certainly keep you in my prayers."

"Thank you."

"Speaking of Paul, I see Lizzie is still Lizzie. You'd swear up and down the woman was forty." Annabelle lightly giggled and the two continued their talk before Nancy said her goodbyes to the family and left.

The family then had the repass at Annabelle's home, and at night, she endured another night of being a widow. Annabelle took her time to heal from John's passing but remained active in her family.

On December 4, 1913, Maria passed away in a suburb of

Chicago, followed by Eli on February 11, 1914, making Grace a widow. Both of their lives were heavily celebrated. Grace spoke proudly of Eli, and her voice echoed through church while she sang a hymn.

The love in the church made Annabelle reflect on Maria's funeral. She glanced over at Maria's children and grandchildren. *I'm proud that we've been able to keep the family together*, she thought.

Over the months, Annabelle could feel the struggle of her family increase when several of the men were drafted into World War I. Annabelle took in several of her great-grandchildren, nieces, and nephews to help their mothers. Every day, the women got together and prayed for the men's safe return. New letters from Naomi also informed Annabelle that Marilyn wasn't well. Due to illness, Marilyn later passed on February 11, 1915 with Naomi and Lee Ann by her side. Annabelle, Grace, Lizzie, and Paul took a trip to St. Louis to pay their respects to her. On January 21, 1916 Michael passed away, and his wife Mimi unexpectedly followed on May 5, 1916.

After the war ended on November 11, 1918, the men were given a welcome home party at Lizzie's home. During the celebration, Annabelle sat down on a couch, and watched the children. *We're fighting so many battles for these children, but these little ones speak no Cherokee*, she thought. *I'm not sure if we'll get enough time to teach them.*

Lisa sat down next to Annabelle. "What's on your mind?"

"To be honest, I guess I'm worried. It's getting harder with each new generation to keep them Cherokee."

Lisa nodded in agreement. "Yes, it is. The way these White people expect us to work cuts into family time. I know my grandbabies are forgetting words. Maybe we need to start teaching them after school."

"That's a good idea, Lisa."

Lisa sighed. "I'm tired, Annabelle. Our children have to pick up the pieces they dropped. Samuel and Maria's children have almost completely adopted Maria's Mexican ways. After Samuel passed, Maria became too sick to encourage Cherokee ways. I can't be mad at her. She certainly tried. Only Rosita and Sky can speak Cherokee now, and Sky is having health problems."

"I want to say we should've stayed in Cherokee land, but I know they're suffering."

"Yeah, they are. Those White men stole everything. I think the best thing we can do is keep our family in prayer, and to keep telling the old stories."

"I had to encourage Joyce to be proud to tell other children she's Cherokee. It's like these schools are trying to erase Indians."

"I wouldn't be surprised if they tried. Sunni is strict on her children about our blood. She does make me proud." The two women smiled at each other and continued their conversation.

On September 3, 1920, Lisa passed away smiling, with all of her children by her side. Because she loved her daughter, she forever kept her rape a secret from Sunni. Over the months, Annabelle's family comforted Jacob and the rest of Lisa's clan. To the family's shock, Jacob later passed away while sitting down on a chair outside of a horse stable on November 5, 1920, on Lisa's ninetieth birthday. He was buried next to Lisa.

On the morning of July 30, 1921, Paul passed away in his sleep. His death was a double blow for the family with Victoria having passed a month prior. He was buried in the same cemetery as the rest of the family. Lizzie stood before his lowered wooden coffin while family and friends walked away. Speaking Cherokee, Maya said, "Momma, we're ready to leave when you are."

"I'm ready baby, y'all go out to the new car," Lizzie replied in her native tongue. "It cost us enough." Her son Joshua came up to her and gave her a kiss on the cheek. She smiled and patted him on his shoulder. Her children slowly walked away. "I'm glad we had the years we had. I know I gave you a rough time in the beginning for a little while." Lizzie sighed. "I guess five years isn't a little while, but you knew I loved you and I love you now, Paul." Tears shimmered in her eyes. "Ugh, you're going to make me cry again. Now, you tell, John I said hi. We will see each other again." She turned around and walked toward Grace. Grace rubbed her back and the two sisters walked to their family holding hands.

Two days later, Lizzie left a bundle of blue flowers on Paul's grave. She left a note on the bundle reading, "When I'm called home, I expect you to give me some more blue flowers."

The Lightning-Strongman family agreed to make it a priority to visit each other's home regularly. The women continued to teach their grandchildren and great-grandchildren Cherokee traditions. Lizzie remained adamant in making sure they knew the story about the two wolves. One day, Annabelle's great-granddaughter Ada came to visit her. While Annabelle braided the brown-skinned girl's long curly hair, she reflected on how much time had passed, and the friends and family that had passed away. Through her house's rectangular windows, she glanced over at the garden she, Lisa, Tsula, Grace, Maria, and Lizzie had created and smiled. "I love you, Ada," Annabelle said in Cherokee.

Ada grinned, replying in Cherokee, "I love you, grandma."

Annabelle leaned forward and kissed the twelve-year-old on the cheek. "Me and Auntie Grace will teach you more since your momma is too busy. We'll teach you how to plant gardens too. It'll keep you young." The girl smiled as Annabelle continued to braid her hair.

On April 19, 1918, Belle visited Annabelle at her home with Rain accompanying her. "Come on in Belle, you're looking just like your momma," Annabelle said. "You know I was excited to learn you and your family moved up here into the Chicago suburbs."

"Thank you, Mrs. Lightning. It's a blessing to see you," Belle said, matching Ruthanne's Southern tone.

"Come on and sit, you're not old. You're sixty-seven."

"Momma," Rain said with a slight frown.

Annabelle's eyes locked onto Rain, and her gaze shifted to Belle's green eyes. "Is your momma gone?"

Belle frowned and sniffed, answering, "Yes, ma'am. She passed three days ago. I didn't want to tell you over the phone."

Annabelle exhaled and closed her eyes. "Your momma went peacefully?"

"Yes, ma'am, with a book in her hand."

Annabelle tearfully half-smiled. "That was your momma. I'll have to make sure Judy Mays knows."

"We just informed her through the phone. She will attend my momma's service."

"Well, all right then. While you're here, I'll make us some tea." Annabelle stood up and made some tea for the women. She spoke with them for a while before the women had to leave. Annabelle returned to Missouri with Tsula, Lizzie, Grace, and all of her children to pay their respects. Ruthanne's funeral was massive, and Annabelle was grateful to say goodbye to her friend with Judy Mays by her side.

On May 03, 1921, Judy Mays visited Annabelle and remained as lively as she was when she was young. It was heartwarming for Annabelle to spend time with her best friend, Tsula, Grace, and Lizzie. Judy Mays brought along Luther who was now fifty-nine years old and had a family of his own. "It's a blessing to see how well you raised Luther," Grace said.

"Yes, it was a challenge," Judy Mays said. "My Pa went into the dirt, never apologizing to my momma. Took Scarlett a year to accept him and three years for Sue, Ellen, and Genevieve. May they rest in peace."

"Still, it's no telling how different his life would've been if it wasn't for you," Annabelle said.

"He must be a sore spot for the rest of your family," Lizzie blurted.

Annabelle pouted. "Lizzie."

"No, she's right," Judy Mays said. Me and my sisters' children are the only ones that accept him. I honestly worry about him every time he goes somewhere alone. The South isn't safe for a colored man, with all these hangings and other craziness that's getting worse each year. I almost regretted me and my sisters encouraging him to marry a mulatto girl, but now it may be the only reason his family isn't treated as bad. All his children are lighter than him."

"It is a dangerous trend in this country," Grace said.

"I hope our children will at least see reconciliation. White men are bitter and dangling power over everyone's head…it'll only lead to hate."

"I agree. It's heartbreaking. People are acting like our people are extinct now."

"Ignorance has a way of moving faster than the truth."

"Yes, that's true," Annabelle said. "I find myself having to remind my grandbabies not to let people talk them into ignoring their Cherokee blood. I feel like these institutions are actively trying to erase the Indian."

Judy Mays replied, "I'm sure they are."

Lizzie took a drink of water. "Our nation is now infested with Five Dollar Indians. These White men with no Cherokee blood paid to get put on the rolls, while those of Cherokee blood not in the territory were left off the rolls. They tried to fix the problem by doing another roll, but Five Dollar Indians are alive and well. It's broken us as a people. Indians have become the trustees of titles of land in the interests of White men, while Negros and Mexicans continue to be cheap labor," Lizzie said.

"Amen to that," Judy Mays said, raising her glass to Lizzie.

She smiled at Judy Mays, and the women continued to spend the rest of the day together.

On May 7, 1921, Judy Mays returned to Mississippi with Luther on the train, but that night, she passed away in her sleep. Luther's and Judy Mays's children quickly called Annabelle.

Although heartbroken, Annabelle rejoiced about the time she had with her best friend and attended her funeral along with her children, Tsula, Grace, and Lizzie. Judy Mays's blue-eyed daughter Breanna escorted Annabelle to the pulpit to speak about her best friend.

"I was separated from my best friend for over a decade," Annabelle said. "As a child and a teenage girl, I was a slave, but Judy Mays and her sisters loved me. And I loved them. I give praise to Jesus for allowing us to spend the majority of our lives reunited. With her great heart, she became a mother, a grandmother, and a great-grandmother. The greatest lesson I learned from her was love will always overcome hate. The greatest love comes from Jesus, and we are to spread this love to the best of our ability. She showed strength for her family when her love, Edgar, passed away twelve years ago. I'm blessed the Father put her in my life, and I'll be happy to see my friend again." She sat down next to her family and reminisced while the pastor finished Judy Mays's service. The train ride home was difficult, and she fought back the sadness she felt.

Over the years, Annabelle's family tried to keep traditions alive, but the demanding American society made it difficult. The women continued to speak Cherokee among themselves and to their children. Lizzie now refused to speak English to her children in any setting. On January 2, 1924, Grace passed away while reading her Bible with a cougar medallion in her hand that her granddaughter had given her, a symbol of her never ending faith. The Lightning-Strongman family took the heavy loss deeply. She had made all of her grandchildren and great-grandchildren feel like each one was her favorite. Annabelle, Lizzie, and Tsula spoke about Grace at her service. Giving praise to the woman who took on the role of mother when she was a child herself, and Uncle George was left alone to raise their family. The young woman who successfully gave Annabelle a new identity and brought her to Elder Joyce to heal. She gave grace, and her name was Grace. On June 2, 1924, Annabelle, Tsula, Lizzie, and their descendants were granted US citizenship because of the Indian Citizenship Act. Tsula mocked the law stating that her family belonged to the land before White men stole it. Tsula maintained her humorous sarcastic ways along with her daughter Katelyn. Tsula and Katelyn were known as the mother-daughter duo, rarely seen apart. However, on October 22, 1925, Tsula passed away after Katelyn unexpectedly died from an illness earlier in the year. Annabelle believed Tsula passed away from a broken heart. Katelyn had three daughters of her own who were exact copies of her. Annabelle understood well that it is hard to bury your child, and even though Tsula had her grandchildren, it was difficult.

As time passed, the culture of America became more dominant and demanding, making it difficult for Annabelle and Lizzie to pass on Cherokee traditions. The women often tried to only speak Cherokee to their great-grandchildren because they were worried the children would completely forget who they were. One day, in August of 1931, Annabelle struggled to walk upstairs. She thought, *I should've kept up with Lizzie's routine. Old woman still moves like she has something to do.* She got to the top of the stairs and exhaled.

"I never thought I'd struggle up those stairs," Annabelle said. She went into her twins' old room and looked at pictures she had put on the room's walls. "How time flies. I wonder if this is how Elder Joyce felt." She sat down in a rocking chair and picked up a photo album. "Thanks to Daniel, we have all these pictures." She turned a page and saw a picture of John and grinned. "I think you'd be proud of me. I'm moving around with no cane, and I'm still dressing sharp." She lightly chuckled and soon fell asleep in the chair while looking at more pictures.

An hour later, she awoke with the sunset shining through the wind. She stood and slowly went to the stairs. She held onto the rail and slowly went downstairs. Once she finished, she could feel her heart pounding. "I'm feeling so tired these past months. Lord, give me strength." Annabelle told her family she'd been struggling lately. It was agreed for Lizzie to move in with her. Annabelle's and Lizzie's children constantly came over to check on the elderly women.

On the afternoon of August 31, 1931, the warm summer rays illuminated Annabelle's home. She sat on a beige couch next to Lizzie. "I'm tired, Lizzie," Annabelle said in Cherokee.

She turned to Annabelle, replying in her native language, "I've noticed how much weaker you've become recently. We should have the doctor come and see you."

"No, it's okay. I don't think there's much a doctor could do. These past few months I can feel my body slowing down on me."

"Are you sure?"

"I don't welcome death, but I know if Jesus calls me home, I'll see all of them again. I know my children will be fine, and their children. We fought hard to have a foundation many colored people don't have."

Lizzie calmly held Annabelle's hand. "Yes, we did. The rest is up to them."

"I'm glad Daniel took those pictures of us."

"Yes, I'm glad I didn't fuss about it."

"We've gone through so many trials. Do you think we did the right thing by writing all those diaries?"

"I think we did. Even with a lot of the truth being hard to tell, I think they need to know. Knowing where they came from will give them strength."

"I know it was hard for Lisa to write the truth."

"We will keep our word. It's made clear that Lisa's writings can't be read until Sunni walks on. She'll see her mother again, unaware of Brock Jackson."

Annabelle weakly chuckled. "I know you wanted that man's head."

"If the Lord gave me another chance, I'd feel the temptation to cut him down. He was dealt with, though. No greater prison than being trapped in your body and waiting to die."

"I'm happy for you."

"Oh, stop it. We've had this talk."

"I know, but I'm happy for you. I'm glad I can call you my sister. Jesus gave you great children and a good man. You've always been independent of a man, but you were certainly given the right one."

Lizzie smirked. "Yeah, I was. I know the first five years were rough."

"Rough is an understatement. That man was showing you love for more than five years." Lizzie rolled her eyes. "Don't dismiss the truth. He had the patience of Job."

The two women began to cackle. "He did, especially when I got pregnant with Sarah…woo the mood swings. I'm happy for you too."

Annabelle sighed. "The world is ruthless even with the

beauty within in it. The constant lesson of our lives is to trust in the Lord will all our heart and not lean onto our own understanding." Later in the day, the two women ate dinner together with the company of Joseph, Lacia, the twins, and Lizzie's son Joshua. On September 01, 1931, Annabelle struggled most of the day, and Lizzie helped her sit in a rocking chair. Holding John's bronze pocket watch, Annabelle smiled while she watched the birds play around their garden. As Lizzie exited the kitchen, Annabelle's eyes widened. She let out a weak gasp, saying, "Constance."

Lizzie approached Annabelle and held her hand. "Constance? Annabelle?" she said. Lizzie touched her cheek and frowned. She looked at the sunset, and her gaze shifted back to Annabelle. "We will see each other again, sister." Lizzie kissed her forehead and stood up. She waited for Sarah and Claire to arrive at the house since they were expected. When the two women arrived at the house, they mourned Annabelle's passing and left to tell the rest of the family. Five days later, Annabelle's service was held. The mourning for Annabelle echoed throughout the church. Lizzie began to sing an old church hymn to calm her family, and they joined her. She marched up to the pulpit, saying, "My sister has left a strong legacy…a legacy of faith, love, perseverance, kindness, education, and culture. The legacy must be taught to the new generation. We had many years together, and I'm thankful to the Father for every year. If the Father be for you, who can be against you…walk forward with love against the evil of this world." She turned toward Annabelle's wooden coffin. "We will see each other again, sister," she spoke in the Cherokee language. The service continued, and Annabelle was later buried next to John.

Lizzie continued to tell the old stories cheerfully, remembering her family. She remained in good health while she continued to work in the garden created by her, Annabelle, Grace, Lisa, Maria, and Tsula. On November 25, 1933, she experienced the pain of burying her son Joshua who passed from an illness.

She comforted her family and mourned on her own. On June 18, 1934, the United States government passed the Indian Reorganization Act. Lizzie scoffed at the new law declaring the damage had already been done and there was no returning to the old ways. She soon explained the truth about the letters and writings to the twins and Maya. She gave the family history to them, including Annabelle's Bible and *The Three Musketeers*. Lizzie passed away on her 108th birthday on July 25, 1936, in her sleep. A year later, David passed away, and he was followed years later by Joseph who passed on September 13, 1940. Over time, the family became more assimilated, and all of the family lost the Cherokee language through the pressures and persecution of society, including the Jim Crow laws. Through the civil rights movements, some of the Lightning-Strongman family members felt pressured into identifying as black. However, Grace's and Lizzie's descendants quickly took the lead over the family to reinstate their Cherokee heritage. Most of the family had now married people that were mixed with black and Indigenous blood, Latinos, or had married mulattos. Samuel and Maria's branch married almost entirely Mexicans but kept strong ties with the rest of the family.

The elders in the family decided the stories of their family must be forever told so they never forget who they are, and what their family went through. Albert sat before his family with his wife Coney sitting next to him. "The old stories from Annabelle, Grace, Lizzie, Lisa, Tsula, Judy Mays, Rebecca, Ruthanne, and Marilyn reflected their world," Albert said. "Even Joseph wrote one. We've lost many records because of a fire from over sixty years ago, but because of these writings, we know the truth."

"Granddaddy, so we're the children of Joseph?" Christina asked.

Albert grinned at his granddaughter. "No, we're not the children of Joseph. We're the children of Rain. This is one of her pictures taken when she was a teenager." Albert gave the picture to Christina. "Daniel took that picture of her, and many of the other pictures we have. David and Joseph worked as painters. Those two were always seen together. They had their own business because the Keys bought the property." Albert put down a picture with all of Annabelle's children. "This picture is one of a few we have. Joseph lived a long, interesting life."

"Daddy, I'm sorry. I've forgotten so much," Liz said.

"We have to keep telling the stories. Do you know who you were named after now?"

Liz smiled. "Was it Elizabeth, because even though she and Annabelle wrote each other she passed before Annabelle got to see her again?"

Albert smiled. "Well, no, but good guess."

Albert handed Liz a picture. "Oh my God, we look almost identical. I don't believe it. Daddy I'm...I don't remember you ever showing me this...is this Lizzie?"

"Yes, that's Lizzie and I didn't show you her picture...that was my mistake." Suddenly, the family heard the backdoor open and they all looked back. Albert looked down the hallway and saw a girl with short, wavy hair and a teenager with cornrows standing at the backdoor. A man with glasses holding a clipboard stood with the girls. "Come on in girls, don't be shy."

Coney stood up while the girls smiled and walked through the kitchen toward the hallway. "Daddy, who is it?"

"Family, sweetheart." The two girls came out of the hallway and stood in the doorway of the living room. Both of them had almond-shaped eyes, high cheek bones, and a brown skin tone. "Everyone, I want you to meet the missing branch of the family. Kelly, who just turned eighteen and Mya who is thirteen. They are who I've been looking for, for years because they're the last descendants of Joseph Lightning."

The family was wide-eyed as they looked at the teenagers. "Wait, the last? But Joseph had like five children, didn't he, Daddy?"

"Yes, but life happens. That side of the family became separated from the rest of us. Joseph's grandchildren had parents that didn't put effort into us staying connected. They knew nothing." Albert approached the teenage girls and placed his hands on their shoulders. "I found them in foster care. Their father died shortly after Mya was born in an accident, and their mother had a heart attack two years ago. So, welcome home, girls."

"Thank you so much," Kelly said, her voice slightly breaking.

"There isn't nothing to thank. You are family," Coney said. "The both of you are as beautiful as when we went to that foster care place and first saw y'all. Come sit with your family there is a lot you need to learn." Mya gave Coney a hug as she cried.

"Mr. and Mrs. Brooks, it has been a pleasure. I'm always happy to reunite a family," the man said.

"Richard Keys, it's always a pleasure and tell your brother to keep up the good work. We will be voting for him again," Coney said. "And tell your momma I said hi."

"Yes, ma'am, I will. Her pies are waiting for you and Evelyn Reynolds will be in town next week."

"Good, I want to see her new baby girl."

"Come back soon Richard," Albert said.

Richard smiled, saying, "I will Mr. Brooks. Good to see all of you. Goodbye."

"Bye, Ricky," the family said. Richard left the house smiling.

"The rest of the family will be here to meet the girls," Albert said. "We're having a family reunion early this year to celebrate the retrieval of our two lost silver coins."

"Come here, Kelly," Liz said. She then gave Kelly and Mya a hug as other family members welcomed the girls. "So do we need to get them enrolled, or has that been done already?"

"No, they need to be enrolled. We should try to get that done for them as soon as possible. Who knows what their future will be with the Cherokee Nation."

Liz gave a skewed frown. "Daddy, why do you say that?"

"Because Joseph was put down on the freedmen rolls making the girls vulnerable of being excluded if a new ruling by the Cherokee Nation was to come again. No different than Heather, Aretha, and the others that can't enroll because Samuel and Maria told the family not to enroll them."

"Daddy, the Cherokee courts reversed that ruling to have the freedmen removed from the nation years ago."

"It's still a fight, sweetheart. We're not allowed to fix the rolls. White men put our family in this position, and our tribe made the mistake of falling for the trap. There are many others being punished for their family not being enumerated on the Dawes Rolls or documented incorrectly. That's why it's important to keep the truth alive, because it's easy to forget the past…those two girls are the last of Joseph's clan. They both carry the name Lightning. Let's make sure they remember where that name comes from." Albert and Liz smiled at each other and spent the rest of the time with the family. The other family members soon arrived and celebrated the first unification of all of their family's clans in over sixty-five years.

Albert sat next to Coney, smiled at her, and calmly held her hand. "We're blessed to see an answer to an old prayer," she said.

The descendants of the Lightning-Strongman family remained close knit forever, and Joseph's legacy continued on through Kelly and Mya.

I hope this adventure was an enjoyable experience for you and that you will visit your favorite retailer to leave a review because your feedback is priceless!

ABOUT THE AUTHOR

Hi, everyone! I'm Marcus, from the south side suburbs of Chicago. I'm a descendant of two Native American tribes. I have two degrees in zoology, love the Olympic Games, and I am into Native American history, especially regarding issues that have divided families. Some of the stories I enjoy creating focus on parts of history rarely talked about and revolve around genealogy and interracial relationships, particularly between African American and Native American communities, that cause us to reflect on the choices we make, especially in our teenage and young adult years. This focus is to help young adults see the bigger picture earlier in their lives. God's greatest commandment is to love each other. I hope to fascinate your minds, to educate, to make you think about your family, and make you reflect on your own choices in life.

Printed in the USA
CPSIA information can be obtained
at www.ICGtesting.com
CBHW061358011224
18276CB00018B/344